insert endorsements here

WARDENS
OF
ETERNITY

WARDENS
OF
ETERNITY

COURTNEY MOULTON

BLINK·

BLINK

Wardens of Eternity
Copyright © 2019 by Courtney Moulton

Requests for information should be addressed to:
Blink, *3900 Sparks Dr. SE, Grand Rapids, Michigan 49546*

Hardcover ISBN 978-0-310-76718-3

Interior design: Denise Froehlich

Printed in the United States of America

19 20 21 22 23 LSC 10 9 8 7 6 5 4 3 2 1

For my agent, Allison Remcheck. Thank you for keeping my head above the water.

Mine is a heart of carnelian, crimson as murder on a holy day.

I am the phoenix, the fiery sun, consuming and resuming myself. I pace the halls of the netherworld. I knock on the doors of death. The primeval gods are here with me. Their voices hum like flies in my ears.

I am what I will.

—AN EXCERPT FROM THE BOOK OF THE DEAD

1

NEW YORK CITY, 1939

The only memory I had of my parents was also the last time I saw them. I'd replayed the scene over and over in my head if only to understand why they'd done it.

My mother had clutched me to her chest as she ran through the crowded street, darting between people and automobiles, her footsteps and ragged breaths lost among shouting voices and beeping horns. I'd watched the world zoom by from beneath the blanket she had wrapped me in.

We had slowed, and she'd set me down beside a vegetable cart. I'd been small, perhaps three or four years old, I wasn't sure. I'd looked up at her, wondering when we would go home, because I'd wanted lunch. Mama's dark, round, deep-set eyes had been wide, the same dark eyes I gazed into when I saw my reflection now. Her long, gently sloping nose had met full lips forming a defined cupid's bow. The honey-and-olive skin of her cheeks had been flushed and damp. Had it been raining, or had she been crying? I would never know.

"We'll play a game, Ziva," she'd told me, her voice high and soft, its calmness betrayed by the wildness in her gaze. "Wait here and don't move until Baba and I come find you. Do you understand?"

I'd nodded. Games were fun. Lunch could wait.

Mama's dense bounty of dark curls, the midday sun setting their reddish-gold highlights on fire, fell around me like a protective curtain. Sometimes, now, I wondered if her hair ever got curlier on misty, humid days like mine maddeningly did.

She'd kissed the top of my head, drawn a long, deep breath, and stood. She had cast one last glance over her shoulder and vanished into the crowd.

They'd abandoned me, like so many of the city's children had been, whose parents couldn't feed them. A single memory and my real name were all I had of my parents and my history. I had long been on my own—sixteen years now. Lots of the girls who worked with me at the textile company were alone and scarcely scraping by.

If anything, New York was a city of survivors.

I bit the inside of my cheek to pull my thoughts back to the present. My laced shoes tapped the cracked pavement and the frayed hem of my skirt swung above my ankles. My blouse stuck to my back beneath my coat and smelled sour with sweat and thread dye. The air was thick and carried a muddy, damp odor from an earlier rain. This route was lonely after dark, but it was my quickest way home.

A figure emerged from the shadows, grabbed my arm, and yanked me out of the streetlight's reach. My back thudded into the brick wall of a building. I found my balance and felt my fingertips heat and spark on instinct. When I looked up, I saw a white woman in dirty clothes, her brown hair chopped below her ears. She had a knife in one hand.

"Hand it over," she ordered. "Whatever you got. Hand it over."

Her voice was calmer than most thieves'—she'd been at this a while. But today was payday and I knew well to keep my wits about me, watching for whoever might be hungry for the measly few bucks I'd worked for all week. There was no way I'd let anyone take it from me. She wasn't the first who'd tried.

"No," I told her.

The woman waved the knife close to my face. Metal glinted. I stepped away from her. She snarled and leapt at me, grabbing my wrist with her free hand. Her fingers dove into my pocket and I swung a fist in protest, but she darted out of my reach.

"Give it back!" I shouted, and my fingertips burned. I clenched my fists, and sparks bit into my palms. "Leave me alone."

She examined the limp scrap of fabric she'd stolen—the only contents of that pocket—in the sickly glow of the streetlamp. She muttered a curse and tossed the scrap. It fell to the damp ground and I lunged for it and patted off the dirt before stuffing it back where it belonged.

She shot at me while I was on the ground, knife poised high. I threw up my hand, palm out, and the thief screamed when my power slammed into her, wrenching her up off her feet and into the air. Her limbs flailed wildly, and she landed on her back with a crack in the middle of the street. She writhed for a few moments, mouth opening and closing, her voice lost when the wind was knocked from her.

I hadn't meant to hit her so hard. Honestly, I hadn't.

I stood slowly and marched toward her with a smooth gait. Although I tried to appear indifferent, I hoped she was all right. But I had to appear ruthless to people like this, people who were as hungry and desperate to survive as me.

Standing above her, I watched her expression turn from panicked to fearful as she found her air. She rolled over with a groan and pushed herself shakily to her feet. She retrieved her fallen knife and raised it to me again, the entire length of her arm trembling.

"What was that?" she rasped. "What did you do?"

"Move along," I told her, my tone frigid. "Or you'll end up a lot worse."

She crept away, step by step. "Why do you slave away all day in a factory when you have power like that? You can take what you need."

I said nothing as I went on my way.

"You and I would make a great team!" the woman shouted at my back.

I wasn't a team kind of girl.

As I continued on my way, another movement in the darkness triggered my attention. If too many people saw my power, there would be problems. I maintained my pace but kept watch in that area. My nerve endings screamed with alarm. The feeling was all too familiar for me. I was hunted by predators all the time.

When I saw the shadow again, I froze. This was no mugger or street urchin. The body was long and moved like a cat, but it was the size of a lion or tiger I'd seen at the zoo. It lifted its head and I could make out the silhouette of enormous, coiled horns.

My heart hammering, I squeezed my eyes shut, certain I'd imagined this shadow. I opened my eyes again and it was gone.

I ran.

"Extra! Extra!" A teenage newsboy carrying a stack of papers shouted his headlines from the corner of an intersection. "Blackouts in Prague continue as the Reich marches toward Poland!"

I couldn't afford to buy a paper, so I slowed my pace, hoping the newsboy would say more. Last week, I'd heard the Czech people were now forced by the Reich to carry documents declaring they weren't Roma or Jewish. The only shops open now were the ones hanging signs in their windows proclaiming they were Aryan-owned. Europe was halfway across the world, but Americans seemed so afraid of what was happening—what could happen again. The end of the Great War hadn't been all that long ago; the sharp blade of that memory still lingered in the hearts of many.

I hurried toward a regular payday stop for me—a bakery close to home. Before I spotted the awning above the heads of passersby, I could smell the baked goods. My mouth watered as I inhaled deeply, imagining the taste of warm muffins, bagels, and baguettes. All day I'd managed not to think about how I hadn't eaten since the night before. Now my hunger was a ruthless force kicking around my empty insides.

Ducking behind the stoop of a launderer, I unbelted my skirt and reached inside the band to the secret pocket I'd sewn there. I deftly unbuttoned the flap and felt around for my money. After taking what I needed, I stuffed the rest of the cash back into its hiding place.

Before I entered, I needed to make myself appear a little more alive and less like the walking dead. I pinched both my cheeks and gave them a few sharp slaps to add some color to my blanched complexion. Then I emerged onto the sidewalk and crossed the street to the bakery. A bell jingled when I opened the door and stepped inside. The air was dry and warm and thick with the heady scents of bread and the sweet icing of pastries. The man behind the counter cast me a smile as he placed rolls from a tray onto the shelf beneath the counter.

"Miss Ellison," he said with a tip of his white cap. "How are we this evening?"

"Just fine, Lou, and yourself?" I asked.

"Hoping to sell what I have left before I close up for the night."

I moved along the counter, my eyes wide and feasting on what my tongue couldn't taste: rich angel cake, chewy raisin tarts, creamy strawberry shortcake, crisp chocolate chip cookies, and dainty custard-filled cupcakes. Once, I'd spent everything I had on a plate of shortcake. It was heaven. I'd managed to make it last for three days, eating a scoop at a time, and it had left me four days without any food at all.

It'd been worth it.

Lou stepped out from behind the counter to wipe the display glass with a rag. "I saved a half-price day-old loaf for you."

"That's swell, thanks," I told him. "I'm really grateful. How about that job too?"

He sighed and frowned at me. "I couldn't pay you."

I flashed him a bright, lively smile. "I'd take food instead."

"Then who would pay your rent?" he asked soberly.

Reality had a sharp bite. "Well, let me know if a spot opens up."

"You bet, kid," he replied, his voice a little sad.

I walked toward the day-old rack and a dark thought came back to me. *"Why do you slave away all day in a factory when you have power like that?"*

I paused, my gaze lingering on the row of bread loaves.

How easy it would've been to push my power at one and knock it into my hand without anyone seeing. Lou would probably sell a loaf cheaper than half-price if it fell onto the floor.

My heart pounded, and my stomach tightened with hunger and nerves. Shadows seemed to creep around my vision, tunneling my mind, leaving only the bread in focus.

"You can take what you need."

But I liked Lou. He always made sure he had something to sell me. Times were tough for him too. I didn't want to stoop to the same level as the thief. I wasn't terrible enough to hurt someone else for what I wanted.

My teeth clenched until they squeaked and hurt. Before I could let myself think any longer about having extra food this week, I grabbed a day-old loaf from the rack, paid for it, and was out the door with a brief good-bye.

CHAPTER

2

A s far as tenements went, the one I lived in wasn't the worst I'd seen. The city had tried to fix up a lot of the immigrant housing, but this one seemed to have been missed so far. I climbed the stoop, carefully avoiding the man who'd slept on the bottom step for the past two nights and walked in the front door. Once safely inside, I pulled out all the rest of my money to count out what I owed my landlord.

The narrow entry was taken up mostly by the staircase, which circled four floors high. The hallway runner beneath my feet was dirty and tattered, and the faded floral wallpaper was torn in streaks and around corners. This might have been a fine house in the days of carriages and bowler hats, but that was a long-forgotten dream now. If I looked closely enough, I could see the hallway runners were spun with gold thread, reminding me of Rumpelstiltskin.

A hollow pang of loneliness in my middle. I wound up at an orphanage where a woman named Jean worked and she would read fairytales to us from moldering old books. Thinking of her made me miss her and I resolved to visit her tomorrow after work. Jean was likely the best thing to ever happen to me. She'd even taught a few of us how to read, a skill I'd cherish the rest of my life. Reading opened infinite doors to infinite worlds.

"Rose Ellison!"

Ziva. My name is Ziva.

The voice came from the first room on the right, which always had its door open, so our landlord, Mr. Boyle, could spot us as we came in.

"Yes, sir?" I replied with a cringe. Nearly everyone called me Rose Ellison, the name the State gave me when it took me in. The name my parents gave me, Ziva, didn't sound "American." It didn't sound "white." This world had rejected my real name, rejected who I was. I would always remember my name, and now it was all I had.

Mr. Boyle appeared in the doorframe, his suspenders loose and the top few buttons of his white shirt open. A patchy, five o'clock shadow stained his jib and jaw. He had a long nose, a sallow olive skin tone, a messy mop of black hair on top of his head, and watery, even blacker eyes.

"Rent's due," he said flatly, his hands on his hips. He snorted, catching a gob of mucus in his throat and swallowing.

"I know," I replied, sorting through the folded bills I'd already taken from my secret purse. When I handed half of it over, he counted greedily and gave me a pointed frown.

"You owe me twenty."

I could hardly understand him through his thick Irish accent. "But I don't have twenty."

He snatched the rest of the cash in my hand. "This'll do."

"Wait!" I tried to follow him, but he'd turned and slammed his door shut in my face, making me jump back.

"Good night, Miss Ellison," he called from the other side, his voice muffled and dismissive.

I could bang on his door, demand my money back, but I owed him more than he'd swiped.

"You can take what you need."

And I needed my money.

My power could break open that locked door without a doubt. I'd seen it do worse—because I couldn't control it. There was a terrible certainty I could do more damage than I intended. Mr. Boyle could be hurt. His apartment could be destroyed. This building could be damaged. It could fall. More people could be hurt.

I stood still, taking long, deep breaths and counting backward to quell the sparks at my fingertips. They dissipated after a few moments and I forced myself up the stairs to my room. Each step was harder and more exhausting to take than the last. When I reached the top, it was by sheer will that I made it to my door. I found my key in my secret purse and entered.

The room I rented was just that—a room. The toilet was down the hall and the building across the street had a women's bath house. I was lucky to have my own stove and sink. A small cot sat against the far wall beneath the window, so I could admire the stars as I tried to sleep. The window was quite large and arched; the curtain only covered the bottom half of the glass for my privacy. There had been a few nights this past winter when I'd pulled down that curtain to use as an extra blanket on my bed.

I set the bagged loaf of bread on the stove and tore off a hunk to devour. The first bite was always the worst; when it hit the bottom of your empty stomach, it did things to your body. You cramped, felt sick, and your throat was so tight and dry you thought you might choke. Then the hunger erupted, filling you past your limit like an overflowing sink, and you remembered exactly how long it had been since you last ate. I tried to eat small amounts often rather than big meals sparingly, if only to avoid this discomfort. But hunger was a blinding force and you believed with all your heart you won't care how heavy the food feels in your stomach. But you do. Very quickly you do.

I wrapped the bag tightly back around the bread; I'd need this to last a week. Stale bread I didn't mind, but I hated to waste the moldy bits.

The rickety clock on the wall clacked on the hour and started to chime. Nine in the evening. Horror stuck me like a bullet. I scrambled out into the hallway, my shoes sliding, just in time to watch Nonna Tessio disappear into the toilet, newspaper in hand. My eyes squeezed closed in defeat; I knew well the old woman liked to take her privy time after supper. I'd missed my chance for hours. No fool in New York would use the toilet after Nonna Tessio.

Dragging my feet, I returned to my room. I hoped I could hold it. Hunger, on top of everything that happened tonight, had distracted me. After collecting my needle and thread from the nightstand drawer, I pulled out the scrap of fabric from my pocket. It was only a few inches wide and long, which meant I'd add a few more inches to my quilt. I stitched it to the end of my chaotic patchwork job, hoping the quilt would be long enough to cover my toes come winter.

I unpinned my hat from my hair, changed into my bedclothes, and folded my skirt and blouse for tomorrow since they could go a few more days before washing. The bed frame creaked in the quiet as I climbed in. On the nightstand, the lamp's bare bulb flickered more like a candle flame due to the frayed wire. Soon it would die altogether.

I lay my head against my lumpy pillow and gazed at the stars out my window. They were faint with the carnival glow of the city lights fighting their shine, but they were still there. I was faint and fighting, but I was still here as well.

And lonely. So lonely.

On cold nights I longed for more than just a friend, but boys didn't like my coiled, curly hair, and they'd told me so. They liked girls with shiny, smooth hair they could run their fingers through. My hair wasn't pretty to them. I wasn't pretty enough to bring home to their mothers.

I wasn't pretty enough at the orphanage when I was

little, either, not that any good folks ever came to adopt any of us anyway. But adults fawned over the other children, and every compliment to their straight, fair hair and creamy white skin felt like one of a thousand cuts to me. I didn't know how many cuts it would take to bleed me out.

Nobody had ever told me I was ugly. Yet, the way they had never told me I was beautiful or precious or desirable made me feel like I was none of those things. The way people pointed out that my hair wasn't straight like the other children's made me want to look like them. The way they always told me what I wasn't made me feel not good enough.

In my heart, I knew how unfair my own feelings about my appearance were to me. Punishing myself because I was different wouldn't change what I looked like. It had taken me a long, long time to understand how people had always treated me—and to find peace with how I looked. This journey brewed an obsession in me to learn who I was and where I came from.

In America, people saw skin color before gender or economic status. People noticed my brown skin and that's where they stopped looking. Nobody cared about who I was on the inside. After the Great War, so many people around the world lost everything and everyone. Like my parents must have, they sought new lives and fresh starts here, in a country whose people had always been defined as white or black. Americans didn't know what to do with the lot of us lost somewhere in the middle.

Eventually, they lumped us all together as not white. Not like them. Not belonging. Not to be trusted.

Sometimes when I thought of my parents, I grew angry at them and myself. Perhaps my abilities had made them abandon me. Perhaps they'd been afraid of me. Perhaps I'd hurt them too.

Whoever I was, I was special. And wherever I came from, I was meant for something more than this meager life. New York wasn't home. I didn't know where my parents were from, or where I had been born. I had no identity and place I belonged. I wasn't from anywhere.

I turned off the lamp, ignoring the snap and crackle of electricity, and I wrestled my thoughts to grasp sleep.

I left the factory the next day with an aching body and raw fingertips from the machinery. I'd scrubbed off the blood, but my cuts continued to sting. The thought of going home and eating a few bites of bread made me miserable. There were still a few coins in my secret pocket and I wanted to feel a full belly. A good dinner and a visit with Jean would be the perfect way to end my day.

I wandered in the direction of Bryant Park, unable to shake the hot, persistent feeling of eyes on my back. The paranoia of being watched was intrusive and unnerving. A face through the crowd drew my attention, a young woman who was nearly my mirror reflection. I halted, causing someone to bump into me, but I ignored their grumbled curse.

The woman vanished behind a taller person, and my heart quickened with alarm. I had to get a better look at her, to prove to myself she hadn't been a vision. Never had I seen anyone who looked so much like me and a wildness stirred within me. I pushed through the crowd, hoping to catch sight of her again—and I did.

Her skin was golden brown like mine and her long tangle of curls was nearly as dark and threaded with streaks the color of desert rock. Her clothing was military style with heavy black boots, black narrow men's combat pants, and a matching long jacket fastened by several belts over her torso. She looked positively scandalous for a woman. She moved quickly and caught up to a similarly dressed young man with windswept shoulder-length hair. I tried to maneuver myself closer to them to better see their faces.

I lost my visual again and I scrambled for signs of them. Nothing. My shoulders sagged, and all the air and excitement rushed from me, replaced by cold disappointment.

From a food vendor at the park's perimeter, I purchased two apples and a boiled sausage. I carried my feast to the New York Public Library and chose a partially hidden spot on the stone steps to eat. I didn't need anyone swiping my apples or a cop telling me to park it someplace else.

When I finished, I took a few sweeping strides to one of the magnificent marble lions of the library. They stood sentry on the steps of the north and south entrances. Though I'm not sure what compelled me, each time I visited, I touched a paw. Sometimes, when I was in a rush, my fingers barely brushed the cold stone. Other days, when times were harder than usual, I'd clasp both my small hands around the lion's great paw as tightly as my strength allowed. There was something about the power depicted in their muscular bodies, their serene, resolute gazes, and their heads raised high, that gave me courage. They'd been the guardians of the world's knowledge and literature for longer than I'd been alive, and I imagined they'd still be here long after I'd gone. I learned their names years ago, but I gave them names of my own. That somehow made them feel like they were mine. They were like the gods of old who became servants to whomever learned their secret names. If I told anyone else what I named them, the lions' strength would be lost to me.

The golden glow of the library's marble interior warmed me to my bones. Even on a busy evening, with every last footstep, breath, and voice of patrons echoing off the high ceiling, this was the most elegant place in my world. Some nights, as I lay in bed, I closed my eyes and pictured myself standing in this beautiful hall rather than my dingy room at the boarding house.

I didn't have a lot of time before closing, so I hurried. The woman, Jean, who'd taught me how to read at the orphanage, had only volunteered there. She was a librarian's aid a few times a week and I got to visit her sometimes.

Jean was often stationed in the reference room, returning books to their spots on shelves and assisting patrons. I found her at the top of a rolling ladder with a stack of volumes balanced in the bend of her arm as she shelved them.

"Good evening," I called to her.

She looked down and around for me and smiled when she spotted me. "Well, hello, Ziva! I missed you last night."

My blood warmed. She was one of the few who called me by my real name, even after others had corrected her in that pointlessly cruel way of theirs. "You did? Does that mean my book finally came back?"

She nodded and shimmied down the ladder surprisingly deft with all those books in one hand. She placed them on the bottom shelf, rose, and beckoned to me.

"I saved it for you, so it wouldn't disappear again," she said with an edge to her fun Metropolitan accent. "There's been a lot of interest in the subject since that bigwig archaeologist came to town."

She led me into a back room, which served as office space for several other aids working this department. The air was stale and musty, likely from all the stacks of old books and lack of open windows, and the desks were covered with piles of documents and writing utensils. A pot of coffee and a few yellowed, well-used porcelain cups sat on an unremarkable buffet table against the wall.

Jean snatched a thick volume from her desk and presented it to me. Joy made me wiggle a little dance as I accepted it. I read the title, devouring every word. *The Many Faces of Ancient and Contemporary Egypt*, by Zaman Useramen, Curator of the Egyptian Museum of Cairo.

"You're the best!" I told her, my smile wide and toothy.

"I sure hope you find the answers you're looking for in there," she said.

I took a seat at the unoccupied desk beside Jean's to thumb through the book and quickly glance at the photographs. "This could be it. I really believe I'm close to finding out where I came from. Look at these people. Their skin—it looks just like mine. Their hair—their eyes. My hair is very curly, and my skin tone is a little different—ashier. There! See?" I stopped abruptly and pushed my finger against a portrait of an Algerian Amazigh woman draped in folds of colorful fabric and glinting jewelry.

"I see a resemblance," Jean observed, though she sounded a little sad.

When I looked at her, I momentarily became too aware of her very white skin and honey-blond hair. We were both women, but we were so different. She had always been good to me, but she wasn't like me. She could never know how I felt, however much she kindly tried to. I gritted my teeth and tried to keep my thoughts on track. "I'm so sure my family is from Egypt or Algeria—maybe Tunisia. Do you suppose they came here to escape the French colonizers?"

"Whoever you are, don't forget you're Ziva first," she said, her voice firm yet gentle. "You are your own unique, clever, beautiful woman crafted from your own experiences and circumstances."

Her kindness couldn't drive away my feeling of how this hole in me may never be filled. No matter how much I researched or hypothesized or imagined, I'd never really know. Anyone who had never seen themselves in someone else could not understand that loneliness, or the potential thrill of finally seeing another person who looked like them.

"Have you ever noticed how much the library lions look like sphinxes?" I asked, hoping to redirect the conversation. "Save for their faces, of course. I wish they had sphinx faces." Thinking of them reminded me of the strange feline shadow I had seen last night. If I had magical power, then who was to say sphinxes didn't actually exist somewhere or at some time?

"You know, I heard in passing there are real sphinxes guarding a tomb in Woodlawn Cemetery," Jean said. "Stone sphinxes, but real ones."

"No way!" I exclaimed, and instantly images of the mythological creatures came to my mind. I'd seen many different variations of them in the books I'd devoured, along with lots of other kinds of beasts. "What kind are they? True sphinxes? Hieracosphinx? Kriosphinx?"

"We ought to hunt them down sometime and find out. What do you say?"

"You bet!" I flipped the page to the table of contents and decided I ought to begin with the preface and read cover to cover—to be sure I didn't miss any information.

"Why don't you take that home with you tonight?" Jean asked.

"I will, thanks!"

She walked me to the reception desk and opened a heavy binder filled with what looked like thousands of pages. This late in the evening, no one else waited here for their books to be checked out, so the process was quick and easy.

Before I left, I turned and asked, "Has a position opened up yet?" My body felt tight, bracing for disappointment.

Jean's mouth bunched up in the corner and she exhaled. "Well, one of the girls told me yesterday she's moving back to Ohio. The big city isn't working out for her. I will keep you updated."

"Please do," I told her, feeling a different kind of hunger. That could be a life-changer for me. Working for the city was a pretty good deal if you could find a job. I'd have much rather worked here, surrounding by books and art, than at the factory. Patience helped me stay sane and holding onto the dream of spending every day in this wonderful place helped me get through the week. If you didn't have any dreams, then you had nothing to work for.

I should've been watching the traffic better, but I couldn't stop exploring the book in my hands. The drawings, photos, and evocative narration about the ancient world consumed me. In my head, I could clearly imagine silk awnings draped over breezy open windows. And I could almost taste the warm, lush river air blooming with the sultry scents of anise, marjoram, cinnamon, and roasting nuts blended with the heady fragrances of red poppies, chamomile, and freshly cut pomegranates.

The furious honk of a horn in my face made me hop

with fright and leap back onto the sidewalk. My heart pounding, I grounded myself back to the real world. Dumpy pigeons squatted on the sidewalks and dodged splashes of brown-tinged water as taxis and town cars rolled through puddles. Above, airships floated through the skyscrapers, belching inky black diesel smoke. The city was crafted from cold, gray concrete, dark glass, and trees planted within cages, but I dreamed of the unfamiliar, fragrant, wild glory and moon-white limestone of a palace far away. The images struck me like a falling star, bright and beautiful and unexpected and were gone as quickly as they came.

When I got to my room and caught the scent of bread, my stomach started to eat itself inside out, even though I'd had my apples and sausage earlier. After neatly folding my clothes to wear again for work tomorrow, I slipped on my plain cotton nightgown, washed my face, and settled into bed. I turned out the lamp, but sleep was a slippery beast tonight.

The idea I could change my life by using my magic pecked at me. This sagging cot didn't have to be my bed. I could have one made of feathers rather than lumps, and there could be butter for my toast. I could improve my circumstances if I used my abilities. Why would I have them if I weren't meant to use them?

Finally sleeping, I drifted in and out of dreams, none of them able to keep hold of me. A rustling noise yanked me back into full awareness. I held my breath, sure I had another mouse in the darkness of my room. My heart fluttering with panic, I reached for the lamp and the bulb flared to life, temporarily blinding me. When my eyes adjusted, I glimpsed a shape so huge it seemed to swallow my room whole.

A long ram's face rose high to scent the air and its massive, heavy spiraled horns gave the impression of a devil. The venomous yellow eyes, alight like electricity, belonged to a creature with an almost feline body the size of a small horse. The lamp's glow shone on the slick reddish-black coat, illuminating faint leopard spots splattered across its ribs. I'd seen this creature last night, after my encounter with the thief.

The beast looked at me. Those eyes locked with mine.

I gasped, sucking in too much air too fast to cry out, and I tore the lamp from its tether to the wall and smashed it against the side of the monster's head with an explosion of glass and heat.

The beast snarled, staggering, and backpedaled into the shadows. I jumped to my feet, grabbed the shades, and yanked them down. The city lights flooded my room, revealing the giant, coiled horns on top of its head and the full length of its body. Powerful muscle clenched beneath its panther coat, talons, built to tear a man in two, spread and dug into the floor.

All my research, everything I'd read from history and mythology, the pictures I'd spent hours scouring over—I knew this beast. A kriosphinx in the flesh.

"Lucky, lucky, lucky," it growled, its voice deep as a chasm. "A lucky night for me."

My power singed my fingertips. "Stay back," I warned. "If you leave, I won't hurt you."

The curve of its smile dragged a chill up my spine. Those narrowed yellow eyes watched my hands. "I wasn't sure it was you at first when I watched you last night. But I'm certain now. The queen's scion is a fledgling Medjai. How quaint."

The kriosphinx lurched forward, forelegs up and talons spread. I threw out my arm and cast a rush of my power. The monster deflected my strike with a swing of its head. It bowed and slammed its skull and horns into my chest, knocking the air from my lungs and me off my feet. I felt my body hit something solid and heard a terrible crash and shatter—then I fell. The window grew farther and farther away as I fell, and I could not fill my lungs with enough air to scream. My body flailed and as the sidewalk roared toward my face, I flung up my hands. My power smashed into the ground, breaking my fall, and I cried out with relief when I felt the firm, solid concrete beneath me.

The ram-headed beast landed gracefully to my right, and a second one emerged from the shadows to my left, its long narrow tail lashing like a cat's, ready to pounce. A third stepping into the street let loose a high, resonating, guttural bugle that sounded less animal and more like a ghost's sorrowful wail, filling me with emptiness, and sent shivers through my bones.

CHAPTER

3

My lungs stalled, my breath stolen with shock. I scrambled to my feet in terror and disbelief. People on the sidewalk and in the street screamed and darted in every direction.

The first of the kriosphinxes bounded forward. My fingertips sparked, and my power rushed forth, cutting through the air like a scream. The beast sprang, claws outstretched, and was struck full force by my power and went sailing across the street. Its body hit the wall of a brick building and flopped to the ground. As it tried to lift itself, its badly shattered leg gave way. The second kriosphinx loped to its side with a low noise vibrating in its throat.

I had done that. My power was greater than I'd realized. For the first time in my life, I was eager to test its limit, to unleash, despite the frightening circumstances. I felt *alive*.

The third kriosphinx dashed at me, talons scraping the pavement, head bowed and ready to bunt.

I swung my arm and the magical wind rocketed toward the beast, catching it and smashing it into a passing motorcar. Tires squealing, the car fish-tailed before spinning out and striking another. A gasp of horror ripped through my lungs. I'd been so eager to test my power and again—as always—I'd lost control.

There came a strange, distant crack, then a flash and flames. Nausea welled up inside me and I shot forward to help the panic-stricken occupants escape. I grappled at the door handle. My clammy fingers slipped as though they'd been greased. The door popped open and the woman in the passenger seat seemed to pour out onto the sidewalk in a tangle of limbs, followed by the male driver as he clambered over the interior. I gaped at them, unable to form even a simple apology, my brain turned to mush. They scrambled away as the kriosphinx, to my horror, pushed itself to its feet, recovered, and shook its body like a dog. In a rage and paying no mind to the flames, it lowered its head and launched into the driver's side fender, horns caving in metal with a crunch. The tire burst and hissed as it deflated.

Through the blaze, a young woman appeared, and the kriosphinx backpedaled as fear slashed across its face. She flung out her arm and a short wooden staff unfolded like a bird's wing with a *crack*. Its three segments locked into place creating a nearly four feet long weapon with glossy black blades fashioned at both ends.

She spun the staff above her head, gaining momentum,

and swept downward in an arc, the air screaming. The kriosphinx backpedaled again, but the blade opened its shoulder. Its ram's mouth gaped and gave a high-pitched, haunting bugle that squeezed my bones and pierced my brain. It charged, and the woman whirled aside too quickly for the beast's slashing claws to strike true. It bowed its head and shot forward, but she ducked and rolled away from its horns. The kriosphinx slid to a halt, reared, and pirouetted to follow her—and the woman thrust the staff, driving the blade into the beast's chest.

She stepped aside, tugged her weapon free, and watched the kriosphinx give a horrid lurch. Its chest cavity caved in around the mortal wound, bones snapping as they broke. The beast's bugle of pain cascaded into a whistling scream as the body was sucked through, jerking violently, struggling as it was pulled, bone by bone, into itself, folding, crunching, and snarling. Light poured through the veil like a beacon, but it went out as the kriosphinx disappeared into a void.

I gaped in disbelief, taking in the incredible sight of this warrior, certain she was the same woman I saw in Bryant Park. Her face, though her expression was fierce, was impossibly lovely up close. Her large, round eyes were deep brown and outlined with black kohl, giving her a catlike appearance. The knuckles of her fingerless gloves were embedded with the same starlight-sharp stone of her weapon.

She noticed my presence for the first time and when she looked at me, I found no gentleness in her gaze. "You should run," she instructed, her accent British.

I started to step away as the third kriosphinx left its fallen ally's side and bugled a battle cry. The woman marched toward the beast, whirling her staff with such force it whistled. One end swept low and the kriosphinx reared beyond its reach. The woman thrust the staff's other end upward, and the blade opened the beast's powerful shoulder.

"*Neit!*" A lightning-quick blast of water was conjured from her hand and snaked through the air. The kriosphinx scrambled to evade her power, but it was hit in the ribs and crushed into the wall of a building. I stared, mesmerized by her incredible ability. She was like *me*. The word she said seemed to activate her power as though it were an incantation.

Her head snapped up and she looked past me. "Sayer! Mind your six!"

I spun to watch a young man, the woman's companion from earlier, swing the spade-shaped, black blade of a battle ax into the chest of the kriosphinx behind him. The beast bellowed in agony and curled inward. The man's now empty fist struck the kriosphinx in the snout, the stone knuckles of his glove tearing its face wide open. It crumpled to the ground. He removed a second ax from its sheath and kicked the dying kriosphinx onto its side before burying the blade into its heart. He yanked both axes from the body as the beast imploded and disappeared through its wounds.

Pain ricocheted through my body and I was thrown to the ground with a great weight upon me. I screamed and thrashed, managing to flip myself onto my back. The last kriosphinx raked its claws across my collarbone, drawing streaks of burning pain and blood. My magic flared on instinct, blasting the beast off me. It righted itself and lunged, talons spread and spitting with rage.

"*Neit!*" I cried with all my strength, the strange word instinctively tearing from my throat, and the electricity in my fingertips cooled like shaved ice. A sudden jet of water exploded from my hand so powerfully it knocked me to the ground. The spell rocketed toward the kriosphinx and it bugled again.

The rush of magic pulled at my core like never before, a beast stirring from slumber, sweeping and tugging like an undertow, taking from me something I couldn't name. I ached to cast again, to see how strong I could make my magic.

"You," came a breathy voice.

I lifted my head and found the young woman staring at me, stupefied. Her bewilderment showed plain as blood on snow.

"Who are you?" I asked her.

She scoffed gruffly. "Who are *you?*"

"Ziva?" the man called, and shock socked me in the gut. His dark gaze captured mine. "Catch!"

He tossed a slender object. I snatched it from the air, a dagger made from cold, glossy stone as black as a new moon and starlight sharp.

The kriosphinx reared above me, forelegs spread and ready to bring me to the ground. I slashed my dagger across its ram-face. The creature hissed and bellowed in pain as its skin opened and sparked. In the bloody rip of its wound, I caught a glimpse as though through a veil to another, darker world.

Claws outstretched, it left its chest unprotected. It came down on me and I shoved the dagger deep beneath its ribcage. Hot, reeking blood spilled onto my white nightgown and I knew the black blade had plunged into the kriosphinx's heart. Bright light erupted from the creature's wound and became a void through which its body was twisted and yanked, filling my ears with the sounds of crunching bones and strangled agony as it died. In moments, only empty air remained.

When all had gone still and quiet, I lowered my arms and saw the young man holding out his hand. He wore the same fingerless, stone-knuckled gloves as the woman's, and clasped on his wrist was a gold bracelet with blue, red, and green smaller stones and a large blue stone carved into the shape of a beetle—no, a scarab. He'd sheathed both battle axes into the belt around his hips where they were partially concealed by the long black coat buckled across his chest.

He was as richly beautiful as the young woman, both so strange, so unearthly. He had golden-beige skin a shade darker than mine and his nearly black hair had pulled free from its tie. A few days' worth of stubble spread evenly around his mouth and along his jaw. His dark, purposeful eyes shadowed by full lashes were outlined with bold metallic paint the color of dark graphite. I'd never seen a man wear makeup before and it only added to his beauty and to the thousand—possibly infinite— questions I had for him.

I let him help me to my feet, but my limbs seemed to be growing cold with shock. "Where did it go? I think I killed it—the kriosphinx, correct?"

"Yes," he said, appearing so calm and gentle. "It is you, isn't it? Your name is Ziva?"

I nodded and noticed the tremors spreading through my body—an uncontrollable trembling—but I didn't think it was entirely from the chilly night air.

"Take this." He shrugged off his jacket and offered it to me. I accepted it and slipped my arms into the too big sleeves. The wool fabric provided near instant relief.

"Thank you," I said.

He gave me an encouraging nod and a gentle smile. "Of course. You'll be all right."

The realization I'd never killed anything before—save for roaches and mice—struck me like a slap. It took me a few moments to gather my senses. "How do you know my name?" I asked and couldn't help but sound accusatory. "Who are you?"

"Sayer Bahri," he replied, his accent also British. "And this is my sister, Nasira. We are Medjai, the last of an ancient tribe. We've been looking for you for a long time, Ziva. You're one of us."

While I processed that information, Nasira whipped her staff in the air, and it closed, folding its three segments into a smaller object. She returned the strange weapon to its holster around her thigh and marched toward me, her jaw tight with resolve. She roughly took hold of my arm and steered me along. "You'll come with us."

"To where?" I demanded, bewildered and wishing I

weren't wearing a torn nightgown drenched in blood. The smell nauseated me, and the fabric stuck to my belly, quickly becoming colder than the night air. The streets had emptied of people, but in the distance, panicked shouts and voices could be heard growing closer.

"For now," she said coolly, "back to the car."

"From there, to headquarters," Sayer finished.

"I can't just leave!" I thought of my food and the quilt I'd spent a year working on.

We turned a corner and when we saw a mob of people shouting and crying over what they'd witnessed, we spun back the way we'd come.

"The next street," Sayer directed. "She'll draw attention."

"Right," Nasira agreed.

"Let *go* of me!" I growled and yanked myself free of her grip. "You're not taking me anywhere."

An impatient frown crinkled her features before she exchanged a look with her brother. "We're trying to help you and I think you're smart enough to know we're the only ones that can. All that's happened tonight isn't a complete surprise to you, is it? You've had magic your whole life."

"And you've been missing since birth," Sayer added, in a gentler tone than his sister's. "We detected the kriosphinxes, but we didn't really expect to find you too. We've come halfway across the world to bring you home."

"Home?" I asked, the word a dream upon my lips.

Nasira nodded. "The kriosphinxes are after you because you're one of us and we aren't safe out here.

We'll take you to our high priestess. She'll explain better than we can."

My heart pumped lightning through my veins. "But—I—"

Sayer stepped closer to me, intensity and purpose burning in his eyes. "Either you continue to do whatever it is that you do every day for the rest of your life, or you can come with us and you'll learn who you really are and what you can do. Your birthright."

I stared at them, overwhelmed by everything—my circumstances, the magic, the kriosphinxes. These two people, these Medjai, the same word the kriosphinx had called me in my room—they *looked* like me. Not as though we might be related, but they had my hair and my eyes, my skin tone, the long, gently curved nose . . . Not once in my life had I ever felt like I belonged somewhere. The only time I had ever seen anyone like Sayer and Nasira, I'd been staring at my own reflection. These were my people.

I *had* people.

If I stayed, I'd work at the factory until my death. One day I would wake too starved and weak to work, and without money to buy food, I would die.

I had nothing to lose but the quilt that would probably never be long enough to cover my toes.

I let out my breath and said, "Okay. Let's go."

I sat in the rear of a sleek, black Delage, marveling at the smoothness of the leather seat and finely polished wood dashboard upon which Nasira had propped her boots. My back was stick-straight, my hands folded in my lap. I was petrified of dirtying the leather, and I knew the inside of Sayer's jacket had to be filthy from the blood on my skin and nightgown.

"Where are we headed?" I asked, breaking the silence.

"Long Island," Sayer replied from the driver's seat. "It's temporary. Our main headquarters is in Egypt."

"So, you're Egyptian?"

"Yes, but we are also Medjai," Nasira elaborated. "Our people belong to a tribe native to North Africa. We have protected Egypt and this world from evil for five thousand years."

I am North African. I am Egyptian. I am Medjai. In my head, the words seemed alien to say. I'd never known who I was or where I belonged. *I am Ziva. I am a girl.* Those things I could say, but they were all I could say with certainty before today. They were all I'd ever known about myself. *I am Medjai.* That statement gave me a profound emotion I couldn't quite pinpoint. I suddenly felt like a whole person—someone with a story, an identity, and even a future.

I am Medjai.

The dagger Sayer had given me rested on the seat next to my thigh. I lifted it and drew my finger across the blade's black, glossy surface, noticing how it was imperfect, as if it'd been chiseled by hand. The handle was wrapped in beige leather, mottled like plucked bird skin. "These weapons we used against the kriosphinxes. What are they?"

"Obsidian," Nasira explained. "Mined from volcanic islands in the southern Red Sea and quite lethal to immortals like the kriosphinxes. The hilts are ostrich leather."

"Stone blades," I mused, turning the dagger over in my hands. "They're beautiful."

"Volcanic glass, technically," she said.

I blinked with surprise. "Glass? But wouldn't it break?"

"Obsidian is naturally very brittle," Sayer explained, "but the blades are buried in the hot ashes of a *khet* spell, and the magical fire tempers the material until it's as strong as a diamond. A *was* blade won't break and it's sharper than any surgical needle."

"Have you never seen one before?" Nasira asked. "Your parents' maybe?"

"I never knew them," I replied, my voice quiet. "I grew up in an orphanage."

Sayer and Nasira exchanged looks, their brows dark with concern.

"You don't know where they are?" he asked me.

I shook my head. "No."

"You've never had any schooling with your magic?" he asked, surprised. "How did you know the creatures you faced tonight were kriosphinxes?"

"I read a lot of books," I replied.

Sayer nudged his sister with his elbow. "See, Nasi? Books are useful."

"Mmm-hmm," was her unimpressed response.

"Are you looking for my parents too?" I asked them.

"Of course," Sayer said calmly. "We'll find them, Ziva. We take care of our own."

The farther from Manhattan we drove, past small towns and brightly lit houses on hills, the darker the world became until it was confined within the beams of the Delage's headlights. I'd never been this way before—there had never been any reason for me to visit Long Island—and I couldn't believe how the trees seemed to go on forever on either side of the road. The most wooded place I'd ever seen was Central Park. The moon and stars grew brighter, emerging through the glow of the city and illuminating darkened shapes alongside the road. I pressed my face against the window, straining to make out what I saw.

It was as though the life of Long Island had died on this winding stretch of road. Sprawling estates were blanketed in shadows and silence like empty corpses dried out from the insides, some of them reduced to charred skeletons. Fountains stood as quiet sentinels and feral gardens were overgrown and tangled, seemingly ruins of a lost civilization.

I'd heard of the neighborhoods like this, incredible palatial homes once owned by families who'd lost everything on Black Tuesday and during the years of the depression after. Once some of the most beautiful places in the world, they'd been abandoned and left to fend for themselves, just like I'd been. Rumors swirled of people who'd leapt from towers or locked themselves in their houses and left on their gas stoves. I didn't know how true the tales were. To be honest, I didn't want to know.

We pulled into a circular drive at the end of the lane and came to a stop before the most derelict home of them all. The shadowed estate utterly reclaimed by nature, more fit for the ghost of a prince than a living one. The stone walls rose like towers, and creeping webs of ivy had grown so wide they swallowed the boarded up or broken windows. Gables were disintegrating at their sharp peaks and perhaps little more than half of the shingles remained attached to the roof. All was dark. All was silent.

We exited the Delage and I had second thoughts about trusting these strangers. If I'd been tricked, then my only option would be to run into the trees. I had no idea where I was, but I was sure the distant rushing sound had to be waves crashing along the beach. If I followed the coast, I could find my way to a town and get help.

Nasira and Sayer scaled the stone steps toward a once magnificent portico darkened by massive columns and a sagging ceiling. Sayer turned halfway and paused.

"Are you coming?" he asked.

Still barefoot, I felt rooted to the cracked and neglected flagstones embedded in the earth. My flight response sang in my veins. At the same time, my heart pressed against my ribcage, a balloon filled with hope that might float to the clouds if it were torn from my chest. I hugged myself against a night chill around my bare legs; I'd have felt naked in my destroyed nightgown if it weren't for Sayer's jacket.

"Oh, relax," Nasira said, exasperated but grinning. "It's an illusion! The inside is much nicer. Don't want the milkman stopping by, do we?" She tossed me a wink.

I inhaled, nodding, and followed them up the stairs. Nasira opened the right half of the grand front door and it yielded with a whine, scraping a couple of years' worth of crunchy, dead leaves aside. She entered first and Sayer stepped to the left to allow me to pass him. I tried not to think about how they had me surrounded, but the instant I saw the splendor of the interior, all sense deserted me.

The entrance hall seemed as wide and tall as my entire crummy boarding house and was lit up bright and golden as day by numerous glittering crystal chandeliers. A magnificent black marble staircase rose into a circular, three-story atrium, each floor lined with a balustrade also of gleaming matching marble. And everywhere people—Medjai, I was certain—milled about with steely expressions.

"But the outside was so dark and quiet!" I exclaimed, unable to hide my amazement.

Nasira cast me a look like she couldn't believe I was surprised. "I told you—an illusion."

I stepped forward, my feet tapping the cold white stone floor, moved by wonder and taking in as much as I could. Suitcases, crates, and boxes, as if no one had bothered to unpack them, were everywhere. As if they hadn't been here for very long.

"Hello there."

The speaker was a beautiful, mature woman with honey-brown skin. She wore an eggshell-white cloche hat artfully tilted to one side. Her rich brown hair, the ends flashing with a copper sheen, was cropped at her ears and styled into perfect waves. Gold dust shimmered on her high, elegant cheekbones and her catlike, hazel eyes were elongated with metallic silver-black lines. She wore a fashionable navy wrap dress, belted at her slender waist, which fell to just above her ankles to show off sleek eggshell pumps. She extended a matching gloved hand to shake mine. Even at this late hour, she was immaculately put together.

"This is Ziva," Nasira declared, and that wonder and disbelief returned to her face, the same emotions I saw earlier when she realized who I was. "We found her."

"How astonishing it is to meet you, Ziva," the woman remarked, her burgundy-painted lips smiling, her accent British like the others. "I'm Cyrene Tera, high priestess of the Medjai."

Cyrene wasn't what I'd imagined a high priestess to look like. Perhaps I'd expected spotted animal skins and golden diadems—anything but someone who looked like one of the finest ladies to walk Park Avenue.

"Let's talk," Cyrene continued, an eager gleam in her dark eyes.

CHAPTER

4

Cyrene Tera beckoned me through the parlor, navi-
gating around plush furniture I didn't want to soil
by touching, down a wide hallway with amber lamps
glowing in alcoves, and through a rich mahogany door.
We entered a study whose walls were built-in shelves
crammed with books and trinkets. Cyrene switched on
a stained-glass lamp at the massive desk, illuminating a
framed picture of a white family. I wondered if they once
called this place home and what had become of them.

"Have a seat, Ziva," the priestess instructed, gesturing
to a leather chair across from the desk.

I glanced at the door, but Sayer and Nasira hadn't
followed us in. A part of me felt a small amount of disappointment they weren't here to provide a small amount
of comforting familiarity to me in a strange place. "Forgive
me if I seem overwhelmed and confused," I told Cyrene.

She leaned forward in her chair. "I can only imagine.

You've been gone many years. We know you as Ziva Mereniset, the name given to you at birth."

To not have known your true name and then hear it for the first time was a bizarre experience. I felt like I'd lived a lie or lived a dream and had just woken up. I didn't feel entirely lucid. But I hadn't lived a lie. Rose Ellison was someone shaped by loneliness and hardship. She was a survivor. She was me. Ziva Mereniset was a stranger, but I wanted to know her and where she came from—to learn who she could become.

"We Medjai are blessed by the goddess Isis," Cyrene told me, "given sway over the elements of this earth. Thousands of years ago a man named Narmer climbed into the Atlas Mountains of Algeria to where our people lived and chose us to lead his armies. Together, we united Upper and Lower Egypt and Narmer became the first pharaoh. Isis bid us to swear our lives and our magic to the kings and queens of Egypt forevermore. There hasn't been a pharaoh for a very long time and we have been lost, for lack of a better word. And you have been literally lost. From us, anyway."

"Who were my mother and father?" I asked her.

"You were born in Cairo and your parents, Qadir and Satiah, vanished with you when you were three days old."

Knowing my parents' names felt satisfying, like fitting another piece into the puzzle of me. "But why? Why did they leave?"

Her face fell. "While your parents never spoke to me about their intention before they left, or since, they must have believed they could protect you better than we

49

could. We tried to follow and bring you home, but we lost you all in the chaos caused by the Great War."

"Protect me?" Confusion filled my head with bubbles. Her words didn't correlate with anything that had happened to me. "They abandoned me. I grew up in an orphanage."

"They would never have done that, Ziva," Cyrene said with earnest. "You are no ordinary Medjai. You're descended from royalty. You have queen's blood."

I shook my head, all understanding lost. "Forgive me—queen's blood?"

She leaned forward on the desk. "Through your mother, you are descended from Queen Nefertari, the Great Royal Wife of Ramesses II. She was a Medjai of legendary ability and ruled Egypt's most prosperous period. A god's magic made it possible for Nefertari to be resurrected after death, but that spell depended on a celestial phenomenon which took three thousand years to occur."

"And that is where I come in?" I asked.

Cyrene nodded. "One of her descendants had to be born under a planetary alignment with the center star of Osiris's Crown, the constellation known to the Greeks as Orion's Belt. This allowed for a piece of Nefertari's soul, the life essence known as her *ka*, to be reborn within a mortal vessel. Her *ka* was reborn in you, Ziva. And your birth in this period of global turmoil is no coincidence. Our world is on the brink of a second Great War and you can help us resurrect Nefertari to reestablish a golden age—help us to bring back purpose to our people. There are, however, forces which would stop at nothing to prevent us from doing so."

"Like the kriosphinxes?" I asked.

"They, those who control them, and other, more earthly evils," she said. "You see, Ziva, before the Great War, there were rules and honor while in combat. We fought hand-to-hand, looked into our opponent's eyes, and the best warrior won. That honor was lost beneath bombs falling from the clouds and in the trenches—in the fields of buried mines, poison gas plumes, and tangled barbed wire. Soldiers fired bullets into nothingness and prayed they weren't killed from the bullets sprayed by an enemy whose eyes they never saw. No one living remembers what the glory of victory feels like. They remember only killing and killing more, until an entire generation was wiped out.

"The Great War caused the economy of Europe to collapse. There are no young people to work. The League of Nations has failed, and a hateful, cataclysmic power is amassing in Germany, one far worse than before. This evil feeds on the fear and suffering of its own people. It will swallow this world, leaving behind unfathomable destruction. You alone are the key to resurrecting a leader of the greatest dynasty in history. Is that something you want to be a part of?" Cyrene looked at me from across the wide desk, her eyes watching closely.

The air burst from me in a short laugh, gruff with astonishment. If I went home, the textile factory would be my prison for the rest of my life, if I was lucky enough to keep the job that long. I would go to bed hungry every night as before.

Or I could have an adventure.

I looked up at Cyrene, her hazel eyes glinting in the lamplight. "I'm in."

She smiled eagerly. "I'm glad to hear that," she said. "Tonight, we'll give you a room, draw you a bath, and provide a change of clean clothing. Tomorrow, you'll begin to receive all you've been denied: an education, training, and dignity."

"Pardon, ma'am," I said tightly and deeply offended. "I might never have had a soft bed to sleep in, but I have always had my dignity."

She frowned. "Forgive me. My words were rude and not representative at all of my impression of you."

"Which is?" I asked.

Her head tilted slightly to the side and a cunning smile threatened one side of her mouth. "I imagine you have an exquisitely ruthless will to survive."

Unsure whether that was a compliment or not, I said nothing.

"I do mean to train you, Ziva," Cyrene continued. "Your blood is that of royalty and warriors. You will become the best of both."

The moment I allowed myself to acknowledge the cold blanket of exhaustion pressing down on me, its weight tripled. I closed my eyes for some relief, but opened them again as quickly as I could, or else I'd pass out in the chair. A warm bed was a thrilling thought, enough to stir me to my feet.

Cyrene rose with me. "Sayer?"

The study door opened, and he appeared. The late hour didn't seem to drag on him at all; he seemed as alert as ever, his expression blank and impenetrable. He was *intense*, and I found myself drawn to watching him, which was likely very strange, but I found looking away challenging. The warm lamplight illuminated the amber in his skin tone and gave his dark eyes an otherworldly glow.

"Yes?" Sayer asked.

"Would you please escort Ziva to an available room?" Cyrene requested.

"Of course," he replied, and turned his attention to me. "Right this way."

I followed him into the hallway and down a corridor void of paintings or any other valuable decorations. I couldn't imagine any treasures at all remaining after the mansion's owners had abandoned it. This neighborhood had to have been a thief's paradise.

Sayer led me up a narrow spiral staircase guided by a finely carved wooden railing and lit by the warm glow of lamps set into alcoves. We emerged in a hall and made a left down another.

"Did you . . . know my parents?" I asked, bitterly aware of how awkward I sounded, grasping at any kind of conversation.

He slowed his pace and shot me a glance from the side, one eyebrow raised with interest at me. "I was three when you were born. I remember that day in little pieces, how happy everyone seemed. You are my first memory, I suppose, if that isn't too odd a thing to say."

"No, we all have a first memory," I remarked, thinking of my mine, the one with my mother. "Is there only you and your sister in New York?"

"Mum is here," he said. "She and my dad can tell you about your parents."

Sayer smiled, his skin warm and golden in the lamplight, and my breath stalled. Tiny flecks of gold in his dark eyes caught the glow and glimmered. I liked him and again I thought his demeanor was gentler than Nasira's, though I liked her too. My first impression wasn't that she was unkind, only that he had a softer heart.

He stopped at a closed door and put a hand on the knob. "I hope this will be comfortable for you."

"Oh—and please have this back," I said, suddenly remembering his jacket. I pulled it off and handed it to him. "Thank you. For the coat. For your help."

He gave me a slow nod of solidarity. "I really didn't believe we'd ever find you. Sure that we'd been chasing a ghost my entire life."

"Then it seems I am in as much shock as you are," I told him.

"And I didn't mean to eavesdrop," he started with an apologetic half-smile, "but I heard what Cyrene said about your ruthlessness. She did not mean ruthless, as in cruel. Rather, unyielding. That you will survive at any cost. And she hadn't even witnessed what I'd witnessed tonight. She can tell that by examining the way you carry yourself despite the bites this world has taken from you. I can tell that."

I stared at him like a fool. There were words

somewhere in my head, but I couldn't grasp at them. They flitted around like butterflies.

"I am in astonishment of it all," he continued. "Everything. You. What you did. Maybe there is something to that queen's blood of yours after all."

"Sayer." All I could say was his name.

He backed away from me, ready to turn and leave. "Goodnight, Ziva."

I watched him go, chewing the inside of my cheek. "'Night."

The next morning, I woke more rested and invigorated than I ever had before. I lay in that massive bed for a few moments, willing the comfort to soak into my bones, and I listened to birds singing outside the wide window I'd opened last night before I'd gone to bed. My room had access to a private bathroom—my *own* toilet! No fighting Nonna Tessio. I could use it whenever I pleased on my own time. I'd filled the bathtub with the hottest water I could tolerate, and it had steamed up my suite so thoroughly I couldn't see my way through the haze. Opening the window had helped, and it had let in the freshest, most fragrant air I could've imagined.

I climbed out of bed and had a sudden sense someone had been in my room while I'd slept. I paused and surveyed the floor and furniture. The ruined nightgown I'd left in a wad by the wall was gone. In its place and spread across the back of a leather chaise was a lovely day dress the color of buttercream. A satin mint belt bound the waist and a pair of matching mint pumps sat on the floor in front of the chair.

I changed, happy to find both the dress and shoes fit nicely, and when I inspected myself in the gilded, full length mirror, part of me wished I had cropped hair like the fashionable girls of New York. Like Cyrene. Of course, I'd never had the money for a proper haircut. On the other hand, my hair was long and curly like Nasira's, and I'd rather look like her.

A bowl loaded with fruit had been placed on a marble sideboard table. My stomach knotted itself and I eagerly approached. Tangy oranges, rich bananas, and crisp black grapes—*grapes*! I dived in, crushing as much as I could into my mouth, savoring the crash of different flavors all at once. I couldn't remember the last time I'd enjoyed fruit, but I thought of Christmas mornings when each of us children at the orphanage found an orange in our stocking. Those oranges had been small and a little mushy, but the oranges I enjoyed now were as big as my whole hand and dense with juice.

A smile pinched my cheeks. The dress hugged my waist, hinting at curves I might have had if I got some real food in me. I swiveled left and right, watching the pleated hem swing around my ankles, imagining myself as one of the pretty girls who went dancing with friends and boys. I was sure I was in a fairytale, one just like I'd read in books with Jean. I wondered if I'd ever see her again.

I tousled and freshened up my hair before twisting the curls into shape with my fingers, and when I was ready, I opened my bedroom door to find Nasira leaning against the wall across the corridor. She surprised me so much I stumbled in my heels.

"Good morning," she said cheerfully, wearing similar combat gear to what she wore last night. When a moment ago I imagined myself a debutante, now my pretty dress felt very out of place and impractical.

"Hello," I said in return. "Were you waiting for me?"

"I thought of you," she admitted, "and decided if I were in a strange place full of strange people, I'd like a familiar face to show me around."

Surprise filled me like sunlight, warm and pleasant. "Thank you," I said. "That's very kind. I suppose I've never had someone like that."

Sunlight glimmered gold on her cheeks. "To show you around?"

"To think of me."

Her smile dimmed a little. "Oh."

Nasira fell quiet and heat rushed into my face with embarrassment. I must've appeared pitiful to her and I hated pity. A poor girl with no family, money, or future. With no one. Nothing. Starved and wary like a stray dog.

"If I seemed cold last night, please forgive me," she said. "I'm cautious. And protective. I don't want to see you as an outsider, because you're not."

"I appreciate that," I told her, but wasn't sure what else to say.

"Well," she started, "are you hungry?"

My gaze shifted from her to my room and back.

"There was a bowl of fruit in my room this morning, so I already ate, but thank you."

"That's not breakfast," Nasira said, her smile returning. "There's plenty more downstairs."

"There's more?"

"Come on."

She gestured for me to follow her. She led me into a hallway I hadn't seen yet. Medjai bustled about their morning business and largely avoided eye contact. Their chins and gazes held steady on the empty air in front of them or on whatever they carried in their hands—stacks of books or wooden crates filled with packing paper and stone figures.

"Why does everyone ignore me?" I asked.

"Cyrene asked them to give you space," Nasira replied. "She worried you'll be overwhelmed."

"A little, I suppose," I admitted.

"If you approach anyone, they'll talk to you," she offered, her expression kind. "There aren't many of us left. And you are family we've never met before. Family is an intimate thing. It'll take some time for us all to adjust."

No one had ever called me family before. The word came with a promise of trust and friendship, togetherness and a place where I would belong. Every time someone said my real name, it felt as though my shackles had snapped apart and I was freed from my old measly life. Over and over again, the feeling of liberation struck me. I hoped it would never fade.

The dining hall boasted a view of the overgrown garden through an entire wall of windows rising from the rose granite floor to the high, gilded gypsum ceiling. All of them were open and the morning air, carrying the sweet fragrances of flowering trees and bushes outside, gently blew the sheer, white curtains, which billowed like clouds. One very long table stretched down the center of the hall and was piled with silver and porcelain platters of food—more food than I'd ever seen in Lou's bakery. My eyes couldn't grow wide enough to take it all in. Seated Medjai chatted with each other over their plates, and the only familiar face among them looked up to smile at us.

"Nasi, Ziva," Sayer called, and waved us over.

Nasira took the empty seat across from her brother, who had a plateful of toast covered in powdered sugar and syrup. I sat beside her and couldn't peel my gaze away from all the food; I wanted to dig in right away.

"How did you sleep?" Sayer asked me.

Hunger raked its claws across the lining of my stomach. "Just fine, thank you. What are you eating there?"

"French toast," he replied. "It's a bit more American than French, but it's delicious."

Sayer lifted and offered the platter to me. I chose the three slices covered with the most powdered sugar and poured syrup over them. I cut a piece with silverware so shiny I could see my reflection. I closed my mouth around the modest bite.

If I hadn't been in public, I would have fallen flat to the floor.

I *loved* French toast.

The next pieces I cut were definitely too large, but I would've stuffed an entire slice in my mouth. The rich maple syrup, the delicate powdered sugar, warm cinnamon, the pillowy bread, and . . . something else.

"What's the bread cooked in?" I asked, rolling the mouthful around my tongue, now entirely indifferent to the idea of manners.

"A mixture of eggs and milk, I think," Nasira replied casually, as though this wasn't the most important food ever. "You can make it lots of different ways, of course. I love it with baked apple slices."

I didn't want to stuff myself just yet and I was already a bit full from the fruit in my room. I had to be strategic.

I poured a glass of ice water, something that wouldn't sit heavily. I spotted a dish of iced pastries plump with unknown filling and grabbed two. I took a bite out of one and savored the sweet and tart blackberry flavor. The second pastry was filled with apples and a pinch of cinnamon. If I remembered correctly, Lou sold pastries like this and called them scones, but I'd never had enough money to buy one. Between alternating bites of both, I caught Nasira's bewildered stare. It was so clear she didn't understand. Neither of my new friends could understand. Neither of them had ever wanted for anything.

My eyes burned as I chewed another bite and I swallowed through a muffled sob. I wiped at a tear in the corner of my eye and took another bite.

"Are . . . are you all right?" Sayer asked, his dark eyes wide, brow furrowed.

I finished chewing and swallowed, rolling the last bit of blackberry around my tongue. "It's just . . . so delicious!"

He laughed, a deep and rich sound, and Nasira's grin

spread wide across her face. "We have plenty more where that came from!" she told me.

My tears weren't for the food, they were for myself and I hated that. Knowing there were people in the world who ate meals like this every day and it was nothing to them. Sayer and Nasira treated me a bit like a cute new puppy they'd brought home, but I understood there wasn't any malice in it and I forgave them. Perhaps I did act like an innocent animal, stuffing my face with more food than my belly could hold. If my dress had had pockets and no one had been looking, I would've shoved bagels into them for later, uncertain when I'd have another meal. As hard as I tried, I couldn't convince myself I'd never need to hide food again. All this could be gone in an instant.

CHAPTER

5

Nasira wasted no time, beginning my training immediately after breakfast. She led me into a room with
wood paneled walls and a glossy, patterned wood floor.
Black outfits hung on rolling metal racks, and many different pairs of boots sat in rows on the racks' bottom
shelves. Stacked around the room were locked leather
cases.

"A temporary armory, if you will," she explained, as
she sifted through the clothing. "Home is much more
impressive."

"This is impressive enough," I assured her.

Nasira selected a shirt and slender pants—both black
twill and very similar to her own—and handed them to
me. "This is typical gear we wear during training and in
the field."

"You'll teach me how to use a stick like yours?" I asked,
unable to hide my eagerness.

"It's called an *asaya*," she explained.

"Teach me how to use the *asaya* then."

"Well, we can't do anything when you're barely saddle-broken," she said gently.

Her words brewed sadness in my heart. "It's so unfair that this should've been my life. Why would my parents take me away from our people? If the *ka* of a queen our people were sworn to protect was reborn within me, then what they did makes no sense. Cyrene said Nefertari's resurrection would bring us a purpose again. Something to fight for."

She frowned and took a deep breath, hesitating to think. "I believe our people would need more than a resurrected queen to give us purpose again."

I shook my head, confused at her vagueness. "What do you mean?"

"The gods abandoned us, Ziva," Nasira told me. "We worshiped them for millennia and they bound our tribe to serve Egyptian rulers, and then left us. Evil rises, we fight it, and wait until the next threat comes along. We're nearly extinct. My guess is your parents didn't think the Medjai are strong enough anymore. They thought they could protect you on their own."

"Protect me from what?"

"The gods are gone, but they still exist," she said. "The one whose magic made Nefertari's resurrection possible—Set—didn't do it out of the goodness of his heart. Nefertari made a deal with him and then didn't give him whatever he was promised. He'll do anything to stop her from getting what she wants: life. That same life essence that was reborn in you. As long as you are alive, her resurrection is possible."

"So, a god wants to kill me," I realized with a darkening dread in the pit of my stomach.

Nasira put a hand on my shoulder and squeezed. "I promise I will train you to become the best of us, so you have the ability and skill to protect yourself."

I nodded, hardening my resolve. "Thank you."

Her spark returned. "Now hurry and change and I'll get you started on becoming a real Medjai."

My equipment felt lighter than I'd expected, but only until I armed myself with the traditional stone weapons. When I was ready, I followed Nasira through a pair of French doors and outside to a flagstone path swallowed by overgrown hydrangeas and peonies. The massive blooms were so heavy they bowed over the stones and left even less room for us to find our way. We passed a granite fountain and rising from a moss-covered and rotted leaf-filled basin was a winged lion whose wide open mouth harbored spiders and fly carcasses rather than a crisp stream of water. Beyond towering hedges, I could hear voices—occasional laughter and conversations I couldn't make out—and Nasira took a left toward them through a red brick archway.

Scattered across an expansive and recently mowed lawn were pairs of Medjai, many of them carrying wooden versions of Nasira's *asaya*, practicing on each other and stuffed dummies wrapped in burlap canvas. Small groups jogged around the perimeter of the gardens to the inside of the tree line. All of them wore equipment like Nasira's and mine. My boots were heavy, and my pants made me feel trapped.

"The first thing we'll do is get you fit," Nasira told me, striding past the other Medjai as if they weren't even there. "We don't rely on magic alone, as you've seen, so you'll need energy and strength to fight. We'll get you started on endurance training and building muscle."

I hadn't considered how weak and frail I must've looked to the other Medjai. I may have stood several inches taller than Nasira, but her body was strong, and her curves were something to aspire to. She looked healthy. I looked like a skinny stray.

Nasira rolled up the sleeves of her shirt and I noticed for the first time the tattoos traveling from her wrist to the inside of her elbow: small symbols scattered about and some geometric shapes linked together to form a chain. Her gaze followed mine to her arm. "Are you looking at these?" she asked and held her arms out straight, underside up to give me full view.

"I'm sorry for staring," I said. "I've seen photographs of women tattooed like this in books, but never in real life. They are beautiful."

"Thank you," she said earnestly. "This means strength, these are suns and stars, and the triangles are saddle stirrups because I love to ride. I got my first mark when I was twelve."

My surprise could not be hidden. "That's incredible."

Her expression turned a little shadowed and wistful. "Outside our tribe, you don't see these markings much anymore. Too many outsiders have come to our lands, too many who believe what we do isn't beautiful, even if the tattoos make us feel beautiful. The world is changing. For the better? Worse? Who could say? But it is changing us. We're disappearing."

After a few wistful moments, Nasira found her spark once again. "Anyway, every morning before breakfast, I run laps around the grounds and I'd like you to join me—but you don't have to right away. I don't want to sound like I'm pressuring you. You can do anything you'd like at your own pace."

"No, no," I insisted. "I want this. Whatever you have to teach me, I'll take it."

She smiled, huge and bright. "That's what I love to hear. Let's start with a little warm-up and stretches. Every day I will teach you proper form for hand-to-hand combat and we will work up to *tahtib*."

"*Tahtib*?"

"Traditional stick-fighting with the *asaya*," she clarified. "We Medjai have combined it with our magic to create a very effective style of fighting."

That sounded very intriguing. "So, I'll learn more spells?"

She laughed. "You'll learn more spells."

I didn't realize how sore my body was until I hobbled toward my room after dinner. Nasira had promised stretches would keep me from getting hurt, but she'd overestimated my current condition. I said nothing to her, though, because I didn't want her to go easier on me tomorrow. I wanted to get strong, and she would guide me there.

In the armory, I changed out of the gear and back into the dress. The clothes weren't mine and Nasira hadn't mentioned what to do with them, so I placed them in a basket filled with wrinkled, worn shirts and pants needing to be laundered. After I finished, I headed to my room. There were plenty of Medjai still up and about since the hour wasn't terribly late, but I was exhausted and every muscle I used, even to walk, burned with protest.

My room was dark, quiet, and blissfully empty of anyone else. For the first time since living on my own, I was happy to be alone. The workout drained me, and being around so many people and exposure to so much wild newness had taken anything left. My body was done for the day.

I moved to the nightstand to switch on a lamp. I found a notebook and pen, and on the first page I jotted down every spell I'd learned today and its effect. Studying this list every morning while I dressed myself and every evening while I prepared for bed would help me learn fast. And application of course. Every chance I'd get, I would practice until my gifts became second nature.

A shadow moved into the soft light pouring through my open window. The sheer drapes billowed in the night breeze, revealing a dark form. I sucked in a breath as I realized something else was here with me.

Cool moonlight settled on the back of an enormous black jackal wearing a jeweled gold collar. Its blue topaz eyes burned like star fire and its oil-black coat was short and glossy, taut over a sleek body rippling with powerful muscle. My breath loosed in a rush and my hands raised, my fingertips sparking on instinct.

The jackal exploded in a flash of shadows and eerie pale light. My *taw* spell shot into it but fizzled in the air with no effect. A young man appeared, with dark hair and bronze skin that seemed to glow from the inside, almost like a lampshade. Though my mind prepared for a fight, my heart pulled in the opposite direction. I felt no fear—only an unexplainable featherlight sense of peace.

"What are you?" I demanded.

His almond-shaped eyes burning inhumanly beneath heavy lashes, he dipped his head and smiled, brightening his dark, mythic beauty. A strong, but handsome nose divided his face and his lips were carefully carved, jaw angled squarely.

"I have many forms and many names," he replied, his voice a soothing lull. "Lord of the Necropolis, Prince of Mourning, Protector of the Dead. Anepu. I am best known as Anubis."

Anubis. A *god*. I froze. Nasira had said nothing about what to do when meeting one face to face, that they could and would take physical form. Was he in a physical form or an apparition? Did I bow? Was he a threat and should I have run? I opted for the most neutral choice. I asked an entirely relative question: "Are you here to kill me?"

The edges of his lips cracked into a smile. "I'm happy to report I'm not." When I stayed silent, he held out a hand and asked, "And you are?"

"I have a feeling you already know who I am," I said.

His smile spread. "My intent was to be polite. It's wonderful to meet you, Ziva. I come peacefully, I assure you."

"I was under the impression that the gods turned their backs on us," I remarked, watching the door at the edge of my vision. If I set the canopied bed ablaze with a *khet* spell, the distraction might allow me a chance to escape.

"I am a protector of pharaoh and you are royalty," he replied, "born from unquiet stars, the last heir of one of the greatest dynasties the world has ever seen. Consider me at your service."

"Because you have to, or because you want to?" I interrogated. "I've been cared for by people who did it because it was their job and I haven't been terribly impressed."

He blinked with surprise and his smile grew incredulous. "I have free will and I'm not duty-bound to anyone. You intrigue me, Ziva Mereniset. The way you've survived alone, something I am sorry for. It must be terrible to be alone."

"I don't need anyone feeling sorry for me," I told him.

"I did not come to the mortal world to tell you I pity you," he said. "My intent was to offer you my favor. Everyone must pick a side, mustn't they?"

"I've always been out for myself before now," I replied. "This is the first time I've ever had a side. What does your favor entail, exactly? Protection from the kriosphinxes?"

"Ask of me anything within my power," he said.

I crossed my arms. "That's vague."

His gaze narrowed. "My power is vast but has its limitations."

"Then I'd like to make my first request," I told him.

His brow barely raised. "Yes?"

"If you are who—what—you say you are, then you're my only hope," I began. "Are my parents alive?"

His smile faded and something very human passed over his face—regret. "No," he said, his voice quiet and sympathetic. "They are not. I'm very sorry for your loss."

My loss? The punch in my belly surprised me. I hadn't known them. They meant hardly anything to me. I'd been an orphan from the very first memory I had . . . but now it felt real. An ember of hope had always glowed deep within me and in mere moments, that ember was smothered. As I went dark inside, I wondered what had happened to them. If they'd taken me away to protect me, had they been killed by whoever—whatever—they'd protected me from? Had they died for me?

My entire life seemed to crumble then and there, the belief that my parents had abandoned me having been the keystone to everything I knew. It was all in ruins now. Shame came over me and I didn't know how or where or to whom to direct my emotions, so they turned inward. The anger I felt at myself for having hated my mother and father sometimes felt like slowly rising water, building up all around me. Soon I would drown, and I knew I would, and that made it so much worse. How could I take back everything terrible I had said or thought about them? How could I say how sorry I was? They were gone, and I was here. They were gone so I could be here.

Anubis closed his eyes, the sudden absence of that blue topaz fire startling, and the muscles beneath the skin of his jaw clenched. He tilted his head and his hands balled into fists.

I studied him, and my alarm by his sudden vulnerability pulled me from my own torment. "Is something wrong?"

"This world never sleeps, never suspends," he said, his voice strained. "Sometimes I struggle to focus in the mortal world. There are so many human souls—living, dying. It's a constant roar."

My body tensed. "Is it—do you feel what I feel right now?"

"I—" He paused and winced, as if in pain. "Don't blame yourself. I feel . . . everything."

Anubis grew still for some time, too still, in a way that unnerved me to the bone. His human moment had passed, and I was reminded he was an immortal god, existing in shadow and in dreams. He was both darkness and light, pieces of the universe that couldn't be grasped. The god of death was unreal, an entity but a person somehow, the warden of things darker and more beautiful than my understanding.

He appeared to recollect himself and looked at me with more clarity. "Forgive me. I'm better now."

"The other immortals like you, do they have the same problem when they come here?" I asked, wondering how many like him there were.

"The others are . . . different," he replied stiffly. "But

this is not our domain anymore. Hasn't been for eons. We can't . . . thrive here . . . anymore."

"You'll die if you stay here?"

"Diminishment is not death," he clarified, his voice low and sad. "It is worse. We can stay for a few hours comfortably, but any longer than two or three days, and we will fade. Some of us have succumbed to that fate over the millennia—some willingly. But Set, the immortal to whom the kriosphinxes answer, will know the Medjai are in New York now that several of his kriosphinxes were lost. He will risk diminishment to find you. Others will follow him." The darkness in his voice made his words sound like a warning.

"What did you mean this domain isn't yours any longer?" I asked him, my head spinning. "How is it not yours anymore?"

Anubis moved toward me, his step slow. His mouth flattened, and his brow furrowed as though he searched for words I could understand. "Before humans emerged, earth existed in a primordial state. We, the immortals, lived all across this planet in Egypt, Greece, North America, India, and so on. When humanity arose, the earth transitioned into a mortal one. Some of us enjoyed helping humankind. Others enjoyed terrorizing them. We were worshiped and feared. We became gods. We stayed for as long as we could, but this wasn't our home any longer. So, we created worlds parallel to this one where we could survive, infinite worlds like tree branches brushing against each other. Eventually our influence on this world began to fade."

"Humans pushed you out?" I asked, trying to understand.

"Some feel that way," he replied. "And the humans who relied on us, put their faith in us, feel abandoned. It is time we repair our relationship with your kind. It's our responsibility to do so. I've waited a very long time for someone I believe will unite us once again. I believe that person is you, Ziva."

"I was told Set has unfinished business with the queen whose *ka* was reborn inside me," I said. "He wants me dead so that she can't be resurrected."

Anubis frowned gravely. "I don't know what he wants, to tell you the truth. He is very dangerous, and I will do whatever is within my power to help you. I *can* help, and so I will. You'll need to leave this city as soon as possible."

I had no roots anywhere, nothing to lose. If I wasn't as safe with the Medjai as I'd hoped, there were other options. "I could go west. Disappear somewhere in California. Spending the rest of my life on the run doesn't sound like much of a life, but it's better than rotting away in the city."

He shook his head. "I meant, leave with the Medjai. You're safer with your people than out on your own."

"I've done very well so far, thank you," I told him. "Whatever is best for me—that's my decision to make, not anyone else's. Your concern is appreciated, but you don't know me."

One corner of his mouth pulled into half a smile, deepening a dimple in his cheek. "I don't know you, Ziva, but I like you. I hope you survive—and I believe you will."

I said nothing as he moved, circling me, and a warmth came through the air. But my skin cooled as though a breath blew softly up my arms. Energy crackled between us; it was not an incredible measure, not enough to draw the attention of any nearby Medjai.

When Anubis spoke, his words were slow and dense with unknown power. A mischievous gleam in his eyes caught the moonlight. "I bless you, Ziva, of the blood of queens." He stepped away and dipped into a shallow bow. He held out a hand and a small object materialized. "Take this amulet. If you need anything, help of any kind, call for me with this. I will see you again soon."

I accepted the amulet, blue faience carved into the shape of a sitting jackal, and Anubis was gone in a flash of darkness.

A prickling sensation remained on the surface of my skin. Blessed by death? I did not understand what that meant or what he had done to me. I could only hope he'd given me a good thing.

I'd spent my entire life looking out for myself when no one else would. Then again, my parents may have thought they could protect me better out on our own, and they were dead. If I hung around the Medjai a bit longer, I'd learn more about my power and potential—and more about enemies I didn't know I had. The Medjai were the only ones who could help me with any of the things that would keep me alive. But if Anubis proved to be the ally he claimed to be, then I was glad to have him in my corner. Who better to take on a god than another god?

Anubis

The netherworld, home of the gods and the dead, was a place of shadows and whispers and fallen starlight. From the edge of his floating domain, Anubis gazed upon the Necropolis below. Each immortal soul was a tiny light, and the endless expanse of the city was blazing and bright far into the horizon.

Anubis felt no discomfort from heat or cold, nor did his heart beat or his lungs draw breath for anything save to speak. But here, he felt the chill. This place had a hollow feel, an echo of ice and emptiness that only death brought. That was what immortality felt like—an eternal absence of life.

With a wave of his hand, his view of the city disappeared. The netherlight orbs revolving above ornate staffs cut from bloodstone illuminated his domain. There was no air to burn fire in this place, nor was there sunlight to shine—only the cold glow of netherlight. The portico was lined with magnificent black marble columns on three sides and his throne stood against a wall whose murals depicted his anthropomorphic form carrying out his funerary duties as protector of the dead. Two open archways on either side of his throne led into his bedchamber and the other, a library.

The nothingness prickled with power. Another immortal had appeared at his back.

"You are not welcome in my domain," Anubis said, his voice as cold and dark as black ice.

"I was ordered here," she answered nonchalantly.

"And I order you to leave, Kauket." Annoyed, he glared over his shoulder at the goddess of darkness, who leaned casually against a column. Her smile, on full, blood-red lips, oozed malice and venom. The slow, unnaturally wide gesture reminded him of her serpent form dislocating her jaws to swallow prey. Her eyes, carnelian red, were surrounded with heavy lashes and black kohl. Her nose was short and elegantly curved, and her skin was the color of burnished gold. A thick, waist-length mane of onyx curls flowed behind her like a cape. But all the immortals were exquisite and beauty among the beautiful was common.

Kauket eased toward him, her dress of black scales scraped and clicked across the stone floor. Her forearms were sheathed in bracelets of vertebrae belonging to both animal and man. Shadows clung to the goddess of darkness like a child to a mother's breast. When she reached him, she slid her vertebrae-ringed fingers up his chest and drew one long, sharp nail into the hollow of his throat. "I don't serve you, little pup," she said with a tap of that nail, and strode past him.

"Kauket, get *out*." Anubis's teeth clenched, and he turned toward her.

"I don't think I will," she called, the playful edge to her voice jagged and sharp as razor blades.

He let his power flare, the pressure crushing the obsidian beneath his feet. He almost always kept his strength suppressed, a habit he'd learned around his father for self-preservation. Kauket was no fool; she knew the warning he'd given her. She froze and her gaze fell to watch the fractures in the floor seal themselves like a wound.

"I will give you the courtesy of not tossing you off my domain if you go on your own accord," Anubis said, scowling.

She lifted her chin in defiance. "Set requests your presence."

"Is that so?" Anubis asked, feeling a twinge of fear. Set would be furious he'd blessed the Medjai girl. Swallowing his emotion, he held out a hand for her to precede him. "After you."

"Don't worry, night child," Kauket said, venom dripping from her voice. "I wouldn't linger around you too long lest I catch whatever it is you have that makes your heart bleed for mortals. It's a wonder you don't bleed to death."

She marched toward the edge of the portico, utterly lacking any of her previous grace. In a fractal flash of angry shadows and icy netherlight, she disappeared, likely to Set's domain where he'd be happy to lick her wounds.

Anubis glared hard in the direction she'd gone, his mind spinning. Showing any fear of Kauket's master to her face would give her ammunition. Now that she'd fled, he permitted himself a few moments to gather his courage before departing.

Set's domain was a sailing temple complex made of

several fortresses to create a multi-level maze of statues, columns, passages, pools, stairs, and rooms. A violent, unnatural sandstorm beat at Anubis, ripping at his tunic and his hair, jangling the jewels of his pectoral, and tearing at his skin. He could barely see the pyramid through the rage and lash of storms endlessly circling the domain. Sand beat against stone, tearing out chunks of statuary, only to have them regenerate to perfection. This place was a stark contrast to Set's hideaway in the mortal world, the city of priests and gilded crocodiles. Here, all was half-drowned in shadows and silence, as though the complex had been forsaken centuries ago in the lifeless desert.

Anubis continued his trek toward Set's throne room, past creeping, whining kriosphinxes and blooming braziers of eerie netherlight. He scaled the steps to the top level, took both golden handles of the basalt doors, and pushed them open. The floor and walls of the throne room were gleaming black marble veined with ghostly white quartz, and the ceiling was supported by massive columns made of beryl. The burning bloodstone braziers made the semitransparent, greenish columns almost glow.

Beyond a shallow impluvium, netherlight glittering off the ripples in the water's surface, the god of chaos and the desert lounged casually in his glossy basalt throne. When Kauket saw Anubis, she sprawled herself across an arm of Set's throne, one leg dangling over his. She leaned close to Set, her lips mere inches from his ear, and whispered something that made him smile.

"Too comfortable in that chair to send for me yourself?" Anubis dared to inquire.

Set ignored him, his power pulsing against the glittering floor. His face was a mixture of smooth umber skin and unforgiving angles, and his eyes, set beneath an intensely scrutinizing brow, were bottomless dark orbs ringed with amber. A glossy scarab crawled out from behind the jeweled pectoral hanging around his neck, clicked its wings, and disappeared down his bare back.

"I understand you've recently gone topside," he said, his deep voice grating like a blade against stone. "Three of my kriosphinxes were vanquished and now I wonder if you know anything about that. I've lived too long to believe in coincidence."

"They weren't vanquished by my hand, if that's what you're implying," Anubis replied. If his heart could beat, it would've been racing.

Set appeared unmoved as his eyes narrowed and the permanent wrinkle in his brow deepened. "There aren't many someones out there to blame. The Medjai have arrived in New York City."

"Not to my knowledge. They were in London last I heard."

"See, Anubis, I know when you're lying because you're less cheeky about it," the god of chaos mused with a drowsy tilt of his head. "Either get better at lying to me, or don't do it at all. Honesty is less likely to get you dismembered."

Anubis lifted his chin. "Despite the obvious dig at my father, everyone in this room knows that's an empty threat." He did not care to defend Osiris—the king of the dead was his father in name only—but Set's pettiness knew no bounds.

Kauket's eyes widened at her lord, delighted, and her body grew very still with anticipation.

"There's that sass we all know and loathe." Set's smile was sticky with sarcasm. "I sent my kriosphinxes to investigate the surge of magic in Manhattan only to send them to their doom. They were a gift to me."

"One you've squandered," Anubis countered.

Set scowled and leaned forward. "You're too young to know—to understand—what I lost—what I *did*—to complete the task that earned me the kriosphinxes."

"I know what you've done," the god of death replied, his voice cold and careful.

Set slammed his fist on the arm of his throne. Stone cracked and Kauket leapt to her feet in fright. "You had better watch that tongue lest you forget what your mother has done. *I* will never forget."

Anubis swallowed and felt his throat tighten. He hated for his mother to be dragged into this and thrown at his face like a dagger. But he couldn't argue she had nothing to do with what animosity boiled between himself and Set. She had everything to do with it.

Dredging deep within himself for strength, Anubis clenched his fists. "Have you anything else to interrogate me about, or do I have your permission to leave?"

Set sat back in his throne, but he did not relax. "Did they find the scion yet?"

"You know I wouldn't tell you either way," Anubis said. "I will not help you murder a mortal girl over a grudge."

The look that came over Set's face was difficult to read. He didn't seem insulted. Rather, he seemed scornful. "Who said anything about murdering her?"

"What else could you possibly want?" Anubis demanded with impatience.

"True, her death would be the simplest solution to my tribulation," Set mused. "The girl is a means to an end—Nefertari's end. I will have what was promised to me."

Anubis thought quickly. There had to be something to appease Set so he would leave Ziva alone. "Perhaps if you tell me what the queen owes you—"

Set's laughter cut him off. "How generous of you! Tell you what—set her shriveled corpse on fire. Her damned magic has protected it from me."

"I cannot desecrate the dead," Anubis reminded him.

"Which is why I didn't run straight to you in the first place. I will do what has to be done." The lord of chaos rose from his throne and vanished in a spiraling plume of shadows and netherlight.

Kauket turned to Anubis, face pale and eyes fearful. "You don't want to start a war."

"I hardly think we're headed in that direction," Anubis said tiredly. "Tonight's conversation was nothing but typical."

She was not swayed. "Tonight. And what of tomorrow night? And the night after? Events Set has awaited eons for have finally begun to unfold."

"Just as I have waited," Anubis countered. "The time for us to return to earth has come."

"He believes the same and he will let nothing stand in his way," she warned. "He can't."

"Neither can I," Anubis replied unflinchingly.

He turned his back to her, avoiding the shining eyes of the kriosphinxes hiding among the pillars and sculptures. They pawed stone and marble and bashed their skulls together, the crack of horn to horn reverberating through the complex. Hungry for discord. He did not stop or slow his pace, and the beasts, so tall they were nearly eye level with him, retreated like the tide, creating a path for him.

CHAPTER

6

I woke early, before the sun breached the horizon, so I could meet Nasira for our training. Someone had set out a day dress and athletic wear and I wondered who had sneaked into my room a second time. Certainly, the gesture was intended to be courteous, but I found it creepy.

Whoever had prepared these outfits had given me a choice this time, but I'd made up my mind yesterday. Hastily I put on the sleeveless exercise shirt and loose-fitting knickers, grabbed an apple from the bowl, and jogged toward the front hall entrance. I considered telling someone about my visit from Anubis, but first I needed to decide whether to heed his warning.

Nasira waited for me at the front door wearing her own equipment and a quiet smile. "I'm glad to see you this morning, Ziva," she said.

I was reminded of my first impression of her, how she looked scandalous dressed in clothing more appropriate for a man, and I glanced down at myself. I looked as scandalous as she did—and it excited me. Of course, our gear wasn't designed to be a defiant fashion statement; we were dressed to be practical. But it still felt good.

Then I realized how narrow and knobby my legs looked next to her strong ones, and for a split second I wanted to wear the dress and hide the sharp angles of my hips and knees. I drove the thought from my mind, focusing on how I would soon be healthy like her.

After our training, my body felt like overstretched rubber, but Nasira promised this was a good feeling. All morning I'd wanted to tell Nasira about my visit from Anubis last night, that he had blessed me—whatever that entailed. But considering her feelings toward the gods as a whole, I wasn't sure if divulging the encounter was a good idea. Not yet. I'd needed to learn more about her first. The last thing I needed was for her to consider me fraternizing with the enemy. Was Anubis the enemy? My heart told me he wasn't.

We headed back to the house to bathe and dress for breakfast, and we ran into Sayer as he walked toward us from the road. He'd tied his shoulder-length hair behind his head, but locks had pulled free around his face to cling to his dewy skin. He looked wild and winded.

"Take a look at this," he called, his expression intense. In his hand was a folded-up newspaper. "A few of the homes on this road still receive the daily paper and I thought the front-page article might interest you both."

I reached for it and spread it wide to read the headline aloud: *"Explorers Unearth Stela of the Lost Queen."*

Nasira peered over my shoulder and frowned. "Why should we care about some lot of Egyptomaniacs?"

"What's an Egyptomaniac?" I asked, scanning the large photo in the center of the page. Several finely-dressed white men surrounded a rectangular slab of limestone covered with markings too small to make out.

"Toffee-nosed aristocrats and industrialists who employ archaeologists to desecrate royal tombs," Nasira explained, her face twisted with disgust. "They keep all the gold and jewels for themselves and their *'collections.'* I'm not interested in these despicable graverobbers, thank you."

"Why don't the artifacts go to a museum?" I asked.

"Some do," she explained. "But there are many privately funded digs. In a perfect world, there would be no thieves and the tombs would remain undefiled. The European explorers who first invaded our country and stole our antiquities did not do so with the intent to protect what they found. To them, our history is treasure and riches. Their 'museums' showcase our culture as spoils of conquest. Their claim of preservation is an excuse for their greed and implies Egyptians cannot care for our own heritage. We could have reclaimed our lost history if we hadn't suffered from nearly constant invasions for thousands of years. The damage imperialism has caused is a cold truth and its darkness should not be ignored. We can help our people with the power we have."

"Look closer," Sayer insisted, snatching our attention back. "That's the cartouche of Nefertari."

She gave an incredulous huff and took one corner of the page to examine the image herself. Her eyes grew wide as she rapidly scanned the article. "What does 'the queen of cardinals' mean? Their translation makes no sense."

"That's because an amateur translated it," Sayer said confidently, his gaze dark. "All I can decipher is, 'The cardinal treasures of the queen of kings are the key.' I must see the stela in person to read the rest."

"The key to what?" I asked.

"Exactly," he replied. "There's a chance the hieroglyphs on this stela could tell us more about Nefertari's resurrection and your part in it."

I read the article in its entirety while Sayer and Nasira argued over the rest of the inscription. When I spoke, I nearly had to yell over them. "It says here the stela's owner will hold a viewing at his residence on Park Avenue tonight."

They both shushed and stared at me with excitement. I grinned and asked, "What do you say we crash this clambake and you can read the rest of the stela yourselves?"

A smile spread slowly across Nasira's face. "That's not a bad idea."

"The three of us?" Sayer asked.

"Any more would look suspicious," I offered. "But three Medjai could sneak in."

Nasira beamed. "Another brilliant idea, Ziva. A little espionage would be fun."

"Count me in," Sayer said with a nod.

"That settles it," Nasira declared with a clap of her hands. "Tonight, we're going to town!"

When I got to my room, I drew a bath. I may have fallen asleep in the bath, but I could neither confirm nor deny that. Afterward I finished and dressed in combat gear, and when I found the dining hall, the tables were empty. The food was gone. An attendant carried a stack of plates past a door and into a noisy room I guessed was the kitchen. I considered chasing after him in case anything was left over. Even as my belly started to chew itself from the inside out, I told myself it was all right. There was still a lot of fruit in the bowl back in my bedroom.

But it wasn't French toast.

With my feet dragging, I headed upstairs. The orange in my hand was barely half-peeled before a knock came. I set it on the table and answered the door to find Sayer. In his hands was a plate of syrup-drizzled slices of bread caked with sugar. I blinked, and my head tilted to the side as I tried to comprehend why he would do something like this. To think of me. To remember the dish I loved. To put together a plate for me. To bring it all the way to my room.

To think of me.

My silence had grown painfully awkward. What should I have said? Should I have taken the plate?

"Ziva?" he asked.

Uncertainty passed over his face, and I couldn't help wondering if regret now hit him. I wondered if he thought this had been a mistake and he'd never do it again. He shouldn't have thought of me.

"Ah—I'm sorry," I stammered, and still I couldn't move. It was like a sheet had been pulled over my head. Everything went blank in me.

He exhaled, half-smiling. "I had imagined you'd be thrilled."

An uncomfortable laugh burst from me, and I asked, "Is that for me?"

"Unless you don't want it," he said. "I never saw you at breakfast and worried you'd missed it."

"I did," I said. "Thank you." Perhaps to him and most people the gesture was insignificant—a kind thought that took mere minutes of his time. He had plenty of minutes anyway. To me, however, the gesture was rare and beautiful, like a strawberry moon. In my world, everyone was too wrapped up in their own misfortunes to take any time for an act of kindness. Why should they go out of their way to help others if no one would do the same for them? I'd been guilty of this myself. I saw now how easily a kindness could be done. How simple it could be and how great the impact.

I thought of Lou, who saved day-old bread for me, and how I didn't want to hurt him by stealing. I didn't want to hurt Sayer either. If I got what I needed from the Medjai and left, would it hurt my new friends? *Were* they my friends?

"Do you intend to eat this in the hallway?" Sayer asked, one eyebrow lifting in that curious way of his.

"No!" I laughed and stepped aside. "Please, come in. Thank you for this."

"You're welcome." He handed me the plate and sat with me at the little round table by the huge windows. He gazed out onto the gardens as I cut bite-sized pieces for myself.

"Share with me," I said to him, tugging back his attention. "I want you to. Surely it was a great deal of work bringing this all the way from the kitchen."

He smiled and replied, "It wasn't, but I'll share with you." He closed his eyes briefly and muttered something under his breath before picking up a small square with his fingers and eating it.

"What was that?" I asked. "I didn't hear you."

"A prayer."

"Nasira told me the gods left us. May I ask why you would pray to them if that's true? I don't mean any offense."

"No offense taken," he said. "I don't necessarily believe we've been abandoned. We all have different experiences and gifts, and mine make me feel close to the gods. You have to trust in your heart, Ziva. It won't steer you wrong."

"All right then," I said, studying his face as he ate another bite, curious to know if there was a story behind his words.

"How have your lessons with Nasira been getting on?" he asked.

"Well," I replied. "She's patient, but she makes me work hard. Looks like I'll be a real Medjai after our mission tonight."

"You already are," he assured me with a smile. "Though I don't expect things will get too thrilling at the party."

I smeared my next bite into as much syrup as possible. "How did you learn to read Ancient Egyptian?"

"Practice," he replied. "Lots of it. I shouldn't have been so critical of the stela's translation in that article. So much of it is educated guesswork."

"Can you teach me?" I asked.

He nodded. "Of course. How's your French toast?"

I smiled around a mouthful. "Wonderful. This is my favorite thing ever."

"I remembered you seemed to really enjoy it yesterday."

"Thank you." *For thinking of me.* "Why did the article call Nefertari the lost queen?"

He took a deep breath and began. "Her tomb, arguably the most beautifully painted of them all, was uncovered empty. They found pieces of bone, but they didn't belong to her. Perhaps a decoy mummy or that of an attendant. Some say tomb raiders found the treasure first and some say Nefertari's sarcophagus was never there in the first place."

"Then where is it?" I asked.

"Before her death, Nefertari commissioned a second tomb—a true tomb—to hide her mummy from her enemies, primarily Set. Those servants who laid her to rest, sealed themselves within the tomb and followed her to the afterlife. You, her descendant born beneath the Osirian alignment of the stars, are fated to lead us to Nefertari's mummy."

I shook my head. "But how would I have any idea as to her whereabouts?"

"We hope the stela will tell us," he said. "Nefertari couldn't leave us many clues. To ensure the resurrection's success, she had to be very secretive. She'd had everything in the world and was probably more scared than anyone to die. Can't fault her for that, I suppose."

"What will happen once she's resurrected?"

Sayer smiled. "We'll have a queen again and the leadership to drive the French, Germans, and English—all threats—from our lands. Something to fight for. Perhaps we can rebuild our numbers again. I hope one day the Medjai will be restored to our glory as in ancient times."

"And I hope you have those things," I told him.

"You will, too, Ziva," he said. "You're one of us. Our glory will be yours."

I finished my breakfast and left with Sayer. "Perhaps my training with Nasira could wait a bit longer today," I suggested. "Would you be interested in starting my Ancient Egyptian lessons now?"

His brow creased with thought and he glanced at me sidelong as we walked. "I certainly could, if you'd like. The library is on the second floor. This way, then."

Sayer hadn't exaggerated when he said translating hieroglyphs was mostly guesswork. I was glad I'd grabbed my notebook before following him—studying the information later would be challenging without him there to explain what I couldn't recall from the lessons. He showed me how some glyphs could be interpreted differently depending on context, *if* we interpreted that context correctly. His explanation for that was helpful in a complex way.

"If a crocodile were to emerge from the Nile miraculously able to speak English, contemporary human minds would not understand a word he'd say," Sayer told me. "His words might translate, but the meaning is lost. The way he sees and interprets the world is so intrinsically different from the way we do. His words mean something we can't possibly fathom because we are not crocodiles."

I foresaw being able to read and write Ancient Egyptian becoming a life's work. Regardless of the complexity, I grew mind-wrenchingly interested in the skill.

"There you are!"

Sayer and I looked up when we heard Nasira's voice. She wore her combat equipment with an *asaya* in her hand.

"Hieroglyphs?" she asked, peering at the books spread out on the table before us.

"Ziva wanted to learn," Sayer told her.

"Well, may I have her now?" Nasira inquired. "I can bribe her with gifts. Look, I've brought you your very own *asaya*."

"For me?" I gaped, excited and surprised, at the beautiful weapon she presented to me. I took it gladly and clutched it to my breast.

She beamed at me. "Care to give it a go?"

"You bet!" I shot to my feet, but I looked down at Sayer. "Can we do this again tomorrow?"

"Certainly," he said with a nod.

Nasira ushered me from the library and down a hall toward the gardens. "I'd like to show you some *asaya* basics. Get used to its weight in both your hands. Notice the points where the blades meet the staff are weighted with granite bands. Obsidian, even our magically tempered variety, is very light. The heavier granite helps the *asaya* spin faster."

"Do you think I'll need this at the party?" I asked.

She shook her head. "Likely not, but you must always be armed—or prepared, rather. And you are. You always have magic. But it's nice to also have a physical weapon."

I moved the *asaya* around in my hands, familiarizing myself with its center of gravity. "If the viewing is a big deal, won't the kriosphinxes catch wind of it?"

"That is a thought," she muttered. "All the more reason for you to become familiar with the *asaya* and other weapons—*and* we can talk more about spells."

"Great," I said. "I'd like to understand magic better."

"It's not an easy thing to explain," she began. "What you call magic is simply a matter of course for us. It infuses every aspect of our lives and daily activities. You grew up where people could not change and manipulate nature and objects—but *you* could. You had abilities outside the limited knowledge and understanding of everyone around you. That is what the word magic denotes. It was invented to describe what people could not comprehend."

"I see," I said, letting her words digest.

"Magic, as you know it, is the activation of your heart's power," she continued. "All words are divine, whether they are written or spoken. The gods gave us language so we may activate and use our heart's power. When words are used during that activation, they become incantations to wield power over yourself or others to protect, to harm, to manipulate, to create, or to destroy. The stronger your heart, the stronger your magic."

The morning had grown into a beautiful sunny day. The dew in the air had lifted and other Medjai had appeared in the gardens to train as well. A few of them turned their heads toward us, but none approached. Nasira directed me to an open grassy spot and she stopped a few feet across from me.

"You're getting a bit of a crash course," she said apologetically. "My ideal training would involve your first spar before we venture into the field, but I feel you're a bit of a way off from that."

"How so?" I asked.

"Firstly, sparring is about trust, and you and I aren't quite there yet. Secondly, have you ever been hit in the face?"

I bristled and narrowed my gaze at her in suspicion. "Are you offering?"

She laughed. "My point is, at least half of fighting is a good defense and knowing what it's like to get hit helps you learn how *not* to get hit. It hurts, and once you know that, you do a better job of avoiding fists. But I'm not going to hit you. Not today."

"That's comforting," I mumbled, teasing.

Nasira grinned and held up her staff while stepping back with one leg. She placed a hand at one end and her other hand a forearm's length above the first. "Do as I do. Are you left-handed, right-handed?"

I mimicked her with my own weapon. "Right-handed."

"Left foot leading then. Good. Now hold your *asaya* above your head. Brace yourself on your rear foot. Imagine that foot is braced against a wall. You cannot take another step back. You may only go forward. All of your energy will come from there."

I followed her directions again and held my breath

as she raised her own *asaya*, slowly spun her staff in a figure-eight, and brought it down against my staff more gently than I'd anticipated. The staffs clacked together.

Nasira met my gaze. "Trust, remember? I won't knock you on your arse the first day." She repeated the motion several more times, increasing her strength each time. "The harder you begin your rotation, the more torque you generate in your *asaya*. The spin increases momentum and how much momentum your *asaya* achieves will determine how hard the obsidian meets its target. Your strike can be light. A nick. Or it can cut deep and sever. However, once you extend the staff to make your strike, you lose some of that momentum due to friction with the air, so you must be fast, or start the spin over again. Does that make sense?"

I nodded, turning her explanation over in my head until I understood.

"Physics," Nasira said with a shrug. "Well done. Now do the same to me."

She raised her *asaya* and I did my best to swing—though, awkwardly—and clacked it against her staff. After praising me, she instructed me to repeat the swing again and again until the figure-eight felt more fluid and natural.

"Very well done," she said, beaming. "We will practice a few swings at different heights. Do as I do."

By the end of our session, I felt pretty good about my ward, hand position, and swing. As long as I kept it up every day, the *asaya* would feel like a fifth limb to me. "Perfect practice makes perfect," Nasira had said to me at least six times today.

She explained the *asaya* was for me to keep, so instead of returning to the armory, she led me to her rooms to pick out our disguises for tonight. Her bedroom and sitting room looked very much like my own, but the walls, furniture, and fabrics were decorated with different colors and patterns.

"While you were off with my brother," Nasira began, "I took the liberty of picking out what we'll wear. I ventured gold would do you quite well."

She opened the huge, finely carved wardrobe and removed a stream of gleaming molten gold silk that had to be ten feet long. Its artfully scattered sequins glittered in the daylight, prismatic.

A dress. A *gown*. "I thought we were wearing disguises," I said, my eyes wide.

"We are!" Nasira said. "We've got to look like party guests, not crashers, yeah? Go try it on!"

She shoved the garment in my hands and ushered me into the bathroom to change. I hung the dress on a clothing stand made of polished black cherry wood and I stared at it for so long I forgot how cold the marble floor was against my bare feet.

"How's it look?" Nasira called from the other side of the door.

"Uh—" I scrambled, undressing. "One moment!"

I freed the hanger and examined the dress. The tag, a completely stitched-in patch on the inside, bore some French script I couldn't read. The silk was slinky and the tiny sequins dazzled just enough to catch the eye and not to blind.

I stepped into the dress and lifted it up and over my hips to hang on my shoulders. The neck was a deeply cut triangle, showing more skin than I'd ever shown before, and the back was bare all the way to the base of my spine. A light cinch just below my hips gave the illusion I *had* hips. The hem trailed on the floor behind me, despite my height, and I predicted with the right set of pumps, it would trail just right.

Excitement sparked at my fingertips. I felt good. I felt confident. I felt like a goddess.

I straightened my back and lifted my chin. If I would wear something like this, then I needed to wear it ruthlessly.

I opened the door to reveal myself.

Nasira drew a long breath as slow and satisfied as her smile. "You look like a princess of the sun. Of Amarna."

I tried to hide my own smile and turned around to show her the back. The material coiled like liquid gold around my feet. "Maybe I am," I teased.

"I found you some shoes," she said, and handed me a pair of cream silk pumps with a large assortment of crystals and gems sewn into the straps and silver piping. The color of the shoes' material seemed to blend into the gold dress, complimenting it, yet detracting nothing of its magnificence.

"The silhouette is probably wide enough to hide my *asaya*," I suggested, reaching down to swing the fluttery hem.

"I didn't choose this dress for you on a whim," she said, with a mischievous gleam in her dark eyes. She reached into the wardrobe and removed a leather holster with my contracted *asaya* already in it. She knelt in front of me, lifted the hem of my dress, and buckled the holster around my ankle and calf.

Nasira stood. "Sit at the table and let me paint you."

I obeyed, watching her closely as she brought a small, eggshell-colored alabaster pot and unrolled a scrap of fabric to reveal a pair of wooden sticks about the length of my hand. She removed the pot's lid and dipped a stick inside. When she removed the stick, its tip was a black graphite color with a faint metallic sheen.

"Kohl," she explained, "is powerful magic. It's made from a mineral called galena. Before we go into battle or perform any ceremony, a Medjai should be ritually purified. This will help your heart be strong and heal your body from injury. Close your eyes."

She began in the inner corner of my eye, drawing across my upper and lower lids and beyond. She stopped halfway to the line of my hair at my ears and then painted my other eye. "How would you like your hair? Up or down? I'm glad you never chopped it all off like Americans do."

I didn't want to tell her I would have if I could've afforded a cut. "You can style it however you'd like."

"I'll do us both in fancy chignons," she said with a grin. "We'll look as sisters."

Those words put a smile on my own face. "How can I make my hair look as shiny as yours?"

She frowned, and my heart clenched. "My mother taught me how to take care of my hair and my skin—and

I'll teach you. Our hair is delicate and requires a lot of care. It's different than most kinds of hair."

Nasira reached for a dark glass bottle and poured a few drops of some sort of gold-colored oil into her palm. "Olive oil. Put it on your skin to make it feel soft and supple. It will do the same for your hair. Rub a drop in your scalp at night." She rose and stood behind me. She carefully separated my hair by each spiraling lock and massaged oil into my curls from root to tip, adding extra attention to the ends. "Fruit oils, nut butters, rose water," she began, "Add it morning and night and your curls will come to life."

I closed my eyes as she played with my hair. I imagined this was how a mother's love felt. This should've been mine. My mother should've been here to teach me how to care for myself. Set was to blame for what was taken from me.

But I didn't want to be angry or sad tonight. I had an objective to carry out. A mission. My concentration was necessary.

I felt myself buzzing with anticipation. I stole a glance at my reflection in the small tabletop mirror. Never in my life had I felt like a grown woman and looked the part.

Tonight would be incredible.

CHAPTER
7

Sayer parked the Delage alongside the curb a few blocks from our destination. He exited and rushed to open my backseat door. I grasped his open hand, and he helped me step onto the sidewalk. I felt very conscious of the *asaya* tucked into its holster around my ankle and I tried not to swing my dress too much as I moved. Anubis's amulet was tucked into the holster. If the immortal made good on his promises as he'd claimed he would, then I made sure I brought the amulet in the unfortunate event I needed his help.

Sayer stepped close to me to shut the door, my hand still in his, and he dipped his head to tell me, "You make that dress look beautiful."

I looked up at him, smiling, and found golden stars in his eyes. "Thank you."

He looked quite handsome himself in his very well cut tuxedo and bowtie. Nasira shined stunningly in her

silk dress of rich, shining ruby so glossy it appeared polished. She'd painted my lips a similar shade of red and
had dabbed gold powder on my eyelids. I felt as though
I wore a mask. No one could see through my makeup
and evening gown, through my stardust and sequins, to
the real Ziva beneath, the starved orphan girl. Perhaps
this *was* the real me—the princess of a solar court once
forgotten in a dusty tomb, the sparkling diamond once
lost in rock. Whichever Ziva I was . . . tonight, I was the
Ziva I wanted to be.

"We are here covertly," Nasira reminded us as she
rounded the car and tucked a stray lock of her bounti-
ful hair back into its knot behind her head. "Sayer, that
means you. Do not go in there brandishing your axes and
causing a ruckus."

"What if I'm not the one to cause a ruckus?" he asked,
his tone playful.

I gaped at him. "Do you mean me?"

He grinned and started forward.

"I intend to be on my best behavior!" I called after him.

As we walked the few blocks, I couldn't possibly fail
to notice the way other people looked at me as I passed
them. It was the way I used to look at the rich women
wearing dresses like mine and seeing those faces from
the receiving end was heartbreaking. For the first time in
my life, I understood why those women pretended not
to notice me when I stared.

When I saw the limousines pulling up alongside the
curb and gobs of fabulously dressed men and women
getting out, I knew we'd arrived. The white limestone

exterior of the townhouse gleamed in the nighttime lights and the elegant wrought iron window grills cast lovely, coiling vine-like shadows. Faint music seeped from the open windows and ushers in tuxedos guided guests through the front door.

"We have no invitations," Sayer said, his lips close to my ear, "so walk in like you own the place. No one will dare question you."

"I appreciate your confidence in my confidence," I replied.

"You have both," he told me, voice firm with conviction. "I know you can do this. Nasira knows it. You are royalty. Don't forget that."

His words repeated in my head as we approached, falling in queue with the rest of the guests. Nasira smiled at the ushers while I tried not to make eye contact with anyone, for fear I might be stopped.

"Pardon, miss," inquired an usher with a robust Metropolitan accent, his vowels harshly exaggerated. He wasn't from this neighborhood by a long shot.

My breath stalled, and my spine tensed between my shoulders. I felt a bit unreal as I turned to him. "Yes?" I asked.

"May I have your name, miss? For the list?"

I opened my mouth to speak, but I had no words.

"We're students of Dr. Sweeney," Nasira chimed in, leaning over me. "With the EEF?"

He blinked, his expression empty. "The . . . ?"

Nasira exhaled gruffly with impatience. "The Egypt Exploration Fund! Honestly, how did you get this job?"

"I—I don't know anything about—"

"Obviously," Nasira snapped, grabbed my arm, and marched us both past him and into the house.

When the three of us were inside, I leaned over to her and asked, "Who is Dr. Sweeney?"

"The archaeologist who discovered the stela," she whispered back. "I got his name from the article."

We meandered through the crowd, comprised entirely of fair-skinned people in their formal best, and I felt their eyes on me from every angle. Never had I felt like anything but an ignored gutter rat. They gaped as though I was a comet blazing an unstoppable path through them, my fire devouring their faint starlight.

I plucked tiny delicacies from the silver platters passed around by servers and something in particular, a slim fold of meat and a juicy blackberry set atop a square of cheesy toast, was quite fantastic. After I'd taken a sample, I'd spun to grab a second. As I hastened to catch up to my friends, a round white man with tomato-red cheeks intercepted me. I jerked to a stop and swallowed the last bite of my snack.

"Where are you from?" he asked, speaking tightly as though he were holding something between his back teeth.

I stared at him, disgusted, but I'd been asked that question a thousand times before. "Mister, I'm from New York."

He exhaled, impatient. "I meant, what *are* you? Are you Egyptian?"

"Yes, I am," I told him harshly, hoping he'd be satisfied and go bother someone else.

The man leaned back, smugness filling his red cheeks until they were puffy. "How exotic. I thought so. You look it. Charlotte—Charlotte, dear. I told you. They are *Egyptians*." He turned to get the attention of a slim white woman in a pink silk gown who took one look at us and held her sequin-encrusted clutch tighter to her side.

Nasira grabbed my arm and smiled a full set of teeth at the rude man. "So, what are *you*?"

He blinked at her, quite perplexed. "I beg your pardon? What am *I*?"

"Why, yes," she said, unflinchingly.

"I don't understand," he said with a shake of his head.

Her saccharine smile spread. "Of course you don't." Turning both our backs to him, she dragged me deep into the thick crowd and made a gagging face.

"Nasi, that was *aces*," I told her, voice hushed.

She wore an ugly frown and her narrowed eyes were dark as they glared across the room. "They look at us like we aren't even human," she snarled. "Like *we* are on display—objects to be touched and used and paraded around. Just a few more spoils of rich Western conquest. They'll always treat you like an exhibit, Ziva, because you threaten their perfect, little white bubble."

I didn't reply; all over the floor and in every room, the well-to-do guests perused the artifacts, but there was something missing. The way they looked at the jewelry, pottery, every-day items like cosmetics applicators and furniture—there was nothing academic. These people had no interest in better understanding how my ancestors interpreted the world around them. They couldn't see past the glittering gems and gold on the surface. They didn't take long enough to wonder about the princess of ancient blood who once wore that necklace and used those brushes and sticks to paint her face. These people glanced, saw color, and moved on. People had looked at me in this exact same way my entire life.

"All of the 'imports' here were raided from burial tombs," Nasira remarked. "From the graves of human beings. They see nothing wrong with what they do, because they've dehumanized our people, who once walked around, ate and slept, lived and loved. And these sods have 'unwrapping parties.' Did you know people can buy mummies? The bodies of human beings? In some places the mummies sell cheaper than firewood, so venture which gets thrown into their hearths first."

My stomach turned with the horror of what she said.

Nasira's lip curled and her voice started to break with emotion. "Point any of that out to them and they get defensive and lash out at you."

"But what do we do about it?" I asked her, feeling helpless. "Let them talk to us like that because it's the way things have always been?"

The anger in Nasira's expression eased into sympathy. "People have made you feel like your only option is to be passive about the way they treat you. I want to teach you that you don't have to be passive. Do not diminish yourself because a little man feels threatened by your strength. It's a waste of time to wait for things to change.

If you stand up to them and tell them, 'No, you can't treat me like this,' they'll probably get angry, but it will make them think. Eventually, hopefully, someday, they will learn."

I stared at her and realized people had beat me down my entire life, called me whatever they wanted to call me, and none of it had ever been okay. They made me feel like I wasn't beautiful or desirable, like I would never be important or smart or educated enough, all because my skin wasn't white enough or my hair wasn't straight and *controlled*. I didn't fit into their boxes. As though the way I looked made me less human or something else entirely. I would be passive no longer.

I was indeed a comet blazing through them, a force they'd never anticipated and could not stop. I had the strength and the power to obliterate their standards, their structures, and their expectations. My fire would burn them up.

"Come on," Nasira said. "We've got a job to do. Let's finish up and get out of here."

Two men in belted jackets, breeches, and boots stood out and away from the rest of the guests, the visors of their caps shadowing their eyes. I couldn't help watch them as we moved through the room. A blonde woman approached them, her back to me, her deep emerald dress rippling in her wake. From here I couldn't hear their conversation.

"German S.A.," Nasira said quietly.

"Soldiers?" I asked.

"Officers," was her reply, her attention to them scrupulous. "Unusual. I'd like to know why they're here."

We found Sayer towering over many heads in the room. He caught our gazes and gestured with a nod of his head for us to follow him. I hoped he'd found the stela and we'd leave any minute. My dress suddenly felt too tight. My *asaya's* holster itched.

The next parlor over was significantly busier than the last and I could hear a man bellowing above the voices of the crowd and the music.

"*Three months* struggling to survive in the blistering desert, ladies and gentlemen. We battled diseases that killed half my men, thirty-foot crocodiles that devoured half of the *other* half of my men, and sandstorms great enough to swallow Manhattan whole. But even the gods couldn't stop *me* from making the most incredible archaeological find in history hidden within a secret room of the Ramesseum. This is an extraordinary mortuary complex built outside Ancient Thebes for Nefertari's husband, Ramesses II, or Ramesses the Great."

I cringed at his needless theatricality. The man, I presumed, was Dr. Sweeney mentioned by Nasira. He was a tall, tan white man with a deeply receding mostly gray hairline and dressed in a very fine tuxedo. He surveyed the crowd, studying their reactions in quite a theatrical, circus ringleader sort of way.

"The stela of Nefertari is more significant than the death mask of Tutankhamun. Why, you ask?"

His dramatic pause lingered far too long. Nasira rolled her eyes so hard I thought they'd fall out of her head.

"Because *knowledge* is a greater treasure than gold."

Low, stunned murmurs snaked through the audience.

"So cliché," Nasira grumbled beneath her breath. I snickered.

"Think of the Rosetta Stone," Sweeney offered. "Ancient Egypt would hold far more secrets than it does today had the Stone not been deciphered. The mesmerizing hieroglyphs would still be a puzzle. Today, I unveil to you proof Nefertari was the most powerful queen in history. Greater than Cleopatra—greater than Elizabeth the First! This artifact is the twentieth century's Rosetta Stone."

Nasira almost pried apart the bodies blocking our view, despite their muffled protests, and I trailed in her wake toward the front. The stela everyone marveled over was a simple-looking limestone slab about two feet tall and a foot wide, set on a red velvet display.

"I can't read the inscription from here," Sayer whispered. "But there's no way I could get close enough with all these people staring at it."

Nasira lifted her chin and a look of determination crossed her face. "Leave it to me."

Sayer nodded and moved behind us to the far end of the crowd. I stood in my place, unsure of what I needed to do, if anything. If Nasira needed me, I hoped my instinct would charge me to action.

"Here Nefertari is described as the queen of cardinals," Sweeney continued, "a title of hers previously unknown to the scientific community."

"Perhaps it's previously unknown because your translation is wrong," Nasira called.

The crowd's response was an immediate collective gasp. Sweeney's jaw hung wide open. After a painfully long hesitation, he let loose an uncomfortable chuckle. "Young lady," he said as though about to scold a child. "I'm quite certain not only do I have the proper credentials but the experience in the field to make accurate translations of Ancient Egyptian hieroglyphs."

People turned their heads toward Nasira and shifted away from her. "Well, you've identified Nefertari's cartouche correctly," she said with a shrug. "But any halfwit could memorize that."

Sweeney's breath rushed from him and he blinked hard. "Excuse me?"

"This doesn't say, 'the queen of cardinals,'" Nasira added. "It says, 'the cardinal treasures of the queen.' You're reading the hieroglyphs backwards."

"Even if you were right—which you're not—the script could still identify her as the queen of the cardinal points of Egypt: North, South, East, and West," he lectured, his tone condescending and haughty. "Typically, rulers were given control over only Upper and Lower Egypt, after the two kingdoms were united, of course. This stela could mean Egypt had expanded its borders and elevated Nefertari to a position of power we've seen nowhere else."

"The stela could also mean Nefertari was given a team of winged horses to pull her chariot," Nasira called with biting sarcasm. "Though the latter is more likely."

Sweeney eyed her carefully and with disdain. "What did you say your name was, young lady?"

"My mother calls me precocious. A lot of people do in fact."

"I would've guessed irritating," Sweeney shot back. "Though both are more likely."

The look Nasira gave him was cold murder and war. As they bickered back and forth, I pushed through the audience to locate Sayer. He was bent over the stela with his left sleeve pushed up past his elbow, revealing one of the scarab cuffs. He'd unrolled several sheets of paper and with a stick of charcoal he created a rubbing as quickly as possible. I tried to do him a favor by blocking him from the view of anyone who might notice him tampering with the stela.

Sayer glanced at me out the corner of his eye and said, "I'll spend more time translating at headquarters. If I rush this, I could make a mistake."

"We don't need that," I agreed.

The corner of his mouth quirked in his smile. "No, we don't."

"Nasira is very good at distractions," I noted.

He snickered. "She's enjoying herself, isn't she?"

"To say the least. The girl was built for battle."

A hand clamped around my arm and yanked me around. A man in an usher's tuxedo and apron filled my vision.

"What are you doing?" he demanded and pointed at Sayer's charcoal rubbing.

"Well," I started, thinking of a way to stall and give Sayer a few more moments. "Upon closer examination—and I'm no expert mind you—I read something quite interesting. 'If any man dares disturb my rest and reads this inscription, I shall break his neck like a goose.' Oh, uh-oh. It's a good thing I'm not a man. Although my friend here has run into some bad luck." I gave an uncomfortable, awkward laugh. Sayer grimaced, rolling with it.

The usher's face twisted into a scowl. "I'll have to remove you for touching the artifact."

"No, thanks," I replied. "*Taw.*" My spell hit him in the chest, knocking the air from his lungs and his back into a curio. Its contents jangled, and the man toppled to the floor, knocking over guests like bowling pins.

I glanced at Sayer as pandemonium erupted. He hastily rolled the paper and nodded at me. "Let's move," he said.

I shoved a path through the crowd, and when I reached Nasira, I clamped a hand on her shoulder. "Time to go," I told her in an unintentionally sing-song voice.

She gave a curt nod and offered a salute to her red-faced opponent. "Well, Dr. Sweeney, it's been a pleasure. Best of luck to you, mate."

The three of us rushed toward the front door, ignoring the protests of the usher I hit with my spell. The confusion of the guests made it difficult for anyone to chase us into the street.

"So—did we get it?" Nasira called, taking my hand.

I tried to reply, but I couldn't stop laughing, so I merely nodded. I'd never had so much fun in my life! Adrenaline sang through my veins and pumped into my muscles, until cold cascaded through my body and I slammed to a stop.

The kriosphinx stood not thirty feet from us, appearing from the darkness like a phantom from hell, its spiraled ram's horns casting a sinister shadow across the urban surroundings. Nasira didn't hesitate; she dropped to the ground, slipped her *asaya* from its holster, and snapped it to its full length. Sayer tore open his tuxedo jacket and yanked free the twin axes from the scabbard strapped to his back. I moved slower than my companions, unable to tear my eyes away, as I knelt and retrieved my own *asaya* from my ankle holster.

None of the pedestrians had screamed yet. Not yet. They slowed, stopped, and stared. Shock plumed, thick and disorienting.

The beast raised its snout to the sky, opened its mouth, and bugled a terrible, eerie, high-pitched scream, the crescendo a ghost's song.

And the screams began.

The kriosphinx didn't seem to notice any of the panicked people running and shouting in all directions. The way it looked at me—not Sayer, not Nasira—was predatory, focusing as if it could see nothing else. Power leaked from it, flowed across the black pavement, and from everywhere people gasped and murmured cries of surprise and fear. It threw back its head again, heavy with horns, and bugled, sending shivers like snakes through my limbs.

"What's it doing?" I asked.

"Calling for reinforcements," Nasira replied, her tone hard.

Sayer put his back to us and we had all our sides covered. The second kriosphinx emerged from a flash of shadows. Erratic headlights strobed at the beasts, reflecting off their yellow eyes with demonic glints.

Stuffed delivery wagons, canary yellow taxis, and cars of all kinds screeched to a stop as they careened into one another, blocking both ends of the street. Drivers and passengers flung themselves from their vehicles and darted in the opposite direction of the two monsters and we three poor fools were trapped between them. Soon, the roar of the city was a distant dream and we were abandoned in a wasteland.

"Three Medjai in one night," the first kriosphinx mused, its ram-mouth moving in a terrible, not-right way.

"One of them is the scion," the second said, nostrils flaring. "I smell queen's blood."

Something scraped across the pavement from the darkest corner of the street. I turned my head only to feel my insides contract and twist with horror. An enormous cobra appeared, gliding fluidly, black diamond scales flickering like starlight, and a sandstorm of fear unleashed its wrath inside my chest. The snake stopped and coiled into a tight knot before rising tall toward the sky. It disappeared in a flash of spiraling shadows and eerie netherlight and emerged as a woman. Not a woman—an immortal like Anubis.

"Oh, have I waited eons to meet you," the goddess said, her words slow and savoring, seemingly disembodied from the sculpted, unmoving mouth of her war mask. "I have lived every one of my infinite days waiting for the time I could present you to my king."

Shadowy flames licked up the folds of her dress of glittering black snake scales and the streetlights reflected off the vertebrae bracelets sheathing her forearms. Her starless midnight hair bloomed around her with growing magic, and from behind a mask of solid gold, her carnelian eyes settled on me in a disquieting, eager way. The face carved into the mask was serene and almost sleepy, the painted brow frozen without emotion, the mouth curved into a smile sweet with malice. Those shadows plumed behind her; her body melted into them as though they were a physical part of her, the gold of her mask shining. She was a beauty too terrible to behold.

"I am Kauket," she said to me. "I am Darkness."

The kriosphinxes launched forward, their eerie screams cutting through the night, and bounded toward both sides of us. Nasira met the first hard; she whirled her *asaya* faster than I'd ever seen, and the whistle of the staff rose above the beasts' cries. The second kriosphinx reared, forelegs and talons outspread to bring Sayer down, but he swung one ax and it tore through shoulder meat. Sayer whirled aside and dropped, and the beast flew overhead. He spun back around and buried his other ax into the barrel of its chest. Obsidian glanced off bone with a crack but gleaned its share of blood.

A pair of patrolling police officers appeared with their revolvers already drawn, arguing over whether or not they ought to shoot the "dangerous animals" before their backup arrived. No doubt they'd been on the lookout since the night I was first attacked. No matter how they'd prepared for the beasts' next appearance, the police department could never fathom the destruction wrought by the immortals.

The officers fired, and their bullets hit the kriosphinxes, who shrieked with anger. Kauket lifted a hand to the mouth of her mask and blew gently, as if blowing a kiss. The officers' bodies exploded into golden sand that scattered across the pavement.

These beasts in New York . . . This wasn't their world. This wasn't *our* world. Manhattan was diesel and bullets, not magic and gods. They didn't know what to do about us, or we about them. We could tear this city apart.

CHAPTER

8

My pulse kicked up inside my skull, a steady over-whelming rhythm promising to draw me away from reality if I let it. My mind grasped at a different world. My bare feet were sinking in mud. The Nile kissed my toes. Tiny fish dared to nibble the tips. But I smelled pavement and garbage and fuel. I was here and now, not then, and I needed to do something.

My hand tightened on my *asaya* and I shot forward and slashed left. Kauket pulled herself out of reach. I slashed with the other end, but she knocked my weapon away with her hand.

I needed to be faster, but this dress was too tight around my thighs. I kicked off my shoes. With a whirl of my *asaya*, I slashed a line through the fabric across the length of my leg, feeling relieved with the newfound freedom of movement.

The masked goddess *tsk*ed at me. "Hmm. That looked couture."

I launched at her, whirling my *asaya* as fast as I could—up, right, behind me, left, in front of me, down—until confusion filled the goddess's face when she couldn't predict my moves. The *asaya* spun and my hand shot forward with a powerful *taw* spell that slammed into her chest. Kauket wailed in fury as she was forced back. She skidded to a crouching stop, her fingernails screeching against the pavement. She lifted her head and her shining eyes locked on mine. I leapt forward and swung the *asaya* in an arc toward Kauket's chest, but a spell cast by the goddess smacked it out of my hand so hard my own weapon ripped a deep gash into my exposed thigh. I cried out in pain and one knee buckled beneath my weight. Blood poured down my leg.

Hot adrenaline pushing me through my pain, I threw up my hand, casting a *benu* spell into the goddess's face. She screeched as the blinding sunlight exploded like a bomb's flash, illuminating the entire street. Kauket stepped aside, shielding her eyes and cursing.

I reached toward the darkened sky, clenched my fist, and brought down a *setekh* spell. The lightning bolt cracked as it struck the goddess, whose screams were drowned by the spell's resulting roar in the raging flash of light. It slammed through her body and into the ground, splitting a gorge that rocketed through the asphalt toward me. The force blasted me off my feet and I was blown backward through the air. I landed hard and the wind rushed from my lungs, leaving me gasping.

A hush of darkness and quiet settled on the street, and in the distance, sirens wailed, growing louder and louder. Magic buzzed and crackled in the atmosphere like electricity. I caught my breath, rolled onto my side, and sat up. My hair had been torn from its chignon and was long and wild around my shoulders. Kauket lay on her back like a fallen angel, the charred black wings of her dress splayed and withered beneath her.

"Ziva!"

I turned my head toward the direction of Sayer's panicked voice and called back, "I'm all right!"

His face was bloodied and his tuxedo torn, but the kriosphinx looked worse. It scrambled some yards away from him, bugling a strangled, pained sound, its head jerking to its right over and over, reaching for the ax buried between its ribs.

Kauket loosed a low, angry growl and stirred. As she pushed herself to her feet, her hair spilled over her shoulders. From behind her war mask of gold, her eyes glowed a violent red.

"*Ow,*" Kauket grumbled with malice, and bared her shining fangs. "That stung."

Tires squealed as a stream of paddy wagons maneuvered around the smashed and abandoned cars. Officers poured out, guns at the ready.

One of them, standing behind an open door, spoke into a megaphone. "I need everyone to move away from the—the—wild animals and lay their weapons on the ground."

I exchanged an uncertain look with Sayer. He said

nothing but gave me a subtle shake of his head. I searched the area for Nasira and found her crouched in front of one of the beasts, both of them battered and bloody, their gazes set on each other, deadlocked.

The kriosphinxes whined and something began to stir in the street—shadows and gloom, netherlight and pulsing magic. Kauket's low chuckle curled the hairs on the back of my neck as she summoned her power. The officers shrank at the sight of the goddess of darkness, several lowering their guns to look at each other in fear, but some held courageously. She raised both trembling hands, as if to welcome the crowd, and her magic detonated like a bomb.

The blast knocked the officers off their feet and charged into the ring of paddy wagons, shattering windows and headlights, exploding glass and ripping open doors off their hinges. I toppled to the ground and flung up my arms to shield my head from debris. The officers scrambled. Shots rang out and bullets embedded in netherworld flesh and twisted American metal.

Kauket loosed a roar of frustration and transformed into her colossal cobra form with a flash of shadows and netherlight. The pandemonium in the street exploded into a violent riot of panic and madness. The goddess thrashed, hurling her pure muscle body into the side of a car, sending it flying into the front of a building. It crashed and rolled down the stoop to slam into a streetlight. Kauket spread her hood and screamed, baring her fangs at the shell-shocked police officers.

"Kauket!" I yelled and pulled Anubis's amulet free from my *asaya's* holster.

Some horrible rasp and howl of rage erupted from deep within the goddess, a cry strangled by the lack of vocal cords in her serpent throat. I bolted, darting away from the police, weaving between smashed cars. I felt Kauket's eyes burn lightening-hot on my back as she launched into pursuit.

"Anubis," I called breathlessly. "Anubis, I could use a hand here!"

When I glanced behind me, the sight of the side-winding serpent smashing her way through parked cars and lampposts was enough to make me forget about the broken pavement and pebbles cutting my bare feet. I looked ahead to narrowly dodge the back of a truck, but I smashed into the sideview mirror, hitting it so hard it was torn free and my body careened to the ground. Kauket's gigantic shadow soared over me as I fell, and she slid across the street and into a vender's cart, causing it to explode with goods.

I scrambled backward, using the grill of a car to pull myself to my feet. Kauket shot toward me and transformed back into a woman to stomp in my direction with hellfire in her eyes.

Another flash appeared between us and the goddess slid to a stop. A look of surprise lit up her eyes. The shadows dissipated, and I recognized the man in front of me.

Power rolled from Anubis, spreading from him across the ground like a cold, dark inferno and I felt as afraid of him as I was of Kauket. Death and Darkness faced off and the world held its breath. Again, I was reminded of their unearthliness; they were not mortal, and they were more ancient than the rock this city was built upon.

"Move aside," Kauket ordered, the jewels and scales of her dress glittering in the city lights, "or I will cut through you."

"You don't belong here," Anubis replied, standing his ground, his back to me. "Return to the netherworld with your creatures and leave this human girl be."

"How bold you've grown," the goddess of darkness sneered from behind her shining mask. "I was already thousands of years old when your mother whelped you, pup. You make a grave error daring to challenge me."

Anubis tilted his head to the side and oh, how I wished I could've seen the look on his face when he said, "After how miserably you fared against this neophyte Medjai, I'm not exactly shivering in fright of you."

Her eyes grew wide, filling with white, and her body swelled as though she would burst with rage.

"Ziva! *Ziva!*"

"Nasira!" I cried, hearing her voice behind me, and I turned, searching the street for her. "I'm here!"

Kauket hesitated. She and I realized at the same time her kriosphinxes were gone. Nasira and Sayer burst onto the street and toward me, but they slowed when they caught sight of the immortals. Kauket took a few steps back, finding herself alone and at odds against another god and three Medjai.

"*Your stars will fade!*" she shrieked and vanished in a swarm of shadows.

Anubis faced me, a strange mixture of worry and relief in his topaz eyes. "Are you all right?" he asked.

I nodded. "I'm fine."

Nasira dropped to the ground in reverence, her body shaking with disbelief. "Lord Anubis. Thank you for your assistance tonight."

He offered her a shallow bow of his head. "It's my honor to do so. The Medjai have long protected the mortal world."

"Well, I for one am very glad you answered when I called," I told him. "I kept hitting her with everything I had, but . . ."

"Kauket underestimated you," Anubis said, his tone serious. "I'm glad she had the sense to flee. A fight between me and her here, in the middle of the city, would be disastrous. I don't want to consider the collateral damage."

"Is she as old as she says?" I asked.

"Yes," he answered. "She is one of the original eight deities born at the beginning of time. As there came earth and sky, there came light and darkness." He looked past our heads and down the street. "You must go."

We could hear shouts coming from around the corner, growing louder as they neared.

"The police have reassembled," Sayer said. "Let's move."

We rushed toward where we left the Delage, limping, battered, and bruised, before we could be stopped and questioned, even arrested. Whatever the Medjai protocol was about that, there was no way I'd allow myself to get hauled away in handcuffs.

"Did you get what you needed for the translation?" I

asked Sayer as soon as we were safely inside the car with Nasira driving.

He nodded from the passenger's seat and presented the charcoal rubbings to reveal the markings. "The hieroglyphs I copied remained intact for the most part." There were smudges here and there, but even my novice eye could make out the symbols. "I'll transcribe them to a proper notebook once we're back at headquarters."

My mouth twisted as I thought. "Where did Sweeney say he found the stela? The Ramesseum? Perhaps Nefertari's true tomb is somewhere in that mortuary complex."

Nasira nodded. "That's possible." She glanced over her shoulder at me, her expression hardening, but only for a brief moment. "You seemed familiar with the god of death. May I ask how that is?"

A flutter of panic came through my chest and then splintered into guilt. "He visited me. I didn't tell either of you because I didn't know what it meant. I still don't. He blessed me."

Sayer looked at his sister and his expression was tense and unreadable.

"I really don't like it when you two look at each other like that," I snapped, exasperated.

Sayer's gaze fell before raising to meet mine. "I'm sorry. I don't think we know all of what it means either. A number of things."

"Where did you learn to use magic like that?" she asked, but her prying sounded more like an interrogation. "Was that his work? Anubis's?"

"You taught me those spells," I reminded her. The alarmed tone in her voice had me feeling the same.

She shook her head. "Not like that, I didn't."

"Did I do something wrong?"

"No, Ziva," Sayer assured me. "You were brilliant. Perhaps more brilliant than we'd expected, that's all."

The confidence I'd felt in my skills tonight now churned into suffocating anxiety. Sayer might have meant his words, but Nasira's reaction concerned me. I was reminded of Anubis's blessing, unsure of the hidden magic in those simple words he spoke to me. The other Medjai carried on their conversation while I sat, silent within my inner storm, thinking, calculating, worrying.

CHAPTER

9

When we returned to the mansion, we parted, and I
headed for my room to change into a nightgown.
In my absence, someone had laundered and hung it in
my wardrobe. I dressed and caught the faint fragrance
of gardenia in the fabric. For some time, I tried to sleep,
but I felt restless as a butterfly trapped in a jar. I couldn't
wait until morning to find out what Sayer had learned
from the stela. Though I couldn't have memorized all
of the hieroglyphs earlier, there were a few symbols I
remembered, and I could use what Sayer had taught me
to practice translation.

I slid out of bed and wrapped a robe around myself.
I cast a *tahen* spell before venturing from my rooms and
in the direction of the library. The corridors were quiet
and dark, but my little ball of netherlight illuminated my
way. Every piece of furniture or statuary looked very different and much more sinister in the middle of the night,

like dark caricatures of their daytime selves. Finding the library in the dark proved a challenge. But I'd made up my mind and wouldn't give up now. There was no use in going back to bed only to lie there all night wishing I were elsewhere.

By some miracle, I reached my destination and exhaled with relief when I pulled the great library doors open. I paused when I saw the glow of an oil lamp. Someone else was already here.

I stepped inside, my bare footsteps padding softly. "Hello?" My voice was like a terrible crash in the silence and made me flinch. Drawing closer, I saw Sayer lift his head at a desk.

"Ziva," he called quietly, and waved me over. Splayed in front of him was a sheet of paper covered in hieroglyphs with English words below them, and several reference books opened flat.

"Is this the stela translation?" I asked, stunned to find him already in here working. I took a seat in the wooden chair opposite him.

"Yes," he replied, his voice a bit dry and tired, as though he hadn't spoken in some time. "I couldn't wait to begin. And here I am, up all night because I have no patience."

I smiled, knowing exactly how he felt. "You're not impatient. You just have to *know*."

He returned my smile, though his was lopsided and weary. He was an attractive young man and when he smiled, there was something boyish and youthful in his face. "You speak as if you're here for the same reason."

"Quit reading my mind, Medjai," I told him playfully.

He continued to watch me, the lamplight giving his skin a golden glow and lighting the stars in his dark eyes. Something pulsed in my belly and pulled at my spine, and I set my teeth to regain my ground. He was a kind of handsome that unraveled you and had a smile that was nothing short of savage magic. An unbidden vision coiled around my thoughts and I imagined him whispering my name against my skin in the dark. There was no harm in a fantasy, and I rather liked thinking of him that way—especially when he always looked at me with the same devilish eyebrow raised with interest.

I couldn't be sure how long the moment lasted, but I forced words out of myself to recharge our stalled conversation. "So, what did you find so far?"

He blinked hard, like he'd been trapped in the same reverie. "Well, the cardinal treasures reference Nefertari's mummified organs, like the cardinal directions: north, south, east, and west." My undoubtedly blank expression prompted him to explain further. "During the mummification process, four organs are removed from the body cavity and are each dried in natron within their own canopic jars. Qebehsenuef, the falcon, is guardian of the bowel. Duamutef, the jackal, is guardian of the stomach. Imsety, the man, is guardian of the liver, and Hapy, the baboon, is guardian of the lungs."

"And everything else—aside from the heart, which needed to stay with the body—was all discarded, yes?" I inquired, unsure if I remembered correctly.

"Right." He looked down to read and I took the moment

to study him, the edge of his jaw and the short hairs speckling it. I wondered how soft the hair was—more precisely I wondered how soft it would feel brushing my skin.

"It says here, 'The cardinal treasures of the queen of kings are the key to complete the resurrection. They will lead the way as the stars guide travelers. Reunite her treasures within the stargate and she will be remade as one of the wardens of eternity.'"

"What is the stargate?" I asked, imagining a doorway.

"The human flesh," he explained. "It's the conduit through which a soul connects with the netherworld. We will have to find her resting place and the four canopic jars. I recall an unidentified canopic jar which had been recovered from an illegal antiquities street dealer. The cartouche had been damaged, so we weren't sure who it belonged to."

Excitement gave me renewed energy. "You think of it now because it could possibly have belonged to Nefertari."

He nodded. "If reuniting her sacred organs is part of her resurrection, then she would've wanted them to be very hard to find. Something perhaps only the Medjai can do. Something only you can do."

"This sounds like our lead then," I said.

"The canopic jar is at our actual headquarters in Cairo, Egypt. We call it the Pyramidion."

"Oh," I mumbled, deflated with disappointment. "I should've guessed that. We won't fully understand what the stela means until we see the Pyramidion jar."

"Right," he agreed. "All this trouble, and we don't have any answers at all."

I leaned across the desk. "Yes, we do. We know what we need to find in order to locate Nefertari's true tomb. The stela revealed she'll be one of 'the wardens of eternity' when she's reborn. Does that mean she'll be immortal? Like Anubis? It sounds like a spell to make a god."

He shrugged, his eyebrows raising with consideration. "That is certainly what's implied here. Perhaps once she's resurrected, she'll be safe from Set. Immortals can still be destroyed, however, with much difficulty."

"Nefertari must have promised Set something very important for him to go through all this trouble," I started, thinking back. "It's been thousands of years and he's still trying to stop the resurrection. How infinitely petty."

"When she betrayed him, he swore never to allow her the taste of life again," Sayer explained. "No one holds a grudge like an immortal."

"What was Nefertari supposed to give in return?" I asked.

Sayer shrugged. "We don't know. There is no option but to beat Set and Kauket to Nefertari's tomb. Because you are important to her resurrection, Set will never allow you to live."

"How could he know what part I play if I don't even know?" I asked. "How do the Medjai even know?"

His brow furrowed, and he took a deep breath. "The lector priest at the time was present when Nefertari made the deal with Set. He supposedly wrote all he knew on a scroll. It hasn't aged well, and what has survived of the scroll is, inconveniently, partial. We've restored as much as we could, but we can't restore what we don't know was there."

"I see," I replied. "Earlier, Kauket had mentioned her king. Did she mean Set? What is he king of?"

Sayer shook his head. "Set is not a king. Osiris is king of the dead."

"Hypothetically speaking," I offered, "what if taking Osiris's throne is Set's endgame?"

He frowned and the muscle in his jaw clenched. "Set and Osiris have feuded for eons. Set could very well want the throne for himself. It's a frightening thought, but not so farfetched."

"Why's that?" I asked. "More frightening than him wanting to kill me?"

"You've seen enough of the immortals' power to know a war between them would only bring destruction to both the human and immortal worlds," he said gravely. "If Kauket and Anubis had battled to the death, they could've destroyed Manhattan in a single night. A second world war between human nations has already begun. We must do whatever is in our power to stop all of this or humanity won't survive to see a new century."

"May I ask you something?" I ventured. "Between you and me. If we are friends."

"Of course," he said, puzzled. "We *are* friends."

"What do you think about Anubis choosing to bless me?" I asked. "Nasira was scaring me."

"Don't let her reaction eat at you," he told me gently. "When Nasira is faced with something she doesn't understand, she gets afraid and she gets defensive. I believe, with my entire heart, something I trust deeply, that your being blessed by a god is a good thing. Nasi does not trust in the gods, but I do."

His words and the softly earnest way in which he said them eased the tension from my shoulders. I exhaled and nodded. "Okay."

His brow raised, and he took a deep breath. "But please do not tell her I said she gets afraid. She will throw my heart to Ammit without hesitation."

My laugh was soft and coaxed a smile from him. "Your secret is safe with me. Tomorrow we should pay Sweeney a visit. He might know something more. He could even have one of the canopic jars with him."

"I'll suggest that to Nasi," Sayer agreed. "Get some sleep. You'll need your energy for tomorrow—that is, if you still want to do this."

"I don't want to sleep," I replied, unable to hide my smile. "How could I after tonight? Now that I'm beginning to know what I'm doing with magic . . . I suppose I'm not sure exactly how to describe the feeling."

"I know what you mean," he said. "You like to feel strong and in control. You depend on nothing and nobody but yourself."

"You're reading my mind again," I told him.

"Don't have to," he said. "You and I are a lot alike, Ziva."

I laughed softly. "I can't be sure if that's a good thing."

"We'll have to wait and see, I suppose." He leaned back in his seat and stretched his arms high above his head and yawned. "I think I will call it a night. There's not much more I can do right now."

"Then I'll meet with you bright and early?" I asked.

That breath-seizing smile of his returned. "Your enthusiasm might rival Nasira's. I will see you tomorrow, Ziva. Good night."

When I headed to the main hall for my morning run, I was pleased to find Nasira waiting for me. To me, it meant she had faith I hadn't been scared off after last night.

"I want to apologize," she said, frowning, her gaze wavering. "I didn't mean to sound so alarmed about how you fought against Kauket. You showed rare instinct. I've never seen any neophyte cast a lightning spell like that."

"Well, I wasn't lying when I said no one had ever taught me spells except you," I told her, feeling defensive.

Her dark eyes grew wide. "No, no, that's not what I meant. Of course, I believe you. My reaction was a stunned one, nothing more. You were very impressive and I'm excited to see your potential realized."

"Thank you," I said, and with relief, my confidence returned.

"Well, I'm not sure if you've spoken to Sayer yet this morning, but he and I agreed we should seek out the archaeologist again, preferably today. As soon as possible."

"I did," she replied, "and I agree with you both. Sayer is making calls to find out which Manhattan hotel Sweeney resides in. Starting at the top, of course. The good doctor seems like that sort."

The prospect of another exciting adventure had my blood stirring. I looked forward to expelling some of my energy with exercise. "This afternoon sounds like a good time to pay Sweeney a visit."

Nasira gave me a quick nod and a smile. "It's a plan."

We returned in good time and headed straight for breakfast so I wouldn't miss out again. Sayer was already seated and lifted his head from his plateful of food to wave us over. I sat across from him and eagerly reached for different dishes to fill my own plate.

"I learned from yesterday," I said. "Eat first, then bathe. I'll never miss another breakfast. Or another plate of French toast."

"Pray tell, what did you find, dearest brother?" Nasira asked.

"Your friend, Dr. Sweeney, is staying at the Waldorf-Astoria on Park Ave.," Sayer explained. "I rang a few places, posing as his assistant, and was given his room number. Apparently, the proprietors of his expedition are footing the bill during his stay in New York."

I smiled, feeling quite devious. "Then let's eat and dress to impress, shall we?"

We found parking not far from the entrance of the hotel. The old Waldorf-Astoria had been torn down to make way for the Empire State Building, which became the tallest building in the world, but it couldn't shadow the opulence of the new hotel. The granite Art Deco facade glittered in the midday sun and when I looked up, the limestone of the upper floors blinded me.

On the streets, we certainly attracted many looks of curiosity in our black gear—weapons concealed, of course—but when we entered the hotel, curiosity turned to disgust and disdain. Every man, woman, and child we passed was dressed impeccably and we were clearly a blemish in their habitat. I wondered if Sayer and Nasira noticed the way people responded to our presence. None of it affected me terribly; I was used to being treated this way. But I still didn't like it. Today, however, I walked with my head held high, knowing the sort of power I had was greater than the false superiority of people who had more money than I. Like Nasira had said, I had potential. Everyone around me in this over-the-top, glitzy lobby had already peaked.

A man waiting by the elevators grew quite nervous when he saw us. He peeked at us sidelong and quickly looked away. The elevator car touched down and dinged, but the man hesitated at the open door. I imagined he was afraid we'd follow him in.

Nasira stepped forward and claimed the compartment, and Sayer and I followed. She paused and glanced at the man, presumably to wait for him to join us if he'd have liked. But he didn't, and I pushed the button to close the door.

"We need to get Sweeney to let us in," Nasira said. "There can't be any forced entry. We'll be in and out clean-like. He'll recognize me from last night, so Ziva, your American accent and lovely face are it."

I nodded without protest. I could do this.

From the corner of my eye, I caught Sayer's pleased smile and I gained a little more strength and courage.

He directed us to the correct room and my friends pinned their backs against the wall on either side of the door, out of the peephole's view. I took a deep breath and knocked.

"Yes?" came a man's answer.

"Room service, Dr. Sweeney," I said, hoping to sound as pleasant and nonchalant as possible. Eagerness might make him suspicious.

Footsteps sounded on the other side of the door and a moment later came a reply. "I didn't order room service."

I supposed I hadn't thought this far ahead. The first thing I thought of became my quick response. "You didn't order this tiramisu with a kettle of hot chocolate?"

Sayer raised an eyebrow at me, half-smiling.

Sweeney paused before he replied, "Why, yes—yes, I did indeed order that."

He cracked open the door, and my *taw* spell shoved it wide, blowing him off his feet and onto his back. My Medjai companions and I stormed into the room. Nasira cast a spell I didn't recognize, and Sweeney began to gasp for air, unable to cry out. He scratched at his throat, eyes bulging with fear. He scrambled away from us, bumping into the side of his bed and collapsing to the floor.

Nasira knelt in front of him and said coldly, "I will

allow you to breathe if you promise not to scream. The instant you try, I will take your air again. Is this clear?"

Wild-eyed with fright, he nodded vigorously.

"Nasira," I said in a low tone, alarmed by her—for lack of a more appropriate word—viciousness. I hadn't seen this side of her before. When I looked at Sayer, his expression was blank.

She released him, and he took a long, grateful drag of oxygen. "You—you were at the party last night!" he exclaimed. "Who are you people?"

"Protectors of this world," she replied. "And we need some information from you. Was Nefertari's stela found at the Ramesseum as you claimed?"

"Well, yes," he insisted. "What would I gain from lying about that?"

She scoffed, an ugly sound. "No, you're a thief, not a threat. Was anything else of Nefertari's found during your dig?"

"A few things, yes. Some jewelry and a canopic jar we can't confirm belonged to her, but—"

"The canopic jar—was Nefertari's cartouche inscribed on it?" Sayer demanded.

"We found a partial cartouche," Sweeney admitted. "But there are so many royal names containing the hiero-glyph 'nefer-' like Neferneferure or Neferneferuaten . . ."

"Where is the artifact now?" Nasira interjected impatiently.

"At—at the British Museum in London," he explained. "I found hieratic script painted on the surface, which was odd since that writing system was used by the priestly and royal classes for informal and legislative purposes. Further, the script's characteristics didn't fit the artifact's age."

"Perhaps you found it odd because it wasn't meant for you to read," Nasira said venomously.

"How was it different?" I asked him.

Sweeney gave a frightened glance at my friend. "This was written in columns and by the time of Nefertari's rule, hieratic was written horizontally. The letters also failed to translate literally. They simply didn't make sense. The jar was sent to the British Museum for further analysis."

"We appreciate your help," I told him. He wasn't an idiot; he was educated and curious. And he'd stumbled across something he couldn't possibly understand.

Nasira turned and started toward the door, and Sayer and I kept up with her brisk pace. Any wasted time spent here only asked for trouble.

Once we were alone in the elevator, I couldn't hold my tongue any longer. "Nasira, was all you did back there necessary? Taking Sweeney's air looked a lot like torture."

Sayer turned and studied my face, his gaze roving and penetrating. I wasn't quite sure how to take it.

Nasira licked her lips and said, "Sometimes, as Medjai, you must do what you must do. It hurt him, but in the end, it didn't kill him."

My mouth formed a tight line and I couldn't help feeling skeptical.

The wind had begun to kick up, threatening a thunderstorm. Our drive home was relatively quiet once we discussed how quickly we needed to move out of the mansion and head to London. If it were possible, overnight would've been ideal. Every day we remained in New York—even hiding out here on Long Island—increased the chance we might be located by our enemies. I was plenty glad it was Anubis who'd found us first.

Us.

The word still seemed so foreign to me. I'd never been part of an *"us"* or a *"we."* But the word felt good, like a dessert I'd never tried before. Unfamiliar, but good.

As we pulled up to the mansion, I saw the front door was alarmingly wide open. I glanced up front and saw the others had noticed it as well. The wind was a ruthless force now and the darkening sky had grown the color of a bruise. Dread felt so close, like an icy wind upon the back of my neck.

Nasira lowered her window and a terrible crashing sound and cry rushed inside the Delage. Sayer punched the gas and the engine roared, tires squealing, toward the portico. The car came to a drifting, then abrupt, stop and the three of us launched ourselves out the doors, leaving them open, and dashed up the steps and into the entrance hall.

Sayer's cautious voice was a purr in the darkness. "Don't be afraid."

I drew a breath and said, "I'm not afraid."

The broken, battered body of a Medjai woman lay sprawled across the marble. A skulking power descended the staircase toward me and slowly devoured the hall like invisible vines stretching, creeping, choking.

I gasped for air as magic flared within me, poured from me, fusing flawlessly with adrenaline to craft a cocktail that lit fire in my veins. I shed the extra layer of clothing meant to conceal my weapons and I drew my *asaya* as a kriosphinx's haunting, guttural bugle echoed through the cavernous hall.

CHAPTER
10

Movement to my left ripped me into action. I whirled to face the leaping kriosphinx and Sayer stepped between us, slamming his right ax into the beast's chest. It dropped hard and didn't rise again after Sayer buried his left ax into bone at the base of its skull. Its body seized violently as it was drawn through its wounds like a vacuum, vanquished. Shadows drowned us, stealing our vision, and I pushed through them into the light. The sounds of a woman's wicked laughter and shattered wood and bone reverberated through the hall.

"Kauket is here," Nasira murmured, her tone low and cold.

The walls and ceiling seemed to draw closer, threatening to crush me. I bit my lip, bidding the piercing pain to refocus my mind and body. "How could she have found us?"

The air around Nasira prickled with magic. "It was only a matter of time."

A thump and a crash came from above.

"I need to make sure Mum is all right," she said. "It's too quiet in here for the siege to have just happened."

"Go," Sayer agreed. "We'll sweep the first floor, then follow you."

She gestured at me with a flick of her chin. "Look out for her."

He didn't affirm her instruction in any direct way, but he didn't need to. I trusted him enough to know he'd have my back—and I'd have his. Nasira shot toward the stairs and darted to the second floor, treading stealthily when she reached the top.

"We need to vanquish whatever kriosphinxes remain and help anyone who's survived," I told Sayer. "I'll go this way, so we'll cover more ground. Yell if you need me."

He nodded. "Likewise."

I proceeded cautiously, my *asaya* held in both hands, ready to defend or attack at any moment. In my head, I went over the incantations Nasira had taught me. My memory felt fresh and gave me confidence. I had all the tools; now I needed to utilize them.

I first checked an office opposite the parlor and found a mess of overturned furniture and piles of books with torn pages and broken spines. The shelves they'd fallen from had been snapped in half and splintered. I stepped around something dark pooled on the rug beneath me. My jaw tightened as I searched a little closer, but I found no one.

A whistling whine came from outside the office and I wheeled around, *asaya* above my head as I stepped into the corridor. A kriosphinx, so enormous it seemed to swallow the walls and ceiling, stalked in through the open door of the next room. I moved quickly and silently toward it undetected, and I leapt, casting a *taw* spell at the floor to propel my body higher—my *asaya* whirled until it screamed and slashed. Obsidian sliced deep into flesh at the base of the beast's neck, severing the spine. Its huge body dropped, and I landed in front of it in a roll, stopping just beyond the burst of its dying shadows.

I continued and heard a crash come from the dining hall. I took off at a run. Two kriosphinxes occupied the room, each taking turns ramming the far door with their thick horns. One backed up, lowered its head, pawed the floor, and launched. Its skull smashed into the door, muscles rippling beneath its dark pantherine coat. The white paint on the door splintered, revealing the crushed wood beneath. They would breach the door soon and attack whatever or whomever they wanted on the other side.

They didn't seem to notice me enter the hall, allowing me the element of surprise. I braced myself on my heel, turned my *asaya* behind my back, and cast out my free hand. My magic flared to my fingertips. *"Taw!"* I roared, and the blast torpedoed toward the beasts, slamming into the banquet tables between them and me, lifting them into the air and tossing them to either side of the hall with a crash. My power slammed into the kriosphinxes, shoving them into the walls in a tangled heap.

The confused kriosphinxes weren't prepared when I shot toward them, my *asaya* whirling and gaining momentum. I deflected slashing talons and jabbed the obsidian blade of my *asaya* into the top of one creature's skull. The second sprang through the air and I whirled my staff, one of the blades cutting the kriosphinx's throat as it landed on me, dragging me to the ground. I climbed out from beneath the bodies as both were vanquished.

I rose, took several steps away from the door, and slammed a *taw* spell into the broken wood. What was left of the barricade exploded into splinters and fine dust. I stepped through the opening to find a Medjai opening the throat of a kriosphinx with a whirl of her *asaya*. Once it was vanquished, she turned to me and offered me a nod of solidarity.

"I assume you took care of the two outside?" she asked, breathless. "I hadn't liked my odds against three. Separating them seemed a wiser option." She was a fawn-skinned woman with a long, elegant face and large eyes made even more expressive by the dark kohl tracing them. Her dark hair was a mess in its long braid down her back and her gear suffered tears from claws.

"We are agreed," I said, impressed, and glanced around the room for any other threats. This was some sort of smaller dining parlor, perhaps once used for tea and socializing, with a lovely view of the gardens.

"My name's Haya," the woman said in an amusingly polite manner for the circumstances. "I don't believe I've had the opportunity to meet you yet."

"I'm Ziva," I replied, grinning and feeling a burst of laughter rising in me.

She gave me a lovely, friendly smile, her dark eyes glimmering in the flash of lightning outside. "It's been a pleasure, Ziva."

"I'll leave you to it, then," I told her with a salute of my free hand.

I hurried from the room, casting Haya a smile over my shoulder, and returned to the corridor. More sounds of battle attracted me toward the main hall. As I slid into the atrium, a sudden force struck my body and crushed me against the wall. My *asaya* clattered to the floor beneath the kriosphinx pinning me by its great horns. The beast backed away from me, relieving me of the pressure, and I took a great breath. I used that breath to cast a spell before it could charge into me a second time.

"*Sena!*" I cried, throwing up my hands. The charging beast struck the magical wall mere feet from me and bashed its horns in a rage, muscle rippling beneath its coat. "*Khet!*" My fire spell blew up in the beast's face, illuminating its fury. The kriosphinx bugled and my fire pushed it backward. Its talons dragged on the marble.

A spell erupted from above and rushed down the grand staircase, hitting me with so much force I lifted my arms to shield myself. The spell was visible, tangible, a beautiful but terrible and destructive thing as it beat against the walls and floor. I lowered my arms and watched the magic pause and reverse direction like a storm called back to the sea.

From the floor above me, a vortex descended. It was

light and heat, power and ancient magic that weighted on me, made me want to drop to my knees beneath its force. The walls rattled, potted plants were stripped of their leaves, and all manner of debris was sucked into the tempest. At the vortex's crest hovered Cyrene Tera, summoning her magic with a fierce concentration that turned her beautiful features to steel and stone. She settled on the marble below as lightly as a feather. Her magic bloomed in light around her, spiraling, radiant and magnificent.

The kriosphinx loosed a low growl with a shake of its head. I snatched my *asaya* from where it had fallen and shot toward the beast. It met me with ferocity and a claw hooked my leg, ripping my jeans, but I whirled the *asaya* hard. One obsidian blade cut deep into the kriosphinx's throat, spilling red. I slashed out with the other blade. Black glass cleaved the beast's head from its neck and within a dark implosion, the rest of the body disappeared.

I no longer feared death—only the cruel threat of failure. Magic wreathed my body, filled my eyes, head, and bones with a sparkling electric current. I drew in the fallout of the spells cast all around me, feeding myself until I built a throne of magic, from which I would rain destruction.

Another kriosphinx descended on me, but I shoved my shoulder into its gut and flipped its body over my head with an assisting *sena* spell. As the beast landed on my other side, I slammed one end of my *asaya* into its heart. Claws reached for me and I deflected the blow with an arc of the staff. I balled my free hand into a fist and punched the kriosphinx in the snout, snapping its head back. The obsidian knuckles of my gloves ripped its face wide open. Sparks of magic and netherlight filled my vision. I slashed the black blade across its exposed throat and at last it died.

Claws grappled around my shoulders, tearing at my jacket, dragging me to the ground. I rolled onto my back as a kriosphinx covered me with its huge body and I kicked with all my might into the beast's head, crushing bone. With a savage howl, I cast out a hand, slamming a *sena* spell into its gruesome ram's face, and the magical wall halted it in its tracks. My power withdrew into an incandescent, gleaming orb of magic in my open palm. I cried out a *khet* spell, and the light exploded into flames. The inferno blasted the kriosphinx, toppling it end over end in a tangled knot of limbs, its ghostly bugle lost in the scream of magic.

Kauket's smooth laughter echoed through the atrium. "You've been overwhelmed, Medjai."

I spun, breathless, to see the goddess and Cyrene face off in the center of the atrium. The priestess's only reply was a rush of magic that hammered into Kauket, whipping her hair and the folds of her dress into a storm. But she did not bend to it.

The masked goddess stood her ground, shielding herself with darkness, as Cyrene's spell slammed into the staircase like a cyclone, ripping out the handrail and half the stairs before hitting the walls. A chandelier snapped and shattered on the floor with a perfect halo of glass.

Windows exploded outward into the night and their curtains blew through the gaping frames. The thunderstorm invaded, heaving giant raindrops onto the marble floors. Lightning cracked its fury across the blackened sky and the crash of thunder shook the walls and my bones.

Kauket emerged from her shadows like a dark birth, flicked a hand upward with lightning speed. She slammed her open palm into Cyrene's chest and a gust of air and agony expelled from Cyrene's mouth. She buckled, and her magic returned to her, leaving the atrium cold and dark and still.

"The gods' power is not for you, *priestess*," Kauket hissed, her crimson gaze examining Cyrene as though she were a mere insect.

The goddess didn't seem to have noticed me and she vanished inside a flash of shadows and netherlight. Cyrene curved inward, her body trembling, and she collapsed to one knee. I rushed to her and caught her arm before she crumbled into a heap. Her eyes were wide, and she struggled for breath. One hand clutched her chest, her fingers crooked and bloodless.

"Tell me what to do," I said, unable to hide the panic rising in my throat like a scream.

She managed to grab a gulp of air, and her free hand clapped onto my shoulder, squeezing me so tightly I submitted to the pain and my own knees hit the floor.

"Sayer," she rasped, with several emphatic nods.

"Can he help you?"

She nodded harder. "Go."

"All right," I agreed. I hated to leave her, but the only thing I could do was trust her and obey.

I shot to my feet and darted through the great hall in the direction Sayer had headed the last time I saw him. The parlor I'd seen him enter was empty, so I ducked out of the room and back into the hall—and nearly smacked into Kauket. Fear was a flame-hot knife twisting inside my belly. I drew a strangled breath of surprise and horror, reeling backward, limbs flailing as I skidded to the floor.

The expression the goddess of darkness wore was thick and sticky with satisfaction. I had to stifle my fear, or it would give her yet another power against me. She would kill me if I allowed her to. Cyrene, the woman who gave me a real home and a place where I belonged, could die if I didn't get help. Nasira and Sayer, my friends who brought me home and showed me what it meant to have a family, could be killed if I weren't there to have their backs as they had mine.

I pushed myself to my feet and raised my *asaya*. I had to be faster and stronger than a goddess I knew was faster and stronger than me. The only way to beat her was to do precisely what she didn't expect me to. It wouldn't have been the first seemingly impossible thing I'd done today.

I cast a blinding *benu* spell and the goddess shielded her eyes, snarling. I leapt through the light, *asaya* high and arching, as Kauket swung a *taw* spell straight toward me. Instinct guided my protective *sena* spell, but with a firecracker flash of magic crashing into magic, I realized it hadn't been enough. Kauket's spell slammed into me, sending me soaring. My back smacked the floor and the air rushed from my lungs. Blinking hard, I refocused my eyes in time to see the goddess appear over me. Kauket raised a hand and blasted. I screamed as the magic savaged me as though she were boiling me alive.

I rolled to the side, forcing myself through the pain, and pushed to my feet. A spell Nasira had mentioned in passing came to my thoughts and now seemed like a perfectly desperate time to try it.

"*Sekhem*," I growled, and raised my hand, spreading and curling my fingers like spider legs, and then crushed them into a tight fist. Kauket stopped cold and something in her changed. Her limbs clamped against her body and she jerked, struggling to free herself from an invisible power.

I was both horrified and awed by the constricting force my own spell inflicted on the goddess. Kauket lifted her chin, her carnelian eyes widening. Her head dropped back, and a disembodied, shrill, skin-ripping scream leaked from her, rising into a crescendo that made my blood run cold. Kauket's power surged and she exploded in a flash of shadows and netherlight, transforming into the colossal cobra of my nightmares. Kauket's scream became a hiss of rage and with a violent jolt of her serpentine body, she thrashed free of my *sekhem* spell and lurched forward, jaws agape and fangs shining.

A bright flash of light and heat made me shield my eyes. A *khet* spell large enough to swallow us whole rocketed toward Kauket. The goddess hissed and swung her body out of the fireball's path, ramming the walls. Paintings and photographs crashed to the floor.

The flames burst and died, and the evanescing light revealed Sayer. The enormous cobra swept toward him, forgetting me entirely. He threw a *taw* spell, but the goddess continued her charge. A force collided with me from the side and I was dragged to the floor. The kriosphinx's horns blocked my vision and I scrambled backward only for it to rake its claws down the front of my jacket, tearing fabric. The beast slashed with a paw and knocked my arm aside so hard the *asaya* was torn from my grip. I ripped a *was* dagger from its sheath inside my jacket sleeve and as the beast opened its mouth to release its shrill call, I slammed the dagger into the side of its head, cutting its cry short. Its body erupted with shadows and nether-light, swarming me, and I stepped out of their reach and returned to clear air.

Kauket had relinquished her cobra form and when she saw me, she vanished in a flash of darkness. She reappeared in front of me, grabbing me by the throat and squeezing. Shadows erupted around her, darkening the world until all that seemed to remain in my vision was her mask of shining gold and its oddly pleasant, horrible expression. My lungs dragged for air, pain screaming through my oxygen starved veins, and my face felt like a swelling balloon. The quickly numbing muscles of my neck told me it was about to break. She strangled me for so long, it felt like hours. I should've lost consciousness, I should've been dying. But I didn't.

"I bless you, Ziva, of the blood of queens," Anubis had said to me. I was blessed by death.

I lifted my hands, and Kauket's gleaming eyes

narrowed with interest, and then shot wide with surprise when I took her by her own throat. My *neit* spell filled Kauket's gullet with water, bubbling up her esophagus and gushing out her mouth like a plugged drain. I was sure the spell wouldn't drown her—the immortals had no need for air—but the agony was enough that Kauket released me. I crumpled to the ground and gasped for breath. I scrambled toward my fallen weapon.

Kauket dropped her battle mask and I saw her face for the first time—horror and rage slashed across her visage. She gurgled violent threats, water continuing to spill from her mouth and soaking the front of her dress. Her spell lashed me across the face and whipped me aside. I gritted my teeth at the pain, and when I wheeled around to her, I slashed with the *asaya*. She jerked back, but the obsidian caught her across the forearm, splitting her flesh to the bone. Sparkling liquid gold flecked the air between us. I spun the staff and jammed one end into the side of her ribcage beneath her arm. She screamed as the obsidian buried deep in her body. I prayed I'd struck her heart. She swung, her fingers curled into claws, and I hopped back, falling onto my bottom. She grabbed hold of my *asaya* and jerked it from her body and snapped the wood in half before chucking it across the room.

Kauket staggered forward and collapsed with a whimper. A trickle of gold blood leaked from her lips as she wilted heavily. Her body shuddered as her power fought the *was* blade's magic, but it was futile. Kauket let out a strangled scream partly in pain, partly in rage, and vanished, leaving her voice echoing through the hall.

11

I whirled in a panic, searching the hall. "Sayer? Sayer!" I hadn't seen him since Kauket charged after him. I hadn't had his back like I was supposed to. Anger at myself was a physical pain in my chest.

A slowly stirring form tangled up in a shattered buffet table attracted my attention. Sayer shoved silver-gilt ornaments and wood splinters off him as he sat forward with a low groan. "I'm here," he called.

I rushed to him, held out my hand for him to take, and I helped him to his feet. "Are you hurt?"

"I'm all right, I'm all right," he insisted.

"Kauket is gone, but Cyrene told me to find you," I explained. "She was injured."

"Take me to her."

I led him to where I'd left Cyrene and was relieved to find her still alive. Sayer knelt over her, inspecting her carefully.

"She can't breathe because her chest plate is crushed," he said.

I stared at him. "How could you know with only a look?"

"I know," he replied without looking at me. He placed one hand over Cyrene's forehead and the other hovered above her sternum. I sat on the other side to observe with fascination.

"Mother Isis," he murmured as softly as though the goddess were standing beside him. "I invoke you and ask for the power to heal this mortal flesh. I invoke you and ask for the power to protect this mortal flesh from infection."

They were simple words, but as he activated his power, those words became magic. He raised her hand and pressed a kiss to her knuckles. He whispered something in a voice too low for me to hear. Cyrene's chest swelled and made a *pop-crack* noise. I marveled as a gash splitting her cheek stitched itself together with invisible thread and the seam melted into her skin. She took a great gulp of air and pulled herself forward.

"Thank you," she said, touching her face to inspect her healed wound.

Sayer stood and helped her to her feet. Cyrene smoothed out her dress and hair. When she seemed satisfied she'd tidied her appearance, she drew another deep breath and exhaled slowly.

"How is the threat?" she asked, then looked past our heads.

"Neutralized," came Nasira's voice. She appeared

beside me, her mussed clothes and hair telltale signs of battle. "The second and third floors are clear."

"Mum?" Sayer asked.

She nodded. "She's fine."

"Ziva drove off Kauket alone," Sayer declared.

Both Nasira and Cyrene fixed their gazes on me. "Truly?" the priestess asked.

"I couldn't kill her," I explained, realizing Sayer had seen my battle against the goddess.

"You fought like a titan," he said, his tone, to my surprise, a little muted.

I stared at him, trying to understand why he seemed so sad as he praised me. I hadn't done anything wrong. True, I wasn't as experienced as the others and I'd have understood if he were surprised I could already hold my own. But I wanted more than anything to excel at what I was born to do as Medjai. Perhaps I misread his emotion.

Cyrene and Nasira started toward the front of the mansion discussing the damages done. As they wandered away, I worried about who we'd lost tonight, if there'd been any casualties. I wondered about the woman I'd met earlier, Haya, and if she'd run into more trouble.

"Ziva—you're hurt."

"What?" I looked at Sayer with surprise and then down at myself, but I saw nothing obvious.

He drew close behind me and gently lifted my hair away from my skin. I reached up, feeling gingerly with my fingertips, and found the back of my neck tender and sticky with blood.

"A kriosphinx must've clawed me. How does it look?"

I winced when I applied too much pressure. The magic in the kohl lining my eyes would heal my wounds more quickly than they naturally would.

"Not bad," he replied, his voice low and soft behind me. "I'll take care of it for you."

"Is this a talent of yours—healing?" My body coiled tightly, tensely with anticipation.

"Yes," he replied, his touch a whisper on my skin.

"Your prayer to Isis . . . this is why you still have faith in the gods," I said. "Why you never thought they abandoned us." I trembled, and my nerves wouldn't let me stop talking.

His thumb brushed the exposed skin of my shoulder. "Ziva."

"You believe some of them are on our side, like Anubis? Not all of them want to hurt us."

"Ziva," he repeated firmly, but gently. "Just relax."

He was all around me, everything I could smell or feel. His magic touched mine, an unfamiliar intimacy, a prickling warmth in the air just above my skin, like static. He smoothed one hand around the bend of my neck, but it calmed the fire in my wounds. His other hand pushed the rest of my hair aside, his fingertips gentle on me, and I realized with a thunderclap in my belly what would happen next. I'd seen him heal Cyrene.

He lowered his head and exhaled, his breath warm and soft on the bend of my neck, and he pressed his lips to my bare skin. His kiss sent lightning zipping into my muscles and I inhaled when an ache rippled through me, low and deep. My chin raised, and my head tilted back.

I breathed deeply as his magic coursed through me. A dense fog, like the kind that plumed after a hard rain, filled my mind.

He repeated the prayer he'd said over Cyrene, including the last part I couldn't hear earlier, his voice tender and breathy. "Mother Isis, this woman is mine and I ask that you take from me what she needs to be whole. Let your love be my love and may it heal as you heal."

The rest of me, from ears to toes, grew hot and quiet as a candle flame. This definitely wasn't from the magic. There was no possibility he missed the way my heart kicked up or the shaky, deep breaths I took in an effort to maintain my composure. I was desperate for him to continue. If he kissed me again, I would survive this agony.

Then he let my hair fall and he drew away, leaving me blanketed in sudden cold. I shivered.

"Thank you," I said, stealing a glance at him from over my shoulder. A peculiar sensation had taken me; I felt intoxicated with whatever his kiss had pumped through my blood and I ached to be close to him, to feel him against me, before the buzz faded. I turned to face him, and he didn't step away. He gazed down at me, his dark eyes heavy as they fell to my mouth. I parted my lips and inhaled, tasting his scent he was so close to me.

"Is that better?" he asked.

It could be, I wanted to say, bleary with wanting him. He seemed a bit loopy himself, as though his energy were spent. Instead I asked, "So, when were you going to tell me you're a healer?"

"When you needed one, I suppose," he replied,

giving me a half smile. Those same lips had been on me moments ago.

"Sayer," called a familiar voice. We parted and turned to watch the woman I'd met earlier approach. There was something about her attractive, narrow face and nose that made her feel less of a stranger, as though I'd met her before tonight, but I was certain I hadn't.

"Mum," he replied, and my breath was lost from me.

Haya smiled at me as though she weren't battle-swept. "Hello again, Ziva."

I flushed with surprise and raised my hand for her to shake. "I seem to meet people at inopportune moments."

"Ready for everything, yeah?" Haya ignored my hand and embraced me in a warm hug, placing a delicate kiss on my cheek. "Welcome. It seems you've fit right in."

"I hope so," I said, but I thought of the darker side to our mission, the one I witnessed in Nasira earlier today. "Sayer—Dr. Sweeney, remember? The British Museum?"

His eyes widened as he recalled our new information. He relayed to her everything we'd learned from the stela and Sweeney. "One of the canopic jars is in London for further analysis. We need all four to get another step closer to the resurrection."

"This location is compromised anyway," I added. "There's a possibility Kauket doesn't know the canopic jars' locations, yet. When we retrieve the one contained in the British Museum, we can collect the jar we already have at the Pyramidion in Cairo."

"How are we supposed to retrieve the jar at the British Museum?" Haya asked, bemused.

I looked at Sayer for assistance, but he remained quiet. "Steal it?" I suggested, knowing that sounded less than noble.

"What other option do we have?" Sayer asked. "I don't suppose they'll simply give it to us."

"We'll do what needs to be done," Haya agreed. "I'll speak to Cyrene and make arrangements. You two continue a sweep of every room on each floor. There could be more casualties. Pray Nephthys has protected us."

Of the fifteen or so Medjai in this house, three were dead. I'd never spoken a word to any of them or ever learned their names, and that drove their fates home for me. I'd been so caught up in learning all I could from Sayer and Nasira and moving forward with our mission to protect Nefertari that I'd forgotten about taking time for the rest of the Medjai. A persistent hollow ache of guilt lingered at the bow of my thoughts.

Cyrene arranged passage for us on the first zeppelin airship out that evening, a voyage which would take us three days. We spent the rest of the afternoon and into the evening packing our belongings. I loaded weapons and books in cases and boxes until we were all ready to go. The beautiful mansion, which had seen life again for the first time in so long, once again fell into the gloom of abandonment. I wondered whose voices would fill its halls next, whose children would explore the magnificent library, if any ever would again.

We would be flying to England. On an airship. To *England!*

The closest I'd ever been to a zeppelin in real life was hiking across Manhattan to its southernmost point at the harbor to watch them sail into the sky. Up until the last few years, airships had been considered only as the future of warfare. Now they were the singular most fashionable method of travel. Our Atlantic Airliners zeppelin was as long as any skyscraper was tall and made of gleaming metal. Its three levels boasted comfortable lodging and amenities, though the noisy engines and exhaust kept me off the balconies and inside where the air was recycled, but clean and warm.

Nasira had been assigned as my cabinmate, something I was glad of. If we'd not booked our tickets so last minute, more of us could have had first class cabins, Cyrene had explained. She seemed terribly apologetic, but I wasn't sure why she thought I minded. I didn't plan on spending any time in my cabin anyway.

We lay in our bunks that night, the room quiet, but I found sleep impossible to grasp. There seemed to be no getting used to the sensation of being in perpetual motion.

"Nasira?" I whispered, unsure if she was still awake.

"Hmm?" came her sleepy reply from the top bunk.

"Is there . . . something wrong with me?"

"What?" Her voice was a bit louder with her surprise.

I exhaled. "With my magic. I keep thinking about the way you looked at me that night in Manhattan, after I fought Kauket that first time."

"Oh, please don't take that personally," she insisted. "I didn't mean to frighten you. Sometimes, I suppose, I react or say things before I think."

That comforted me a little, but unease continued to squirm through me. "I only used the incantations you taught me to stop her."

"My brother was right," she said. "You were brilliant. The way you used magic—it was unprecedented. Not in a bad way. I'm trying to find a way to explain how I felt. Surprised, yes, but not scared. No, that's not the right word. Hmm. You were creative. You struck a goddess with a bolt of lightning. And Sayer told me you tried to drown her with a *neit* spell from the inside out."

"Well, I knew it wouldn't drown her," I corrected. "I needed to make her let me go."

"I've never heard of anyone using that incantation the way you did," she continued. "You have a gift, Ziva. A frightening one, only because you are better and stronger than anyone expected you to be. Don't apologize for your talent. Those who are weaker than you will shrink from you, but do not shrink with them. Don't you dare."

Something swelled within me. I did not think of myself as humble, nor did I think of myself as prideful. I wanted to be practical, to have my head in the game and not in the clouds.

"Thank you, Nasi," I said. "Will you continue training with me? Three days is a long time to waste on this ship, so I want to make the most of it."

"Yes," she answered. "You know you can ask anyone for help. Don't be shy. The others have a high opinion of you. They'll be willing to offer whatever they can to help you get even better. That's what family does. We're a team."

"You talk to people about me?" I asked, surprised and a little nervous.

"People like you, Ziva. So does my mother. She's heard a lot about you, especially from listening to my brother and me. Sayer does not need Nefertari when he has you for a queen. The way he talks about you . . . I'm convinced he'd go to war for you."

"War seems to be the direction we're headed in," I said and suddenly felt more tired than ever before.

Nasira paused before replying. "This mission is thousands of years in the making. We were, by chance or fate, meant to carry it out. Perhaps we're the only ones who can see it done. You and I must be who we are for a great purpose."

I wanted to ask what exactly she meant by that, but I suspected I already knew. She was willing to do anything to achieve what she needed to.

Was I as well?

The next day Nasira worked with me on focusing my magic until lunch. Afterward, I enjoyed a self-guided tour of the zeppelin and found it quite opulently decorated in the common areas. We were permitted to enter some of the first-class lounges—though I did see some misbehaving children escorted out of the tea room—but our tickets didn't let us into the grand dining hall. I didn't see much of Cyrene at all, who'd secured a first-class ticket for herself and spent most of her time in her cabin. Nasira told me her mother was in charge of working out our plan to retrieve the canopic jar at the British Museum, and so I assumed Haya and Cyrene were collaborating.

I headed out to the promenade deck to soak in some of the sun pouring through the floor to ceiling windows. I paused to watch the endless, calm expanse of the Atlantic Ocean before finding a bench overlooking an interior deck upon which a group of children kicked a ball between them, laughing and screaming with joy. The game was one we'd played at the orphanage I'd grown up in, and I smiled to myself thinking about how we'd all run up and down the streets after our chores were through. I thought of Jean, her sweet smile and her books, and I felt a heaviness in my heart, unsure I'd ever see her again.

"Good afternoon."

I looked up with surprise to find Cyrene approaching. "Hello," I replied.

"May I sit with you?"

"Of course."

She came forward, seating herself with one leg crossed over the other, her body turned slightly toward me, her smiling features shaded beneath her wide-brimmed hat. Her body was lithe and athletic, much like Nasira's, and the cream-colored pantsuit, cinched at her waist, was more casual than my coral day dress. I loved how fashionable and feminine she was on top of being so powerfully fierce in battle. No one told her she had to be one or the other.

"I've heard great things about your quickly growing skills," she said, her smiling lips painted a deep cherry red. "It's been exciting to watch you grow as Medjai."

"There appears to be some colossus bearing my name and a reputation I must live up to," I mused.

She made a little face of disagreement at that. "I had hoped we wouldn't suffocate you with our curiosity, but many like myself are finding that hard to achieve."

"Then I thank you for giving in," I told her with a grin. "Admittedly I've felt much like a ghost. Nobody talks to me besides Nasira and Sayer."

Cyrene frowned. "That's my fault. I meant well."

"I understand," I told her. "And I appreciate your effort to make me feel more comfortable. Everyone can relax around me, I promise."

"Well, you'll have the opportunity to meet as many of our people as you'd like soon," she replied. "There is a large group deployed to our headquarters outside London. Our accommodations will improve once we port, I promise."

"Really, I'm very comfortable," I insisted. "Everyone seems concerned about that. This is all much more than I've ever had, believe me. I've hardly spent any time at all in the cabin."

"We take care of our own, Ziva," she explained. "That means you."

I couldn't help my small smile. "I suppose I've misunderstood, then. I'd worried you had thought I preferred the fancy duds and accommodations. Of course, it's all lovely, but really, that's not required or expected."

"I'm still getting to know you," Cyrene said. "We all are. My intention isn't to treat you like a guest. You're one of us." She looked up and past my head. "Sayer."

I turned my head to see him approach and my body seemed to ease into contentment at his familiar presence. Not that Cyrene made me uneasy—rather, a friend made me more at ease.

"Hello," I greeted him.

"Hello back," he said, giving me a warm look. Today he was clean shaven and his hair was loose around his face. His clothes were less combat-ready, the fabric soft cotton and linen, rather than thick twill and leather. "Is Cyrene regaling you with her tales of adventures around the world?"

"Not exactly, no," I replied. "Should she be? I wasn't aware you were such a globe-trotter." I shot Cyrene a grin.

"Oh, yes," he said, watching the priestess closely. "You'll want to hear those stories."

"They aren't as thrilling as he implies," Cyrene told me.

"Well, the rest of us find the chimera of Mount Nemrut a very thrilling tale," Sayer said. "Cyrene was the first of us there and saved an entire village from being butchered. There was the Jötunn in the Hamra National Park in Sweden. A cult had been sacrificing children to this creature."

I stared at Cyrene in reverence. "Truly? So, there are monsters all over the world?"

"There are benevolent immortals too," she insisted.

"We leave them be, but the ones who would spread malice and carnage across this earth must be stopped. That is why our work is so important and why we must do anything we can to save our people, so we can save others. Do you understand?"

I nodded. "Yes. I want to help people too."

She smiled, red lips catching the sun. "Good."

Sayer turned his gaze to me. "So, Ziva, I think we should continue your training if you are up for it."

I nodded. "As much as I possibly can. My body already feels stronger."

He gestured with a nod to follow him. "Let's go."

CHAPTER

12

My days were a blur of hand-to-hand combat training in the most secluded places we could find
aboard the zeppelin. Using magic could have endan-
gered the lives of passengers, so we stuck to drills and
repetitions. I'd noticed as the voyage went on, my ses-
sions with Nasira and Sayer became more energizing
than exhausting. Sayer stayed true to his word about
my hieroglyphs lessons and he seemed happy to see
me working as hard at them as I worked on my combat
skills. Learning another language wasn't necessarily more
difficult than learning to maim, disable, and kill with a
dagger, but it was a different sort of repetition learned
best through immersion. Everything came down to
muscle memory—brain as well as body. Thankfully Sayer
hadn't yet attempted a conversation with me in Ancient
Egyptian. In between my lessons, I practiced everything—
language, combat, spells—in the hope it all would grow

to be second nature. One afternoon, Nasira told me she found my relentlessness to be "disconcertingly inspirational." I took her words as the highest compliment.

We arrived at Southampton and I was excited to explore a bustling city in a whole new country. I braced myself against the zeppelin railing, my knuckles gone white on the steel bar. I'd been smiling so wide for so long my face began to hurt. Every street and path I could see was packed with people. It seemed a lot like New York City, but the stately old buildings of stone, brick, and plaster sported no trace of the Art Deco style American architects were currently obsessed with. Despite the diesel trams and motorcars adding to the noise pollution, something about this place had a fairytale charm.

Our airship found its place seamlessly between other arriving and departing vessels as though there was no chaos to this organization. We filed in tightly-packed lines down gangplanks and onto the docks. Many of the passengers greeted their waiting loved ones with waves of their caps and kisses on cheeks.

Amid the excitement, Nasira took my hand and led me toward a number of waiting black town cars being filled with luggage and Medjai passengers. Our procession began, and I soon found much of Southampton's perimeter surrounded by a gigantic, ancient stone wall. At the end of one street, I saw trams disappearing beneath a medieval gatehouse squeezed between modern brick buildings. I'd been plopped into the middle of a strange mixture of the industrial and historical, and I wasn't sure which was choking out the other.

We left the city and rolled down a narrow, winding road through the countryside dotted with cottages, sheep, and half-grown lambs. On the way, Nasira explained the Medjai owned a property some ways southeast of London, in the county of Kent, where we would stay. Apparently, this was a permanent residence for a group of Medjai as they monitor immortal threats in Europe. When I'd asked Nasira why there was no true headquarters in the States, she'd explained the Medjai had had every intention of establishing one, but then the Great War had happened.

Our car turned onto a single-lane drive shaded by the canopies of enormous trees, the tires following the worn grooves in the grass, past a gate and gatehouse. I squinted to read the words inscribed on the plaque.

WYTHEFORD HALL

1362

1816

"Why are there two dates?" I asked.

Nasira stirred from some reverie, focus drawing her pupils tight. "Hmm? Oh, the original castle was destroyed a few hundred years ago, and when the Medjai purchased the property at the end of the eighteenth century, the ruins were demolished and the castle rebuilt."

My brow raised with surprise. "Castle?"

"It's more like a big house," she assured me. "Or an inn. There are no moat or turrets—nothing like that. Don't look so disappointed!" She laughed, making me smile too.

"We shouldn't stay long—once we have the canopic jar, we'll be off. Not everyone is stationed here."

My smile faded, and I shook my head, confused. "Stationed? How do you mean?"

"Well, we all have assignments," she explained. "There's a possibility you could be deployed somewhere, and I could go elsewhere. Oh—there it is!"

I tried to feel excited about seeing this supposed castle I'd be housed in, but I couldn't help feeling a certain dread at being separated from Nasira and Sayer. My whole life had been spent alone and now that I'd found friends, I couldn't bear to be parted from them.

Wytheford Hall loomed ahead, its lawn shadowed by trees in the afternoon light. Dense ivy, clematis, and white jasmine devoured the chiseled brick and stone, spreading toward the steep roofs and gables, tamed only at the vast paned windows. I'd never seen anything so wild and beautiful.

The vehicles ahead of us had rolled to a stop and Medjai had already begun to exit and gather their belongings. People appeared out the massive front doors and helped the new arrivals assemble. As everyone filed inside, Nasira and I exited our own car. The air here prickled with magic, and I couldn't be sure if this was caused by the great number of Medjai, or something else.

I looked up and around, unsure of what or whom I was looking for, but when my gaze met Sayer's, relief warmed me. It wasn't as though I'd worried he wouldn't be here. The way the breeze caught the freed wisps of his hair from its tie and the way the sun illuminated his dark eyes—I felt at home even thousands of miles across the ocean in a country I'd never visited before. One corner of his mouth tugged into a smile for me until his attention turned toward an older Medjai who needed assistance in lifting his bags.

"Ziva?" Haya Bahri approached me with a canvas duffel bag flung over her shoulder. "You can follow me. I'll show you to a room, so you may rest, if you'd like, before tonight."

"I appreciate that, thank you," I told her.

"Is this your first time in England?" she asked politely.

"Yes," I replied, unsure exactly how much she knew about my past, or what her son and daughter had told her. "I've lived in New York for as long as I can remember."

"I'm afraid you won't have time to grow too comfortable here during this trip," she said with sympathy. "You'll return, I promise. There is an alarming amount of activity we monitor in Europe."

"Immortals?" I asked.

"Yes," she replied. "But that's not our mission today."

"Is Wytheford Hall well protected?" I asked. "If the Medjai have owned this property for so long, how have the immortals not found it yet?"

"There are many ancient magical protections over Wytheford," Haya answered. "Many Medjai over the years added their own spells to the old." She grinned. "It's quite like layers of a really tall, magnificent wedding cake. Does that make sense?"

I nodded with a laugh. She reminded me a lot of

Nasira. "So, the strange electricity I feel in the air must be the protective spells."

"You'll get used to it," she replied.

If lots of Medjai had added their own, I wondered if my parents' magic was in there somewhere, touching my skin and filling my lungs with the air I breathed.

"Is there anything else you need, Ziva?" Haya asked kindly.

"No, thank you," I replied. "I'll be down shortly, after I've changed into my gear."

"Cheers, then."

Our black Daimler sedan, sleek and sharp as an arrow, shot through the night and rolled past the extraordinary colonnade of the British Museum and around to the receiving dock. Our after-hours arrival ensured we'd only have security guards to deal with and no patrons. Away from the busy streets of London, the rear of the museum had a spooky feel. The windows of the grand building were dark and empty, and the only light was a dim lamp lit outside the receiving door. On a typical day, art and antiquities would pass through here, both coming and going.

Nasira, her mother, and I exited our car at the loading dock as a black coupe came to stop behind us and Cyrene and Sayer appeared. Our Medjai contact, a self-proclaimed 'overlooked laboratory grunt,' greeted us, having ensured the receiving door would be unlocked when we arrived. Dina was a plain looking woman at first glance, but that was all part of the character she played as a museum employee. She blended in so seamlessly no one noticed her. The perfect mole.

Inside the receiving room, steel shelves were filled with cardboard, wood, and metal boxes. Most were sealed with heavy padlocks and a few had loose lids with packing paper spilling out of them. Numbers and letters were painted on their sides, perhaps codes to identify the contents. A large framed corkboard hanging on a wall was covered with charts and lists. I was eager to know if they detailed every artifact in the room—where they came from, who made them, what purpose they once served.

"We've never had any canopic jar bearing Nefertari's cartouche come through here," Dina said with confidence. "Believe me, we'd all be chuffed."

"Do you know where the one we seek could be?" Haya Bahri asked.

Dina paused at the exit. "We only display artifacts we've identified, of course. What we haven't can be found in storage or in the laboratories downstairs. Someone made a bit of a mess in the precious stones and minerals room upstairs, so our security guards are preoccupied for the time being."

Cyrene smirked. "Who would've done such a thing?"

"My diversion was harmless," Dina assured her. "Security heard the ruckus and I apologized profusely for my clumsiness. They agreed to pick it all up while I rang maintenance to have the display tended to. We won't have a lot of time, so we must be quick about it."

We emerged into a hallway which led in two directions.

"Say we split up?" Cyrene offered. "Cover more ground?"

Haya nodded. "You, Dina, and I can search the storage room. The rest of you head to the laboratories. Nasira, do you remember the way?"

She nodded.

"Good. Go." Haya turned her gaze to her son. "Sayer, be on the lookout for any hieroglyphs denoting the cardinal treasures. We aren't only after canopic jars. There may be other clues here."

"Right," he replied.

Cyrene beckoned to Haya and Dina and the three started toward the darker end of the hall. Nasira jumped into a brisk pace in the opposite direction and took a sharp left into a cavernous domed reading room. As we steered around the perimeter, I noticed how the dozens of long desks packed with chairs seem to fan outward from the room's center like the spokes of a wheel. I imagined myself spending weeks at a time reading as many books as I could. Part of me hoped we could linger at least a few more days in London so I could explore the exhibits.

Nasira traveled so swiftly and lightly on her feet her steps didn't echo. She ducked into an alcove and flew down a winding staircase. I heard voices and stopped cold. I grabbed Sayer by the jacket and pulled him against the wall beside me. The voices came again. Security guards, I presumed.

"I rang the geologist, but he won't be in until the morning. He said not to damage anything."

"They're *rocks*! He's got to know that, yeah?"

"I didn't dare tell him so, though."

Their laughter faded, and I exhaled when I became certain they weren't coming our way. Nasira nodded to us in the pale light and we resumed our pace. The basement laboratory wasn't as large as I'd expected, but it was about the size of the receiving room we'd arrived in. The only sounds were the buzz of the lights overhead and the tinny whir of some machine. We wasted no time in our search. Clean scientific tools were spread on canvas mats beside a sink. The fragments of broken pottery were neatly arranged on a wooden table. The seat appeared very well used, judging by the indent of a rear end in the cushion. Sayer disappeared down an aisle and Nasira rummaged through boxes at her eyelevel on a wooden rack. It wasn't long before I'd gone through everything in front of me without success and Nasira's low curse told me she'd also found no clues.

"I found two jars from the fourteenth dynasty," Sayer told us. "That's it."

"Should we meet up in storage?" I asked.

"Let's take the long way," Nasira suggested. "I want to search the Egyptian exhibits. Someone might've misidentified the artifact and put it on display."

We tidied up the laboratory, ensuring the next morning no one would suspect it had been searched, before heading back in the direction we came. At the top of the stairs where I'd seen the guards, we paused to listen. The exhibition hall appeared void of life and so we crossed it to the enormous and elegant staircase, sticking close to the walls and displays and avoiding moving through the open where we could. We ascended to the second floor and passed rooms dedicated to various Mesopotamian civilizations until we reached our destination.

I felt transported to another time and world; colossal stone sphinxes and sculpted heads of Ancient Egyptian rulers stared at us as we entered. Their small, secretive smiles reminded me of Kauket's war mask and I felt a sliver of ice snake up my spine. Incredible painted wood and golden sarcophagi covered with hieroglyphs and funerary scenes stood on end to display as much of their art and decoration as possible. Wood curios filled with faience shabtis and animal amulets stood against the wall. Glass cases of dazzling gold jewelry inlaid with gems filled the center of the room. Stone pottery, both painted and plain, were displayed on marble stands. Behind more glass were miniature coffins with feline heads and canopic jars engraved with pictures and prayers.

Sayer was an expert at deciphering hieroglyphs, but he'd taught me a lot. I could help him find the artifact we needed. I leaned close to the glass to examine the markings on the canopic jars. I hadn't learned all of them, not even close, but I recognized a few lines.

"Let my eyes see, let my heart beat, let air fill my lungs and give me breath," I read quietly. "Let my soul return from the netherworld and through the stargate. Let me live. Let me live."

I didn't see anything about Nefertari on these, so I started to turn away.

One of the cat jars twitched. I stopped, staring. If I had blinked, I'd have missed it.

A sound came from another—a scratching noise.

No. No way.

A bundle of linen wriggled, and a neat slice opened down the middle with a dry, papery sound. Something long, thin, and grayish-brown pushed through the slit, and the tip stretched. Jagged, yellowed talons attached to paws covered in leathery, hairless, dead skin appeared.

The breath seeped from me in a slow leak as horror set in.

It was a cat—or at least it had been three thousand years ago. An eyeless face pushed through and seemed to peer up at me from empty sockets. Where its nose should've been, empty holes flared, taking in the scents around it. Its ears, dried and shriveled, twitched to listen. It opened its mouth, flashing chipped, browned fangs, and it made a hoarse, raspy meow. The rest of the cat mummy emerged, gangly, joints snapping, papery, hair-less skin scratching, a low, whining growl shredding its dry throat.

"Nasira? Sayer?" My voice was nearly inaudible, but I couldn't cry any louder. I couldn't blink. Couldn't breathe. I could only stare at what I'd done, the creature I'd resurrected.

A ceramic jar bobbled and tipped over. Something inside thrashed and the vessel shattered. Another cat mummy escaped, stretched, spine cracking. The first creature approached cautiously, and the two sniffed noses. They seemed disoriented, unsure. They hissed, fangs bared. Paws lashed out, scratched.

They turned and looked unseeingly at me. Another mummy tore itself from its wrappings. Another smashed through its tiny coffin. Another. And another.

They hurled their bodies into the glass with thud after thud, proving they weren't as frail as they appeared. The glass cracked and cracked further. Their claws raked, leaving streaks. Their voices filled my head, my mind, my bones.

What had I done?

13

I threw up my hands and turned away as glass exploded in my face. The cat mummies collided with me, and their claws tore my skin, sending searing pain up and down my body. I lost my balance and fell onto my back beneath them, unable to hear my scream over the mummies yowling. Horror, panic, and disgust seized my thoughts, muting them, and all I could do was react.

"*Khet!*" Blinding flames swarmed my vision, blooming like petals, unfolding and stretching around me. The cat mummies screamed and scattered into the shadows. I pushed myself to my feet, lingering in the fire of my spell for protection until they died.

"Ziva!" Sayer ran to me and slid to a stop when he saw the broken glass case. Behind him a cautious Nasira had her *asaya* raised.

"I'm sorry—I should've known better—I thought reading the words was harmless . . ." My stammering trailed off.

"The cat coffins," Sayer murmured as understanding grew in him. "What happened?"

"They came to life," I told him, still in disbelief.

A low yowl came from the darkness and we turned to face it.

"They seemed confused, enough so to become violent." I shook my head. "Honestly, I don't know. They were monsters."

"We can't let them live," Sayer said, removing his axes from their scabbard. "Not if they're dangerous to innocent people. Send them back to where they belong: the netherworld. We'll apologize to the gods later."

A cat mummy sprang at him, claws outstretched with a scream, and he swung an ax with clean precision. Its head spiraled through the air and the body smacked to the floor in a heap. He took off after one of the creatures scurrying through the hall and Nasira backed up against me.

"And the lesson learned tonight?" she asked jokingly.

"Magic is dangerous and when used carelessly can wake up horrifying cat mummies," I answered, drawing my *asaya*.

"Good girl."

One of the creatures darted from the room, and I chased after it into the hall overlooking the main floor. A mummy leapt into my path and landed, skidding before smacking into the base of a display. I raised my *asaya*. The mummy's reedy limbs unfolded stiffly from its tight ball like a spider's corpse in the midst of resurrection, its dark, empty eye sockets huge and fixed greedily on me. It pushed itself onto its hind legs and launched, but I swung my *asaya* and the obsidian slashed through its neck, taking its head.

A second mummy emerged at a lope, yowling, but a devastating *neit* spell dragged it off its feet. The water rushed across the floor and spilled over the side of the second floor balcony. Before the creature could recover, Nasira knelt and killed it.

"Who's there?" an echoed voice shouted through the cavernous first floor. "The police are on their way!"

Gasping for breath, I looked at Nasira and said, "We've got to go."

Another cat mummy barreled into her, knocking her into the balcony railing, which erupted in shattered wood. The force of a second mummy pitched both of them over the edge and Nasira screamed as she grappled for balance. I snatched her hand before she fell, but the creatures' claws latched onto her clothing, tore her skin, biting and scratching.

"Hang on!" I cried, summoning all my strength to keep Nasira from falling. I braced my boots against the base of the balustrade and leaned back. What was left of the railing creaked and threatened to crack. I freed one hand, risking losing my grip on Nasira, and shot a *taw* spell into the cat mummies, rattling them, but they quickly reassembled. Nasira slipped through my grip with a yelp and I grabbed her arm with both hands again.

Nasira groaned and looked up at me, her face pale and stricken. "Let go and get out of here. You have to trust me."

I shook my head furiously. "I can't!"

"They're ripping me apart!" Nasira begged, tears pooling in her eyes. "Please."

"Okay," I said, swallowing hard. "I trust you." I squeezed my eyes shut and opened my hands. I heard Nasira let out a gasp and then a thud. When I heard squealing and thrashing, I opened my eyes and watched her wrestle with the creatures. I looked wildly for her weapon and found it lying on the floor.

"Nasira!" I called.

Her head snapped up. I chucked her *asaya* and she snatched it from air. She shot for the beasts, spinning the staff so fast the air screamed.

"The storage room!" she shouted to me. "Find my mother and Cyrene!"

I nodded and did as she instructed, though I hated leaving her to clean up my mess. I was the one who'd resurrected the cats and it was my fault they had to be stopped, my fault the sacred animals had turned vicious during resurrection.

Racing through the museum, I tried to be as quiet as possible. Back here I wasn't likely to be spotted. The guards had all rushed to where the action was, and any moment the police would arrive. Guilt for putting my friends through this horror gnawed at me, but I had to remain focused on my task. We hadn't yet found what we came for. I could not leave empty-handed.

I found the hallway we'd split up in and moved quickly in the direction Cyrene and Haya had gone. One door led to a cramped washroom, so I opened the other. Bingo. The storage room was larger than the lab and receiving room combined.

"Cyrene?" I called.

"Ziva?" The priestess poked her head out from around a freestanding shelving unit packed full of boxes and metal trunks. "What was that noise out there? Everything all right?"

"Uh, well, something came up," I explained, purposefully vague. "Sayer and Nasira are on it, but we have to be quick. Our guards are no longer distracted."

Her mouth formed a tight line. "No luck yet. Care to assist?"

"Yes, of course," I told her, and started down the far aisle, peaking into open crates. I moved quickly, wishing I could speed this up somehow. If Nefertari's *ka* was alive in me somewhere, then I should have had a connection to her body, especially her sacred organs. I brushed my fingers across wooden boxes and steel safes, closing my eyes and hoping something in my power would speak. Something about a pine box drew my attention and I decided to indulge the impulse and remove the lid. It was filled with shredded brown paper I was careful not to spill onto the floor as I searched for the artifact within. There couldn't be any obvious evidence we'd been through here.

"Come on, queen's blood," I whispered. "Sing to me."

My words seemed to transcend into an incantation and as soon as my fingers brushed something cold and solid, I felt the prickle of energy zip up my hand. I lifted my prize and held it to the light. The canopic jar was made of smooth, creamy alabaster, and traces of paint. The lid was carved into the shape of a baboon, whose name, I recalled, was Hapy. Inside, packed in natron salt, were sure to be lungs. I made out the rope of a cartouche and understood why Sweeney had found it difficult to read. The inscriptions were quite faded, but I recognized the heart-and-windpipe hieroglyph denoting *'nefer'* and excitement filled me. When I looked further, I found the delicate, cursive slashes of hieratic script, and while so far, I'd only learned the very basics of reading it, the strangeness in the syntax was immediately noticeable. This was what we came for.

"Haya!" I called. "Cyrene! I've got it!"

They rushed to my side and I presented the jar. "I'm positive this belonged to Nefertari," I insisted. "There's strange hieratic here just as Sweeney said."

Cyrene took the jar from me and examined it closely. "It's not strange. He simply didn't know how to read it. This is Medjai hieratic. We were the ones to develop this writing system. Let's call it a night before things get any more exciting, shall we?"

I carefully returned the box to its original state and hoped no one would notice the missing contents for a long time. We exited the room and emerged into the hallway, just as Nasira and Sayer slid to a stop in front of us.

"We're on our way out," Sayer said, breathlessly. "Care to join us?"

"After you," I replied, grinning.

"Do you have it?" Nasira asked, peering into Cyrene's hands.

The priestess nodded. "Right here. Let's go home."

Our Medjai mole remained behind to avert suspicion from herself. The rest of us ran from the museum and back to the cars, which sat dark and silent as waiting soldiers. Dina remained behind at the museum for damage control. Nasira and I joined her mother in the first car, while Cyrene and Sayer slipped into the second. We sped off into the night.

"That was excellent work back there, Ziva," Haya praised. "Nasira has trained you well."

Nasira glanced over her shoulder at me from the front seat and grinned wide. "Only a minor hiccup."

"Minor?" I laughed. "Cat mummies are not minor!"

"Wait—*what*?" Haya stuttered. "Cat mummies?"

My cheeks burned. "I promise I'll be more careful when I practice reading hieroglyphs."

"In a controlled environment," Nasira added.

"And I won't speak them aloud just to be safe—"

My words caught in my throat when the Daimler pitched through the air. It hit hard ground and bounced, sending us soaring again. Glass shattered and scattered through space like sparkling rain and the shards ripped through my skin. My stomach flipped, dove into my throat, and dropped low in my gut and back up again. No one screamed; I heard only grunts as bodies thudded against surfaces, and the groan and crash of metal against pavement. I felt nothing but abject confusion and amazement. When the motorcar came to a mangled rest, my senses returned to me and I understood we weren't right side up. My limbs were tangled with someone else's. My skin and clothing scraped against glass and debris.

Shuddering from shock and pain, I looked through the busted-out windows. Headlights blinded me, and I heard panicked murmurs.

"Mum?" Nasira asked fearfully, her voice shaking.

"*Ssh*, baby girl," Haya whispered, as she jangled the door handle and worked to keep herself from falling forward into the dashboard.

Realization gripped me breathless; magic suspended the car in the air, propping it perpendicular to the ground. Taillights blazing into the black and starless sky, the grill gave a low whine as it grated against the cold pavement. Knotted metal whined and groaned, and the air cracked and buzzed with energy.

Footsteps clicked on the pavement, belonging to heels trailed by a dress of black snake scales dazzling like jewels.

Nasira shoved her shoulder hard into the car door to no avail. "It won't budge. She's keeping the doors closed." She put her feet onto the dashboard, pushing herself higher in the driver's seat, and she kicked the windshield over and over. Her *taw* spell added force to her blows. Spiderweb fractures spread. The glass creaked.

Kauket's shadows swallowed the moonlight and drowned us in suffocating darkness.

I freed a tireless instinct for survival. We had to escape. Escape. *Escape*. I looked around wildly. The doors wouldn't open. This was a trap. A prison.

My stomach hurled into my spine as the car lurched forward, careening through the air until it smashed into something horribly solid, crushing the roof into us. After a moment, we fell, and the car toppled to the ground, scattering glass and dropping chunks of undercarriage. The sensation dragged me deeper into unreality. My vision grew blurry, and everything became tight around me. I couldn't move. Couldn't breathe. Revulsion took me like a riptide, powerful and without mercy, and my ears rang; an abominable sound like kettles shrieking and bones breaking.

"Mum? *Mum!*"

I'd never heard terror come from Nasira before. When I turned my head to find her, I saw she'd been pushed into the backseat and was now pinned against me. I couldn't see Haya. The coppery odor of blood made me sick.

Nasira's screams released a clarity in me. I choked on the air stuck in my throat and I scrambled, the animal instinct deep within again screamed at me to break free. The rear window had been shattered and turned into a gaping hole. The roof hadn't been crushed as badly in the back. We could certainly squeeze out this way.

"Come on," I said, my voice hardly audible. "Nasira, we can get out. Come on."

I dragged myself through the glassless skeleton of the sedan and onto cold, glossy pavement. Nasira had stopped calling for her mother and I assumed she followed me. I pushed myself to my feet, straining against the fear and dread and pain desperate to drag me to the ground. I lifted my head to meet the familiar carnelian eyes, cold as old blood, of the goddess of darkness.

"Nasira!" I screamed. She wasn't behind me. "*Nasira!*"

From behind her expressionless, inhuman gold mask, Kauket observed me. Her painted brow and carved mouth remained calm, without empathy or humanity. With malice sharp as a stone's edge to cut clean and deep, the monster whispered Nasira's mother's words: *"Ssh, baby girl . . ."*

I mustered what confidence I could and threw a *taw* spell into Kauket's face, but a wave of her hand deflected it.

"Hunting you is quite easy when you make such a racket everywhere you go," the goddess sneered. "All that magic wasn't for nothing. Time to tell me what you've been up to, little mouse."

Tires squealed to a stop behind me and I dared not look away from her. Car doors opened and slammed shut. Sayer yelled my name, but he seemed distant, a cry carried from across the sea. I was in shock, I told myself. This would pass. It had to, or I was dead.

"Nasira is still inside the car!" I called to Sayer.

"And my mother?"

I couldn't answer. I didn't know. All I knew was that I had to fight and defend my friends and Nefertari's treasure. We couldn't resurrect her without it and there was no way I'd let Kauket take it.

My *asaya* felt like an old friend in my hand, its weight empowering. I swung it around my head, and the staff extended with a *crack*, the obsidian blades shining in the night. Magic kicked up like a whirlwind around me, lifting and grabbing my hair. I summoned all and it pulsed into the pavement. I felt the ground crack and sink beneath me. My life force, every fragment of my heart and soul shaped by a bloodline thousands of years old, gave me the power to protect this world and those in it who couldn't protect themselves. I'd inherited this ancient blood and it was my responsibility not to let anything kill me before I fulfilled my destiny.

My teeth clenched together beneath the weight of my power. A coppery taste of blood stung my tongue. The gods had started all of this over a grudge. They've tried to kill us over a grudge. They murdered my parents over a grudge. But they had no idea that what they created had grown even bigger than the immortals themselves. This fight was about more than my life or the life of our queen. I understood why, in the end, we would win. We had more to lose than gods who would live forever.

The pressure of my magic began to implode on me, squeezing every last inch of my skin and clenching the muscles in my arms and legs. I refused to let it be too much for me to handle; I needed all of it to fight. No matter how much I summoned, the goddess of darkness would have more.

There was, however, something about me that set me apart from the other Medjai. They didn't think like I did. I was a survivor, I was a woman, I was blessed by Death, and I had queen's blood. Queens do not die for nothing. For my entire life, I had been endlessly underestimated. Never again.

"*Khet,*" I snarled through gritted teeth. Magical flames burst from my hand and tore up both ends of the *asaya*, consuming it, wreathing it. The concentration required to control the spell was burdensome, but Kauket's disarmed reaction made up for my struggle.

I raised my *asaya*, presenting it to the goddess of

darkness—a promise the obsidian blades would slake their thirst on her immortal blood.

Her wide, stricken eyes told me she understood, yes, I was mortal, but I was also Medjai, an ancient people of god-given power. I would not yield until death took me, and I'd give it one hell of a fight first.

With a scream I shot forward, whirling the *asaya* until the air shrieked with power, the flames hot. I leapt into the air and brought down my staff in a fiery arc, one end slashing open her collarbone as she yanked herself aside. I landed, swept the *asaya* again, anticipating her attempt to dodge it, and obsidian met the flesh of her abdomen in one slice. Golden blood sizzled in the flames.

A force lifted me up off my feet and my stomach plummeted. A surprised wail escaped me as my body soared, my limbs flailing, and my *khet* spell was extinguished. Something grabbed my ankle and stopped me dead in the air before yanking me toward the earth. I smacked the ground, sending a shock of pain through me, and I grunted as I was dragged toward the goddess of darkness. I glanced wildly over my shoulder at her and flipped onto my back. Kauket's hand reached toward me and her *sekhem* spell hauled me like a doll across the ground. I kicked, but the magic wrapped around my ankle held my leg rigid and still. She raised me into the air and I slashed with my *asaya*, but she caught my arm and squeezed. Dangling, I cried in pain and was forced to drop my weapon. My free hand shot for the sheath inside my jacket and whipped out a smaller *was* dagger, which I sliced across Kauket's cheek. The goddess's head snapped to the side and she snarled, baring fangs. The wound bled gold and crackled with netherlight.

"Release me!" I screamed, my body thrashing in the spell's grip.

Kauket's eyes blazed like flames. A line of gold slipped down her face. "I don't think you're in the position to give orders, Medjai."

I threw up my arm with another *khet* spell. The flames flashed and slammed into Kauket's body, knocking her back and making her lose focus. I crumpled to the earth in a heap, and though my limbs were tangled and weak, I shakily pushed myself up. From over my head, an ax hissed through the air at a lightning fast spin and slammed into Kauket's chest with a thud. She shrieked and doubled over, clawing madly at the obsidian blade and helve.

I turned, daring to take my eyes from her as she struggled, and inhaled deeply with relief when I saw Sayer. He collided with me, his gaze hard and dark and his touch gentle. He raised his hand to cup my cheek, lift my jaw, move my face left to right, as he inspected me for injury. His burning eyes met mine.

"Are you all right?" he asked.

I nodded. "Yes, yes, I'm fine."

He seemed as visibly dazed and shaken as I was. "I got Nasira out. Cyrene is working on my mother. I tried to heal her. I did."

I stared at him, understanding what that meant. Everything I felt and saw seemed unreal and dreamlike. Shock hadn't yet waned.

"Medjai!"

We both spun to face Kauket, who had Nasira's slackened body suspended by the throat. Cyrene knelt by the unmoving and bloodied form of Haya. Once she noticed Nasira in the goddess's clutches, Cyrene rose slowly with caution.

"Enough games!" Kauket roared. "I know you have the canopic jar, boy. I can sense it on you. Give it to me or she dies. Then you watch your friends die. Then you die."

Sayer's face drained and he exhaled shakily, staring at his sister in dread.

"I will *break* her, Medjai," the immortal snarled. "Hand it over!"

Cyrene did not take her eyes off him. "Sayer. Don't."

He acted as though he hadn't heard her. Indecision rooted him, silent, to the ground. After another moment, he drew a trembling breath through his mouth and exhaled. He opened his leather jacket and presented the alabaster canister.

"*No!*" Cyrene barked in anger.

Kauket dropped Nasira and the goddess's form vanished from sight. Shadows flashed where she'd been standing. She appeared directly in front of Sayer, swarming them both in a plume of inky darkness.

"Sayer!" I cried fearfully and shot toward where their forms vanished.

When the shadows died, Kauket was gone and Sayer had lost the canopic jar.

CHAPTER
14

Sayer's dark eyes, shining with adrenaline, met mine. He opened his mouth to say something to me, but he closed it without a word. He didn't need to say anything to me. I knew why he did it. Even though I'd never had a sister, I'd always wanted one badly enough to know I'd do anything to keep her. I gave him a gentle nod to let him know I stood with him. His gaze bounced around my face, searching for something I could not know, before he bolted toward where Nasira lay. I followed him at a jog. When he reached her, he knelt to check her wrist, and rose again to return to his mother's side.

Cyrene threw up her hands and gave him a disgusted look. "You have no idea what you've done."

"Yes, I do," he spat back. He knelt beside Haya and took her limp hand in his. He rocked back and forth and whispered something too low for me to hear.

Haya was dead and Nefertari's treasure was gone.

My lungs felt shriveled, my chest constricted. The air seemed thin and my limbs had turned to jelly. I sat wobbly next to Nasira, picking her hair, matted with blood, out of her face. She was alive, but deeply unconscious. One of her arms hung loosely, stretching the skin connecting it to her shoulder socket, which appeared far too sharp to be normal. I didn't need to be a doctor to tell her right lower leg was badly broken. I didn't know how we'd get her home, or if she'd even survive the trip. When I lifted my head, I saw Cyrene running a hand through her hair roughly, growling curses under her breath. Sayer's cheeks were stained with tears.

The anguish erupted from inside of me. "Anubis!" I screamed, squeezing his amulet until it bruised my hand. "*Anubis!*"

I smelled desert sand and stone.

"Ziva," the guardian of the dead said gently, and he knelt by my side. "What's happened here?"

"We found the canopic jar," I told him, meeting his gaze blearily. "But Kauket took it. Haya is dead. And Nasira . . ."

"She's alive," he assured me. "She'll be fine."

His eyes rolled into the back of his head until only glassy white orbs remained, and then his lids fluttered closed. He paused at the wound in her leg and muttered his spell more forcefully. The gash splitting her skin stitched together with invisible thread and the seam melted away. This was a far different healing magic than what I'd seen Sayer use—what he'd used on me—but Anubis was a god.

There came a disturbing pop sound from Nasira's

chest and Anubis's eyes returned to their prismatic topaz, but she didn't stir.

Panic fluttered inside me. "Why won't she wake up?"

"Her body was brutalized," he told me firmly. "Her heart was barely beating. Give her time."

"You have to get the canopic jar back from Kauket," I told him, my voice rising with desperation. "I can't chase her to the netherworld, but you can. Please, Anubis, you have to help us."

He licked his lips, trepidation filling his face. "There's only one place she'd take it: to Set."

"Do you know where he might keep it?" I asked, hopeful.

Anubis shook his head. "He won't keep it anywhere. The jar is only good to us and Nefertari. He will destroy it."

The breath rushed from me with disbelief. "Then we don't have any time. You have to get it back. Now! *Go!*"

He closed his eyes and let his shoulders slump, the sadness unmistakable. Then he was gone.

Anubis

The moment Anubis took in the cool netherlight of his domain, his power darkened with anger. He stepped to the edge of the dais, hoping that if he hesitated before seeking Set he might calm down, but his rage only grew. Anubis was sick after what Kauket did to the Medjai. The cruelty was unfathomable.

He sensed her energy and found her slumped against the side of a corridor in Set's domain. For a critical moment, he gaped at her in shock. The goddess of darkness looked like anything but, with her hair haphazardly tangled around her shoulders and her dress slashed in several places. Her crocodile-tight grip on the canopic jar was her only sign of life.

She looked up at him with dull eyes set in dark, bruised sockets. "If you're going to kill me, then do it and spare me that look of pity you reserve for kicked puppies."

"You'll find no pity from me," he replied coldly. "I hope you feel as terrible as you look."

She exhaled harshly and frowned as though she'd tasted something foul. "That Medjai girl has wrecked my dress and my pride. I'm having a wretched night."

Anubis felt a bitter smile start at the edge of his mouth.

"Don't look so pleased with her," Kauket grumbled. "I've made it this far to rest, but I'll be on my way now. No doubt you're here for the canopic jar. You caught me off guard. You could've taken it if you hadn't stalled." She spat a gob of blood onto the ground. "One day your tendency to hesitate will get you killed."

He crossed his arms. "That's quite the threat from someone lying helpless on the ground."

She huffed and gave him a frail smile. "I like you, Anubis. You're a nuisance, but at least you've got a spine."

A rumble came from deep, deep below them, beneath the deepest chasm of the netherworld's emptiness where Anubis had never dared to venture. The stillness that had settled between them fractured; fear squeezed through as blood from a wound.

Shadows closed in on Kauket's skin, veiling her, to

protect their mistress. A whisper passed her lips as but a breath. "He stirs."

She used the last of her energy to vanish before Anubis, and though he didn't know what her last words meant, he knew where she was headed to heal. He believed with a dark ember in his heart he'd had the strength to finish her off then and there.

But he let her go.

It was foolish of him. He didn't fear retribution. Set wouldn't dare. After all Kauket had done, she deserved it. Then why wouldn't Anubis kill her? His own actions—or lack thereof—angered him.

Anubis continued to his destination. The god of chaos sat rigid in his throne and his expression seemed less pleased with himself than Anubis had expected. The canopic jar perched on one arm of the throne, inches from Set's hand, taunting. He had no idea how he'd claim it from Set. There was no way he could fight Set and win, not without an element of surprise.

As Anubis approached, Kauket emerged from the impluvium at Set's feet, her nude backside shimmering in the netherlight that danced across the water's surface. Her black satin hair gleamed down her back, and with both hands she squeezed the remaining water from her tresses. She grabbed a linen sheet to cover her slender body, but the material was too sheer to have any worth. Her body already appeared healed and cleaned of blood, thanks to the regenerative power of the water. The goddess of darkness looked over her shoulder, offering Anubis a sly, victorious grin.

"Kauket," he called with a lilt of false surprise in his voice, though his hostility added to it a drop of poison. He was eager to wipe that smile off her face. "You're looking well so suddenly. I'm almost impressed you've overcome your gutlessness enough to function."

Her grin sunk into a grimace, and her carnelian eyes narrowed into slits. She licked her lips with a flick of her serpent's tongue.

"Rude, Anubis," Set scolded lazily. "Have you come all this way just to pick a fight?"

"Is it your greatest wish, Set, to cause maximum damage in plain view of human beings?" Anubis demanded, unable to hold the bite from his tone. "The mortal world is as delicate as ever, perhaps more so, now that it's a world of science instead of magic. Civilization could erupt into madness and chaos."

Set spread his hands and gave Anubis a flat smile. "That's kind of my thing."

Kauket stepped forward and darkness cupped her jawline, poured over her shoulders, as her rage surfaced and spilled. "The lives of a few mortals are but a few fallen rocks from a mountainside. I follow Set because I believe in him. He has saved us all from annihilation before and yet the rest of you branded him the villain. What he *lost* to save us all! Then you crowned a coward king! Set has what it takes to be a king. I will fight for victory, at whatever cost."

"Kauket," Set murmured soberly, but he could not soothe her passion.

"That cost is human lives," Anubis said through gritted

teeth. "Neither of you understands. You're immortal and you have no concept of death. You don't think killing is right or wrong, do you? You can't even fathom the cost of life."

Her eyes narrowed at him. "What makes you so different?"

"I spend time with them," Anubis answered, and he no longer cared about the desperation building in his throat like a scream. "I've watched them take their first breaths and live their lives and die. I've walked among the fallen in battle, among hospital beds filled with the sick. I have seen life and death for so long and so close that these are tangible things to me now. I feel death in my fingertips and I taste life on my tongue. I'll never be able to teach you the value of mortal life, because you can't feel a thing."

Set lowered his head to glower at Anubis from beneath his strong brow. "I've had enough of your self-righteous blathering."

"The mortals have plenty of evil to worry about without you killing them over a three-thousand-year-old personal slight," Anubis snarled.

Kriosphinxes crept forth into the netherlight, forsaking the shadows. One corner of Set's mouth pulled into a grin. "I merely desire what is rightfully mine by covenant and return our people to earth."

Anubis gritted his teeth and shook his head in disgust. "We all know there is more to your story. What is so important about what a dead queen promised you?"

"She betrayed me," Set sneered. "My heart was broken."

"Your heart was broken long before that," Anubis said,

boldness stirring within him. He trembled, realizing he'd said what no other immortal had ever dared.

The malice in Set's gaze became a physical force and Anubis felt it brush against his throat in warning.

Anubis continued, "If the mortal world is what you're after, then know this: These humans do not have the same fears the ancient people of Egypt had. You cannot expect to rise from the netherworld and be greeted with a sea of mortals groveling at your feet."

Set laughed, his voice thick and booming, echoing like war drums. "Is a savior not precisely what the Medjai are after? This entire world went to war, a more destructive clash than I have ever seen, *millions* dead. They poisoned their own air to kill each other. That is a twisted sort of sickness which impresses even me. I understand the Medjai want to stop that from happening again. They don't need a once-mortal queen. A godless world can only be saved by gods."

Anubis hated to admit there was truth in that. "Perhaps if we joined forces with the Medjai, rather than leaving them alone to protect the mortal world—"

"Are you, oh prince of death, suggesting the immortals *should* intervene?" Set inquired, incredulous.

"I suggest we help the Medjai stop what has started in the mortal world," Anubis said, hoping he could convince Set to merely hand over the canopic jar willingly. "We have the power. If all of us—*all* of us, Set—join together, we can help the Medjai rebuild and stop this second world war. With Queen Nefertari, we may resurrect the Golden Age she created long ago."

Set grimaced and rubbed the bridge of his nose with his thumb and forefinger. "All right. Enough. I don't care about what the humans do to each other." He leaned forward and malice twisted his visage. "They let my temples turn to dust and I'll let their bones suffer the same. I care about the survival of our people—nothing else. I will not allow that traitorous mortal worm to leave the netherworld. She owes me her heart and it will be *mine!*"

Anubis paused. "She promised you her heart? Literally, her actual heart?"

A darkness came over Set's expression as it hardened, and he said nothing.

Anubis did his best not to glance at the canopic jar. He had to act now before it was too late. He threw a *taw* spell at one of the kriosphinxes and it squealed as it smashed into a bloodstone column. Set turned his head toward the commotion in surprise and Anubis took his chance. He flashed out and in, appearing instantly beside Set and grabbed the jar. He flashed to the opposite end of the dais with his prize, beaming with triumph.

Set shot to his feet with a roar and in the same instant, the amber rings in his black eyes flashed like molten gold. Kauket paled ashen with fright.

"Anubis," called an imperial voice from behind him.

He turned and watched his mother, Nephthys, goddess of night and mourning, appear at the edge of the dais, her gown of midnight blue trailing in her wake. Her deeply umber complexion gave a cool glow and her cropped, coiled raven hair emphasized her oval face. Perched behind her shoulders were a pair of wings made of night, the feathers a living celestial skyscape, a canvas of heavenly colors—deep blues, violets, greens, pinks—and twinkling stars against the endless, black universe. They bloomed like storm clouds on the horizon at twilight. Where her dress pinned at her shoulders, black feathers became shining indigo and beryl in the netherlight glow.

Night followed Nephthys like a faithful servant, her starlight banishing the shadows tethered to Kauket's command. The lesser goddess retreated, melting into what little inky darkness remained and wearing it like armor. Kauket scowled at the brightening of Set's domain, but he let Nephthys do as she pleased and allowed her natural inclinations without protest. He stood and took a step forward to welcome her with respect.

Nephthys embraced her son, stretching on her toes to kiss his cheek, beaming with pride it seemed she could barely contain. She settled onto her heels, gazing at him through her expressive, starlit eyes, and offered him a dazzling smile of full lips, setting her high cheekbones aglow. She was an uncommon beauty among the beautiful with a serenity matched not even by the stars. When Anubis witnessed the glowing reverence in Set's expression, he knew the god of chaos believed the same, that his mother had no equal.

"My love," Set said. He bowed his head slowly and deeply to her, dipping his shoulders, never taking his eyes off her.

A cunning smile curved Nephthys's lips and she glanced in the direction Kauket had fled before raising one eyebrow in question toward Set. His reply was a cool, unapologetic shrug. They were too stubborn, too angry with each other because of deeds long done, and for immortal gods who had very little understanding of time, a grudge did not wane as easily as the moon. Set would lay at her feet if she asked him to, even if she would never take him back. She was bold, and Anubis liked to believe she'd passed that trait on to him, though her nerve was a subtler beast than his.

Nephthys placed a hand on Anubis's arm. "What is this you have here?" she asked, gesturing to the canopic jar.

"Ah, returning a lost item to its rightful owner is all," he replied. He struggled to maintain his coolness, unsure if Set was determined enough in his goals to act against Nephthys.

"I see," she said, and continued with a glance at Set, "My lord, I've come to retrieve my son, if you don't object."

"Of course not," Set almost crooned. "Though it would please me if you stayed for a while. It's been too long since I've enjoyed your company."

She cast a long, cool glance at Kauket. "You have plenty of company as it is. I don't want to intrude."

A frown flitted over his face and was gone in a flash. Anubis swore he recognized regret in Set's amber-ringed eyes—possibly even shame. Perhaps one day, if Set and his mother could both overcome their egos and cease to be so cruel to each other, they could have the loving and devoted relationship they'd once had. They wanted each other more than anything in any world and Anubis wished happiness for them both.

"Farewell then," Set said softly, watching Nephthys with an intense longing.

Anubis's mother took a firmer hold of his arm and they vanished, consumed by shadows and netherlight, and reappeared before a modest limestone palace in her own domain. Stretching as far as his eyes could see, was a rolling desert beneath a vast, magical night sky. The stars cascading across the galaxy gleamed as brilliantly as they did over the Egyptian desert, surely a creation of Nephthys's power.

Anubis and Nephthys crossed a pearly granite bridge over a gently flowing river and into the lush courtyard gardens. Before them fluttered buzzing insects and singing night birds among palm leaves and flowering plants. The palace was still and lonely, but brightly lit by starlight and torches blazing pale netherlight. The two immortals entered through the high front doors carved from obsidian and emerged into the coolly lit atrium. Beyond the lotus columns, moonlight glittered off the surface of an impluvium as it beamed down through the opening in the ceiling.

"You've grown to enjoy antagonizing Set," Nephthys teased, though something in her eyes gave away her wariness. He noticed the celestial train of her dress reflected the night sky as the still, dark pool did.

Anubis almost laughed. "I certainly don't enjoy it. Although, this could've gone much uglier if you hadn't shown up when you did. My guess is your arrival wasn't coincidental."

"No," she replied. "My connection with him is still strong, but not as strong as mine with you, my son. Tell me, what is so important about this canopic jar you'd risk your life and my heart for it?"

A moment suspended between them as he searched for the explanation that would stir Nephthys's thoughts. It wouldn't be easy to convince her that what was happening in the human world would echo through the netherworld.

"Egypt is under threat once again," he told her. "And I don't believe we should stand aside any longer. For centuries we've left the mortals alone and we've done a great disservice to them, especially the Medjai. We've lost their trust and it's imperative we repair the damage. Foreign invaders come in waves to Egypt's shores and this new threat—Mother, they've barely recovered from the Great War. They were certain it would be the war to end all wars, and it nearly was, but this could really be the last. Humankind might finally destroy itself."

Her brow pinched together with concern and she put a jeweled hand on his arm to comfort him. "You believe this." It wasn't a question; she always knew his heart.

"The Medjai are close to resurrecting the queen Nefertari," he explained.

Skepticism came over her face. "Surely that's impossible. After death, mortals live forever in the kingdom of the dead. They cannot return to the human world."

He braced himself, drawing breath not for air but for strength. "Set seems quite convinced that they can. He mentioned the queen's heart as though he's desperate for it. As though that is the key to her resurrection. How could all of this effort be to simply get back at a mortal queen?"

She frowned and said gently, "You know him."

He couldn't argue with the truth. Set had proven he was infinitely petty. "In his eyes every slight is personal."

"Forgiveness resides outside his spectrum of emotion. He punishes everyone but me and that's terribly wrong of him."

Anubis shook his head. "He should punish no one but himself."

She sighed and closed her eyes. He knew on this they would never agree. He could only hope, when she talked like this, she didn't regret what she did to give him life. He looked down at the ancient alabaster jar in his hands. "The Medjai search for their queen's canopic jars to move forward with the resurrection. Set only needs one of them to stop their plans." He raised the canopic jar to inspect the inscriptions. "It's odd," he mused, puzzled.

"What is?" Nephthys asked.

"I would've thought I'd be able to sense something here," he noted. "Considering it's a sacred organ. This is only cold stone to me."

His mother frowned. "That is odd indeed. Do you suppose it's all right to peek inside?"

He shrugged. "I don't see why not."

Anubis carefully dislodged the lid, carved into the shape of Hapy's serene face. His heart plummeted. "Oh, no," he breathed.

The jar was empty.

The moment Anubis left us, I held my breath as I waited for Nasira to stir, but she lay still as a sleeping fairytale princess of war. Sayer approached us and knelt slowly, gazing softly at his sister. Her hand was limp and cool in mine, but I held it anyway.

"Anubis promised she'll be okay when she wakes up," I told Sayer. "Whenever that will be."

He looked up at me and my heart broke to see such rawness in his face. "I can heal your wounds, if you'd like," he offered.

"No, please, don't worry about me," I told him. "Save your strength for someone who needs it more." The anguish in his eyes was naked and reality felt like a punch to my gut. I had no words for him. How could I possibly understand how he felt? My parents were gone, but I'd never known them. I'd never lost anyone I loved.

"All isn't lost," he told me gently, as though I were the one who needed comforting.

I summoned my courage. "You're right. Anubis will get the canopic jar back from Kauket."

"Ziva." Sayer opened his jacket and pulled out a small bundle of very crisp, very yellowed linens.

My eyes shot wide. "Is that—?"

He nodded, raising the mummified pair of lungs. "Brute strength can be persuasive, but it's not always the answer—especially when you're up against something bigger and badder than you."

I grimaced and frowned. "Oh, you had that in your pocket. And you touched it."

"I won't unwrap this, I assure you," Sayer said. "We still need the canopic jar to translate the hieratic."

"Anubis will get it," I urged. "I trust him." In my heart, I feared for him. There was something about his relationship with the other immortals I didn't yet understand. I didn't believe there was anything he'd deliberately hidden from me, yet there was more. A darker element. A personal element.

I removed his amulet from its safe place in my pocket and called his name, hoping he'd hear me and arrive unharmed. A few moments later, he appeared, alarmed but in one piece, with the canopic jar in hand.

"We have the organ," I told him, wasting no time.

Anubis didn't need air, yet he blew a long breath of relief. "I was, needless to say, quite concerned when I found this jar was empty. There's something else. Just before I took this, Set mentioned Nefertari owes him her heart. Did you read anything about that on the stela?"

Sayer and I exchanged glances. "No," he said. "The inscription mentioned only her canopic jars."

"We have to find the jars as soon as we can," I said. "Hopefully they'll tell us the importance of Nefertari's heart."

Sayer nodded and rose to leave us. "I'll let Cyrene know."

Anubis's brow drew together, with pain or sorrow or both, I didn't know. More humanity glowed on his face than I'd ever seen in a single day in Manhattan. "Are you all right, Ziva?" he asked.

I exhaled gently. "I have to be, so I can take care of my friends."

"Take care of yourself as well," he said. He touched my shoulder, offering me comfort, and stayed beside me until we were ready to leave.

The food I'd scavenged for myself in the kitchen of Wytheford Hall refused to sit well in my stomach. I had a peculiar feeling through my whole body. A little nausea—from stress I imagined—and the bone-squeezing sensation of uneasiness.

After picking up my mess, I headed toward the bedroom Nasira slept in with Sayer watching over her. A low buzz and tinny voice coming from a room as I passed caught my attention. I peeked inside and found Cyrene sitting at a small, round table by a lamp, her head bowed to a radio as she listened to the grave voice of a British newscaster. She sipped from the steaming teacup in her hands.

"Transmissions from Warsaw bring dire announcement on this morning of September 1, 1939: German planes have bombed numerous Polish towns, leaving many dead and injured among the ruins. Berlin has released the following statement from Herr Hitler: 'The Polish state has refused the peaceful settlement of relations which I desired and has appealed to arms. Germans in Poland are persecuted with bloody terror and driven from their houses.'"

Cyrene looked up at me and turned the radio's volume low. "Hello, Ziva. How are you faring?"

"Better than others," I replied, thinking of Sayer and Nasira. "Has the canopic jar been translated yet?"

She nodded solemnly. "We're working on it. There must be clues as to what to do with the sacred organ and where to find the others. We'll leave for Egypt as soon as possible. We will take Haya home for burial."

Unrest stirred within me. I licked my lips and sat in the chair across from her. The room was so quiet the antique chair's squeak made me tense.

"Is all this worth it?" I dared to ask. "The lives of our friends and families lost, the injuries, the suffering . . . Do you really believe we can make a difference?"

"We have to," Cyrene said. "Already too many with power will stand aside and expect someone else to stop evil. We can't join their idleness and allow the world to fall into darkness."

Static on the radio buzzed, and I listened once more. "B.B.C. has announced television service has been suspended until further notice. During a meeting with the Privy Council today, the king signed orders of complete mobilization of the Army, Air Force, and Navy, among other proclamations."

Ice pushed through my veins. "War has begun," I whispered.

"Britain and France will officially declare war soon, without a doubt," Cyrene said. "Germany has seized all of Austria and Czechoslovakia. Now they take Poland. I find it amusing no one came to our defense when the French occupied Egypt, Algeria, Morocco . . . They sit marionette rulers on our thrones, giving the illusion our countries are still ours, yet the colonizers pull the strings."

She spat that last word as though it were venom in her mouth. She took another sip of her tea. When the cup left her mouth, her bottom lip quivered until she bit down to stop it.

"They only see us as a people to be subjugated," she continued, "and Germany will do the same to Poland, though I admit their visions of violent grandeur are more sinister. Their goals aren't merely to expand their territory and enslave the Polish people. This is *lebensraum*. A harmless word by itself—it means 'living space'—but to the Reich, it means expanding their race. Their armies will spread, swallowing the world as they feed and grow. This is what's at stake, Ziva, and you're the key to it all."

"Our power could be the weapon they never saw coming," I said, understanding. "Our magic doesn't run out of bullets or grenades. We are stronger than they are, but we're so few in number. And the gods—they would help us if we appealed to them."

"The gods removed themselves from human politics eons ago," Cyrene said sadly. "They've turned their backs to our plight."

"Anubis is on our side, though," I insisted. "He may be the only one so far, but he's the keeper and protector of the dead against evil. The things he's capable of—they must be more powerful than anything humanity could comprehend."

Cyrene offered me a small, weak smile. "Your optimism might be the only thing to keep us afloat."

"Hope has kept my head above water for my entire life," I told her. "When Sayer and Nasira found me, it was like they'd pulled me onto dry land. Now I'm up and running and nothing will stop me."

Her face fell, weary. "But we will need more than optimism to save our lands. After the Great War, Europe was crushed and unable to drag itself out of its own ruin. Both Britain and France were under tremendous domestic pressure not to rebuild their infantries. The memory of the trenches and the gas attacks and the endless killing was still too fresh in their peoples' minds. This was the perfect time for hate and fear to take hold."

"How could an ancient queen who died thousands of years before electricity and airplanes save us from another world war?" I asked. "Forgive me, I don't mean to sound contrary."

She leaned forward and turned the radio's knob all

the way off. "Once Nefertari has fully regenerated, she shall possess powers no army could withstand. Human technology, even modern, would mean nothing to her. Not guns, not bombs. Nefertari will be immortal. A goddess. Nefertari ruled the most prosperous and richest dynasty of the ancient world. She will heal this scorched earth."

I wouldn't continue to question her. Of course, I wanted Hitler and his forces to be stopped. Still, I couldn't help feeling skeptical. The Medjai had power the Nazis couldn't fathom. The gods could lay waste to nations. Was it necessary to upend the entire world to save it? How far did we really need to go?

A warm glow on the horizon told me the sun was about to rise, but Nasira still hadn't stirred. I sat in a chair beside her bed, watching for any signs of distress or even life. So far, she'd rested peacefully. Sayer slouched on a couch in the corner with his arms folded and head hanging. Every time he had dozed off, his face would pinch with pain and he would grumble in his sleep. I didn't know what his dreams contained, but I knew they couldn't have been sweet.

Nasira stirred groggily and drew a deep breath only to shudder in pain. A low groan escaped her. I leaned forward and whispered her name. She gave no response.

"*Psst*, hey!" I hissed harshly at Sayer. He continued to snooze. I grabbed one of the unused pillows and tossed it at him. He jumped awake, looking about himself in confusion. I waved to catch his attention and pointed down at his sister. He understood at last and shot to his feet. In one long stride, he reached her.

"Nasira?" he whispered with such tenderness. He smoothed his hand over her head. "It's me. Ziva's here too."

She opened her eyes, looking first at her brother and then at me, blinking hard and frowning.

"Good morning, spitfire," I said gently with a smile, warm with relief.

Her bottom lip trembled, and her complexion reddened. Her hands took tight fistfuls of the silky sheets. Her huge, round lamb's eyes filled with tears. She looked like a little girl and my heart ached for her. She inhaled shakily and exhaled a single word, "Mum?"

The warmth I felt cracked and split like ice. I looked at Sayer.

He licked his lips and opened his mouth to speak, but his hesitation and silence told her everything. She burst into tears, covering her face with the sheet and rolling over onto her side toward me. I draped over her like a shield, holding her tight and murmuring to her softly.

"I'm sorry, Nasi," Sayer said. "It should've been me in the car with you. It should've been me, not Mum."

"She died for something great," I urged, fractured by the guilt in his voice.

Nasira stared at me, her face red and stained with tears, and she said tightly, "If you've never loved anyone, then you don't know what's worth dying for."

The breath rushed from Sayer and he pulled his sister

into his arms. I stared at her shuddering form, my brain smacked clean. Sayer met my gaze and he offered me an apologetic look.

I understood Nasira hadn't meant to hurt me. She was right after all. What was worth dying for? What had this world ever done for me that I would die for it?

I was in no position to say a word to either of them. No matter how many times I told Nasira and Sayer how sorry I was for them, how sad I was, how fervently I wished everything had gone differently, how much we would make Kauket suffer for what she did . . . No words could bring back Haya or make anyone feel any less pain. I may not have had any experience in dealing with loss, but I knew that much. They said time eased pain, but I didn't know how much time was needed. I didn't know what Nasira and Sayer needed at all. I could only sit, helpless, and watch them suffer.

Once Nasira had cried herself back to sleep, Sayer and I stepped out into the hallway. He pulled his mussed hair from its tie and refastened it tighter. He tucked wisps of his dark hair behind his ears.

"Have you had any sleep at all?" he asked kindly.

I shrugged. "Not sure I could."

"You should try," he said. "You'll be surprised how tired you are once you hit that pillow. Sleep is healing, I promise you."

I offered him a small smile and nodded in agreement. "I admire you for being strong for your sister."

He dropped his head, his brow furrowing, and he seemed to search for his words. "I don't know if I'm being strong. Sitting and feeling sorry for myself won't change things. What happened was out of my hands. The only thing I do have control of is what I choose to do next. I choose to carry on."

He turned to leave and paused, gazing down into my face. A strange emotion seemed to come over him, one I couldn't identify. I'd once teased him about reading my mind, and the intensity in his gaze made me wonder if he really could. He seemed to search desperately for something in my eyes and I wished, between the two of us, I was the mind reader. I admired his resilience, but he needed to allow himself to grieve.

Still, if I were in his place, I wouldn't allow myself to grieve in front of others. What could he or I or anyone do with sympathy? It couldn't change anything. The only thing to do, as he said, was carry on.

"What you did tonight was fearless," he said at last. "I'll be eternally grateful for your trying to protect my family. Your heart is strong—and it's not just your queen's blood. You are astonishing, Ziva. I haven't known you long, but I know you're capable of anything."

It seemed as though 'thank you' couldn't express how grateful and inspired his words made me feel. "I'm honored you have such faith in me," I told him. "I only hope I can live up to it."

One side of his mouth pulled into a tiny smile. "You have—and I pray you find equal faith in me."

"I do," I urged.

His hand lifted and held the side of my face, his skin warm as his fingers threaded into my hair, his thumb brushing the line of my jaw. "Get some rest."

He pulled away and left me standing alone in the sudden absence of his heat. I hadn't noticed my hammering pulse until now.

Across the hall was an empty, dark, and quiet room I'd chosen for myself. I pulled the curtains to block out the morning sunlight and climbed into the huge bed. Nothing had ever felt softer or sweeter. I lay there, praying Sayer was right and I'd catch sleep quickly, but every time I closed my eyes, I saw Nasira's broken body. Haya's lifeless form. Blood on pavement glittering in the beam of headlights. I heard the whine and grind of the car as it was crushed. Kauket's horrible voice as she repeated Haya's last words to her daughter. Those visions and sounds followed me into my nightmares.

I woke to harsh knocking on the door. I had no idea how long I had slept. I threw the blankets off and climbed out of bed. In the hallway stood Cyrene.

Before I could say anything, she announced, "Gear up. We're flying to Cairo."

Cyrene had chartered an entire Imperial Airways airship for our voyage. The single-deck vessel was a fraction of the size of the gigantic zeppelin we'd crossed the Atlantic on, but it was at least as luxurious. The interior was made of several compartments besides the main passenger seating, including two lavatories, a lounge, and a dining room. As we approached Cairo, I was glued to the port-hole at my seat. I couldn't contain my excitement. Our descent from the clouds was achingly slow. My desper-ation to see Egypt with my own eyes was maddening.

Nasira passed me on the observation deck and I lifted my head, hoping she'd notice me and say something. We hadn't spoken since the night her mother died. I'd never been around a grieving person I cared so much about. I didn't know what I could do to make her hurt less. Sayer explained to me how everyone grieved differently, just as they worked or loved differently. He mercifully had not shut me out as his sister had, though he assured me not to take her behavior personally. Nasira felt all her emo-tions with as much passion as anyone could, and she did not hide them or her thoughts.

She made me realize I tended to do the opposite, per-haps because there'd never been anyone to express my emotions to. I bottled them up so only I suffered them. Nasira made sure everyone around her felt the way she did. I supposed there were two kinds of people, those who took their feelings out on others and those who took their feelings out on themselves. Sayer and I were a lot alike; I knew which type he was. What I didn't know, and what he wouldn't give away, was how much he suf-fered beneath the surface.

Soon the milky haze of clouds turned to gold as

Egypt's endless desert gleamed into view. I glued myself to the window to take it all in. When I saw the colossal sphinx of sand and stone, tears crept down my cheeks. She was the most beautiful and unreal thing I'd ever lain eyes on. Beyond her, the trio of pyramids she'd watchfully protected for thousands of years rose toward the sun. No photographs could have possibly captured their majesty in real life.

The muddy waters of the Nile, its flooded banks green with crops, divided the desert from the cramped, bustling city of Cairo. We passed low over its flat-topped roofs and shining domes, our gentle wake brushing the fronds of palm trees. I couldn't wait to get out of this steel balloon and into the streets to explore.

Our ship steered toward the airport, a sprawling building surrounded by aircrafts of all shapes and sizes from single passenger jets to luxurious airliners. Zeppelins, both large and small, hovered above the ground, tethered by mooring lines. Cairo was already one of the busiest airports in the world and had grown into the gateway to the rest of Africa, Asia, and Australia. Two flags waved from the roof, the British and Egyptian Nationalist flags. We slowed, and I watched the ground crew snatch our own mooring lines and tie us down. Our captain's voice came over the intercom, announcing our arrival and instructing us to proceed to the dock. We gathered our things and emerged into air so dry and hot I felt as though I were standing in front of an open oven. I drew a deep breath with difficulty.

"Take this," Sayer said, appearing at my side. In his

hand was a long scarf, and he helped me wrap it around my neck and over my nose and mouth, giving me immediate relief. He adjusted his own scarf and pulled a hood over the top of his head.

"Thank you!" I shouted over the deafening diesel engine of the airship.

He nodded once to acknowledge my thanks.

Men wearing the traditional *jellabiya* lead tawny camels, taller than any horse, by roped halters. I smelled spices from a tea cart just outside the terminal entrance. The woman attending the cart smiled at me. I knew she wasn't Medjai—there was no spark of magic about her—but her skin, eyes, all of her . . . She looked like me. Most of the people here looked like me. This land was where I'd been born.

Sayer leaned close and put a hand to the small of my back. "Welcome to Egypt. You are home."

CHAPTER

16

I didn't listen to a word of Cyrene's instructions, and I paid no attention to any of the others. My focus was solely on taking in absolutely every last detail around me.

European, American, and Asian couples and families headed to and from the planes and airships carrying their luggage or leading attendants carrying their luggage. Quite a few of them, people of all nationalities, spoke French. I saw a team of what could only be archaeologists. The men and women were dressed too practically and carried too much gear on their backs to be tourists. I'd need to pick up one of those wide-brimmed hats myself. Spending my life in the perpetual diesel smog of Manhattan had not prepared me for this strong sunlight.

A small hand snatched my suitcase from me, taking me by surprise. A boy, maybe nine or ten, seemed to hold it hostage with one palm open. "*Baksheesh*," he demanded several times. "I will carry your bag for you. It's too heavy for you." Nasira swatted at him, speedily snarling something in Arabic, and won back my suitcase.

Someone shouted in German, grabbing my attention. I turned and saw two dozen or so uniformed soldiers marching away from a tethered zeppelin designed plainly like it was designed for cargo, not luxury. The red sashes around the soldiers' left arms were unmistakable. Nazis. Descending from the cargo ramp from the zeppelin's underbelly were several ten-foot-tall bipedal mechanical suits, spewing black diesel smoke, piloted by soldiers whose faces were protected behind reinforced metal mesh. Hydraulics hissed and made the suits jerk, rattling the automatic guns in their chunky hands.

"What on earth are those?" I asked, bewildered and a little nervous.

"I've never seen anything like them," Sayer remarked, his voice dark and low.

Observing the troops and machines was a smartly dressed pair whose faces were concealed by sunglasses: a very tall white man in an officer's cap, the tails of his decorated coat waving in the wind, and a slim civilian woman with blond hair curled and pinned impeccably behind her ears. She wore a lovely duck egg blue dress with fluttery sleeves and a matching belted cloche. Whoever she was, she was high society. Other soldiers arranged boxes and unloaded crates from the cargo platform that had recently been dropped from the airship's belly.

Before I could wonder too long about why Germans would come here, considering how much was going on in their homeland, two soldiers in brown British uniforms approached the officer and his female companion. They were armed, but their rifles were secured in holsters behind their heads. After a few moments, the British soldiers walked away. I understood the British currently occupied Egypt and, though there was no official war yet between them and Germany, the relations had to have been tense.

"What do you suppose they're here for?" Sayer asked, appearing beside me.

"I'm not sure," I replied. "From the looks of all they brought, they intend to stay a while."

"Hopefully they keep out of our way," Sayer muttered. "We don't need to get caught up with Nazis or the British."

I nodded in agreement and continued to watch the soldiers. The woman in the dress called to the team of archaeologists and they conversed rapidly in German over the contents of a canvas bag.

"That concerns me," Sayer murmured low. "German archaeologists working by themselves—nothing unusual. German archaeologists working with soldiers is an issue. They've been digging all over Europe for Ancient Nordic artifacts, anything magical and related to their people's history. I'm afraid to know what they're doing here."

The German woman turned her face toward me and lowered her sunglasses. Her red lips formed a tight line as she studied me in return. I wondered who she was and why she traveled with soldiers. One of them dropped a crate and she whirled on him hotly, barking orders.

"Come on," Sayer said, and I started to follow him. "We're off to the Pyramidion now. You'll love it there."

We climbed into cars along with the rest of the Medjai and drove away from the airport. The heat made the horizon dance and sway to the beat of Cairo's urban bustle. Both swanky and rickety motorcars honked at donkey carts and camels packing the streets, which grew more cramped the farther into the city's heart we roamed. The flat-roofed buildings shone gold in the sun and the infinite shades and colors of shutters, curtains, flowers, fruits, intricately designed rugs, and market carts were an exciting feast for the eyes.

I rolled down my window to see better—to experience Cairo. The aromas of spices and curing meats I'd once imagined in my head had come to life deliciously. It took everything in me not to open my door and leap out into the chaos, but I would remain where I was instructed and obey. For now.

Sitting at small tables outside restaurants and tobacco shops were *jellabiya*-clad Egyptians and Westerners in the latest European and American fashions. Men smoked fat cigars and women lounged beneath parasols and hats. People in every direction chatted in a variety of languages. I noticed the Western hairstyle of pinning up the hair in the front with longer curls in the back was popular among Egyptian women. Some of them even wore Western buttoned dresses with short, puffy sleeves. Common were thick lines of kohl around eyes, reminding me of the ancient style, and bold scarlet lips.

"Lots of Egyptian women don't dress much differently than American women," I observed.

"That's due to European occupation," Sayer said with a

shrug. "Colonialism has . . . a smothering effect. The official language of Egypt's government isn't Egyptian Arabic. It's French."

As we turned a corner, I noticed the crowds on both our sides grew denser and gradually took up more and more of the street. Through the shouts, there came a rhythm—a chant, I was sure of it. I strained to make out exactly what the people chanted, but the words were lost among the blend of French, Arabic, and English outbursts. Our car slowed to a crawl as the people swamped us and barely let us pass. Their angry faces and balled fists filled my vision. Hands beat on the hood and trunk of our car and those in front of us.

A woman's furious shouts crashed through my window: "Egypt is ours! Get out! No British!"

Sayer put a soft hand on the back of mine. "Protests against British occupation grow worse every year," he explained. "Britain returned Egypt's independence years ago, but their military presence remains. The treaty was a meaningless piece of paper. They'll never give up Egypt, especially after the Great War. They need control of the Suez Canal. Britain doesn't have the land to farm enough food to sustain its population, which is why they invaded and seized so many countries. The Suez is their primary trade route and strategically important passage between the West and the East. Britain can't afford to lose it, especially not now."

I nodded, understanding. "And the Egyptian people want control of our own country and resources, which we deserve. With war imminent once again, I understand why the British won't leave."

"The situation is frightening," Sayer admitted. "Different kingdoms have fought over Egypt since the beginning of its history."

We pulled onto a quieter street where off to our right rose a fifteen-or sixteen-foot solid stucco wall. Above it draped heavy branches thick with leaves. The acacia trees and their heavy yellow flowers towered over the road, but I caught glimpses of the massive building they concealed. We rounded the curb and approached an iron gate, which parted wide for us to pass through and became enveloped in dense bushes of pink Egyptian star clusters. Their blooms brushed the side of our motorcar as we pulled forward toward an incredible courtyard. The walls and dense foliage made this place seem quieter, as though we'd wandered into another world altogether.

The Pyramidion itself turned out to be a magnificent palatial estate. Two wings of long, beautiful colonnades guarded both sides of the courtyard. The second-story windows, twice the height of the average man, boasted elegant shutters and breezy linen curtains. Each sat in its own arched alcove with a small, private balcony over-looking the gardens. We rolled in front of the palace's main wing, where an incredibly long portico spanned the entrance's entire length. A trio of gigantic doors, shuttered and topped with half-moon skylights, greeted us beneath a wide balcony. A couple of Medjai waved at us from its balustrade.

We stopped by a glittering fountain filled with gigantic

blue lotus blossoms, a color reminding me of Anubis's eyes. When I opened my door and stepped out, I deeply inhaled the fresh air fragrant with flowers and earth. The temperature was very warm, but dry and bearable, and the courtyard patio was made of a variety of flat stones fitted together like a puzzle. Pots of flowering white jasmine and rich dragonwort sat in corners and on steps, and green vines coiled and hung from trellises over iron patio tables and chairs. Medjai emerged through bright turquoise-painted and natural-stained wooden doors to welcome their visitors. The sounds of footsteps blended with the tweeting of birds and human voices.

"Baba!"

I turned my head in the direction of Nasira's shrill, gleeful cry and saw her burst out of the crowd and leap into the arms of a bearded man halfway down the steps of the portico. He squeezed her tightly as though the wind might carry her away if he loosened his grip. His mouth moved, but I couldn't make out what he said to her. Sayer slipped past me and when his father saw him, he raised an arm to grip his son's shoulder and tug him into their embrace. They grieved together for the first time over their loss and I grew slowly aware of how quiet everyone else had become.

When they parted, Nasira's father kissed her on top of her head. He was a handsome man with a kind gaze and warm, umber skin. He hadn't spoken a word to me yet, but I saw where Sayer got his gentleness.

Sayer came to my side and placed a hand on the small of my back. "Father, this is Ziva Mereniset," he said.

His father's eyes widened and then grew so very, very sad. "You look like your mother. I'm honored to meet you. My name is Tariq Bahri."

"I can't even begin to express how terribly sorry I am over the loss of your wife," I said, trying not to think about Nasira's biting words after I'd offered my condolences. "Haya was kind to me."

"Your words are appreciated," he replied. "Please, follow me to your suite. Your belongings will be dropped off there shortly."

As soon as I began to follow him, I felt a tug at my hand. I turned. Nasira offered me a kind smile. It was the first time she'd looked at me since that night. Perhaps she felt more at peace now that she was home and reunited with her father. Of course, I forgave her for shutting me out. Her grief wasn't about me. I was glad, though, to see her smile, weak as it was. However she was able to heal, I hoped she did. I knew from experience, even if she'd been right and I'd never loved anyone before, I still knew pain—the pain of loneliness and fear and abandonment. She would heal, like I had, but that deep, deep wound would scar, like mine had.

I smiled back at her, offering as much kindness as I could with a simple look. Then I followed Tariq into my home.

My home.

The rose granite floor of the foyer was complimented with geometric mosaic designs, each tesserae shining with gold leaf. A soft current of perfumed air flowed from the main doors and through the perimeter of lotus columns around an open peristyle. The garden within was a lush refuge and reminded me more of an original Egyptian peristyle than a Greek or Roman one.

In the foyer, plush leather and upholstered furniture with brass hardware sat around polished and glittering wood coffee and buffet tables. Limestone extracts carved with Egyptian hieroglyphs were mounted on the wood paneled wall, and it took everything in me not to reach out and run my fingers over the faces of beautiful rose granite busts of kings and queens sitting on pedestals. I marveled at framed displays of glossy faience amulets, gemstone-encrusted pectorals, and invaluable jewelry from antiquity. Iron chandeliers hanging from a concave limestone-inlaid ceiling, and glass lamps on end tables offered a warm glow to the long and narrow room.

"I understand this is your first time back in Egypt since you were born," Tariq said as he led me around the peristyle and into a wide corridor with a very high, arched ceiling. "Cyrene has explained your situation to me. I'm also very sorry for the loss of your parents."

"Thank you," I replied. "I wish I knew what happened to them."

He cast me a reassuring smile. "They saved you."

The corridor was very long, and I ventured this was one of the colonnade wings I'd admired from outside.

"I went ahead and prepared for you the rooms that had once belonged to your mother and father," Tariq explained. "This was their home when they weren't deployed in Kent or elsewhere. They were quite devoted to each other, your parents. They went everywhere together. Here we are."

He stopped to open a door, revealing a beautifully ornate suite decorated in shades of bright turquoise and rich ochre. We stood in a sitting area full of brocade furniture and fabrics woven into beautiful, colorful patterns. The ceiling was high and inlaid with mismatched beveled wood, and the floor was cool stone beneath my boots. On the other side of a gorgeously carved marble archway was the adjacent bedroom with a fireplace against the golden ochre stucco wall. An armoire and a desk were placed on the wall opposite the enormous window and balcony which overlooked the courtyard.

"No one has told me what my parents were like, only what they did," I admitted.

"Have you ever seen a picture of them?" he asked. When I shook my head, he beckoned me toward the nightstand by the canopied bed. He picked up a frame and handed it to me.

I greedily absorbed the image of my mother and father, Satiah and Qadir. They didn't look much older than I was, and they smiled at the camera with their arms around each other. Tariq was right; I looked like my mother. Her face from my single memory of her flashed into my mind. Now that I saw her with such a happy, carefree expression, I could identify the naked anguish she wore when I saw her last. It hadn't been raining. Her face was slick with tears. Why? Because she had to leave me? Because something terrible had happened, or would happen? Where had my father gone that day?

"Did they surprise you?" I asked, looking up at Tariq. "When they left?"

A peculiar expression came over him. His brow furrowed, and his gaze fell and darted around the floor a few times. When he lifted his head to look at me, he said, "That's an interesting question. With perfect honesty, yes and no. I understood their decision, because I am a father, but I was astonished to find they went through with it. Your parents loved you even more than they loved each other."

His words warmed my heart, and at the same time a sense of loss grew in my chest like a huge void. I was left with a feeling of longing, because I'd never know how much my parents had loved me. I ached to know what that felt like—to love and be loved, to know how it felt to have a love you'd kill and die for. How could anything possibly incite such a beautiful violence?

"Thank you," I told him, knowing the simple words could never articulate the extent of my gratitude.

"Of course, darling girl." He dismissed himself and turned to leave.

And I was alone in my parents' suite. The air in the room had a soft, warm scent with a light, spicy musk beneath a breath of jasmine. Is this what they'd smelled like? The furniture was finely carved and gave an antique impression. The wood paneling alternated between engraved wood and hand-painted murals of Egyptian gardens. Stuffed bookcases stretched to the ceiling. Framed paintings depicting daily life in a Cairo souk hung on the sitting room wall on either side of the double doors leading back into the hallway.

In the bathroom, the wall sconce gave the cream marble flooring an amber glow. A few items sat on the vanity, including a cosmetics box. I peeked inside to find it neatly organized with brushes, a kohl pot, several lipsticks, and a palette of eye paint. I imagined my mother sitting at this very mirror and applying her purifying kohl for battle. These were her things, I was certain of it.

Thinking of my mother made me feel heartsick for Sayer and Nasira, who knew and loved their mother before she was torn from them so violently. Perhaps there was something that could be done. I had connections after all.

The jackal amulet was cool in my palm. "Anubis?" I said aloud, hoping he'd hear me.

"Yes?"

I jumped and spun around to find Anubis standing in the middle of the room wearing a serene expression. Something changed in his face after a moment and he looked around himself in bewilderment. "This is the Pyramidion. I've been summoned here once before, but I wasn't aware it could still be done. There have been wards against immortals over the Pyramidion for eons."

I cringed. "I didn't break a rule, did I?"

"Not unless someone finds out," he said, with a certain darkness in his playfulness.

My heart pounded, but I forced myself to find courage. "I have a request, or maybe it's even a deal, if that's how these things are done. I'd like to make a deal with you."

He eyed me, not with suspicion, but cool interest. "I don't make deals with mortals, but you may make your request."

"I need to learn a particular magic," I elaborated. "And it's not for me. I have nothing to gain from it."

"What kind of magic?" he asked, intrigued, but cautious now.

"Creation."

Anubis frowned, his brow wrinkling over those beautiful eyes. "Ziva, the only way for mortals to create life is to have a child. No magic can do what a woman can."

"Then you must do it," I begged him. "Bring Haya back. There must be something that can be done. Nefertari died thousands of years ago and she can be resurrected. Why not Haya? Her family needs her. The ritual for her entombment is tonight and I'm out of time to make this right."

"Set used very, very dark magic to enable Nefertari's resurrection," Anubis explained. "Magic we don't fully understand yet and could be darker than we can even imagine. A Medjai can use creation magic to bring a wax bird to life, but it has only a life force."

"But it would be *alive*," I insisted.

He shook his head. "If you were to use magic to give life to a human body, the mortal flesh, the heart might beat but the *person* isn't there. There is no unique character or self, no soul. They possess no emotion or intention. Those creatures are shells. Do you understand?"

"Yes." I felt heavy, deflated and sorrowful. "It would be cruel." I remembered the poor cats I resurrected at the British Museum. They had become monsters. I couldn't imagine doing that to someone I cared about.

"I'm sorry," Anubis said. "Truly. I know why you want this magic and I sympathize. Those who've died can't return to the mortal world without a powerful god's interference and that interference has consequences."

I nodded. "Nefertari can only be resurrected in a very specific way in order to be whole."

"I wish I could help your friends too," the god of death admitted, and I believed him. "Try not to despair. Death is only the beginning. It's the gateway of a mortal's transcendence to immortality. Death is not always beautiful to behold, but the endless peace awaiting a soul is indeed."

"And for those left behind?" I asked. "They suffer. Nasira and Sayer suffer. What about all the experiences they'll never have with their mother? What about everything I never had with my own parents? Death is the end of dreams."

His voice and expression gentle, he replied, "Death is not the end, but only a change. Those left behind will bear the weight of sadness, but you bear it and walk on. This is what makes life so precious. You must remember nothing would bring more happiness to the loved ones you've lost than for you to live a beautiful life. Miss them, but live."

Anubis's compassion filled my heart with so much love and hope and peace. I had imagined the god of death to be dark and fearsome, rather than more human than us all. And I understood what he tried to explain. Sadness was all right to feel. I had my own life to live and couldn't let that sadness bury me. My own dreams would continue, as my life would continue, even when those of my parents and Haya had died with them. And yet—who decided what was worth the death of dreams?

"Ziva." Anubis frowned. "You look troubled. What's the matter?"

"Nasira said something to me I don't suppose I'll ever forget," I told him. "She said I don't know what's worth dying for, because I've never loved anyone before. She's right. I had a friend in New York, but Jean wasn't my mother. Losing her isn't like Nasira losing her mother. I had hoped to find family when I agreed to go with her and Sayer. I want friends. Someone to love. Someone to love me back."

My eyes burned from the salty sting of tears I knew were coming. I supposed that was the trouble with holding in all your emotions. One day they'd break free, all of them at one time, a broken dam. I sputtered through my tears and loosed a long wail, mourning everything I should've had and was stolen from me, mourning what I could've had with Jean if I'd let her become my family, mourning what my friends had brutally lost. I couldn't have been the only person in the world who felt so desperately alone that they'd do anything not to be. My fists were so tight my fingers grew numb and cold; relief came when his warm hands pried mine apart. Anubis let me squeeze his hands as hard as I needed to until I'd cried myself out. When I calmed down and all my tears were smeared across my cheeks, I opened my eyes and looked into his face.

"You aren't alone," Anubis urged, his hands tightening on mine. "I am so deeply sorry you have hurt like this your whole life."

I pulled my hands from his and wiped my tears, unable to shake my embarrassment. I hadn't wanted anyone to see so deeply into my heart, to see all of the vulnerability spilling out of me. Now that I had, I saw the value in letting someone see my pain. I'd always been so afraid that receiving someone's pity and sympathy would make me feel weak and sorry for myself. I'd been so wrong. This was compassion, and it made me feel like I wasn't alone anymore.

"Why do you hide your feelings from people who care about you?" Anubis asked.

I shrugged, sniffling. "They have their own problems to deal with. I don't want to be one more."

He studied my face earnestly, his gaze digging deep. "You're not a burden, Ziva. Your pain doesn't make you unworthy of love. You've survived, and you'll always live with it. Wear your past and your pain like a medal of honor. Your friends can help you with whatever you're going through if you communicate with them."

"Thank you," I told him, sniffling like a child. "I know I'm not alone. Even though Sayer is going through so much, he's looking out for me. It ought to be the other way around right now."

Anubis softened with sympathy. "He cares for you

because he's a good friend. I'm sure your presence comforts him too. Everyone needs to have that person."

"Who's yours?" I asked, but I wasn't prepared for the startled and unsure look on his face.

"My mother, I suppose," he replied.

"Do you have any friends?"

"No," he said. "I've known mortals, been familiar with them, but they die."

I couldn't believe I'd asked him such a thing, to remind him of all that he'd lost. But that had never occurred to me. "I—I didn't mean—"

"Death is natural," he assured me.

My cheeks felt hot. "I know someday I'll die . . . but if you need a friend . . . I'll be there for you."

He smiled, and his gaze faltered for a moment before raising to meet mine again. He was a terribly beautiful creature and so much more human than I would have expected. "Thank you. I'd like that."

"What's she like?" I asked. "Your mother."

His expression grew pensive. "Nephthys is the powerful Nile, and nothing can control her. She is the beautiful and imperishable and loyal moon illuminating the night. She is the stars, promising endlessness to the universe and guiding us through the dark and the desert."

"I'd love to meet her someday," I said with a smile. "What is your father like?"

A troubled look came over him and his brow bunched tightly, darkening his eyes. "My father . . . is not my mother's husband. She is married to Set. Has been since nearly the dawn of creation. Not long after they were united, the netherworld was threatened by the great serpent Apophis. Set was the greatest warrior of the immortals and he destroyed Apophis, but he betrayed us all with a terrible act of greed. He subsumed Apophis's power—and the evil along with it. Set made himself a monster.

"My mother continued to love him, but he had changed," Anubis continued. "She tells me of how sad and lonely she was. She longed for a child's love, not because she thought it would save their relationship, but because she wanted to save herself. After what he'd done, Set had been corrupted and couldn't give her a child. She turned to Osiris, the King of the Dead. Already jealous of Osiris's position and power, Set discovered Nephthys had conceived, and he murdered Osiris. He tore the corpse into a thousand pieces and those thousand pieces still weren't enough to slake his fury. His unconditional love for Nephthys let him forgive her. He'd saved every last drop of his rage for Osiris."

I swallowed hard, troubled by Anubis's story and the despair it brought him. "But your mother has you. And she's happy now."

He mustered a weak smile. "Yes. I believe she's happy. Magic resurrected Osiris, at a cost, but Set would love to tear him apart again."

A thought struck me, one that chilled my bones. "The queen's heart Set was promised when he made the deal with Nefertari . . . It possesses a great power, one that could immortalize her. Possibly make her a goddess.

237

What if Set wants to use it to go after Osiris once more—for the last time?"

"We all believe Set would do anything to take from Osiris all he holds dear, especially the throne," Anubis agreed. "If Set could channel the power of the queen's heart to do so, then his actions would make a dark quantity of sense."

"The queen's heart must have limitless powers if Set would use it to destroy another immortal," I said, my voice low with fear. "He seems desperate to get it before Nefertari's resurrection. Perhaps it will lose its magic afterward, or she will become too strong for him to carve it from her chest himself."

"This may seem hard to believe, but," Anubis said, "even though Set's nature is dark, he is not inherently evil. He was terribly betrayed by those he loved. He was wronged, and he has done wrong in return."

"That doesn't mean he's allowed to drag innocent people into his vendetta," I told him. "I won't let him hurt anyone else."

A knock came, and I looked at the door. Cyrene's voice called, "Ziva. It's time."

"Coming!" I replied.

When I turned back, Anubis was gone.

CHAPTER

17

Deep beneath the Pyramidion and the busy streets of Cairo, was the *khertet netjer*, hidden catacombs where the bodies of Medjai were prepared for their journey to the afterlife and then entombed for eternity. Every one of us who died, regardless of whether he or she had perished in battle or succumbed to natural causes, was given the same rites after death and the same spells were performed.

Once the bodies were placed within the preparation rooms, we dressed in ceremonial *hem-netjer* clothing. My dress was made of fine linen, my sandals of papyrus. A jeweled collar with a linen shawl wrapped around my shoulders and was pinned at the center of my chest. Women wore blue sashes over their dresses, while men were bare chested beneath their shawls and their skirts were held with a jeweled belt at their waists. Cyrene, as high priestess, wore an ancient leopard skin over her shoulders and atop her head were poised two falcon feathers.

As rituals were carried out, Cyrene read the spells from a modified version of the Book of the Dead written for Haya, ensuring she would live for eternity in the netherworld among the gods. We recited the incantations alone with Cyrene and beside me, Sayer's voice broke on several occasions. As his mother was wrapped in linen, he gazed upon her for what would be the last time, the expression on his face quiet and stoic.

When we finished, we returned to the surface and I to my room to change out of the ceremonial *hem-netjer* clothing. In my broken heart I knew this wouldn't be the last funeral we'd conduct. I was as certain as the coming night that I would see more of my friends and family laid to rest within the many levels of the cold, dark catacombs.

Days and many hours of studying hieroglyphs and combat training later, Cyrene summoned me to the library of the Pyramidion. It was a gigantic hexagonal room large enough to rival the one boasted by the British Museum. Though it lacked the unique wagon wheel spoke bookshelves, every wall was packed to the ceiling with books. The dome above allowed elegant acoustics and was painted night-sky blue with a smattering of white stars. Egyptian and Hellenistic art decorated open spaces on bookshelves, desks, and end tables between plush, well-worn, leather couches and wood-and-iron desks filling the middle of the room. A stone Assyrian relief and Carthagian busts of women with pleated hair were also displayed with care and I wanted to take a closer look at them. In the center of the gleaming marble floor was a circular mosaic of elegant azure lotus blossoms emerging from the Nile, each tesserae glittering in the daylight.

Cyrene led me to a desk surrounded by a small crowd of Medjai, all of whom inspected two canopic jars. I recognized the baboon head of Hapy on the lid of the jar I found at the British Museum. The second, undoubtedly the one the Medjai had possessed all along, sported a human-shaped face as its lid.

"Imsety," I said, pulling the information from my memory. "Inside is Nefertari's liver."

"Well done," Cyrene praised.

"The translated hieratic on Imsety confirms Dr. Sweeney's claim of finding Hapy at the Ramesseum," Cyrene explained. "Imsety's inscription tells us the third canopic jar, Qebehsenuef the falcon, was buried at the feet of Ramesses II."

"We believe the inscription refers to the Ramesses II colossus discovered in 1820," Tariq added. "It's quite possible the referenced canopic jar may be the one in the Egyptian Museum's possession. With luck, it will reveal the location of the fourth and final canopic jar—"

"—Which in turn should reveal the location of Nefertari's heart," Cyrene finished.

I frowned with worry and said what we all had to be thinking, "If the third canopic jar is at the Egyptian

Museum, couldn't there be a repeat of what happened in London?"

Sayer stiffened beside Nasira, whose gaze faltered for a second.

"We can't allow that again," Tariq said. "Not to any-more of our people. The curator in Cairo is Medjai. Surely there is an inconspicuous way to retrieve the artifact."

"If he travels anywhere near the Pyramidion, he could be spotted by Set's agents," Sayer suggested. "He will be a target."

"Then we'll meet him elsewhere halfway," I offered. "Someplace random, public and unremarkable. We'll travel in small groups to avoid drawing attention. A couple of us will meet with the curator, pick up the arti-fact, while the others stand nearby."

Cyrene nodded and exchanged glances with Tariq. "This ought to work."

"Very stealthy," he agreed. "Where should we meet?"

"Baklava," I said without thinking. Everyone stared at me. "Let's meet at a baklava café, in someplace crowded like a *souk*. If the curator were to stop for something sweet after a work day, that wouldn't be unusual, would it?"

"All right," Tariq said. "I'll make the arrangements."

"Let's move in pairs on motorcycles," Nasira suggested. "We'll be more maneuverable in case we run into trouble."

"Motorcycles?" I asked, backpedaling.

"You noticed the traffic, yeah?" Sayer asked, smiling.

"I'll need your help then," I told him.

His eyes narrowed. "Why?"

I folded my arms. "I've never driven one before."

Sayer led me into the sprawling subterranean garage beneath the Pyramidion. We passed rows of sleek black sedans sitting in silence, mostly Duesenbergs with mean faces and whitewall tires, and approached a dozen or so motorcycles all bearing the blue-and-white-check BMW emblem on their fenders. Their black paint was shiny and flawless—not precisely as inconspicuous as I'd had in mind, but that didn't matter as long as they were fast.

"We'll still stand out on these," I warned him.

"We don't exactly have time to go bike shopping," he said. "So . . . baklava, hmm?"

I knew what he was getting at. "It was the first thing I thought of."

He chuckled. "I'm sure we'll stop there long enough for you to try some."

"You don't even know me," I teased. "Fine. I confess. This was my plan all along."

"How diabolical of you." Sayer rounded the machine, tilting his head to gaze down at it, his expression growing serious. Strands of his dark hair pulled loose from their tie and fell over his eyes. "Come here. Sit."

I obeyed, lifting my leg over the seat and sliding onto the leather. I found a comfortable position and leaned forward to grasp both handles. He stepped close to my left side, his heat radiating against me. He smelled like earth and leather and soap. The planet slowed its rotation; time came to a stop. A low, deep pang struck my belly.

His boot tapped my left one. "Feet on the pedals. Get used to the forward shift in your balance."

His hands wrapped over mine and he kicked out the stand from beneath me. He leaned against me, his broad chest leaving me in his shadow, and he held the motorcycle still.

He squeezed my left hand. "This is your clutch." He squeezed my right. "And your throttle. This silver lever is your brake. Be gentle with them or you'll eat dirt. Be gentle as though they're reins attached to the horse you're riding."

"I've never ridden a horse," I admitted.

"Then be gentle as though this bike is a lover," he suggested coolly.

No matter how hard I tried to stop my smile, it managed to break free in one corner of my mouth. I didn't want to tell him I hadn't had one of those either. My focus drifted to his body over mine, his heat and delicate, musky scent surrounding me, his cheek so close to brushing mine. The thought of him moving his hands to my hips released savage butterflies in my stomach.

"Now, steering and balance are much like riding a bicycle," he advised, getting serious again. "Have you ridden one of those before?"

"Of course. Who hasn't?"

"But do not lean into your turns at first or you'll eat dirt," he warned. "Or rather, the dirt will eat you. Slow down and turn the handles for now. After you've taken a few rides, you can try leaning."

He directed my hands, his fingers tight over mine.

I practiced turning the handles left and right, but my efforts were jerky and lacked confidence. I needed to get a feel for the bike in motion, certain the action of steering and stopping was the only way I would truly learn.

"If you don't feel comfortable, Zee, you're very welcome to ride with me," Sayer offered.

"You just want me to ride with you like I'm your girl," I dared to tease him. No one had ever used a nickname for me before. I'd never had one. Sayer made me feel like I had a place in his world, like I belonged. No one had ever made me feel like I belonged with them. My smile began to grow again. Zee. I liked that. I'd let him call me Zee.

His brow raised as he considered this, and he grinned. I loved when he smiled at me. "I wouldn't say no. But you wouldn't ride with someone because you're their girl." He paused and took a deep breath. ". . . Even if you were my girl."

"Yeah, I'd like my own bike," I admitted, my veins singing at his word. He didn't seem like the kind of man who needed me to need him so he could feel important. I got the impression he wanted me try on my own. He knew I could do anything on my own.

When I felt a sliver of courage, I seized it and added, "Even if I was your girl."

He exhaled. "In all seriousness, it's your call," he said soberly. "I want you to feel safe."

"I am serious," I told him, searching his eyes for anything that would give away what my words meant to him. My silly grin faded but my pounding heart remained at full speed.

Sayer brought down the kickstand and eased the machine to a rest. I swung my leg back over the seat and found solid ground. I shut my eyes and the closeness and warmth of his body radiated against me. I felt everything inside me slow down—my heartbeat, my breathing. He was my whisperer when the world around me was screaming.

I dared to touch the edge of his open jacket and tilted my head back to look up at him. His eyes, soft and dark like staring into an endless night sky, fell on my exposed throat and lifted to meet mine. That one eyebrow again— always the same brow—oh the effect it had on me. The way he looked at me made me ache. How could he do this to me? Unravel me from the inside out with just a gaze?

I smoothed one hand across the hard ridges of muscle in his abdomen, sending a sharp shock through my nerves. His breathing became slow and deep. He took hold of my free wrist, magic warming his fingertips, and pulled me even closer until our bodies touched. He had only ever been kind and friendly before. Now, the way he held me, his thumb tenderly brushing over the delicate skin of my wrist, his gentle gaze studying the touch with curiosity before rising to my face, felt more than friendly to me. The sensation he gave me was strange and electric in my body, honeybees zipping through the hollows of my bones.

Sayer licked his lips and dipped his head as I held my breath, waiting for him to kiss me. He hesitated, his richly dark eyes dancing left and right across my face.

He exhaled and kissed my cheek instead, the short hair along his jaw prickling my skin. His nose and mouth brushed my ear and my hair as his hand tucked a stray lock. He pulled back, his heavy gaze roving over my face. His other hand wrapped around the curve of my waist and he closed the remaining space between our bodies.

I felt right at home in his arms, like this was how we were supposed to be. Like he'd held me a thousand times before, even if this was the first. He brushed his other hand across my throat, gently as he would touch a rose in full, delicate bloom. He traced the line of my jaw and tilted my chin up and my head back. He leaned over me and paused, searching my face for hesitation. He wasn't sure what I wanted either. Did I want to change who he and I were? Would a kiss be the next step or our undoing?

He drew back and lifted his hands to cup my flushed face. His dark gaze met mine, questing deep and filling with purpose. "I'm with you, Ziva," he said. "Never forget that. I will stand by you and protect you. Always."

I searched his eyes for answers to why he pulled away from me, my need for him physically painful. "I'm with you too," I told him.

At the clank of an opening door, we sprang apart. Adrenaline flooded through my blood, kicking my pulse back into a race.

"How is the lesson getting on?" Tariq asked, striding toward us and fastening the buckles over the chest of his jacket. Its tail waved behind him. His footsteps on the stone floor echoed through the garage.

I swallowed hard and reached out to the handlebars of the machine I'd tried. "I feel good about it."

"You'll do famously, I'm sure," Tariq told me. The closer he came, the harder he stared at Sayer and me, his eyes darting back and forth between us. He wasn't a fool. He knew he'd interrupted something. I couldn't read Tariq's expression, but he didn't seem angry, and that was good. At least he didn't catch more than what he had. Sayer, in turn, watched me from behind loose strands of his hair, head lowered, chest rising and falling with slight breathlessness.

"I'll gear up," I said. "May I keep the scarf you gave me?"

Sayer nodded briskly and said nothing. He swallowed hard, his eyes hot on me.

I left him with his father and headed back to my room to prepare myself for battle.

Covering as much skin as possible with my pants, boots, and long coat would protect me from the wind and sun. I fastened my buckles tightly and stopped at the mirror to touch up the kohl around my eyes. I felt the magic working, tingling my skin and sharpening my eyesight. The scarf Sayer had given me was black and somewhat sheer, but thick enough to cover the vulnerable parts of my face and neck. After securing my *asaya* and several *was* daggers, I was ready, and I rushed down to the garage where the others had already assembled.

The Medjai were all dressed in their gear—black boots,

pants, buckled coats, and scarves—like me. Nasira handed me a round helmet with a pair of padded steel goggles.

"Two down," she said.

"Two to go," I added. "Then it's the home stretch." This was the first verbal exchange we'd had since her mother died, a detail I hadn't missed.

"Look," Nasira started, drawing her voice low. "I can't stop thinking about that night and what I said to you. It was terrible and no matter what had happened to me, I had no right to say that. And I'm sorry it took all this time for me to say this. I hadn't known how to."

My heart grew heavy in my chest. "No, it's all right. There's nothing to apologize for. We're friends. There's nothing I couldn't forgive you for."

"Famous last words," she warned me with a playful wink. She smiled and after a moment, she threw her arms around my shoulders and hugged me tight. She'd caught me by surprise, but I gathered my senses and embraced her.

Perhaps I was on my way to understanding what it was like to have someone or something I'd die for. I would certainly kill for Nasira. I would kill Kauket for her and for Sayer.

The roar and growl of a motorcycle's engine tore us from the moment. The smell of diesel fuel filled the garage. Tariq lifted the tall, wide doors to reveal a violet twilight hanging over Cairo.

Sayer fitted his helmet over his head and said to me as he buckled the strap beneath his chin, "Remember not to lean into your turns. Take it easy. Play daredevil another day." He slid his goggles over his eyes.

"Nasira," Cyrene called above the engines. "You're with your father. Stand by two blocks from the rendezvous point. Sayer, go with Ziva. I will secure a perimeter. Pick up the package and meet here. No scenic routes, no pit-stops. Move out."

Nasira and Tariq sped from the garage first. I started my machine gently as Sayer had instructed me. He nodded to me in approval and gestured for me to go ahead of him.

I charged forward, climbing a slope to emerge at ground level and along the Pyramidion's exterior wall. I passed through the rear entrance's open gates and purposefully took a deep, leaning turn into the busy streets. I didn't look over my shoulder to make sure Sayer had seen, but the revving of his engine assured me he had. I weaved through traffic, handling my machine quite well enough to impress myself.

Sayer pulled up beside me at the next intersection. "How do you feel on that bike?" he called to me.

I gave him a thumbs-up. "Five by five! You ready to take the lead?"

"As long as you're good to follow. You've memorized our route, yeah?"

"Yes—there and back."

He nodded in acknowledgment and kicked his bike into gear. We zig-zagged, making quick work of the much slower motorcars and trucks. I tried not to ride too closely to any of the donkeys or camels to save from spooking them, but the animals were so accustomed to the Cairo chaos they didn't even notice us. Overhead, zeppelins, twin-engine planes, and compact airships passed, blanketing us in shadows. We passed centuries-old mosques, a beautiful *madrasa*, and Roman-era churches. Shopkeepers lit oil lamps beside their signs and around terraces. Tobacco and rug stands didn't appear to be closing up their wares anytime soon. In that sleepless way, Cairo reminded me a lot of New York.

Another large protest filled the street outside a municipal building guarded by British soldiers. The people screamed in several languages, yet they remained a safe distance from the armed guards. I couldn't make out their words beneath the roar of our engines. Their anger was plain on their faces; they wanted freedom—demanded it—and they would fight for it.

Our trek took us to a bustling *souk* filled with street food vendors, shops, restaurants, and cafés. The scent of spices made me forget all about the constant haze of diesel fuel and animal dung. We passed an aromatic coffee shop I'd love to have stopped in. Perhaps the baklava spot served coffee too. It sounded like the perfect combination to me. With regret, I reminded myself Sayer and I weren't out for a night on the town. This was business. The dangerous kind.

CHAPTER

18

Sayer parked his bike in the only open spot nearby and removed his goggles and helmet. I pulled up beside him and did the same.

"Across the street," he said, gesturing with a nod.

He set out at a brisk pace, slipping between traffic slick as a snake, and I followed him with caution, whipping my head back and forth to avoid being run over. Horns honked, and people shouted in different languages at me, but I paid them no mind. We entered an indoor market of sorts whose alley was too narrow for any vehicle to drive through. The floor, walls, and ceiling were made of aged, golden limestone. Vendors selling embroidered pillows, ornate brass lamps, and delicious-smelling cured meats and fresh bread filled the cramped, dry space.

We found our way to an open-air café made of three walls and a roof allowing the sultry scents of its goods to draw in prey from the street. On outdoor terrace tables, white couples smoked cigarettes over their coffee and chatted in French. I even noticed some Egyptians speaking French as well, though they did not sit at the same tables as the white people.

My mouth watered, longing desperately to taste the crisp nut and honey baklava swarming my mind and numbing my thoughts. We pressed through the crowd in front of the baker struggling to keep up with his customers. Sayer pulled out a chair at a small table occupied by one man and joined him. I took the third empty chair.

The Medjai man, his magic buzzing around him, wore elegantly embroidered robes that covered his entire body with the exception of his hands and face. Beneath his hood and behind round, gold-rimmed spectacles, he smiled at us—or rather, he smiled quite pointedly at me.

"Here she is," he beamed just loud enough for only us to hear. "Ziva Mereniset, I presume. My name is Zaman Useramen, curator of the Egyptian Museum and humble servant to the cause—though I am more of an academic."

"It's a pleasure," I told him.

"Oh, dear, the pleasure is mine," he replied, the tone of his voice quite slimy. "You're very beautiful—*very pleasing*. You are a perky young thing!"

"You insult me," I snarled, and with disgust, swallowed the taste of worms his words gave me. As Nasira had taught me, I would never be passive again.

He chuckled and waved a dismissive hand. "One would argue I gave you a compliment."

"The compliment," I informed him darkly, "would have been keeping your *compliments* to yourself."

Sayer leaned forward. "Keep to our business," he warned, his tone grim with malice.

"Business it is then," Zaman agreed, suddenly, wisely nervous. "Since hearing of your rescue, I have been most eager to meet you."

"Rescue?" I asked, my patience lost. "Sayer and Nasira found me, yes, but I was fine."

"Oh, well then, your recovery, rather," Zaman corrected himself. "Welcome home. You've come at a tumultuous time, that's quite certain. So far there hasn't been any violence between the people and the military, but the recent German presence has caused some excitement."

"How so?" Sayer asked, his voice low with concern.

"Many Egyptians want the Germans to drive out the British," Zaman explained tiredly. "I fear we will trade one regime for another. We don't need Europeans to save us from other Europeans. If there weren't so few of us left these days, we Medjai could."

"Soldiers bearing red Nazi sashes arrived at the airport with archaeologists," I told him. "I don't think they're here to liberate Egypt at all."

The curator grew very still in his seat. "There are no German teams on any existing sites right now."

"What about any sites off the record?" Sayer asked.

Zaman shook his head. "None, meaning any excavating they plan to do is without permits and therefore illegal."

"Meaning," I added, "anything they plan to do, they don't want anyone to know about."

The curator's mouth formed a firm, straight line. His

brow crinkled deeply. "The situation grows more con-
cerning every day. I'll organize a team of my people to
investigate."

"Do you have the package?" Sayer asked.

"Yes, yes," the curator said.

He lifted a strap from across his chest attached to a
long cylindrical leather satchel from over his head. Sayer
took the cylinder and popped the lid. He took a peek
inside before holding it close to me so I could see. Inside
was a falcon-headed canopic jar. He needn't remove it
and risk exposing us.

The magic buzzing around the jar felt as familiar to
me as my own magic. Nefertari's life force within me
knew this object. "That's it," I confirmed to Sayer.

"How, may I ask," Zaman said, leaning closer to us, "do
you know without fully examining the artifact?"

I started to reply, but Sayer interjected.

"Something to do with her queen's blood," he said
vaguely.

"Ah," the curator huffed. He didn't appear satisfied
at all.

Sayer replaced the cylinder's cap and got to his feet.
"We'll be seeing you, Zaman. Thanks for this."

The curator frowned. "Do let me know if there's anything more you need!"

I rose to follow Sayer toward the front of the restaurant as he swung the satchel over his head and secured
the straps. In the corner of my eye, I swore I glimpsed
the German woman from the airport who had looked at

me. When I tried to find her face in the restaurant crowd again, she was curiously gone.

"He's a slippery one," I remarked when I'd caught up to Sayer.

One corner of his mouth crunched into a frown. "And, unfortunately, useful." Sayer stopped in his path and turned to me to speak in a low voice. "There are several German SS soldiers outside."

I looked past him and noticed two men in Nazi uniforms standing on the edge of the street. They weren't speaking, and their gazes were watchful. I glanced across the café so see if I could spot their female companion but failed to.

"We should wait," I said to Sayer.

He nodded. "We don't know what they know or want, or if they're looking for something. Someone. But don't be nervous."

"I'm cautious," I corrected.

"Good," he said. "Act natural."

He watched me back for another moment before looking to his right and raising his hand. He called something in French and I frowned. I needed to learn more than one language quickly if I wanted to make life easier for myself. I couldn't rely on someone else to do all my communicating while in Egypt.

"How many languages *do* you speak?" I asked Sayer, half-amused, despite the tension in the atmosphere.

He looked at me side-long and a tilt of his head. "Barely, well, or fluently?"

A harsh breath of surprise rushed from me.

"Egypt has been much more diverse than anywhere in Europe for thousands of years," he explained. "And when another country occupies yours, learning their language might save your life. Often the language of the indigenous people—and their way of life—is made illegal by colonizers, to make colonizing easier for them. It is how languages and cultures die. They are consumed."

"I see," I said. "You seem to be the person everyone goes to for translations of any kind."

He shrugged, rolling my compliment from his shoulders. "I happen to have a knack with languages—as Nasira is a talented fighter. You are too. You think differently than we do, I imagine because you had to in order to survive."

My mouth pinched with a frown. "I still have so far to go to catch up."

"Be kind to yourself," he told me. "You'll learn what you wish with time and hard work."

I looked toward the exit and could no longer spy the Nazis. "I think they've gone."

He followed my gaze. "See? Nothing to fret about."

The cashier reached over the counter and took Sayer's money before planting two squares of baklava in his hands. My eyes shot wide with excitement, filling with the sight of my prize. I greedily accepted the baklava and devoured half of it in one bite. It was gooey, and the flaky bits added the perfect contrast, its flavor honey sweet and a little salty. I savored the taste and texture, and the moment I swallowed, I'd started to stuff the second bite into my mouth.

"Are you all right?" Sayer asked, barely able to contain his amusement.

I held my hand to pause him until I'd finished. "Yes, I am more than all right. That was fantastic."

"Will you cry again?" he teased.

"I might." I noticed he'd tucked the other baklava square into a small paper container. "Aren't you going to eat yours?"

Instead, he handed me the tiny white box. "You'll appreciate it more than I will. This might've been part of the reason I rushed our meeting with Zaman. Don't tell Cyrene we wasted valuable seconds."

I scoffed and secured the package in an interior pocket of my jacket. "Baklava is hardly wasted time." Then I smiled. "Thank you. So, what do you suppose we should do about the Germans?"

"Pray they won't get in our way," he told me. "Let's get moving."

We left the café, and once we found our motorcycles, we fastened our helmets and goggles. Sayer double-checked the satchel's strap across his chest before starting his bike. Though I didn't know exactly where they were, our friends stood by in the surrounding blocks. The souk seemed as busy as it had during the middle of the day when we'd driven through Cairo, and the city's nighttime lights had set the sky aglow. Voices, music, and diesel engines still roared in full swing. Once we were past the souk we could hasten our pace.

Excitement stirred me; I couldn't wait to get home and help translate the jar's inscriptions. We only needed one more after this and once we found the queen's heart, we'd have everything we needed for the resurrection.

My goggles didn't provide the best visibility and I wished I had a free hand to wipe away the dark smudge over the lenses. When I tilted my head, I realized the smudge wasn't on my lenses, but in the road.

The darkness in the street detonated, slamming into the sides of motorcars and smashing them into other machines. Chaos erupted around us and I jammed my breaks so hard the bike nearly flipped over its front end. Sayer skidded to a stop next to me and he tore his goggles from his face. Shadows unfolded like blooms, their petals flowing toward me in their liquid creep. A kriosphinx's form emerged, and people began to scream. The beast's eyes glinted in the motorcycle's headlight.

"From above!" Sayer bellowed.

A second kriosphinx leapt from a roof and landed behind us, shaking the ground and kicking up a cloud of dust. We were surrounded.

"Ziva!" Sayer shouted and yanked the satchel over his head. "Take it and get out of here."

I stared at him, shocked. "No! I'm not leaving you behind!"

He ignored me and shoved the satchel into my arms. "Yes, you are. They want this and you. Don't let them have either. I'll slow them down. Ziva, *go!*"

The kriosphinx raised its head, and its wailing, high-pitched bugle pierced the night, stirring ghosts and demons and all things that inspired unquiet dreams. The hair on my skin prickled and my bones turned to butter.

Furious, I tightened the strap, gave Sayer one last desperate look, and punched the gas. The bike screamed, fishtailing and spraying rocks before finding the ground and rocketing me through traffic. I zipped by the first kriosphinx and as it lunged toward me, Sayer's *taw* spell swept it up off its feet in a cloud of dust and through the air. I heard its body crash into something, but I didn't look back.

Our path replayed in my mind and I remembered where Tariq and Nasira were positioned. I could only hope I'd find them and pass along the artifact to them. Someone had to get it to the Pyramidion. I had to go back for Sayer.

The street ahead darkened and lamps burst, showering glass, before going black. Shadows moved within the shadows, and I gritted my teeth with anger. I leaned deeper and drove faster, hoping I'd slip by the kriosphinx before it blocked my path.

A man emerged from the swarm of netherlight, and surprise took me by the throat. I hit my brakes and leaned back, bracing myself for impact. The bike tipped onto its side and gouged into the dirt, pinning my leg and dragging me as it skid. I cried out with pain, holding the handlebars as hard as I could so I wouldn't be torn apart. When the machine came to a rest, I untangled myself from the wreckage, pulling out my leg from beneath the engine. Blood soaked through my torn jeans. I wiggled my toes inside my boats and was sure nothing had broken. I pushed myself up, staring at the immortal in the street, and I limped a few steps back.

His face was concealed behind a solid gold mask, its expression lifeless, merciless, and inhuman. He crossed his arms, his power pulsing. His form was that of a man's, but he was a monster. The mask evaporated in a plume of gilded smoke to reveal his face, but he seemed no more human than before. He was beautiful in the way Anubis was beautiful, too frighteningly perfect to be earthly. Netherlight flickered bronze on his rich umber skin and his keen, deeply shadowed and penetrating eyes blazed molten gold.

"We meet at long, long last," the god said. "You must be the Medjai they call Ziva. I am Set."

My courage was a flailing creature; I grappled for it and gripped it tight.

"*Taw!*" I cast out my arm, and with it a blast of wind shot toward Set. His face disappeared behind the gold mask again and he waved a hand as if shooing a fly. My magic seemed to evaporate into thin air. Anger stirred my soul, anger at those who had killed my friends, and I welcomed the strength. If the gods would torment me and strangle my heart with pain, then I would use it against them.

I summoned everything I had within me, remembering the sight of Nasira weeping for her mother, remembering my own mother's tear-stained face before she went to die. "*Khet!*"

The spell burst from my hand and rocketed toward Set, spiraling around him, drowning his form in violent light and rolling flame. I peered through the blinding spell, freed my *asaya*, cracked it open, and lunged for him. I screamed as I leapt, whirling my staff with all my strength, my boots pedaling in the air as though it would carry me higher. I swept my *asaya* with a *taw* spell, giving it a lightning pace, and brought it down through the flames.

Set's masked face appeared within the fire, his molten eyes blazing hot like twin suns, and he raised his hand. Magic smashed into my body, hitting me like a truck at full speed. I shrieked and was hurled across the street—a tossed, lifeless doll. My back cracked into a wall, caving in stone and tearing the wind from my lungs, and I crumpled to the ground. My mouth gaped, dragging for air, and I forced my body to unfold from its tight knot. Dirt bit into my palms as I pushed myself to my knees. My muscles and bones screamed at me to stop, but if I obeyed, I would die, and I wouldn't allow that to happen.

The satchel, I realized in horror. My hands shot up, questing. It was gone. My eyes darted around me, searching for where it had fallen.

The god of chaos marched toward me, the last of the dying flames from my spell smoking at his shoulders. Light flashed across his mask, the gold gleaming and blindingly bright, before the shadows in the street turned that cold face colder. "If you grovel, then I might not feed your hands and feet to my kriosphinxes."

I lifted my chin and prayed the keen sharpness in my gaze pierced his arrogance. "You will find to your sorrow I kneel to no one."

"You *will* kneel to a god," Set snarled, the amber rings in his eyes flashing raw gold in dark rock. "Do not allow your ego and that royal blood in your veins to fool you into thinking you are anything but mortal. Magic will never belong to you."

The god of chaos's power pulsed against the ground, tendrils of it snaking toward me. A leather scabbard hung from his waist, a hilt of gold within his reach. I looked past him and spotted the satchel tossed beneath a car crushed into another. As long as Set didn't drop to the ground, he likely wouldn't notice it. I had to distract him long enough for me to retrieve the satchel, grab my bike, and get out of there.

I rose to my feet shakily with pain, but once I was up, I found my strength. He was more wrong than anyone I'd ever met. This magic had been passed to me through thousands of generations just to be mine. It was fated to be mine.

"*Neit,*" I snarled, and sparkling water formed in my left hand. I closed both my palms around the staff of my *asaya* and pushed my spell harder. The magical water formed a current up and down the weapon's length, ready to give my strike the force of a raging river.

I charged at Set, arcing my *asaya* high toward his neck, and as I brought it down, he tore his sword from its scabbard. His blade clashed against mine and my *neit* spell slammed into him. His feet slid backward beneath the power. A shockwave reverberated through the earth, rattling the buildings. I landed, withdrew my weapon, and slashed, lower this time. He met my blade again and an animal growl rolled in his throat. His power rushed me, pushing me back several steps. My *neit* spell faded and I settled back on my heel to regain my balance. He was the god of chaos—he could've liquefied me, but he didn't. Was he holding back? Testing me?

Set let his mask dissipate to reveal a face alight with excitement where I'd expected to find frustration and anger. "Something in your heart gives you more spark than the average Medjai."

My returning grin was dark with challenge. "You didn't know I'm also a New York girl."

Eyes wide and glowing, he murmured, "Magnificent."

I raised my *asaya*, ready to clash again. "Have I disappointed you?"

"Quite the contrary," he replied, his gaze hungry. "You *enjoy* the battle. I appreciate a creature with such a competitive spirit. You are wound tense as a viper. You might think I'll take a chunk out of your hide, but we both know you'll bite first."

"We don't have to fight," I said through gritted teeth. "The entire world is about to erupt into war if those with power don't stop the wrong people from taking it."

"You mistake me for someone who cares about the political squabbling of mortals," he said, annoyed. "Even for one with infinite time, I don't like it to be wasted."

"We won't have to resurrect Nefertari at all if you help us," I urged. "She'll never get what she wants, and your grudge will be satisfied. I have no allegiance to her. There are more important things than blood at stake."

He smiled, serpentine and unsettling. "Oh, this is a great deal more complicated than that."

"Do you mean Osiris?" I dared to ask. "Your king humiliated you and he's the real target of your vengeance."

That smile twisted into a bared-tooth scowl. "If you knew anything at all, you'd beg me for sanctuary."

"We will find Nefertari's heart before you do," I countered unflinchingly. "And once she's resurrected, she'll become too strong for you to take her heart."

Set dropped back his head and loosed a deep, booming laugh that reverberated through the street and against the bones beneath my skin. "Our interests—yours and mine—are the same in the end. You are right. We don't have to be enemies. I might even give you my favor. The stars are yours to seize. If the Medjai told you I mean to kill you, they lied."

"You must think I'm an idiot," I snarled at him.

The amusement on his face hardened. "I think you're quite rude, but I like you and I am more forgiving than others would have you believe. My kind cannot survive in this mortal world, and that is Osiris's doing as a weak king. I want to save my people and allow us to return here. An alliance between us and humankind may be the key to victory for us all. There won't be many chances for you to come with me and that isn't a threat." He extended his right arm to me, palm up, and star-fire burned in his eyes. "Take my hand, Ziva. You think the Medjai have shown you true power? I am Chaos. Let me make you a living god and I can give you the universe."

My teeth bit together. I needed my distraction before I ran out of time. I started to lower myself to the ground, one knee resting in the dirt, and I placed my *asaya* gently beside me. My hand slipped into my pocket.

I hated to do this to my friend, but—"Anubis."

Set gaped wide with confusion. "What?"

Beside me, shadows flashed, and I turned my face away from the burst of netherlight until it faded.

"Oh, no," Anubis murmured, staring at Set.

"I'm so, so sorry," I urged, hoping he knew how truly sorry I was.

Set's gold mask reformed from nothingness, concealing whatever fragment of humanity he might have shown me. He roared in fury, his power detonating like a bomb around him, slamming into every last solid object nearby and crushing it like a can. A storm raged around the god of chaos, sweeping the sand and debris around him into a cyclone. Thunder and lightning crashed within it as if Set was the tempest itself. I lifted my arms over my head as the wind and sand barraged my body. Anubis bared his teeth as he braced himself, his hair whipping around his face. Around us, the storm devoured the city.

"When the sands of eternity swallow the kingdom of Egypt, my power shall be at its greatest," Set bellowed, his hands raised high, his eyes glowing molten gold. "The Heliopolis shall crumble, and shadows will eat its ruin. Darkness will cover the sun and the earth will tremble and split and swallow kings. Chaos will flood the earth and drown the Osirian reign. Chaos will be mine as this world and the netherworld shall be mine."

"This is between you and Osiris!" Anubis pleaded. "Don't take everything down with you!"

Set vanished and reappeared in a blur beside us. He knocked me to the ground and grabbed Anubis's throat. He slammed the younger god's back into a lamp pole, uprooting wood from cracking earth. The pole groaned as it toppled through the air and landed, screeching, on top of a motorcar. The roof caved in, exploding glass. Anubis tumbled over and righted himself. He raised a hand to his face, drew it downward from the top of his head to his chin, and his own mask of gleaming, terrible gold appeared. Black paint outlined the slits revealing his eyes, all that seemed to remain of my friend. A knife of fear shoved into my gut and opened me from navel to ribcage.

Anubis launched at Set, shoving his hands and power into Set's chest and sending him flying into the wall of a building, shattering stone.

Anubis lunged forward, throwing a punch into the side of Set's masked face, and his head snapped to the right with a crack. Set's arm shot forward, taking hold of Anubis by the throat, and he threw the younger immortal at the ground so hard he crushed the pavement.

"Did you think I wouldn't anticipate you protecting the girl?" Set spat at him, the sculpted and painted lips of his mask frozen yet unable to hide the rage hidden beneath.

"Anticipate this." Anubis charged Set, barreling into him and knocking them both into the air, but instead of falling, their forms vanished into shadows. When the darkness dissipated, both immortals were gone.

Staying low, I scrambled toward the lost satchel. I flung

it over my head, tightened the strap across my chest, and darted toward my motorcycle. I started it up and sped off into a narrow alley. The spooked chickens and ducks would have to forgive me. I needed to stay off the main streets to shake any possible pursuers.

I took a hard right onto a wider road and headed toward the next alley.

Blinding headlights and a thundering horn overwhelmed my senses.

I hit the brake hard and threw up my hands with a scream of terror and surprise. My instinctive *taw* spell slammed into a massive truck, smashing its grill and lifting it off the ground. Its undercarriage filled my vision as it flipped and landed upside down with an earth-shaking crunch.

My heart was a feral animal my chest, beating and leaping. I gaped at what I'd done.

Men in soldier's uniforms leapt from the truck behind the one I'd destroyed to help those trapped within. More appeared from behind me, whipping past me to join their mates. One of the enormous mechanical suits I saw at the airport plodded forward, belching a cloud of diesel smoke, and bent over to lift the truck off its side.

A woman shouted something at me in French, her voice stricken. When I ignored her, she yelled in Arabic, too fast for me to translate in my head.

I turned around, in so much shock I didn't recognize her at first—the Nazi woman. Her blue eyes were wide as she stared at me, at the wreck behind me, and at me again.

"You did that," she said, her accent German. It wasn't a question. She'd seen everything.

I shook my head, dazed, and I tried to start my bike again.

"Tell me how you did that," she demanded. "Girl? Can you hear me?"

"I have to go," I said blearily in English. "I'm sorry."

"You're American?" she asked. "I can help you."

The bike roared to life. "You can't. I'm sorry for what I did."

"Wait!" she cried.

She grabbed my arm, but I tore away from her as I sped off, leaving the scene behind me.

ANUBIS

Anubis hadn't had a plan when he'd grabbed Set and transmigrated them both to the farthest place from Egypt he could imagine. The moment they stopped, Set blasted himself apart from Anubis, hurling both immortals through a blinding storm of wind and snow. The ground rumbled with volcanic tremors and rivers of molten rock flowed around them, offering a vision of hell. Glowing cracks split earth, releasing gas so hot it turned the whipping snow into rain and then vapor. His kind did not stray here; this wasteland belonged to the gods of fire and ice.

Set leveled his black gold gaze through the slits of his mask on Anubis with a snarl. "To hell with Ammit. I'll eat your heart myself."

Anubis blasted a *taw* spell into the nearest molten

river, splashing lava and fire onto Set's skin. The elder god howled in pain and fury as he clawed at himself. His knees hit the shaking ground and a mix of ash and snowflakes clung to his body.

Anubis's first thought was to return to Ziva, but he had to keep the chaos god busy for as long as he could, to hold out until his inevitable defeat and likely death.

Set pushed himself to his feet, gasping in pain. He relinquished his mask, withdrawing his power to heal himself. "You test me, boy. In five thousand years, I have never experienced a bigger thorn in my backside."

"I'm flattered, but we both know you have bigger problems than me," Anubis shot back. Magic sparked in his hands.

Set's laugh was low and dark. Molten rock dripped from his body, leaving behind jagged strips of raw, burned flesh that healed into rose marble scars and then to perfection. "It's not too late to make the smart decision. All past transgressions can be forgotten. Join me, Anubis. You were born to."

"I was born to serve humanity," Anubis declared. "You had—and have—nothing to do with my existence."

Without the mask, shadows passed over the chaos god's face. A fresh wound was cut over old scars; sorrow knitted the gash together again. After a long pause burned guilt into Anubis's heart, Set replied, "That fact doesn't mean I wouldn't accept you as my son as you should have been. I had dreamed of a child, too, as desperately as your mother had. I have never blamed you for our mistakes, and I've forgiven her."

"I don't think your forgiveness concerns her, it's your actions," Anubis said venomously, but the look of dejection he received made him want to take it back.

Fire flashed, and the blinding snow lashed the immortals.

"Anubis—"

"If you loved my mother, you would have destroyed Apophis and let it alone. But you desired power more than her. More than you longed for a child."

"I did it for her!" Set roared, gold blazing in his eyes. "I did it to make her queen!"

"You did it for yourself!" Anubis yelled back, a thousand fires burning in his heart. "Everything you've done has been out of selfishness. You say you want to save our people, but the only way to do that is for you to get everything you've ever wanted?" He paused, anticipating a response from Set but received none. He continued, "And yet, my mother's heart still belongs to you, because she isn't selfish, and she knows she is all you have left. She knows if you lost her, you will have lost everything, and she would not do that to you. She still believes in you!"

A tremendous explosion in the distance filled the storm-lit sky with flames, molten rock, and ash. The earth trembled and pitched, knocking the immortals off balance. The volcano prepared to erupt.

"Anubis, I must have the queen's heart," Set said, his voice low and urgent. "I must avenge my honor and your mother's honor. *Your* honor. The netherworld will see the rise of a new dynasty."

"The mortal world is at stake!" Anubis shouted, his

anguish tearing his throat. "The Medjai are resolved to protect it and we must help them. Join us and save your eternal spitting match with Osiris for later. Don't pollute your soul any more than power already has. I believe in you too."

The rivers of fire reflected in the flashing gold of Set's eyes. "I loathe to say your mother has whelped a fool," he growled with so much malice that for the first time in a long, long time, Anubis felt real fear slither through his insides.

CHAPTER

19

All noise was drowned from my ears by the scream of my bike's engine, but I did a better job at looking both ways before I burst out onto a street. Relief hit me when I saw Nasira blazing toward me on her own machine. She skidded to a stop as I parked in the middle of the road.

"Ziva!" she cried breathlessly, shoving her goggles out of her face. "We've been looking everywhere for you. Are you hurt?"

I shook my head. "I have the artifact. It's safe. Is Sayer with you?"

Her eyes widened. "No! I thought he was with you!"

Fear rattled my thoughts and I fought for clarity. "Take this to the Pyramidion. We got caught up with kriosphinxes and Sayer stayed behind to let me escape. That's when I ran into Set."

The color drained from my friend's face.

"His creatures must have been spying all over the city," I said, calculating. "I have to go back for Sayer." I handed her the satchel and was surprised she didn't argue with me. "You aren't going to stop me?"

Nasira's gaze grew hard. "He's my brother, Ziva. Family is everything. Find him."

Fixing my goggles back into place, I kicked the motorcycle into gear and sped toward where I last saw Sayer.

The street was like a warzone. Motorcars, food carts, shop displays—all had been reduced to scattered debris. The block was void of life. Sayer's motorcycle lay mangled at the base of a crushed stone wall. He was nowhere to be seen.

"Sayer?" I called, feeling a flutter of panic. "Sayer!"

I ran down the street, calling his name, knowing that doing so put me at risk, but I had to find him. He had to be all right. I turned a corner, searching the darkness, driven by fear.

"Ziva?" a weak voice replied.

I whirled with a wildness at the sound of his voice and spied his form shuffling toward me in the haze of dust. Immediately I knew something was wrong—and then he collapsed.

"Sayer!" I rushed to his side and helped him lean against a dusty sedan for support. His body was slumped and tense, his jacket missing, and his black shirt was shredded to tatters across his back.

"I had really hoped you'd not come back for me, but I'm glad you did," he groaned. "Where is the satchel?"

"Your sister has it."

"Good."

"Loafing around on the job, are you?" I asked, trying to sound playful around the tremble in my voice.

"If there hadn't been two of the damned beasts, I wouldn't have had to put my back to one." He eased forward, and I grimaced at the grisly marks slashed deep into his shoulder. I leaned over him to get a better look, touching him gently in the hope I could soothe his pain. When I looked down, I saw more slashes in his jeans and his skin was slick with blood. His knee appeared to have taken a terrible blow.

"We'll get you fixed up," I promised him, meeting his dark gaze and finding something intense stirring there. Those eyes roved over my face, seeping deep through my skin.

"Something bad happened a few blocks away," he said softly. "I could hear it. I tried to get there. You scared the hell out of me."

"I'm all right," I told him. "Set showed his face, but I got away. His motivations are more complicated, as we suspected. They don't end with stopping Nefertari. He wants the heart to kill Osiris and become king of the netherworld and the mortal world."

Sayer released a long, dragging breath, and after a few moments to absorb what I'd told him, he nodded. "Then we've really got to find that heart before he does."

"First, let's get you back on your feet," I told him. "How does your healing magic work on yourself?"

"Not as well as I'd like," he grumbled.

"I'd try summoning Anubis, but I can't promise that

won't give up our location to Set," I said dismally. "I don't know what became of either of them. If Anubis got hurt, I'll hate myself. I thought he could hold his own better than I could."

"He wants to help you," Sayer urged. "Don't beat yourself up about it. I would've faced Set for you."

"You faced a pair of kriosphinxes alone for me," I reminded him.

"And you're safe," he said, smiling. "Let's swing, shall we?"

"Can you ride?" I asked doubtfully.

"Certainly not," he replied with a soft chuckle.

I started to help him to his feet, wrapping an arm around his back and lifting him. He buried his face into the bend of my neck and groaned, favoring his injured knee.

"The hard part's over," I told him gently. "You're up."

"What do you say we hotwire one of these tin cans?" he suggested. "I'm not so keen on limping all the way home."

"You can do it with magic?" I asked, surprised.

"I can do that with my hands," he replied.

I laughed. "All right, hotshot. Show me your stuff."

Cyrene frowned as she listened to my recap of the encounter with Set, her brow etched with anger. When I finished, she said nothing. She only glared at thin air. I waited for a reaction, exchanging glances with Sayer, who was so wrapped up in bandages he looked quite like a mummy.

Tariq looked up from the desk where he worked at translating the third canopic jar's hieratic script. "The important thing is you made it home safe. That's all you needed to do tonight."

"Something else happened and I'm not sure what it means," I started, feeling uncertain. "I ran into the Nazis we've seen around Cairo. The woman who'd been with them was there and she saw me use magic."

"Don't fret too much over that," Nasira said gently. "Ensuring no one is hurt is more important than staying covert."

"She was . . ." I trailed off, trying to find the right word. "Interested. Very much so. She demanded I tell her how I did it."

Cyrene at last broke her silence. "I have heard rumors of Adolf Hitler's interest in the occult." She swallowed hard. "Experiments on people. Archaeological expeditions. I was concerned they might be in Egypt for the latter, but if they catch our scent, they'll want to know more about our magic."

"What could they possibly want with us?" I asked. "There's no way we'd ever join their ranks."

Her expression grew very dark and very serious. "Their attempts to convince us would be as terrible as if they were trying to destroy us."

"We can't worry about that now," Tariq said. "We'll avoid them, do our best to stay low, and do our jobs. The hieratic here states, 'Her greatest treasure shall reveal her secret resting place.' It must mean the fourth sacred organ protected by Duamutef, the jackal. The inscription states it is hidden at the Temple of Nefertari, depicted as the goddess Hathor, beside the Sun Temple of Ramesses II."

"These days, the complex is called Abu Simbel," Nasira told me.

"Ah," I said, recalling the site from books. "There are two temples within the complex, one dedicated to a war victory and a second smaller temple to Nefertari. Logically, something important to her would've been placed in her temple, and not her husband's. Correct me if I'm wrong, but isn't Nefertari's temple quite small? If something was hidden there, wouldn't it have been found already?"

Sayer nodded. "There are two known chambers, yes, the vestibule and the sanctuary. But our ancestors built hidden rooms inside tombs and temples all the time to protect them from plunderers. For example, the queen anticipated her official tomb could be robbed and so she had a second tomb built for herself. That's where her mummy is."

"Nefertari was Medjai and she trusted her secrets only to her own people," Cyrene said. "We have always known she'd constructed a false tomb, but this was one of two clues to her resurrection she gave us. Your destiny was our second clue. She was very, very careful and very, very clever."

"What will we do once we reach the temple?" I asked. "Is there some spell we need to use in order to find the hidden artifact? Something to reveal an invisible object, or a doorway?"

"Possibly," Sayer said. "We'll know once we arrive. There are all sort of spells, but most are for protection from malevolent creatures. There's even a spell to pacify beasts—*sehar.*"

"What?" I sputtered. "If that's true, then why do we bother fighting the kriosphinxes?"

"They are already pacified," he explained, crushing my excitement. "They belong to Set."

"We must leave at first light for Abu Simbel," Tariq declared.

Cyrene folded her arms. "Sayer, come with me and we'll heal those wounds. Girls, get some rest. Tomorrow will be a long day."

In the morning, we indeed left at first light. To be fair, we left before first light. Thankfully I'd packed my equipment the night before, so I was ready when Cyrene knocked on my door earlier than I'd expected. The Medjai took several cars to the docks, and when we arrived I yet again found myself ignoring instructions. As soon as we were permitted to board, I darted to the bow and stayed there until long after we'd departed. Our air ferry was approximately the same size as the steam ferries which still traveled by water below us. They cut through the Nile noisily, their paddle wheels slapping water. Traveling through the air felt smooth, but we left a trail of black diesel smoke in our wake.

The banks of the Nile stretched into fields and rows of green grain crops sprouted from black mud. People waded waist-deep in the water, filling pots, washing clothes, and bathing. Behind them, flat-roofed houses dotted dry land between groves of unripe apple-green olives and pomegranates. The tangerine sun of early morning splashed across the golden pyramids and the peaceful face of the Great Sphinx beyond them. In my mind's eye, I imagined what they had looked like thousands of years ago, when their golden limestone still gleamed white as moonlight.

I saw clouds floating on the river's surface, but at second glance I realized my clouds were huge, white sails dwarfing small narrow boats. They moved smoothly, perfectly, as though they weren't a physical part of this world, more ghosts of the sun than anything else.

"They are *feluccas*," Sayer explained, appearing beside me. "The Nile is a very long river and the generous wind makes sailing ideal."

I turned to him, leaning against the rail and letting my head fall back. He gazed down at me warmly, his quiet smile forming a dimple in one of his cheeks.

"I'm glad you're here," I told him, lifting my hand to touch his shoulder and finding the injuries magically healed. He didn't seem tender at all there and he melted into my touch.

"Me too," he replied. "Staying behind wouldn't have been any fun."

"You would've missed the view," I said, smiling and gesturing to the pyramids with a nod of my head.

He continued looking only at me. "What a shame that would have been."

My smile widened, and I felt a flutter in my belly that traveled low. "You aren't talking about the river, are you?"

He fell quiet for a moment, wearing that stone wall of a face again. "I'm with you," he said, with that ardent intensity sobering his expression again. "I offer you my life and my death."

I stared at him in starstruck wonder. I needed to ask him a thousand more questions, but I didn't know what they were. "Why do you sound so sad?"

He drew a deep breath, his urgent gaze faltering for an instant. "Me, my sister, my father—we're with you. You're one of us. My family comes first to me. Whatever crossroads I will come to, I will choose *you*."

He called me family, something I'd wanted to hear my entire life, but those words—I was sure of it—meant more. There came a deep spark in my heart; a thunder-clap warning of a distant storm.

CHAPTER

20

Our air ferry made port the next day at a trading post to refuel, and after I had breakfast, I went to explore. There appeared to be no permanent buildings or obvious homes of any kind. Elaborate tents and tables were set up like small shops, filled with beaded jewelry, painted pottery, colorful clothing, and an array of tools. One man had tied a dozen camels to a post presumably to sell, and a shepherd threw grain to his flock of goats. A handful of campfires were tended by men and women cooking their breakfasts and local cuisine to sell.

Men were dressed far more plainly than the women. Most were dressed in bright white *gondora*, but their head scarves, braided around the crown of their heads, were dyed in a variety of colors. Tattooed women in colorful, patterned robes carried naked children on their shoulders. I passed another group of women with painted eyes and many gold coins and other embellishments dangling from their dresses and hoods. One of them stared at me, a gorgeous woman wearing a hood woven in intricate, colorful geometric patterns and a string of coins hanging over her nose and across her cheeks. I supposed I looked rather strange and unbeautiful to her, wearing what looked like a man's soldier uniform. I was the only woman here who wasn't tattooed. If anything, I was a pebble to her diamond.

A table of beautifully beaded jewelry attracted my attention and I wandered over to get a closer look. The camel tied just outside the entrance watched me curiously and reached out to sniff my hand. I smiled and scratched his nose only to be treated with his open-mouthed groan. I wandered away and poked my head inside the tent. The floor was covered in many uniquely different rugs, and several wooden posts kept the canopy securely suspended.

I found a woman inside, placing more jewelry out to be sold. Her black veil was embroidered with colorful stars and embellished with metal pieces and coins. She looked up at me and said something I recognized to be Arabic and heat filled my cheeks.

"Do you speak English?" she asked helpfully, her words soft, though her accent was thick. Small symbols tattooed in faded blue ink adorned her cheeks and chin.

"Yes, forgive me," I said.

"There's nothing to apologize for," she said with a dismissive wave of her hand. "I know English so I can trade with them. You are American?"

"You have a very good ear," I told her.

She smiled, continuing to arrange her jewelry. "I have met a lot of people."

"I was born in Egypt, but I grew up in America," I explained. "My family is Medjai."

She paused and turned to me, her delicately painted eyebrows lifted. "How curious. I know of the Medjai. Your tribe is a very, very old one. Some believe our marks—*oucham*—came from Medjai practices, from wandering *adasiya*. My grandmother used to sing me songs of Medjai sorcery and how they protected Egypt from enemies. I did not think there were any left. You and I are like cousins. I am from Tlemcen."

"Your people is an old one, as well," I noted.

"If the Medjai truly brought the tattoos to Africa, then I thank you," she told me. "They make me feel beautiful, even though I'm not a young girl anymore. In my village, a girl becomes a woman with her first tattoo."

A fullness overcame my heart, one of sadness and loss. I felt as though something were being taken from me, something I never had a chance to grasp. My people had our own standards of beauty outside those in New York. There was more than one way to be beautiful. I didn't have to chop off my hair or try to straighten it or wear belted dresses. I could do whatever made me feel beautiful. I would reclaim all the pieces of my heritage that had been stolen from me.

"What is your name?" the Amazigh woman asked, interrupting my thoughts.

"Ziva," I said.

"Ziva," she repeated, tasting my name on her tongue. "Ziva means 'radiance.' Like the sun."

I smiled. I never knew my name had a meaning. "Thank you. May I ask your name?"

"Rabaiya," she replied.

I examined a garment, listening to the tinkling of the gold coins and beads as I moved them with my fingers. "If you know anything about the traditional Medjai dress, will you help me? I want to embrace who I am. I'll pay you very well for your time and goods."

Her smile shone brightly as the desert sand in her eyes. "I would be honored. Let me have a look at you. Is there anything you wish to keep?"

"My boots and trousers," I admitted. "They are very practical for what I do."

"Which is?" she asked, skimming through an assortment of fabric hung on a line.

All I could offer her was a partial truth. "A soldier. Of sorts. I'll need a lot of mobility, but I need protection from enemies and the elements, so I cover as much skin as I can."

"I can work with that," Rabaiya said. She selected a long piece of partially-sheer black linen embroidered with white stars and a dagger with an interestingly curved blade. She cut through the fabric, shortening it, while I removed my button-up shirt and cast it aside. She turned to me and folded the linen around my upper body.

"You wrap it like this—see? And tie this sash under your bosom." She finished and stepped back to take me in. "Hmm. It's still long—too long for a soldier in battle. Tuck it into your trousers. There."

The sleeves were billowy and allowed air to cool me while the fabric protected my skin from the sun. Around my neck, the linen bunched into a cowl shape which I expanded to test its coverage of my hair and part of my face. It would be perfect for desert tempests. The fabric was loose fitting around my waist and permitted me a great deal of movement and comfort.

"This is wonderful, Rabaiya," I told her. "Thank you."

She waved her hand again. "I'm not finished. You are a warrior, but you are also a woman. It's okay to love your femininity."

I didn't understand her meaning until she took my hand and steered me toward the jewelry. She chose different beads and gemstones and sewed them into my linen shirt, their many colors glittering against the black like a rainbow of stars splashed against the universe. She picked a few thin and scattered locks of my hair and strung them through gold and mother-of-pearl beads.

"Now that I know you are a soldier, I have to ask. Are the stories of Medjai magic true?"

I studied her, considering her question and the consequences of my honesty. She asked me something she already knew the answer to. That I saw in her keen eyes. I had control over my magic now and my gut told me I wouldn't scare her. For my entire life, I had struggled with my identity and Rabaiya had given me an incredible gift. I wanted to give her a gift in return.

I raised my hand and whispered a gentle *tahen* spell.

The small flicker of netherlight grew, a twinkling star dancing across my palm and my fingertips. She stared in awe, the glow glimmering her wide, dark eyes.

"This is a beautiful gift," she breathed as though she'd lost her voice. "Thank you, Ziva."

I let the netherlight fade in my hand. "It's the very least I can do for you. You've given me something I will cherish for the rest of my life."

"I wish I could do more for Egypt's protector," she said. "You will save us from the evil spreading its shadow across this world. Egypt must be returned to the hands of its own people. You can do that. If there is anything— ever—I can do for you, find me, cousin."

The conviction in her voice stirred my soul. "I'd like to offer the same to you, too, Rabaiya. I will protect Egypt and its people."

"You will do what is best for us all," she said. "This I know in my heart." She reached into a clay pot painted indigo and sunset orange. She retrieved a handful of silver and gold coins. "Your jewels and coins let everyone know you have royal blood."

I stared at her sidelong in disbelief as she wove the coins through my hair. "How did you know?"

"Your eyes," Rabaiya replied. "A queen's heart shines in her eyes. Embrace her."

One corner of my mouth pinched into a smile. "I will."

"There . . . is an *adasiya* looking for work, last I knew," she offered with caution. "If you would be interested."

I turned my head and looked at her tattooed face. "Yes, I would."

She put a hand on my shoulder. "Wait here."

A few minutes later, Rabaiya returned with another woman of similar age wearing a red dress with colorful embroidery. Her face was marked with a sun in the middle of her forehead and a line drawn from either corner of her mouth to her jawline and a third line from her lower lip down the center of her chin.

The *adasiya* seemed not to speak English since Rabaiya spoke in Arabic too quietly and rapidly for me to keep up. The one word I did catch: Medjai. The woman nodded and smiled at me as she reached up and held my chin, moving my face side to side to examine me.

"Ziva, this is Touta," Rabaiya explained. "She will give you the *oucham*. The marks hold energy from good spirits, which will help protect you from machinations of evil."

Touta set a bundle of goat hide on a table and unrolled it to reveal her tools: a small knife, a dark glass bottle, a candle and flint, and rag squares. With Rabaiya's aid in translation, Touta guided me to lie back so she could wash my skin. She lit the candle and a small flame burst to life at the wick. She dipped the blade into the fire, sterilizing and purifying the sharp metal.

Then the *adasiya* got to work.

The full moon over Egypt was the most beautiful thing I'd ever seen. Its silver glow turned the endless desert midnight blue. Out here, where there was no nighttime city fire to eat the stars, the sky was *alive* with celestial bodies and splashes of sapphire blues, amethyst purples, emerald greens, and pearly moonstone shades of white. The sight was something I could never have imagined in my most unreal dreams. I understood why the ancients believed our gods lived among the stars. My nightgown glowed in the moonlight and a cool, gentle breeze played with the hem around my ankles. I'd never felt so free in my life.

I heard a footstep behind me and a gentle hand caressed the small of my back. Sayer's scent and presence flooded me. His body pressed against mine, his heat an ember aglow, and he brushed his face against my hair. He pushed the curls aside, exposing the bare back of my neck and shoulder. He inhaled, my scent as intoxicating an incense to him as his was to me.

"Do I gaze upon Nephthys herself?" he whispered, and the delicious memory of his healing kiss struck me, giving me a chill.

"There are ageless tales warning against comparing a mortal's beauty to a goddess's," I teased, trying to act cool when all of my nerve endings were on fire.

"Unless she is also a goddess of night and starlight," he declared, and he brushed his lips back and forth across the bend of my neck. "I would worship at your altar." He gently guided me around to him. He stepped forward and my back bumped against the railing. Strands of his hair swayed across his face in a whisper of Nile air. He was excruciatingly beautiful, alight beneath the heavens.

"If I am a goddess, then what are you?" I asked, searching the stars reflected in his eyes.

"Anything you desire." He raised a hand to touch the

beads in my hair and smooth his knuckles across my collarbone. He leaned toward me, not quite close enough to kiss my mouth, but enough to wreathe me in his heat. Fire blazing in their depths, his eyes fell to my lips and rose to meet my gaze again.

A needful pang reverberated through me, warming my blood. Even the night air couldn't hide the flush in my cheeks. He raised a hand to touch the bottom of my chin and admire the *oucham* given to me. In my head I imagined the line drawn from the middle of my bottom lip, the shorter lines branching off and the little circles hanging from each branch.

"Olive tree," he said, gently avoiding the tender areas of my skin, "for your strength and resilience." His thumb brushed my left cheekbone to the circle surrounded by dots. A matching tattoo adorned my other cheek. "Moon and stars. For femininity and womanhood." His eyes found mine and I believed him when he told me, "You're beautiful."

I felt beautiful. I felt Medjai. I felt like I belonged. I felt like me. Like the breath of life was in my lungs at last. The path behind me was no longer a gray fog and the path ahead of me was no longer made of living shadows waiting to gobble me up. The path ahead rose into wind-swept heights bright beneath stars, right where I stood now. And Sayer was there. And Nasira was there. Tariq and Cyrene. Anubis.

And Sayer was there. He was here.

My smile rich and warm as molten chocolate, I dared to toy with him and slide away, my bare feet silent on the deck. I backed away from him, gathering fistfuls of my nightgown to keep myself from tripping on the hem. "So, you would obey my every whim?"

There was a flick of his brow and a sideways smile. "I will honor my pledge to my death."

I raised my hem a little higher off the floor. "Catch me."

Then I bolted, laughing, the wind five hundred feet above the Nile whispering coolly on my skin, billowing my loose hair and the folds of my white dress in the moonlight. Only once did I glance over my shoulder at him as he pursued me to find a wide and dazzling smile brightening his face.

I narrowly avoided slamming into a passing Medjai couple as they leapt apart with grumbled protest. "Sorry!" I laughed breathlessly.

Taking a tight left turn, I flew down a set of stairs, hit the floor, and my bare feet slid. Behind me I heard the loud thump of Sayer's boots as he landed.

I ducked into a hallway and caught sight of a door with a single porthole window. I tore it open and darted through—only to find myself outside on a small empty deck with no other exit. The air rushed from me in defeat.

Sayer burst into the room and seized my waist. I squealed and whirled in his arms. His hands traveled up my back and held me against his chest. His smile brushed my neck, my ear, and skimmed across my cheek.

"Now that I have you?" he whispered against my skin.

"Kiss me like I'm your girl."

He lifted his head and gazed down at me. His dark eyes, hooded by thick lashes, fell to my lips and he lowered his face to mine. I covered his hands with mine as they settled on my hips, letting him know they were where I wanted them. My palms pushed up his chest and wrapped around his neck, loving the feel of his body, and I pulled him down to me. When I kissed him, his shoulders went rigid with surprise for an instant, but he pushed through it, melting, squeezing my hips and pulling me against his body.

His lips were soft and warm and sweet. His heat blazed from his skin. I opened my mouth against his and he kissed me deeper, impossibly slower. My face was sore from its fresh tattoo, but the pain was a delicious bite and I would hold on for as long as I could stand it.

When his mouth moved to the tender skin of my jawline and then my neck, my teeth bit together and a pang hit me from deep inside. His lips returned to mine and I sighed against them. My fingernails skimmed down his neck and across his shoulders, and his hands gripped my waist more firmly, the way I wanted him to hold me, as though I might float away if he loosened his grip. I rewarded him with a tiny whimper of pleasure.

Sayer pulled back, and his brown eyes consumed me, up and down and everywhere, his pupils wide with desire. He rushed into me, his lips finding mine again, wilder than before. He felt like a storm in my hands, energy building and rolling into me, his kisses the crack and lull of thunder.

But the pain became too much and had begun to spread up my cheeks and down my neck, a sparkling, piercing ache.

I pulled away with regret and relief, offering him an apologetic smile. "My chin—the tattoo—"

He exhaled with a soft laugh, his cheeks flushed. "No—I shouldn't have. I was rough."

"No!" I exclaimed, aghast. "No, you weren't at all. My face is sore, that's all."

"You're healing," he agreed. "I knew better."

"You didn't do anything I didn't want you to do," I assured him, and my words made him smile. I took his hand and returned it to my waist, where he held me tight and pulled me back to him. I said slyly, "You should have kissed me before I was marked."

"I'll kiss you again," he promised. "A thousand times more." He kissed my cheek, brushing his nose over my skin, and kissed the corner of my mouth before resting his forehead against mine, the both of us breathless. For a moment, I felt suspended in time and air, unreal and distant, as the kiss replayed in my mind, the low, low weight in me so heavy I felt I would bottom out. *More.* I wanted more.

I'd fallen for him like the rain, the crashing of an unstoppable force that couldn't be reasoned with, only braced for. I'd had two choices: run for shelter or stand in the storm and let myself be devoured. Needless to say, I wasn't the kind of girl who ran.

CHAPTER

21

I had waited eagerly on deck long before I saw my first glimpse of Abu Simbel. Our ferry approached the telltale mountainside, where at its feet wound the mighty Nile. As we rounded the mountain, I took in the glory of the colossi. Statues of Ramesses II and four gods seated in thrones protected the entrance of the Sun Temple. Just beyond it, the Temple of Nefertari welcomed us. This was the only temple in all of Egypt where the queen's representation was equal in size and significance to the king. Nefertari had been that revered and one of a kind. Her noble likeness, depicted as the goddess Hathor, stood facing the sun along with five other figures.

A steep river of sand flowing from above the cliffside parted the two temples, having not been entirely cleared from the excavation. Because there wasn't enough land between the cliff and the river, the crew tethered our air ferry at the top of the mountain and released a ladder for us to climb down. The air was devilishly hot, and the wind blew only heat at my face. We all wore more kohl on our eyes than usual to protect them from the harsh sun. I lifted my hood over my hair and surveyed the endless expanse of desert before me. My home was a beautiful vision.

Tariq handed everyone bundles of climbing gear and helped us get ready. I fitted my straps tightly and asked him to check my work. Falling to my death was far less illustrious than dying in battle. Not that I intended to do either. The funny thing about heights is you can't predict your reaction to dangling hundreds of feet in the air until you're actively dangling. My boots scraped the rock wall, and the tremendous pressure from the harness around my backside bit into my skin even through my layers. We were all tied together in one long chain of straps and harnesses.

"Everyone always says don't look down," Sayer called from above me. "But it's for good reason."

"Didn't imagine you'd be afraid of heights, Medjai," I teased him.

"Not heights," he corrected. "I'm afraid of my sister cutting the rope. Retribution for all the teasing I did growing up."

"Too easy!" Nasira bellowed. "I'm still plotting!"

I laughed and continued my descent. When my boots touched soft sand, I breathed a sigh of relief and removed my harness. I didn't wait for the rest of the Medjai to land and I wandered toward Nefertari's temple, overwhelmed by emotion. It was as though I'd stepped back in time.

They'd called this one the small temple, but the six sentinel statues stood tall as my old tenement building. If they came to life, they could stomp me like a bug. Nefertari's likeness wore the feathered and horned crown of the goddess of love, Hathor, symbolizing how fathomlessly her husband and all of Egypt had loved her.

"The queen of kings," Sayer said, stopping at my side.

"Thank you," I replied as regally as possible. "I am, aren't I?"

"Indisputably."

Cyrene marched past us and into the temple without stopping to admire the incredible relief. It would've been no surprise to hear she'd been here a thousand times before. If I recalled correctly, Sayer had mentioned she was quite the globetrotter. That kind of life sounded inimitable, and if I continued to train hard, I might get the chance she'd take me along with her. I craved adventure. I needed it like blood in my veins and air in my lungs. It wasn't as though I wanted to leave an impact on the world. I wanted the world to leave an impact on me.

Sayer's hand on the small of my back reminded me of another craving. I needed love too. The kind of human connection I'd never had before. He was like me in every way, my equal. My match. Mine.

He followed Cyrene toward the entrance and my eyes were glued to him.

He was mine.

He was my adventure.

I entered the vestibule of Nefertari's temple and found the interior to be a shock of cool air compared to the furious sun outside. I pushed the hood off my head and pulled down my scarf.

"*Tahen*," I cast, and an orb of netherlight formed in the air above my open palm, illuminating the temple's beauty.

The roof was held strong by six incredible pillars covered in hieroglyphs. Only faded traces of paint remained, but in my head, I imagined them covered in white plaster and their markings a striking splash of reds, yellows, blues, and greens. The vestibule was surprisingly short and led into an even smaller sanctuary. Treasure hunters would've assumed it empty, but they failed to understand the significance of the engravings covering the walls and the four statues carved into the sanctuary's rear wall. Here, Hathor's protection was ensured for Nefertari and Ramesses II. Having an immortal's strength at your back was greater than any quantity of gold. I wondered if she'd had Hathor's favor as I had the favor of Anubis.

"What is it we're looking for?" Tariq asked, certainly voicing what everyone else thought.

"Clues," Cyrene said. "Anything which might mention the sanctuary's true purpose."

We scoured the chamber, looking over every inscription and painting on every last square inch of surface. I noticed how the beam of sunlight rose like the tide on the statues as the morning dragged on. Tangerine light crept closer and closer to their serene faces.

Nasira hunched over a line of hieroglyphs, her *tahen* spell illuminating the inscription. "What about this? 'Only her blood shall reveal the secret of her heart.'"

"Heart?" Sayer asked, surprised. "The last canopic jar is supposed to be here, correct?"

"I thought so," Tariq said.

Looking around, I considered the words, musing aloud, "Nefertari's blood. My blood."

"Are you supposed to do something with it?" Nasira offered. She grimaced. "Bleed on something?"

Sayer looked skeptical. "The ancients didn't always intend their words to be taken literally."

"Perhaps they meant blood, as in relative, or specifically the scion, will unlock whatever is hidden," I surmised. "Well, I'm here, whoever is listening. Now show me the secret. Please?"

Nasira pinched my side. "I don't believe anyone who could help us is listening."

"Your optimism will save us all," I teased her.

She shrugged. "I'm pragmatic."

No one seemed to have any ideas, and once my brain turned to scrambled eggs from all the translating, I exhaled and put my hands on my hips. I frowned and looked around me. Above the exit to the vestibule were several of Nefertari's formal royal titles. The Great King's Wife, the Lady of Two Lands, Sweet of Love, For Whom the Sun Shines . . .

I paused and blinked. I looked behind me at the statues that had been slowly illuminated by the rising sun all morning.

I thought of Rabaiya, the Amazigh woman's words. *"A queen's heart shines in her eyes."*

The sunlight was almost level with the painted eyes

of Nefertari's statue. I had an idea. To try it wouldn't hurt anyone. The others wouldn't even notice my left-field attempt. Still, there was a chance. I knew my numbers; I recognized when things started to add up.

With a glance to my left and right, sure no one paid much attention to me, I slid one long stride into the center of the sanctuary and faced the rising sun. It warmed my chest beneath my clothing, then my chin, and then my eyes. A blinding flash of light flooded my vision.

A deafening roar of sliding rock shook the sanctuary. The two center statues rattled, shaking free thousands of years' worth of dust and cobwebs, and they sank into the stone floor. They disappeared, revealing a tunnel, leading into blackness.

Stunned silence settled with the dust around us.

"Who did that?" Cyrene asked, puzzled.

Everyone looked at each other.

"The sun had to meet my eyes," I said, still shocked it had worked.

"Well done," Tariq praised. "There's an interesting sun trick in Ramesses II's temple as well. The sun shines on the sanctuary statues' faces precisely two days a year. Supposedly it was designed purposefully to align with the equinoxes."

Nasira clapped a hand on my shoulder. "Brilliant work, Ziva."

Cyrene's *tahen* spell strengthened, and netherlight filled the narrow passage. We ventured forth, unsure of what lay ahead. In the darkness, I lost sense of time and distance. We could've walked a hundred miles and I'd never have known for sure.

"Wait!" Sayer called from behind me. I turned, and he pointed above our heads. "There's another inscription here."

I lifted my head, raised my netherlight orb, and found the hieroglyphs carved into a section of stone hanging from the tunnel's ceiling. I read aloud, "If the seal is broken, all who pass the threshold will face the terrors of the world of the gods. Those who are not true to the Lady of Grace will find only monstrous death here."

"How delightful," Nasira grumbled.

"The ancients carved warnings into many tombs," Cyrene said. "Don't fear them. They're meant to frighten off thieves."

I felt doubtful. "Why would it have targeted people who had no way of getting inside this passage? The seal needed me to break it."

Sayer nodded in agreement. "It could refer to Medjai who are or aren't loyal to the queen."

"Then we have nothing to worry about, right?" I asked, hopeful.

We continued, and the farther we walked, the denser the air became. Something else hung around our heads.

"I sense magic," I said, my voice tight with uncertainty.

"As do I," Tariq added.

"There's some sort of barrier here." I reached out and my fingertips prickled with electricity as they brushed an invisible wall in front of us. My hand pushed through with no effort and no consequences. I turned to the others. "It's safe to pass."

We crossed the magical veil and into a large chamber left untouched by time and raiders. Paintings covered the walls from floor to ceiling and the square columns were carved with Nefertari's likeness. I stepped toward one to get a better look at the beautiful inscriptions, but a strange light grew in the chamber's center only feet away from me.

I froze. No one said a word. A shrill electric sound pierced my skull.

A pool of eerie netherlight spread on the smooth stone floor. A large form emerged in the glow, rising through the floor as though the stone was water. Fine, glossy golden fur dappled with faint leopard spots sheathed a sleek, feline body that dropped into a muscle-flexing stretch, paws spreading and arching talons. Its cherubic girl's face and round fuzzy ears were framed with black hair threaded with cobalt, carnelian, and gold. The beast was enormous; its wide emerald eyes, ringed with thick black lines, were level with mine. Its body was assuredly animal, but there was something in those eyes that whispered of cunning and acuity.

It was no kriosphinx. Without a doubt, a true sphinx stared back at me. Its shadow stretched long across the floor. Braziers all around the chamber exploded with dancing flames of netherlight, casting an otherworldly glow across the faces painted on the walls.

When its feminine, musical voice echoed through the ancient chamber, each word the distant, delicate press of a piano key, a chill swept through my bones. "You have come to die."

Nasira withdrew her *asaya* and extended it with a clack. "Never mind the warning of terrors of the netherworld and monstrous death," she grumbled. "They are meant to scare people off."

"There are wiser occasions in which to be smug," Cyrene grumbled, readying her own *asaya*.

"Perhaps the next time we come across an ancient curse we heed it with a healthy respect?" Nasira suggested venomously.

The sphinx's human mouth opened, revealing not-so-human fangs. It roared, shaking the chamber floor. The muscles beneath its feline hide rippled and tensed. It launched, obsidian-sharp talons spread, and it slashed at the closest Medjai. Cyrene whirled, narrowly having her arm torn from the socket.

The sphinx's claws dug into the stone floor, catching its slide, and within a single bound, it met Cyrene again.

"*Sena!*" the Medjai screamed, voice shredded, and her protective magical barrier stopped the sphinx.

It reared onto its haunches and tore viciously at the spell with both huge paws.

Nasira drove her *asaya* toward the sphinx's ribcage, but she spun with a snarl, and charged. Sayer leapt between them and his *taw* spell collided with the sphinx. Her body slid across the floor, her talons dragging gouges into the stone. She was on him in an instant and with a slash, shredded his belted jacket. He screamed with pain and his knees hit the ground.

I threw up my arm with all my strength. *"Khet!"* Fire exploded in a ring around me, splitting Sayer and the sphinx apart. She backpedaled, screeching, and turned her blinding green gaze to me.

The vision of her roaring face through the flames was enough to give me nightmares. I hesitated with fear like a fool. Her power slammed into me, tossing me off my feet. My back slammed into the chamber wall with a crack and I crumpled to the ground.

When I regained my sense, I lifted my head to watch the sphinx bring down Tariq. If this continued, we would all die. We were true to the queen, so then why are we attacked? Perhaps we were supposed to prove our loyalty? I could think of only one spell to try, and it was a desperate move.

I summoned my magic, igniting my spirit's power, and I cried, *"Sehar!"*

The sphinx paused, turning her bared teeth to me.

"I stand before you without fear," I declared. "I repel you. I lay you down!"

She hissed, tail lashing with fury, and took a step backward. Then she settled to the floor on her belly, retracting her claws.

I dared to walk toward the sphinx slowly with caution and confidence. "Through my veins flows the blood of your mistress, Nefertari. I am your mistress as well."

The violence fled the beast's face and she watched me with a passive interest. I felt almost trapped in the sphinx's endless emerald eyes as though they were divining crystals. If I searched them long enough, I might have uncovered the universe's secrets.

"Then you must forgive me, lady," she said in the sweetest, most ethereal voice I'd ever heard. "I wish only to protect and serve the queen."

I looked around me, scanning the stunned faces of my friends. If I searched for directions from them, then it was a losing battle. Admittedly, I had no idea what I was doing. Sayer's gaze captured mine and he gave me a supportive nod of his head, offering me courage to continue. If I made a mistake, the sphinx could take my head from my shoulders in one swing of her paw.

"My name is Baket, lady," she said to me. "May I ask yours?"

"Ziva," I replied.

"I am yours, Lady Ziva," Baket said. "Do you seek my treasure?"

"All I seek is a necessary piece to Queen Nefertari's resurrection," I replied, choosing my words carefully. I was no treasure hunter or tomb raider and I didn't want her to think me one.

"Follow me." Baket rose to her four feet and started toward the far end of the large chamber.

Sayer caught up to me and remarked in a low voice, "Your surprises are endless."

I grinned at him. "Someone told me once brute strength isn't always the answer when you're up against something bigger and badder than you."

One corner of his mouth tugged into a smile. "Fair enough."

The sphinx led us through a vestibule and into another chamber with paintings on every last inch of the walls and ceiling. In the center of the room was a single rose granite pedestal. Atop it, glistened a gigantic uncut ruby the size of my fist, or rather, the size of a human heart.

"What—what is this?" Cyrene sputtered.

I was dazzled by the stone's sparkling brilliance. *Only her blood shall reveal the secret of her heart.* Only something of the highest significance would have such a fearsome protector. "Her greatest treasure . . ." I murmured.

"Yes, lady," the sphinx said sweetly.

"This is the queen's heart," Sayer whispered, astonishment hushing him. "The canopic jar isn't here at all."

"Then where could it be?" Tariq asked.

"Is this a clue?" Nasira pointed to the wall behind the pedestal.

Carved into rock was a clearly female figure raising a spherical object high over her head. The sun disk depicted in the sky showered rays of sunlight down on her and the ray which hit the sphere in her hand was refracted. The beam shot away from her and struck the chest of another female figure wearing the unmistakable vulture headdress of Nefertari. Her cartouche was carved next to her head.

"I know what I have to do," I said.

I grabbed the ruby heart and we headed the way we came, with Baket following behind. Once we arrived at the passage entrance, I ran through the vestibule, praying we hadn't taken all day to reach the sphinx's lair. Outside in the soft sand, I took a great breath of fresh air and relief to see the sun had not yet set.

"Please work," I murmured, and raised the heart over my head.

Sunlight warmed both my skin and the stone, and a moment later a flash blinded me. I turned my face away from the brightness and when it dimmed, I squinted to see what had happened. A red beam of light projected from the ruby and went seemingly on forever, or at least as far as I could see. Curious, I rotated the ruby, moved it around, held it behind me, raised it high—no matter which position I held it, the beam of light continued to point in the same direction.

"I think it is literally guiding us toward our destination," I said to Cyrene as she walked up beside me.

"I think you're right," she replied. "Wonderful news."

"Do we take the air ferry and follow it?" I asked.

She shook her head. "We can't. The ferry routes don't leave the Nile, and if we ran out of fuel out there we'd be stranded. The desert isn't a very hospitable place, needless to say, even for us. We turn around. Head north to Aswan. We'll continue by camel."

CHAPTER

22

The Nubian city of Aswan was neither as large nor as busy as Cairo, but one would never have known by glimpses of its train station and air and steamship ports. It served as the last major terminal between Egypt and Sudan, and the construction to the existing rock dam made travel more chaotic than usual. *Feluccas* drifted past scenic patios filled with potted flowers and palm trees on one side of the Nile and on the other, marshes filled with fishing birds and deeply fertile lowland.

Cyrene negotiated the purchase of camels from a Tuareg man in an indigo-dyed turban I learned was called a *shesh* and we packed our things into saddlebags and bedrolls for the journey. My camel was mild-mannered, and he didn't have a name, so I gave him one. I always thought Clark Gable was a terribly handsome man and as my camel was also terribly handsome, I named him Clark Camel. It was a much better name than just Camel. He drooled quite a bit and his burps stank, but he seemed to like me. He didn't pay much attention to me until I hid grain in my clothes. It wasn't long before he started to root around my pockets for snacks. His loyalty was clearly won by food, but I was glad to have it.

"I hate camels," Nasira grumbled as she pulled to no avail on her ride's lead to get him to lay down in order to be saddled. The animal groaned and resisted heavily on his hind end. "I want a horse!" she added loudly enough for Cyrene to have heard from across the livery.

I looked up at Clark Camel, who watched me intently with his big, beautiful brown eyes and thick lashes. He chewed his cud peacefully and patiently. I held his lead in one hand and left my free hand palm-up. When I pulled gently on his lead and tapped his foreleg, he lay right down in front of me. I gave him a pat and a snack before saddling him.

"How did you do that?" Nasira inquired with suspicion. "Camels don't like to do anything. You literally cannot train them."

My mount turned his head to groan open-mouthed at me. I gave him a scratch on his broad face. "He wants to be treated like a proper fellow, I imagine."

Nasira huffed gruffly. "He's a big, ugly sod."

I wondered how riding a camel differed from riding a horse. Clark Camel's stride was long and slow, and I rocked side-to-side in the saddle. The rhythm was very pleasant, despite the violent heat of the air.

Once we crossed the river and headed into the Western Desert, we found Anubis and the sphinx Baket waiting among the ruins of a small temple. Here they seemed much less out of place than they would have in the city. We dismounted and tethered our animals to each other, and as I removed my scarf from my face, I gave a handful of grain to Clark Camel. His stunningly prehensile lips roved over my entire hand without dropping a single seed. I wiped my palm on my pants and gave his head a pat. He thanked me with an open-mouthed, toxic burp.

Anubis wore a natural-colored linen tunic resembling a jellabiya, its hem dancing in the breeze around his sandaled feet. He pushed back his hood and offered me a warm smile. "Hello, friend."

"Hello to you," I returned and acknowledged the sphinx. "I'm glad to see you again, Baket."

She closed her eyes and pushed her forehead into my palm in greeting as she purred. "My heart sings to hear your voice, lady."

When she opened her eyes, they were level with mine and belonged to a not-quite-human face. Not only was she like nothing I'd ever seen before, far more magnificent than the kriosphinxes or Kauket's dark beauty, but the sphinx's face alone possessed such enchanting magnetism. The effect reminded me of those women you see on the street who are so truly beautiful you can't help but stare, as if they were a mirage. One blink, and they might be gone. I feared I could lose my soul to Baket's gaze.

I could only imagine how my old friend Jean would react if she knew I'd befriended a flesh and blood real sphinx.

"I trust you're prepared for this final leg of your journey," Anubis said. "I'll ride with you. My protection may be needed."

His voice yanked my mind back to the present. The sun blinded me. The sand burned my feet through the soles of my boots. My camel stretched his nose forward and sniffed the god of death's hands for a snack.

"You've got to know how sorry I am about summoning you to fight Set," I confessed to him.

His brow furrowed. "Don't apologize. I gave you the amulet to call on me when you needed me."

"I was so scared I'd made a terrible mistake," I admitted.

Anubis touched my cheek tenderly to reassure me. "You acquired what you needed. And you've made a friend of one of my mother's soldiers."

"It's true," Baket purred. "The lady of night and protection braided and beaded my mane herself. I thank you for freeing me from the temple."

"I freed you?" I asked, surprised and perplexed.

"Nefertari summoned me to protect her heart long ago," the sphinx told me. "Longer than I can remember. Her magic compelled me to stay there—alone—until you set me free. I serve you, Ziva, of the house of the Great Ancestor, Favored of the Sun."

Cyrene passed behind me and said, "It will be dark soon. We'll camp here."

I'd never set up a tent before and it took me longer than the others to finish. The positive side was by the time I'd finished, several fires had already been built and dinner was close at hand. I feasted on kabobs of roasted lamb and vegetables. I shared my treats with Baket—partly because I so enjoyed listening to the delicate rumble of her purr. The orphanage had had several cats who kept the rodents away, but few had been tame enough to touch. One in particular, a tuxedo tom, had a motor like a truck's and he loved to sit on me as I petted him. Baket was sadly far too large to sit in my lap.

The universe was ablaze above our temple sanctuary, and I sat beside Sayer in front of our fire with my head on his shoulder, my belly full and satisfied. I imagined our ancestors praising the gods at this very site, their incense and ritual chants filling the chambers, calling forth magic to bless the surrounding earth. Baket lay curled in a giant ball, her dainty features and toes twitching as she slept. I wondered if the sphinx dreamed the same dreams cats dreamed, whatever those were. Mice and feathers, I supposed. She mewed awake and stretched, spreading her taloned paws and human jaws filled with feline fangs.

The big fire in the middle of camp had the most seated around it. A Medjai man brought out a *rebab*, an instrument which resembled a fiddle, and he caressed its strings with a long bow. His fingers plucked and quivered against those strings with an elegant, practiced speed as if they belonged to a lover. When Nasira sat beside him and began to sing, my visions of the past came to life. Her voice, along with the *rebab's* delicate notes, the vulnerability of it, possessed a magic of its own. I was utterly bewitched. As Nasira sang, her expression crushed with passion, I felt my heart wrench into knots and my will forbad it to tear into pieces.

"I didn't know she could sing," I said to Sayer in a quiet voice as not to interrupt.

"Music around a campfire is a Medjai tradition, but she's much better than the rest of us, so we let her do it. She would teach you some songs if you'd like."

I smiled, listening carefully. "What is she saying?"

He explained the song to me softly, so I wouldn't miss the beauty of her voice. "This is a very old Medjai song, from long before we were taken into pharaoh's service as soldiers, when we lived between the desert and the sky. 'Storyteller, storyteller, sing me a story, a tale of princes and princesses, and of spies and lovers and gods. Sing me a story of evil vanquished and the triumph of good. Sing to me of stones falling from the sky, of rain to turn the desert to gardens. Storyteller, storyteller, we are all children in our hearts, who have only dreams to look forward to, and no nightmares chasing us from behind. Storyteller, sing me a story.'"

Time passed, and I stirred, somewhat disoriented, until I realized I'd fallen asleep, curled up beside Sayer with my head in his lap. I didn't open my eyes, enjoying his body's warmth in the cool night air and the sounds of music and conversation—some English, some Arabic—all around us.

"Do you love her?" The honeyed voice could only have belonged to Baket.

"That must be a sphinx's riddle," came Sayer's reply.

I peeked with one eye to spy her slow, feline smile before I pretended to sleep. My heart quickened, and I prayed he wouldn't feel it.

"Is it?" she asked with little innocence in her voice.

"There are few things which survive death and time," he said vaguely. "Hatred and love are two of them. You can't feel true hatred without having first felt true love. To know one, you must know the other."

"Forgive me for not understanding human emotions, but why do you speak of hate when I ask you of love?"

I wondered the same thing. If anyone here spoke in riddles, it wasn't the sphinx.

Sayer exhaled. "Because an ageless and hateful fate has brought me to Ziva."

"What fate do you mean?" Baket asked.

"All this time," he said, "I'd fooled myself into believing what I felt was real, because it was expected of me, but what has directed the course of my life was always artificial. I hadn't realized how true hate felt until I met her—not hate of Ziva, of course. Rather, hate of those who intend to hurt her. Hate ensures I won't let that happen. A curious pair, love and hate. I'm certain hatred can't be felt until the heart's been broken."

"You speak as if you know this wound," Baket replied.

He hesitated. "My mother died recently."

"I see," the sphinx said, her voice gentle.

"Have you ever been in love?" he asked.

"No," she replied, her voice surprised as though she expected him to already have known the answer to his question. "It's not in my nature to love."

"Is hate in your nature?"

"No. So I suppose you must be right. My heart has been sad, but never broken."

"To answer and to not answer your question," Sayer said, trailing off, his hand brushing my hair behind my neck. "I haven't known Ziva for very long, but for the sake of sounding like every failed poet ever, some primeval part of me has always known her. Perhaps it's because she's been sort of mythologized among our people, or because we're so terribly alike." A soft laugh came from him. "But her instinct and her wit and her conviction—these things are so beautiful to me. That same primeval force within me wants them to be mine—needs them. I don't mean to possess her, like she's some pillar of gold, but I need her fire to light my every day and warm my every night. I would end the fool who tries to smother her flame."

A soft purr came from the sphinx. "That indeed answers my question."

"But I didn't say yes or no," he replied.

"You don't need to."

Sayer twirled a lock of my hair between his fingers. "I don't understand."

"Love on a human's face is unforgettable," the sphinx said. "It's the only place where such a thing becomes tangible. Love is on your lips, your cheeks, and it's brightest in your eyes, like starlight against nothingness. When you look at the lady, I know love. I see it."

"If you can see love on my face, then why did you ask me if I loved her?"

She answered, "I wasn't sure if you knew you did."

They grew quiet and once more the music and levity of the night lulled me to peace. I became jarringly aware of the world again as my body came into contact with a soft surface, surrounding me with the scent of fabric and Sayer himself. He'd carried me to my bed in my tent. I opened my eyes to gaze into his face as he lay me down.

"I'm not sure if I love you, since I've never loved anyone before," I told him groggily. "But I need you."

His hair, loose from its tie, brushed my cheek. His mouth pulled into a warm, sweet smile. "I need *you.*"

He kissed me, a tender brush of his lips on mine, and I scarcely had the energy to kiss him back.

"Stay," I said to him.

He lay beside me and I wasn't sure how long he would wait before he'd leave, depending on how proper this was, or if he paid any mind to propriety. I burrowed myself into his embrace, our limbs tangled. For however long he'd stay with me, I was glad for it.

The next morning, I waited for the sun to rise and I held out the queen's heart in front of me. The dawn light struck the enormous ruby and fired far into the desert, shining the way for us. Clark Camel and I readied ourselves, though I was moderately embarrassed at how poorly I rolled my tent. The lumpy mess sat awkwardly on the back of my saddle and I'd done my best to strap it down. With luck, I wouldn't lose it out in the wilderness.

Our camels proved hardy and didn't seem bothered by the heat or how far they had to take us. Most of the ancient temples, tombs, and cities had been built close to the Nile since the desert was so inhospitable. Even our ancestors didn't want to go too far from water. There seemed to be no end to the sands or my thirst. Baket seemed immune to the elements as she walked beside me. While my hood and scarf protected my skin from the sun, the kohl shielded my eyes from the brightness of the sun and any flies tagging along on Clark Camel.

As the sun rose higher, the burnished gold color of the sand lightened to the same shade of tawny brown as our camels. We scaled mountainous dunes and avoided impassible rocky formations. We crossed a plain of strange stone monuments naturally carved into mushroom shapes, whose stems had been eaten away for eons by the whipping wind and sand. Something appeared on the horizon at last and I squinted hard but was unable to make out the form that seemed to be waving in the extreme heat. The terrain became rougher and more dangerous, and the animals worked harder to scale the rising altitudes without injury. We passed a strikingly unique landscape of limestone and colorful rock jutting skyward from the sand. Great clusters of crystal pillars taller than me shone blindingly beneath the sun.

As we got closer, a mountain took shape on the horizon. The red beam from the ruby struck the mountain's peak, shining as bright as a second sun.

"This is it," I called to the others. "Up there!"

Anubis dismounted, peered toward the sky, the desert wind snatched at his tunic and pulled the hood back from his face. "I'll investigate. See you in a moment."

He vanished and we waited, tired and hot, for his confirmation. After a few moments, he returned.

"There's a dais and an entrance to a cave a hundred feet above," he said. "It's high enough that the opening was never filled with sand. There will be no trouble getting inside."

"Sure, no trouble after we climb this hundred-foot-tall rock wall," Nasira said with a grin.

Sayer hopped down from his camel and dug through his saddlebags to pull out climbing gear. He seemed on edge, tense for some reason I supposed was anticipation for the end of our journey. All we'd done and worked for had come down to this moment. But victory wasn't ours quite yet.

Once we were set up, Anubis and Baket winked away to wait for us at the cave entrance. As far as rock climbing went, going up was a lot harder than going down. If I hadn't worn so much protective clothing and swapped my fingerless combat gloves for full climbing ones, the sharp, jagged rock would have shredded my skin. When we all reached the dais, I removed my harness and ropes, troubled by Anubis's concerned expression.

"What's wrong?" I asked him.

"There's something preventing Baket and me from entering the cave," he explained. "Try going in yourself."

I nodded and inspected the opening carefully before I reached forward. My fingers passed the threshold and I felt nothing besides a prickle of magic. Confident, I stepped forward and entered. I looked back at Anubis. "There must be some kind of warding against immortals."

"Nefertari was clever to protect her resting place from anyone but Medjai," Cyrene noted. "She exhausted all measures to ensure her resurrection."

I turned around and peered into the darkness. "*Tahen*," I cast softly. The netherlight glow illuminated a short way into the deep tunnel, but there wasn't much to be seen from here.

An explosion of energy knocked me to the ground. The mountain trembled beneath my body. I whirled in shock to see Baket leap, claws outstretched, toward Kauket, the gold mask concealing her face ablaze in the sunlight. With a wave of her arm, the goddess blasted Baket with a fiery *khet* spell. The sphinx landed, twisting, shrieking, engulfed with flame. Kauket's second spell upended the ground between them and catapulted Baket. Her claws wildly lashed at the air as she flew, scraping rock, but she could not stop herself from falling over the side of the cliff.

"*Baket!*" I shrieked, the sound tearing from my throat.

Anubis drew the sword from the sheath at his waist, his own mask of gold forming across his face, and screamed, "Ziva, *go!*"

Horror took me like a riptide. Nasira grabbed my arm.

"Let's move!" she shouted, but her voice seemed distant.

I swallowed hard, my friends' fates uncertain, and I did what I came here to do.

CHAPTER
23

Inside the passage, everything became too quiet too quickly. My sharp gasp cut through the silence.

Cyrene's *tahen* spell illuminated the blackness. "We must keep going," she directed.

We descended deep into the tunnel, which had been chiseled from rock with less embellishment than expected for a royal tomb. The queen's enemies and tomb raiders would never have expected to find anything important in this hole in the mountainside. It was deceptively plain, and I understood why the lavishly decorated empty tomb had been such a perfect decoy. Here, the walls were narrow. The ceiling was low. The ground was uneven. I stepped lightly and carefully so as not to trip and twist an ankle.

Sayer's arm shot across my chest, stopping me in my tracks. "There's a drop off." He pointed to the ground, and I shone my netherlight orb at the toes of my boots.

Pebbles and grit broke away from the rock and fell into oblivion.

We prepared our climbing equipment once again. Tariq was the first to scale the rope, sliding down easily with his gloved hands, kicking off the rock wall to give himself a boost. A few moments later, his boots scraped earth.

"All clear," he called up to us coolly.

We followed and reassembled below to find ourselves in a chamber larger and wider than the tunnel above.

I turned around and strengthened my *tahen* spell. Netherlight glittered on an enormous rose granite sarcophagus. Hieroglyphs and ritual imagery were carved into every inch of the stone, save for the exquisite face carved on the lid. The figure's carefully drawn eyes were open, serenely gazing toward the heavens, her lips full and calm.

"We've found her," Nasira said, her voice hushed with disbelief.

Gilded chests were arranged neatly; we lifted lids to find garments, ornate ceremonial wigs, cosmetics jars and applicators, and an immense fortune of jewelry. Everything the queen would need to look her best when she awakened. Against the far wall was a more sinister sight: desiccated corpses slumped beside one another, their bodies anything but properly mummified. It appeared as if they'd died then and there thousands of years ago. I recalled what Sayer had told me of the rumors regarding Nefertari's true tomb—that those servants who sealed her sarcophagus from within also sealed themselves in, protecting the secret of the location for all time. I hoped they hadn't suffered long. The sight itself was disturbing, but I was more unsettled by the fact this had happened at all. I supposed the world was different then, even for a queen who'd been heralded as a great ruler. Still, it was disturbing.

"Let's lift this," Cyrene said, instructing us all to stand on each side of the coffin.

Our collective and careful *taw* spell raised the incredible load and set the lid on the ground. The inner coffin was crafted of wood, painted with melted gold, and covered with funerary scenes. Nefertari's cartouche was inscribed between her likeness's crossed arms and the beautiful, winged image of the horned goddess of love, Hathor. We lifted the second lid and set it beside the first. Contained within the inner coffin was the fourth and final canopic jar—and a mummy wrapped in creamy-white, aged linen strips, her face concealed within a solid gold death mask carved delicately into her likeness. She wore the gold vulture crown of Tefnut over a wig of dark henna-dyed hair carefully curled and threaded with pearls and other gemstones.

Cyrene reunited the last canopic jar with the other three inside the coffin beside the mummy. She cautiously lifted the wig first, then the death mask. She drew her dagger as we waited in breathless silence and cut through the linen covering the mummy's entire head. To my astonishment, Nefertari had been remarkably preserved, despite her skin having dried and darkened with age. She wore a peaceful expression in death, her cheekbones pronounced and lips closed, though they'd thinned. Her thick hair remained wrapped and pinned to her scalp, and I imagined the tresses were still quite long.

"The heart, Ziva," Cyrene said, and I blinked to attention and handed the giant ruby to our priestess. She placed it on Nefertari's chest and the stone flashed, flashed, and dimmed, flashed, flashed, and dimmed just as a heart would beat.

Cyrene raised her palms skyward and magic pounded the air around her. "Osiris!" she bellowed. "King of the netherworld and of the righteous dead! Banisher of the damned to oblivion! He who was murdered by Chaos and resurrected! I invoke you!"

Light grew from the queen's heart, pulsing, surging, flooding the chamber with red. Braziers in the four corners of the room burst brightly with netherlight. Magic swallowed us all.

"I invoke thee, Osiris!" Cyrene continued. "I invoke the messengers of any god! I invoke all the gods! Hail to you, the wardens of eternity, founders of the everlasting! Queen Nefertari is the possessor of the pure heart. She is the pure lotus who awakens from the long night and comes forth by day. I have collected the magic from every place it was hidden and brought it here. I have the queen's heart and through it, Nefertari's soul will find her mortal body, return to life, and become immortal. Her heart is hers alone and obeys no other. Her mouth is hers, so she may speak. Her legs are hers to walk. Her arms are hers to raise and destroy her enemies. Nefertari is aware in her heart! She speaks with her mouth! She walks with her legs! She raises her arms to destroy her enemies! Let the sky open its doors to the domain of eternity. Allow her soul to come forth through the stargate, return to her body, and arise a living goddess. Arise, Nefertari, Favored of the Sun! Arise! Arise! *Arise!*"

The mummy's eyes opened, a brilliant, sparkling green. The magic flowing through her and spilling over the walls of the granite sarcophagus was intoxicating. It seeped through my skin and soaked my muscles and bones. Nefertari sat forward, her dry skin scraping and scratching. She raised her hands and began to claw at her linen wrappings. She lifted the ruby heart in her palm, but it had grown dark and lost its glimmer. She dropped it beside her as if it were a spare brick. She turned to look at us, that orphic green glowing in our netherlight.

She opened her mouth, licked her lips, and tried to speak. "Medjai," she rasped, the word barely audible, and she touched her cracked fingertips to her desiccated throat. Her bare feet touched the ground and she settled onto them shakily. She was quite petite with small shoulders, standing a good half a foot shorter than me, but her hips were shapely and womanly. She raised her hands to unbind her hair and those long, walnut-brown tresses tumbled over her shoulders.

Everyone around me settled to the floor to bow, kneeling with their heads lowered, some with their palms flat out on the ground. I followed suit, hoping not to make a mistake in front of our queen.

Nefertari asked something in Ancient Egyptian, her

voice rough and weak. We rose once she addressed us and I stood with them.

Cyrene replied in English, "More than three thousand years, my queen. I am high priestess of the Medjai."

Nefertari paused, surprise lighting her face for a moment, before she nodded with acceptance. Her gaze surveyed us with interest; I imagined our clothing was nothing like she'd ever seen before. When she noticed me, she came forward, eyes fixed on my face. "This is the scion," she said, miraculously in English as well, her tone assured as though she already knew the answer to her question, could sense it.

"Yes, my queen," the priestess said.

"Do you know the transference spell?" Nefertari asked.

"Yes, my queen."

"Then proceed."

Cyrene turned and raised a hand. Magic shot toward me, clamped my arms to my sides. I tried to wrestle free of her grip, stricken speechless with confusion.

"What are you doing?" My heart began to pound and the air around me seemed to condense and grow so heavy I could barely breathe. People around me stared in shock, mouths open. I looked up to the priestess, who wore no expression at all.

"Cyrene!" I yelled at her. She ignored me. *"Cyrene!"* Somehow I pushed forward, taking a step and she looked at me with surprise. Then an invisible force collided with me, shoving me backward, my boots squeaking on the stone floor. Nefertari's hard green glare pinned on me, her magic tightening on my body like a fist.

"What is happening?" Sayer demanded. "What are you doing?"

When he started toward me, Cyrene cast out her hand, her power picking him up and slamming his back into the wall, suspending him in the air. His face was wild with panic. "No! *No! Ziva!*"

Nefertari's mummy stepped shakily toward me, her desiccated face pinched with curiosity. "Why must you be restrained? Are you not honored by your sacrifice?"

At that last word, Nasira tore her *asaya* free and shot toward Nefertari, but Cyrene met her with one stride. Her own weapon cracked against Nasira's. Cyrene's *asaya* swept high, slashing Nasira across the chest. My friend wailed with pain and her legs buckled, but before her knees could hit the ground, Cyrene's magic cast her body across the room.

"Nasi!" I yelled but did not see her stir.

Tariq stepped forward, and in a low, shaking voice he said, "What is this, Cyrene? You attack my children." He drew an *asaya*. Other Medjai pulled their own weapons, but some moved to stand beside Cyrene and not against her. The room was carved in two as though by a blade.

The high priestess summoned her power and it manifested as a shining light, spiraling up her legs and down her arms to pour into her open hands. "Our queen's resurrection must be complete. Her soul was returned to her body, but her life's vitality was reborn within Ziva. It rightfully belongs to Nefertari. Our queen must be restored."

The sinister truth in her words resonated quickly.

"That's a very fancy way of saying you mean to kill me," I accused her.

Cyrene looked at me, void of empathy. "I would gladly take your place. But unfortunately for us both, that cannot be done."

"You had this planned the entire time," I replied, pressing against my magical bonds for freedom.

"You are Medjai, Ziva, but you're not truly one of us," she told me. "*We* understand the life of our queen matters more than any and all of ours."

Her power encircled me and pulled me toward her. My limbs were frozen in place and I could barely move. My growled *taw* spell slammed into Cyrene and broke her concentration for an instant.

Sayer clawed free of the magic restraining him and charged toward me, only to be hit with the powerful *sena* spell Cyrene threw in front of him. His wild eyes darted all over the shining shield before he started trying to break through it. His *taw* spell struck hard, and magic sparked. As he cast over and over, I could feel every gust and blast, but the high priestess's spell was too strong.

With a roar, he tore back his fist and punched as hard as he could. He beat at it, his voice rage-strangled deep in his throat. The magic cracked, the splinters of light blinding and electric. He shoved his shoulder into the barrier, pushed and pushed. Blood streaked his arms, flashes of red in the searing brightness.

He was killing himself. Tears scalded my eyes.

"Stop," I begged him, as he tried to get to me. "Stop, Sayer, *please.*"

Cyrene withdrew the magical wall only to throw another spell into his body and dash him away from me. He hit the ground rolling and her magic snatched him up into the air and bound him with the same spell restraining me. I turned back to Cyrene who marched toward me once more.

Sayer's screams of fury filled my ears. "*Ziva*! No! *No!*" He screamed and screamed, the sound of his anguish tearing my skull and heart in half—then he went silent. My head snapped in his direction and his body had gone rigid as stone. I could see the tendrils of fire-crackling magic coiled around his throat, cutting off his air.

"Stop it!" I screamed at her. "Don't hurt him!"

"Ziva, I don't want to," Cyrene said to me as she drew me close.

Rage curdled inside me. I spat at her. Spittle flecked her cheek and she raised a hand to wipe it away with a grimace. My teeth gnashed at her; I must've looked like a wild animal.

Set had been right. His words echoed in my mind, each syllable a slap to my face: "*If you knew anything at all, you'd beg me for sanctuary.*"

"You disgust me," I hissed at the woman I had so admired.

Whatever calm Tariq had grasped onto had slipped from his fingers. "These are my children, Cyrene!" He launched at her, but two of the Medjai who'd stood with her grasped both his arms, wrested him to his knees, and poised their blades at his throat. "My wife *died* for this!"

The pressure of Nefertari's magic descended on me,

a cold, electric prickle. The queen was supposed to have arisen as a living god, and that meant her power had to rival Set's and Anubis's. How could I possibly escape from this with my life?

"We were given magic to protect and serve Egypt at any cost," Cyrene said, addressing us all. "Our lives have never been our own."

"My parents knew what you had planned for me," I growled at her. "They fled to America to protect me, because I was more important to them than some dead queen who should've stayed dead."

Nefertari turned toward me, and I couldn't imagine how I'd found any beauty in her grey, dead face. Her lips twisted into a snarl and those eyes—that electric green—flared like the color the sky turns during the worst and deadliest of storms.

A shadow passed over Cyrene's face and anger quivered in her frown. "Your parents became traitors that day. My mission was to retrieve you, but I found your father first in New York seventeen years ago."

"You murdered him," I growled venomously. "Did you murder my mother too?"

"I found her nearly a year later in France," Cyrene corrected. "She'd left you in New York and fled alone, leaving far larger tracks than you ever had. I suspect she intended to lure me away from you. You'd disappeared, nameless, among countless New York orphans. She never gave you up during my interrogation. She died to protect you. I took no joy in ending her life."

Heat, horror, and understanding hit me like the blast

from an oven. Desperation to tear this creature limb from limb ran through my veins like fire. "You stole my parents' lives! You stole *my* life! I will end you for what you've done!"

Cyrene's teeth snapped together and the muscle in her jaw rippled. "Ziva, they ran from their destiny—your destiny. None of this is about us. Our duty is to protect this world and our queen. I did my duty—just as I must do again."

Cyrene faced Nefertari, raised her hands, and bellowed: "I know all your names and I praise you, the wardens of eternity! The magic is mine and the power is hers, Queen Nefertari. Her soul has returned on the great wind of the sky. She will be vindicated against her enemies! She will strike them down with stone and blade and magic! From her womb, she was made immortal. Her daughters and their daughters and their daughters have lived on her heart's blood and here she will reclaim it! This life is hers! This vitality is hers! Her daughter yields her life! Nefertari will be whole!"

"Ziva, don't stop fighting," Tariq begged me. I looked at him, into the ardent tears of his eyes. "Don't let them do this."

The queen flicked her wrist and Tariq's neck cracked. His head lopped to the side and his body went starkly limp. Those who held him let him drop.

A scream of horror tore from my throat.

Nefertari moved toward me, her arms outstretched. The ancient linen covering her body was so very, very dry.

I opened my hand wide and said, "*Khet.*" Magical flame

erupted, catching the crispy, papery linen. The queen gasped with surprise and her wail filled the chamber. The magic binding me fell like ashes at my feet. I bolted for the entrance toward freedom.

My body slammed to a halt and my internal organs crushed together against my diaphragm. Nausea flooded me. I yelped as I was hauled upward through the air. My spine cracked into the ceiling. The floor was too far below me. The air expelled from me as magic dragged me across jagged stone. The world whirred past my vision. My body was yanked again, down at an angle, and I hit the wall before the magic released me. I crumpled to the ground and lifted my head.

Nefertari stood above me, her bejeweled, skeletal body engulfed in red flame and black smoke, her eyes shining green. She was a vision ripped from a nightmare I'd never had the imagination to conjure.

"I will claim what is mine and the gods will tremble before me!" the queen roared. "My shadow will spread across the sands of Egypt and beyond the currents of the seas, the infinite imperishable stars—all that creation has touched belongs to me!"

Those eyes shot wide and bulged. Her mouth dropped open and she tried to lift her arms, but they seemed glued to her sides. I recognized this spell. *Sekhem.* But it wasn't mine.

Sayer held one hand high, fist clenched. Magic surged from him, wave after wave crashing into the floor. The tomb's ceiling shook, the walls rumbled.

He was trying to bring it down on the queen.

His eyes met mine. "Go, Ziva. Run!"

I shook my head. "Not without you."

A scream freed itself from Nefertari's throat and she broke free of Sayer's magic. She turned on him. Netherlight and shadows erupted in the space around her, and in an instant, she was in front of him. Had him by the throat. Closed her fist. And she let him fall, his body loose and limp. A broken toy at her feet.

Satisfaction filled her gaunt face.

Not without him. Not without him. I couldn't go.

He was dead. Sayer died for me. Tariq died for me. My parents died for me. Nasira had likely suffered the same fate.

They were dead so I would live.

So I *would* live.

I shot to my feet and wasted no time in darting toward the exit once more. Chaos had erupted behind me; roars of anger and confusion rose to the heavens, but I didn't look back.

With a small *tahen* spell lighting my way, I ran. At last I reached the rock wall we'd climbed down and I quickly strapped myself into my equipment. Alone, the ascent was dangerous and difficult. Every muscle in my body screamed at me and I ignored them all.

"I'm strong now," I told myself, my voice strained. "My body is no longer starved and weak. I made myself strong. I can do this."

I reached the top, and as I hauled myself up over the edge, the pain of the effort tore a cry from my throat. Safely on firm ground, I allowed myself a moment's rest.

My chest heaved, desperate for breath and relief. I stood, my muscles screaming at me, and I discarded my climbing harness and rope. I paused and looked behind me. Anger flushed through my cheeks. I knelt at the edge of the drop-off, removed my *was* dagger, and I cut that rope.

CHAPTER

24

At the mouth of the tunnel, I found Baket pacing impatiently and I almost sobbed with joy. Her expression twisted with concern at my disheveled and panicked condition.

"Baket!" I cried and ran to her. I threw my arms around her neck and hugged her tight. "You're okay! Where is Anubis?"

Uncertainty filled her eyes and my stomach plummeted. "He and Kauket have gone and . . . others have come."

I stared at her, baffled, too exhausted. "Others?"

"Humans," the sphinx said.

She led me to the edge of the dais where I could see the assembling of military vehicles and dozens of soldiers—each wearing a red Nazi sash on their arms.

"We have to go," I said, swallowing my panic. I fumbled with my harness and ropes until Baket nudged my arm.

She did not ask me why or what had happened inside the tomb. She did not question why I was alone.

"Climb on," she said, and gestured to her back with a nod of her head.

I did as she instructed, bleary-brained and desperate for escape. With both my legs astride her back, I clasped my hands together around her chest. She took a couple steps toward the cliff edge and leapt. I squeezed my legs as hard as I could, held on with my hands, and I felt my body rise off her back. Before I could cry out, we hit the ground with the grace of a bird and relief flooded through me.

That relief was immediately stolen from me as the large trucks and tanks rolled to a stop twenty yards from us. Soldiers hopped out, their boots thudding softly in the sand, their rifles jangling and clicking. The same ten-foot-tall bipedal mechanical suits I saw at the Cairo airport plodded toward us, expelling diesel smoke, hydraulics hissing. Within the protective mesh cages, their pilots pulled levers to raise the large guns built into the machines' arms.

I slid from my sphinx's back and stood tall, no matter how tired and brutalized I felt. Magic sparked at my fingers. I would do what I had to do for survival.

My heel dug into the earth and I launched, the toes of my boots skimming the ground. The Nazi soldier below me fired twice and my *taw* spell cast both bullets from their course. I smashed my fist into his helmet and the tempered obsidian chips of my gloved knuckles shredded steel with a scream. He collapsed to the ground, and

I tore his helmet from his head, breaking the buckle. I landed in a crouch as another soldier raised his gun and I swung the helmet, catching bullets and mangling what was left of the steel. I let the helmet fling from my grip, and I ripped my *asaya* from its holster and spun. The staff extended with a *crack* and I whirled it faster. When a third soldier's attention turned to my weapon, I kicked his knee with all my strength. Bone yielded, and he sank to his feet, the cry of agony from him shrill. My *asaya* spun and struck the outstretched hand of the next soldier, and he dropped his gun as his fingers splintered. My *asaya* struck again, this time across his back, slashing his coat in two.

The delicate, metallic jostling sound of a pistol behind my head made me freeze.

"Juggernauts, *halt!*"

My weapon thudded in the sand. Breathless, I swallowed hard and raised my hands.

Baket hissed and stepped forward. "Don't!" I shouted to her. I couldn't bear to watch their bullets tear apart her body. The soldiers, to my astonishment, did not react as violently to the sight of her as I would've expected them to. Perhaps this wasn't their first confrontation with the supernatural.

A woman barked orders in German and the soldiers lowered their guns but did not relax.

I whirled and recognized the Nazi woman and high-ranking officer emerging through the crowd. He had pinkish-white skin and his cold blue eyes stared at me with such contempt I imagined he could watch me bleed out in the sand without so much as frowning.

"Can I help you, gentlemen?" I called to the crowd. "Or are there none left man enough to challenge a woman?"

The officer scoffed, a guttural, phlegmy sound in his throat, and muttered something in German that I imagined from his tone was a very, very nasty word.

"Ziva Mereniset," the Nazi woman said, removing her sunglasses to gaze at me with wide, hungry eyes. "I didn't have the opportunity to introduce myself before. I am Doctor Ursula Vogt."

"How did you learn my name?" I demanded.

"With a great deal of trouble," Vogt replied. "I like your sphinx."

Baket and I exchanged glances and she took a step forward. I gave her a subtle warning shake of my head. "You don't seem all that alarmed by her presence."

"No," she replied, her voice cool, but a shadow of madness grew in her eyes. "I have seen things, Ziva. Done things."

Her words sowed dread in the pit of my stomach. "We will be on our way now," I announced.

The juggernauts took a collective step forward, hydraulics wheezing. Their officer barked an order in German and they froze.

"I believe you have something we seek," she declared. "Please relinquish the queen's heart."

Adrenaline sparked a flame in my blood. "You're too late. Its power is gone."

Tendrils of shadows snaked across the ground

between the soldiers' boots, creeping toward me. My throat tightened, snatching any whimper of terror I might have made.

"*You*," came a woman's voice I knew, one sizzling with malice. "You mortal *fool*."

Kauket's form materialized in the inky darkness and the pressure of a terrible power closed in on my skull. When I saw her face, all the blood in my body crashed and I nearly crumpled to the earth.

"What have you *done*?" Her voice trembled and her own fear seeped through the cracks in her rage. Gold blood stained her dress.

"Where is Anubis?" I demanded. This couldn't be. He was stronger than her. She couldn't beat him.

Tremors of unease and muffled voices rose from among the men as they shuffled in their places, their weapons rattling. They'd become nothing more than an audience to me; my attention was wholly on the goddess eager to crush me in her hands.

"You've got greater concerns now than his wellbeing," Set warned as and he appeared behind me. I jumped and Baket positioned herself between me and the god of chaos, a growl rumbling from deep within her chest.

"You knew." The words were a rush of air from my mouth.

"I gave you the chance to come with me," he said, but his tone wasn't exactly condescending. "You should have taken it."

I gaped at him. "You were trying to kill me!"

"I wasn't trying to kill you, I was getting to know you."

There wasn't enough time in the world to explain how bizarre that was.

"We were searching for a savior and unearthed a monster, and you knew we would," I accused him, my voice sharp and unforgiving. "Why didn't you just tell me?"

He crossed his arms, tossing me a pointed yet sympathetic look. "Would you have believed me? If I'd wanted to kidnap you, child, I would have."

I looked around me, at the faces of the Nazi soldiers who didn't know which creature to aim their guns at. The decorated officer barked orders in German and they reassembled quickly. The juggernauts raised their machine guns.

I started to walk toward Set. The soldiers shuffled once more with uncertainty. My heart hammered in my chest, but I would not allow my fear to surface. Baket followed, and the men gave her a wide berth. The juggernauts took lumbering steps back with a collective hiss and whine.

I walked past the bewildered Vogt and the officer to Set, who beamed at me with what I swore was pride. A weight seemed to lift from his brow and his eyes brightened as though he'd removed a mask. He seemed younger in that moment—almost human.

"Ziva," he said, his voice earnest and low. "I wanted the heart's power so I could rule my kind. Now, the heart is gone. I need your help. Nefertari's heart was not the only queen's heart. The blood and the power are in yours too. You and I can stop her together."

An explosion behind me deafened my ears. Set looked

up and bared his teeth. I whirled in horror as rock debris rained from the sky all around us. Men scattered in a panic. Their grunts of pain and surprise vanished in the smothering cloud of dust. Set's *sena* spell stopped a boulder from careening into the two of us.

The top of the mountain had blasted apart. The cliff dais was now in fragments at our feet. A profound hush settled on us.

A man's scream rose and then was drowned by a deafening metallic clang. I ducked as a truck hurtled over our heads and crashed onto its side before skidding into another. More men screamed, firing their weapons in all directions as their bodies were tossed into the air, crushed and twisted by the *sekhem* spell cast from someone unseen. A juggernaut's machine gun tore apart the tanks as its pilot fired in a wild, sweeping arc. Vogt and the officer darted through the pandemonium, their hands shielding their faces, shrieking orders in German.

Set grabbed my arm and yanked me around him as a tank exploded and sprayed shards of metal. His broad body shielded me; I clung to him, and a chunk of steel the length of my arm tore through his shoulder. Our eyes met in bewilderment and shock. The look of utter fear on his face was more terrifying than anything happening around me. Then the fear washed from his visage and the look the god of chaos gave me promised he would lay waste. His golden battle mask materialized, consuming his face and any trace of humanity left in him.

Shadows and netherlight flashed. Vanished. Flashed again twenty feet to our right. Vanished. An unseen force yanked a soldier off his feet and through the air. His body was eaten by the burning tank's flames.

A horrible darkness spread across the sky, drawn like a curtain by a great fist. An invisible blade slew the sun. The screams, the screams. Breaking bones and blood and dust. The world was on fire.

I squeezed my eyes shut, clapped my hands over my ears.

A surge of electricity pierced my skull, and my eyelids flew open.

The silhouette of a woman against the flames moved toward me. Hair billowed around her like a cape. A shining mask of gold concealed her face, her eyes behind it flashing green.

"*You will watch*," came Nefertari's breathy whisper in my head. "*You will see.*"

She raised her hands and opened her mouth in a scream, massive, explosive, world-ending. Her power and rage were one murderous beast, swallowing all other sound. Machine gun flashes lit the darkness, the snap and pop of gunfire lost in the queen's roar.

Set rose above me, his power building like a storm, and detonated with his scream. The earth lurched and swayed and rolled, the sand blasting from him, tearing into the air around us. Trucks and tanks, juggernauts and human bodies were cast aside like wads of paper. The queen may have been an unholy monster, but the desert belonged to Set.

"Lady! *Lady!*"

I didn't know how long Baket had shrieked into my

ear before she nudged me hard with the top of her head, snatching my attention.

Nefertari was horrible. Her power . . . she was more than I had imagined. More than Set had imagined. She was doom and destruction. She was not the savior the Medjai had made me believe in. This world was hers for the taking and take it she would. Piece by piece. Bone by bone.

I looked up to meet Baket's wide, terrified eyes. "We have to run."

The sphinx nodded briskly. "Yes, we do."

I sprinted toward where the camels had blessedly remained tied, though they grunted and danced with fright. Out of mercy, I took valuable seconds of time to cut the tethers of all the animals so they could get themselves to safety. Clark Camel stared at me and groaned eagerly.

I slapped his rump and yelled at him, "Go! You stupid thing, *go!*"

He spooked, spinning hard and bolting. A panicked German shout made me jump and spin to face a line of soldiers with raised guns. This close, I could see their faces. They were so young. Boys my age. A few surely younger. And so afraid.

One of them shouted at me in German and backed up his threat with three gunshots into the sky before pointing the barrel at me again. Boys or not, they would kill me.

A rising, crawling fog rose between us, shimmering and crackling with magic. The soldiers looked about themselves with fright before they dropped with a collective exhale and thud in the sand. I held my own breath and stared, horrified, at their lifeless bodies littering the ground before me.

"Ziva."

My name in his voice was a hoarse, broken effort. Anubis appeared in front of me, looking beaten, worn, exhausted. He could feel me, my heart, the grief and terror and hopelessness. He looked past me and at the carnage he himself had wrought.

"I am so sorry," he said softly, and I wasn't sure to whom he was apologizing. "To use my power only causes pain to others, to myself. For me to take mortal life . . . it is an abomination."

"They intended to kill me," I told him. "You saved me. Set saved me."

"If he'd told me the truth about Nefertari and I'd trusted him, then we wouldn't be here right now," Anubis admitted tiredly.

"Perhaps he didn't think he could trust you either," I offered. "And whatever creature arose from that tomb . . . it is not of this world."

"You have to keep moving," he urged. "The only thing that matters now is survival."

My senses became clearer again. "We will meet again soon," I told my friend.

Anubis nodded, and Baket nudged my hip. I climbed onto her back and couldn't help myself but to search the distance for my camel, who was long gone. The need to scream and sob returned. I took a deep breath and urged Baket into a gallop for our lives.

I did not steer the sphinx into the direction we'd come from, but slightly northeast, based on the sun's position above my head, and toward the Nile where we'd find civilization. I turned to look behind us and cast a powerful *taw* spell. The magical wind beat into the sand, kicking it up, lashing it through the air, and erased our tracks. I urged her to lope faster, deeper into the desert.

CHAPTER

25

*❯❯*Lady, we are close to Asyut."

Baket's voice stirred me from a strange, restless sleep maybe more accurately described as a state of unconsciousness. If I'd had any nightmares, then I didn't remember them. I slumped against her back, unable to feel my hands or feet anymore, and I realized she had slowed to a walk at some point.

I lifted my head, squinting against the harsh sunlight, and searched my surroundings. We were still in the desert and traveled alongside a mountain range. Cut into the rock were numerous levels of rectangular openings half-filled with sand and debris. Old Kingdom tombs, I was sure. I wondered who'd been buried there eons ago.

Baket and I continued our trek, and I felt wearier than before. A city of haze emerged on the horizon smudged with deep, lush greens. The promise of water and shade spurred me with excitement.

"This is where I leave you, lady," the sphinx said, her sweet voice softened with regret.

"I understand," I told her. "We can't attract attention from the locals."

She nodded and frowned. "Stay safe."

Her form dissolved into the wind. The realization that I was alone hit me with a bitter punch to my gut. I wanted to scream now more than ever, into the emptiness of the desert, but if I allowed myself to then I'd lie down and die. Death would be the last thing I'd succumb to if I had any say in my fate.

Asyut was less colorful than the tourist-centric Aswan. Flat-topped buildings rose straight out of the Nile, their mud brick walls stained at different heights, indicative of past flooding. The river's opposite shore was lush palm groves and crop fields. I trudged into town, overlooked by passing motorcars and donkey carts. The occasional airship above cast its shadow over the street as it followed the Nile.

I felt like a broken, spinning compass that couldn't find its way. I had two choices: travel south into Sudan where I had no clue what to expect or any of the language, or head north and get passage out of Egypt through Cairo. But that was risky even if I stayed on the run and ahead of the Medjai. Escaping to Europe and somehow finding my way home to America wasn't an option. They'd expect me to do exactly that. If I knew French, then I could've gone west, to Morocco. I'd have to make my decision once I got to Cairo.

Fear and uncertainty had me by the throat, but I didn't have time to let them in yet. Not yet.

There were no airships docked today, but I wasn't discouraged. Since an airship would've been faster, Cyrene might watch for me to travel that way rather than by river.

I headed back to the docks and purchased my ticket on the first boat out. My stomach rolled and squeezed itself around my insides. I hadn't been this hungry since I met the Medjai, but if I wandered into a restaurant looking as ragged and filthy as I did, I'd get chased away. I found a lamp vendor nearby, and in the glossy reflection of brass baubles, I surveyed the damage.

Another disadvantage of having thick, curly hair was being unable to brush it out. I did what I could with my fingers to reshape the curls from out of the dirty, bushy mop my hair had become. With a little bit of saliva on my thumb, I could smear away most of the blood and dirt. After a couple minutes I looked like a person no one would run from screaming.

I had enough money to buy a meal, so from a street cart in the souk I ordered a dish of *ful medames*, mashed fava beans with garlic and lemon juice and a few triangle slices of pita bread. I selected a table on a café patio and ate.

"Good afternoon," came a voice I was sure I'd heard before.

I looked up and choked on my food. "You!" I exclaimed, bewildered to see Ursula Vogt alive in front of me.

"Yes, me," she replied in English. "So astonished, Ziva. I'd love a chat with you, if you have a moment."

"How did you find me?"

"If there is one thing Germans exceed at, it's finding what we want," she replied slyly. If she weren't wearing those huge sunglasses I was sure there'd be a wicked gleam in her eye. The wide brim of her fabric slouch hat concealed much of her face and her shoulder-length blond hair. She smelled faintly of diesel fuel and cigarettes. She wore a khaki trench coat belted at her waist and black leather gloves.

"Well, you surely exceed at dodging questions," I grumbled, glancing around us. A tall white man in a Nazi uniform paced outside the entrance, making me more uneasy. How could any of them have possibly survived?

"We have ways of detecting paranthropic energies," Vogt explained vaguely, then paused. At my baffled expression, she continued. "Intelligent, nonhuman life and beings long considered myth."

I glowered at her. "Sorry to disappoint you, but I am human."

"Not according to our qualifications," she replied coolly and removed her sunglasses and placed them on the table in front of her, revealing a piercing blue gaze. "I believe yours is a strong species, and I choose to be open and honest with you because I hope you will cooperate with us. The men in control of my country support my research, and within the National Socialist organization is a group devoted to a higher cause. You may call us the Thule Society. Our purpose is rooted in lineage and history."

"Your armed soldier pals didn't look like scholars to me," I challenged. "They look like Nazis."

Her red lips flattened, though not quite in a smile. "My associates allow me the means to do my job."

"Which is?"

"To bring greatness and strength to our cause," Vogt explained, and her mouth formed a true smile, sparkling with self-pride. "We want to find beings like you."

"Why?" I asked, stunned.

"Paranthropes are capable of magical or scientific feats ordinary humans are not," she replied. "We are interested in your power."

"For global domination," I finished callously for her, narrowing my gaze. "The French have overrun Morocco, Algeria, and Egypt. The British won't let India go. Your cause is to exploit and destroy as many groups of people as possible. There is no glory in imperialism, there is only decimation."

"The Führer's interests are more complicated than that," she said. "He wants to avenge the German people for our humiliation during the Great War and to create the perfect race, the *true* human race. The Thule Society has begun several successful programs, including the very ambitious Lebensborn Project. But our last meeting has inspired me, Ziva, and I have seen my true purpose."

I pushed my plate aside and leaned forward onto the table. "Which is, Doctor Vogt?"

The madness I'd seen before in her eyes began to glow again as she replied, "To create a god."

If I'd had energy, I would have laughed in her face. "You can't."

Her brow raised, and one corner of her red lips tugged into a smile. "Can't I? You saw with your own eyes mortal flesh made immortal and gifted power beyond anything in this world. Not even the old gods could stand against her might."

At the mere memory of Nefertari rising from the carnage and mayhem she wrought herself, the blood in my veins began to freeze with fear. "I would not call what I witnessed a gift."

"If you would let me study you, I might be able to recreate your abilities in our people," Vogt explained excitedly. "Imagine the incredible things the Aryan race could do if we had power like yours. A god leading our war machines. We wish to bring unity to a broken and tumultuous world. Your kind can aid us."

"You want to *use* us," I interjected. "But you picked me because I'm an outsider, even to them. You've been watching me."

Vogt paused, her chest rising and falling slowly. Those blue eyes seemed to slip into my skin like needles to probe the flesh beneath. "I want to be friends with you, Ziva," she said. "But I don't have to be to get what I want. Consider this my first petition of only three. If you refuse my third, then I will take you by force."

I almost laughed, but I was too tired and angry. "If you think you can take me by force then you know even less about *my kind* than you thought," I warned her, my voice shaking, as I leaned across the table toward her. "Gods have tried to take me by force and yet I sit here today having my lunch. Never mind the sphinx awaiting my safe return. You remember her, surely."

Ursula Vogt smiled at me in a very disquieting way. "I could not forget. Your implication is clear, but please understand something about me as well. We all have our monsters. Some we keep in chains and save for a rainy day."

Her threat did not faze me. "I would like you, Doctor Ursula Vogt, to get out of my sight and never speak to me again. I will not be so accommodating to your presence again."

Several long, achingly frigid moments of silence passed between us.

She rose from her chair and smoothed out the skirt of her belted coat. "Have a lovely evening, Ziva Mereniset. I shall see you soon."

CHAPTER

26

Nothing I could do would alleviate the tension in my shoulders from my confrontation with Vogt—not a full belly, nothing. After I boarded the ferry and got the key to my cabin—really, it was more like a glorified closet—I climbed onto the hard cot, wishing I had a change of clothes. Everything I'd had was left in the saddlebags and gone with my camel for good.

I woke, groggy from sleep and as sore as I had been after Nasira's first training session. That felt like a hundred years ago, even though it'd only been a few months.

A shadow in the dark room made my heart jump in surprise. "Good evening, lady," Baket said sweetly.

Relief soothed my aching muscles. "What time is it?" I asked.

"Not long after midnight," she replied. "How did you sleep?"

Midnight. That meant we'd departed from the docks

and were floating somewhere down the Nile. I yawned and rubbed my stiff neck. "Not so well."

The sphinx's head tilted to the side. "Why is that?"

"Well," I began, "this bed is less comfortable to sleep on than on the ground, and I have a lot of things on my mind. I need to decide what I'm going to do."

"What *we* will do," she said. "I am your friend, lady. I'm with you."

An invisible dagger plunged into my gut. Sayer had said the same thing. And he was gone. So was Nasira and both their parents. And both my parents. Murdered by someone I had trusted with my life.

Oddly enough, I trusted Baket. She was a creature with human intelligence and animal-like, pure-hearted, unconditional love. Animals always felt more honest to me than humans, who were capable of such cruelty. Animals never thought to hurt anyone else, even when they killed for food. They only thought of their own survival, and that left no room in their hearts for betrayal.

I let myself succumb to the chasm in my heart, let the emptiness swarm all of my senses, but I found no relief. My body curled into a tight, trembling ball on the cot. I sank into despair with a keening wail muffled by my pillow, allowing the tragedy and brutality of what happened consume me. My sobs were ugly, shuddering gasps like I was a fish hooked and tossed onto a boat's deck to suffocate. One moment I'd been weightless, fluid, in my element, and the next moment I'd been thrust into a world where gravity pinned me to something hard, a world that didn't lift and propel me—a world I couldn't survive in.

But I would survive. After allowing one minute of grief and hopelessness, I willed myself to live, something I'd done every day since before I could remember. I closed my eyes until I stopped trembling and could breathe again, remembering I was no fish. My world was one of gravity and air. Cyrene had planned so much for so long, but she'd never really planned for me. I grew up an outsider in a harsh city with the world against me. That carved me into a woman stronger than my enemies.

Baket's emerald gaze filled with more glittering life than I had seen in them yet, as if the sphinx had grown a little more human or was at least beginning to understand us. "Is there some way I can help?"

I smiled at her. "Don't ever stop being kind. Thank you for being my friend."

The sphinx smiled with her human mouth. "I'm happy to."

"What should I do?" I asked her. "Should I keep running from them? Shouldn't I kill Cyrene for what she did?"

"You must ask yourself what you are willing to sacrifice for revenge," she replied.

"I've already lost everyone I've loved," I argued, though I felt more exhausted than angry at that moment.

"What you seek will take more from you," Baket said sadly.

I shook my head. "I have nothing else to lose."

The sphinx frowned. "Your goodness, lady."

I turned from her, setting my teeth tightly. My throat

grew tight, trapping my air, unable to expel without unleashing my scream with it. After a moment, I forced the tension from my body and could breathe again, though I felt emptier than ever before. "Maybe it's worth it," I whispered at last.

"I can't tell you the answer to that," she said. "Only your heart can."

When I looked back at her, I found her with a tilted head, watching me with sympathy. "The question I need to ask myself—my heart—is am I willing to sacrifice who I am for justice?"

"Are you?" the sphinx asked.

"I believe I am willing to sacrifice who I am to protect Egypt and the people who can't protect themselves from evil," I told her. "That is the only thing for which I can justify breaking my heart. I don't want to, but my heart belongs to Egypt, not me, and protecting this world is the righter thing to do."

The sphinx beamed. "A queen's words from a queen's heart."

"But everyone who cared about me—everyone I cared about—are dead," I said, my voice so weak.

"Forgive me, lady," Baket said, her brow furrowing in thought, "but I don't understand why mortals die. Why are they here and then . . . not?"

I tried to think of way to explain death to something that would never die. "You have a heart that doesn't beat. Eventually a mortal's heart gives out. All the parts in our bodies grow tired after a long life. We die because we live."

The sphinx closed the distance between us, her power

prickling my skin, her huge, sleek body warm, and she pressed a round, furred ear against my chest. Baket fell silent and I fell with her, sucked in by the void and left breathless, until the only sound left was my pulse.

"I hear it," the sphinx whispered. "Your heart beats like a ticking clock, counting down until it stops."

Only when she drew away could I breathe.

"I hope your heart beats for a very long time," Baket said.

It was such a strange thing to say, I almost laughed, but I didn't have the energy for it. "So do I."

She sat on her haunches and pulled away from my face. "You will. I know you will survive."

"You're a prophet then, huh?" I asked, though it was a half-hearted joke.

"No one can see the future. We can only learn from the past and design our own fate." Baket offered me a lily-sweet smile. "You were born a princess of ancient blood, but the gods also gave you strength, lady. Those gifts haven't gone wasted. You have earned who you are with your wit and teeth and claws. These are admirable virtues."

Peace warmed my heart. "You must be the only sphinx in history who deals in reason rather than riddles."

She beamed at me. "Thank you, lady. You flatter me."

Someone knocked on my door and my body chilled. The sphinx pinned her ears, pulled back her lips to bare her neat, little fangs, and hissed. She withdrew, her powerful, slender tail lashing angrily.

"Should I attack, lady?" she whispered.

I shook my head, staring past her at the door. "No, we can't afford to get kicked off the boat."

There came another knock. "Zee."

His voice filled my heart with light and broke it at the same time.

I tore open the door and flung myself into Sayer's arms. He made a gruff, throaty noise of surprise and his back hit the wall. We sank to the floor, our arms entwined. Tears soaked my cheeks, dampening his wool jacket as I buried my face into his chest. I crawled into his lap, pinning my body against his, letting him pull me as close as we could physically be. I cried, gasping deeply for air. He had to be real. Had to be. I could feel him and smell him. He was real.

"Ziva, Ziva," he breathed into my hair, whispering my name over and over.

The boat rocked, and its sway and his touch soothed me. A *chanson* lulled behind the wall of another cabin. My body ceased its shuddering, and I looked up into his face, into those dark eyes. His hand touched my face, lifted my chin, and he bent over to kiss me. His lips were warm and soft, gentle against mine, though his arms held onto me for dear life.

It seemed as though hours had passed when he put his forehead to mine.

"I watched you die," was the first thing I said to him.

A low, *mmm* sound vibrated in his throat. "It would take more than the violence of a god to wrest me from you."

"Why did this happen?"

"Because there are terrible people."

"Is Nasi okay?"

"She's okay." He kissed the top of my head and exhaled, warming my skin. "Let's go inside."

Weakly, we climbed to our feet. I smoothed out my nightgown and led him into my room. He closed the door behind himself. Finally, I could look at him. There were deep circles around his eyes, his cheeks purple and green with bruises. His sleeves covered his arms, but I remembered the blood from when he tried to tear through Cyrene's spell. I wondered if I looked as broken as he did.

"Where is Nasira?" I asked him.

"A safe place," he replied, his voice hoarse. "I got to her injuries quickly, but she'll need time. My magic doesn't work as well on myself. I'll need even more time."

I swallowed hard, struggling to hold my heart together. "Your dad."

He drew a deep breath and his exhale came with a shudder, then a sob. He bit down on his lip and the muscles on his jaw clenched. I raised my hands to wipe the tears from the bruises beneath his eyes and he turned his face into my palm and kissed my skin. His arms wrapped around me and I threw mine around the back of his neck.

"Lady," the sphinx said delicately. I pulled away from Sayer and looked into her concerned, fearful face.

"Oh, Baket, we're okay," I told her and deflated. "It'll be okay." As if she was the one who needed convincing.

She nodded and curled up in a ball on the floor, though she didn't relax.

"What do we do?" Sayer asked, looking at me, defeat in his eyes.

"Finish what they started," I told him, finding a flicker of strength within myself. "We unearthed a monster. Cyrene will do everything in her power to stop us from righting this terrible wrong."

He shook his head. "But how? I'd trained my entire life to be faster and stronger than anything so when the moment came, I would win. And I didn't. I couldn't."

An ember of an idea began to glow in the back of my mind, one I know would burn him. "We're only mortals."

"We're no match for the queen," he said, fear and desperation raising his voice.

"Maybe that's just it," I whispered. "We need to find her match."

He stared at me, puzzled. "Cyrene is the strongest of us and she sided with Nefertari."

I braced myself for the pain I was about to cause him. "I don't mean another Medjai. I mean Set."

Sayer's jaw clenched, and he shook his head again, the gesture and his gaze harsh and rough as a brick. "No. *No.* His creature killed my mother. I will not beg him for help. I have nothing left but my honor, and I won't toss that in the dirt."

"This is not the time to cling to our egos," I told him delicately.

"This has nothing to do with my ego!" he spat, his voice curdled with rage. "Set is as much a monster as the thing we must destroy. That doesn't mean we team up with him!"

It took everything in me to keep my voice even and calm. "I understand my decision is a betrayal against you—"

"So, it's *your* decision? We won't even discuss it?" he interjected.

"—but what we're up against is greater than any of us," I finished. "Only a god can kill a god!"

"You have Anubis!" he shouted, throwing up a hand in exasperation.

"Set is stronger," I argued tightly, trying not to yell back at him. "He's the strongest of them all and he wants the same thing we do. We'd be fools not to side with him. I'm doing this for our people, for the rest of the world. The Germans we saw in Cairo are led by a scientist who's been researching the supernatural. She knows about us— the Medjai, magic, the gods. Yesterday she came to me in Asyut. She told me the research they've done is only the beginning. They want to create an artificial god."

His brow crushed into a frown of disbelief. "She's mad."

"The threats we are up against are growing," I told him. "We can't do this alone."

"Ziva . . ."

"What terrors will Nefertari unleash on this world if we don't stop her with everything we have?" I pleaded with him. "How many more lives will she destroy? What devastation will the Nazis bring upon our own people if we don't take every measure to stop them? I'm doing this."

Sayer gaped at me for several moments before he closed his mouth, shaking his head, and turned away. He covered his face with his hands, then roughly ran them through his hair. His hands fell, rolled into fists, and tightened until his knuckles paled to white. When he looked back at me from over his shoulder, it was crystal clear how I had hurt him.

"I love you," he said to me, his words muted with sadness. "But you're making a mistake. He will bring your doom."

"I don't believe he will," I said, sticking to my decision and knowing exactly what I was sacrificing for it. For us all. "This is the only way to win."

A fresh tear perched on his cheekbone, but his expression was empty and unreadable aside from the sadness, denser and more drowning than anything I'd seen before. "When we first met, Cyrene said you would save humanity from itself because that was your fate. She was wrong, you know. The only thing she was right about was your ruthlessness. You'll save us because only you have the grit. The gods tested you well your whole life. Those trials shaped you, despite all the suffering this world has caused you, into the one person who believes it should be saved and can get it done."

My shuddering sob nearly sank me to my knees.

"But not this way," he continued, and his shaking voice rose with anger. "Not with something so evil."

"I'm sorry," I told him, but I knew I was right.

He came toward me, leaned over, and kissed my cheek. Warmth, then cold as he backed up toward the door. He looked at me, dead-eyed, for a moment and said, "Good-bye, Ziva. Take care of yourself."

Shock filled my veins with ice, freezing my feet to the floor. "Sayer!" I called to him.

And he left me.

A harrowing scream ripped free from my throat, unleashing my anguish from its cage in my heart. The walls tilted toward me from every side, and the floor beneath me felt as though it were rolling like a violent sea. I collapsed to my knees, spreading my palms on the floor for balance. My eyes shut, and I saw my mother's tearstained face, the only memory I had of her.

My heart was breaking. This is what it felt like. Two hands, taloned fingertips embedded deep, ripping my heart into two. I felt like I was dying, drowning. I smothered my face in my hands and wailed as I rocked back and forth. Fear, pain, grief, and horror lashed at me like tempest-whipped, sea-salted winds. The sound of Sayer's screams filled my memory.

I withdrew my hands from my face and watched them shake as I pressed them into the cold floor again. I pushed myself up by sheer will alone, as though my arms and legs had burned into charred stalks. He and I were over. Everything we had, every laugh and smile and touch—they were only memories from another life now. They would never be again. The connection we had, the closeness, the comfort, the hope—all gone. A void grew in my chest where my heart once was kept safe, the emptiness all-devouring, until all that remained in me was a numb, dull roar. Time slowed and my body sank, heavy, spent. My grief almost buried me alive and I could only sit here and let it.

Baket pushed her softly furred forehead into my hand, and I turned to meet her gentle gaze. I put my arms around her to bury my face in her braided mane. The gold and gemstone beads made a soft, comforting tinkling sound. She leaned into me and purred, her sweet voice a candle's flicker in the darkness, "There, there, lady."

I needed the reminder I wasn't alone. I'd lived my life trying to survive, but I'd hoped the world could be a better place for myself and others who had suffered. Baket had been imprisoned in a tomb for thousands of years, utterly alone, and still she had hope.

I drew a deep breath and pulled away from the sphinx. I'd spent my life searching for the answers to my past and future, hoping someone would steer me in the right direction. Now I realized that no one else held sway over who I was. I had to carve that out for myself. My identity was my own. As were my decisions.

I had to do what I believed was right. This thought steeled my nerve. I felt like myself again.

From my belongings, I removed Anubis's amulet. He appeared moments after I whispered his name into the air. The god of death took one look at the wretched sight of me and said nothing before scooping me into his arms, hugging me tight. His scent of sand and stone, once comforting to me, now reminded me of what I had endured in the unforgiving desert. I slipped from his grip, and he did not protest, only gazed down at me with quiet sorrow in those orphic topaz eyes.

"What do you need?" he asked gently.

"For you to do something for me, my friend, my brother," I told him. "Something you won't like. But you have to trust me."

As Anubis searched my face, trepidation passed over his own, but he braced himself and said, "All right, Ziva. I trust you."

I paced back and forth through my cabin, the sphinx watching in calm silence. She did not question me, and I was glad for it. Only a few minutes had passed since Anubis departed, and it took all of my will not to doubt my decision for an instant.

A disturbance in the air made me stop. Inky power spread across the floor, exploring every object like a sentient thing, and Set materialized in a plume of shadow in front of me. He smiled when I held my ground. Baket hissed from where she crouched, ready to spring to my defense.

"I feared for you after you fled," he confessed. "Words cannot express my joy when I learned you sent the pup for me."

"Your invitation still stands, yes?" I inquired. "I will help you end Nefertari if you help me."

"I would not have offered if I didn't think you had the will," Set crooned. "To watch your courage . . . You are a rare jewel of this earth."

"Let me be clear," I said boldly. "I want vengeance, but above all, I want justice."

"Glad we are agreed upon their destruction," he remarked, studying me for a sharp moment. "On my immortality, I swear I will not let her have you. If she is fully regenerated, I will not be able to stop her. You were right about that all along. And I accept responsibility for unleashing this evil upon your world. I was arrogant enough to believe I could stop your people from resurrecting her."

"You made a terrible gamble for what you wanted," I told him.

His smile grew serpentine. "You would do the same."

My teeth bit together. "I wouldn't be so careless with the lives of others. That's the difference between you and me."

"No, you don't gamble, do you," he said, and it wasn't a question. "But us side by side—that's a sure thing. I want to save my people and return us to this world, where we will thrive. You can be my intermediary with humankind. Please, allow me to add but one condition of my own. A request, not a demand."

I drew a deep, defiant breath, carefully controlling the magic at my fingertips. "Which is?"

"Allow me to make you a living god." Set's eyes of molten gold flickered with flames. "You are the only living descendant of a pharaoh. By all rights the throne of Egypt is yours, and I will help you claim it and more. Come with me to the Crocodile City and rule at my side. Be my crocodile queen."

My blood quickened. Only a god could kill a god. To end this, I would embrace the darkest facets of my heart. I would reach for my darkest power and fear would not hold me back.

I did not want to claim this world for my own; I was

no Nefertari or Adolf Hitler. All I desired was for my enemies to suffer beneath more than anything the mortal
world could provide me. Set had proven himself to be
dangerous, but he had shielded me from the tank explosion and taken the debris himself. He would honor his
pledge to protect me from Nefertari. I didn't owe him my
life. I didn't owe anyone a thing.

Taking a deep breath and pushing away the shame
I felt when I pictured Sayer's disappointed face in my
mind, I said without regret, "Agreed."

The air between us prickled with magic and the gold
in the eyes of the god of chaos glowed with eagerness
and satisfaction. "Together we will soak Egypt's sands red
with the blood of all those who betrayed us, and you will
rule their ruin. None will foresee the storm rolling toward
them from across the darkened sea, and that storm is
you and me."

I would not forgive, and I would not forget. I thought
of all who had tried to hold me back, to stop me from
rising to where I belonged. The bullies and the evil people.
The monsters and their gods. Of all the hunger and the
pain and the suffering I had survived. I had *survived*. They
would not. No one had made me a victim.

They'd made me strong.

ACKNOWLEDGMENTS

[content to come]